Heron Books

CHARLES DICKENS

COMPLETE
WORKS

CENTENNIAL EDITION

Charles Dickens

CHARLES DICKENS

OUR MUTUAL FRIEND

II

Illustrations by
Marcus Stone

HERON BOOKS

I.S.B.N. for this volume:
0 86225 099 4

CONTENTS

BOOK THE THIRD. A LONG LANE

CONTENTS

CONTENTS

BOOK THE FOURTH. A TURNING.

CHAPTER I.

CHAPTER II.

CHAPTER III.

CHAPTER IV.

CHAPTER V.

CHAPTER VI.

CHAPTER VII.

CHAPTER VIII.

CHAPTER IX.

CONTENTS

LIST OF ILLUSTRATIONS

BOOK III

A LONG LANE

CHAPTER I

IT was a foggy day in London, and the fog was heavy and dark. Animate London, with smarting eyes and irritated lungs, was blinking, wheezing, and choking; inanimate London was a sooty spectre, divided in purpose between being visible and invisible, and so being wholly neither. Gaslights flared in the shops with a haggard and unblest air, as knowing themselves to be night-creatures that had no business abroad under the sun; while the sun itself, when it was for a few moments dimly indicated through circling eddies of fog, showed as if it had gone out, and were collapsing flat and cold. Even in the surrounding country it was a foggy day, but there the fog was grey, whereas in London it was, at about the boundary line, dark yellow, and a little within it brown, and then browner, and then browner, until at the heart of the City—which call Saint Mary Axe—it was rusty-black. From any point of the high ridge of

1

land northward, it might have been discerned that the loftiest buildings made an occasional struggle to get their heads above the foggy sea, and especially that the great dome of Saint Paul's seemed to die hard ; but this was not perceivable in the streets at their feet, where the whole metropolis was a heap of vapour charged with muffled sound of wheels, and enfolding a gigantic catarrh.

At nine o'clock on such a morning, the place of business of Pubsey and Co. was not the liveliest object even in Saint Mary Axe—which is not a very lively spot—with a sobbing gaslight in the counting-house window, and a burglarious stream of fog creeping in to strangle it through the keyhole of the main door. But the light went out, and the main door opened, and Riah came forth with a bag under his arm.

Almost in the act of coming out at the door, Riah went into the fog, and was lost to the eyes of Saint Mary Axe. But the eyes of this history can follow him westward, by Cornhill, Cheapside, Fleet Street, and the Strand, to Piccadilly and the Albany. Thither he went at his grave and measured pace, staff in hand, skirt at heel ; and more than one head, turning to look back at his venerable figure already lost in the mist, supposed it to be some ordinary figure indistinctly seen, which fancy and the fog had worked into that passing likeness.

Arrived at the house in which his master's chambers were on the second floor, Riah proceeded up the stairs, and paused at Fascination Fledgeby's door. Making free with neither bell nor knocker, he struck upon the door with the top of his staff, and, having listened, sat down on the threshold. It was characteristic of his habitual submission, that he sat down on the raw dark staircase, as many of his ancestors had probably sat down in dungeons, taking what befell him as it might befall.

After a time, when he had grown so cold as to be fain to blow upon his fingers, he arose and knocked with his staff again, and listened again, and again sat down to wait.

Thrice he repeated these actions before his listening ears were greeted by the voice of Fledgeby, calling from his bed, "Hold your row!—I'll come and open the door directly!" But, in lieu of coming directly, he fell into a sweet sleep for some quarter of an hour more, during which added interval Riah sat upon the stairs and waited with perfect patience.

At length the door stood open, and Mr. Fledgeby's retreating drapery plunged into bed again. Following it at a respectful distance, Riah passed into the bed-chamber, where a fire had been some time lighted, and was burning briskly.

"Why, what time of night do you mean to call it?" inquired Fledgeby, turning away beneath the clothes, and presenting a comfortable rampart of shoulder to the chilled figure of the old man.

"Sir, it is full half-past ten in the morning."

"The deuce it is! Then it must be precious foggy?"

"Very foggy, sir."

"And raw, then?"

"Chill and bitter," said Riah, drawing out a handkerchief, and wiping the moisture from his beard and long grey hair as he stood on the verge of the rug, with his eyes on the acceptable fire.

With a plunge of enjoyment, Fledgeby settled himself afresh.

"Any snow, or sleet, or slush, or anything of that sort?" he asked.

"No, sir, no. Not quite so bad as that. The streets are pretty clean."

"You needn't brag about it," returned Fledgeby, disappointed in his desire to heighten the contrast between his bed and the streets. "But you're always bragging about something. Got the books there?"

"They are here, sir."

"All right. I'll turn the general subject over in my mind

3

for a minute or two, and while I'm about it you can empty your bag and get ready for me."

With another comfortable plunge, Mr. Fledgeby fell asleep again. The old man, having obeyed his directions, sat down on the edge of a chair, and, folding his hands before him, gradually yielded to the influence of the warmth, and dozed. He was roused by Mr. Fledgeby's appearing erect at the foot of the bed, in Turkish slippers, rose-coloured Turkish trousers (got cheap from somebody who had cheated some other somebody out of them), and a gown and cap to correspond. In that costume he would have left nothing to be desired, if he had been further fitted out with a bottomless chair, a lantern, and a bunch of matches.

"Now, old 'un!" cried Fascination, in his light raillery, "what dodgery are you up to next, sitting there with your eyes shut? You ain't asleep. Catch a weasel at it, and catch a Jew!"

"Truly, sir, I fear I nodded," said the old man.

"Not you!" returned Fledgeby, with a cunning look. "A telling move with a good many, I dare say, but it won't put *me* off my guard. Not a bad notion, though, if you want to look indifferent in driving a bargain. Oh, you are a dodger!"

The old man shook his head, gently repudiating the imputation, and suppressed a sigh, and moved to the table at which Mr. Fledgeby was now pouring out for himself a cup of steaming and fragrant coffee from a pot that had stood ready on the hob. It was an edifying spectacle, the young man in his easy chair taking his coffee, and the old man with his grey head bent, standing awaiting his pleasure.

"Now!" said Fledgeby. "Fork out your balance in hand, and prove by figures how you make it out that it ain't more. First of all, light that candle."

Riah obeyed, and then taking a bag from his breast, and referring to the sum in the accounts for which they made him responsible, told it out upon the table. Fledgeby told it again with great care, and rang every sovereign.

"I suppose," he said, taking one up to eye it closely, "you haven't been lightening any of these; but it's a trade of your people's, you know. *You* understand what sweating a pound means; don't you?"

"Much as you do, sir," returned the old man, with his hands under opposite cuffs of his loose sleeves, as he stood at the table, deferentially observant of the master's face. "May I take the liberty to say something?"

"You may," Fledgeby graciously conceded.

"Do you not, sir—without intending it—of a surety without intending it—sometimes mingle the character I fairly earn in your employment, with the character which it is your policy that I should bear?"

"I don't find it worth my while to cut things so fine as to go into the inquiry," Fascination coolly answered.

"Not in justice?"

"Bother justice!" said Fledgeby.

"Not in generosity?"

"Jews and generosity!" said Fledgeby. "That's a good connection! Bring out your vouchers, and don't talk Jerusalem palaver."

The vouchers were produced, and for the next half-hour Mr. Fledgeby concentrated his sublime attention on them. They and the accounts were all found correct, and the books and the papers resumed their places in the bag.

"Next," said Fledgeby, "concerning that bill-broking branch of the business; the branch I like best. What queer bills are to be bought, and at what prices? You have got your list of what's in the market?"

"Sir, a long list," replied Riah, taking out a pocket-book, and selecting from its contents a folded paper, which, being unfolded, became a sheet of foolscap covered with close writing.

"Whew!" whistled Fledgeby, as he took it in his hand. "Queer Street is full of lodgers just at present! These are to be disposed of in parcels; are they?"

"In parcels as set forth," returned the old man, looking over his master's shoulder; "or the lump."

"Half the lump will be waste-paper, one knows beforehand," said Fledgeby. "Can you get it at waste-paper price? That's the question."

Riah shook his head, and Fledgeby cast his small eyes down the list. They presently began to twinkle, and he no sooner became conscious of their twinkling, than he looked up over his shoulder at the grave face above him, and moved to the chimney-piece. Making a desk of it, he stood there with his back to the old man, warming his knees, perusing the list at his leisure, and often returning to some lines of it, as though they were particularly interesting. At those times he glanced in the chimney-glass to see what note the old man took of him. He took none that could be detected, but, aware of his employer's suspicions, stood with his eyes on the ground.

Mr. Fledgeby was thus amiably engaged when a step was heard at the outer door, and the door was heard to open hastily. "Hark! That's your doing, you Pump of Israel," said Fledgeby; "you can't have shut it." Then the step was heard within, and the voice of Mr. Alfred Lammle called aloud, "Are you anywhere here, Fledgeby?" To which Fledgeby, after cautioning Riah in a low voice to take his cue as it should be given him, replied, "Here I am!" and opened his bedroom door.

"Come in!" said Fledgeby. "This gentleman is only Pubsey and Co. of Saint Mary Axe, that I am trying to make terms for an unfortunate friend with in a matter of some dishonoured bills. But really Pubsey and Co. are so strict with their debtors, and so hard to move, that I seem to be wasting my time. Can't I make *any* terms with you on my friend's part, Mr. Riah?"

"I am but the representative of another, sir," returned the Jew in a low voice. "I do as I am bidden by my principal. It is not my capital that is invested in the business. It is not my profit that arises therefrom."

" Ha ha ! " laughed Fledgeby. " Lammle ? "

" Ha ha ! " laughed Lammle. " Yes. Of course. We know."

"Devilish good, ain't it, Lammle ? " said Fledgeby, unspeakably amused by his hidden joke.

" Always the same, always the same ! " said Lammle. " Mr. —— "

" Riah, Pubsey, and Co., Saint Mary Axe," Fledgeby put in, as he wiped away the tears that trickled from his eyes, so rare was his enjoyment of his secret joke.

" Mr. Riah is bound to observe the invariable forms for such cases made and provided," said Lammle.

" He is only the representative of another ! " cried Fledgeby. " Does as he is told by his principal ! Not his capital that's invested in the business. Oh, that's good ! Ha, ha, ha, ha ! " Mr. Lammle joined in the laugh and looked knowing ; and the more he did both, the more exquisite the secret joke became for Mr. Fledgeby.

" However," said that fascinating gentleman, wiping his eyes again, " if we go on in this way, we shall seem to be almost making game of Mr. Riah, or of Pubsey and Co., Saint Mary Axe, or of somebody: which is far from our intention. Mr. Riah, if you would have the kindness to step into the next room for a few moments while I speak with Mr. Lammle here, I should like to try to make terms with you once again before you go."

The old man, who had never raised his eyes during the whole transaction of Mr. Fledgeby's joke, silently bowed and passed out by the door which Fledgeby opened for him. Having closed it on him, Fledgeby returned to Lammle, standing with his back to the bedroom fire, with one hand under his coat-skirts, and all his whiskers in the other.

" Halloa ! " said Fledgeby. " There's something wrong ! "

" How do you know it ? " demanded Lammle.

"Because you show it," replied Fledgeby in unintentional rhyme.

7

"Well then; there is," said Lammle; "there *is* something wrong; the whole thing's wrong."

"I say!" remonstrated Fascination very slowly, and sitting down with his hands on his knees to stare at his glowering friend with his back to the fire.

"I tell you, Fledgeby," repeated Lammle, with a sweep of his right arm, "the whole thing's wrong. The game's up."

"What game's up?" demanded Fledgeby, as slowly as before, and more sternly.

"THE game. OUR game. Read that."

Fledgeby took a note from his extended hand and read it aloud. "Alfred Lammle, Esquire. Sir: Allow Mrs. Podsnap and myself to express our united sense of the polite attentions of Mrs. Alfred Lammle and yourself towards our daughter Georgiana. Allow us, also, wholly to reject them for the future, and to communicate our final desire that the two families may become entire strangers. I have the honour to be, Sir, your most obedient and very humble servant, JOHN PODSNAP." Fledgeby looked at the three blank sides of this note, quite as long and earnestly as at the first expressive side, and then looked at Lammle, who responded with another extensive sweep of his right arm.

"Whose doing is this?" said Fledgeby.

"Impossible to imagine," said Lammle.

"Perhaps," suggested Fledgeby, after reflecting with a very discontented brow, "somebody has been giving you a bad character."

"Or you," said Lammle, with a deeper frown.

Mr. Fledgeby appeared to be on the verge of some mutinous expressions, when his hand happened to touch his nose. A certain remembrance connected with that feature operating as a timely warning, he took it thoughtfully between his thumb and forefinger, and pondered; Lammle meanwhile eyeing him with furtive eyes.

"Well!" said Fledgeby. "This won't improve with talking about. If we ever find out who did it, we'll mark that person. There's nothing more to be said, except that you undertook to do what circumstances prevent your doing."

"And that you undertook to do what you might have done by this time, if you had made a prompter use of circumstances," snarled Lammle.

"Hah! That," remarked Fledgeby, with his hands in the Turkish trousers, "is matter of opinion."

"Mr. Fledgeby," said Lammle, in a bullying tone, "am I to understand that you in any way reflect upon me, or hint dissatisfaction with me, in this affair?"

"No," said Fledgeby; "provided you have brought my promissory note in your pocket, and now hand it over."

Lammle produced it, not without reluctance. Fledgeby looked at it, identified it, twisted it up, and threw it into the fire. They both looked at it as it blazed, went out, and flew in feathery ash up the chimney.

"*Now*, Mr. Fledgeby," Lammle said, as before; "am I to understand that you in any way reflect upon me, or hint dissatisfaction with me, in this affair?"

"No," said Fledgeby.

"Finally and unreservedly no?"

"Yes."

"Fledgeby, my hand."

Mr. Fledgeby took it, saying, "And if we ever find out who did this, we'll mark that person. And in the most friendly manner, let me mention one thing more. I don't know what your circumstances are, and I don't ask. You have sustained a loss here. Many men are liable to be involved at times, and you may be, or you may not be. But whatever you do, Lammle, don't—don't—don't, I beg of you—ever fall into the hands of Pubsey and Co. in the next room, for they are grinders. Regular flayers and grinders, my dear Lammle," repeated Fledgeby with a peculiar relish, "and they'll skin you by the inch, from the nape of your neck to the sole of your foot, and grind every inch of your skin to tooth-powder. You have seen what Mr. Riah

9

is. Never fall into his hands, Lammle, I beg of you as a friend!"

Mr. Lammle, disclosing some alarm at the solemnity of this affectionate adjuration, demanded why the devil he ever should fall into the hands of Pubsey and Co.?

"To confess the fact, I was made a little uneasy," said the candid Fledgeby, "by the manner in which that Jew looked at you when he heard your name. I didn't like his eye. But it may have been the heated fancy of a friend. Of course, if you are sure that you have no personal security out, which you may not be quite equal to meeting, and which can have got into his hands, it must have been fancy. Still. I didn't like his eye."

The brooding Lammle, with certain white dints coming and going in his palpitating nose, looked as if some torment-ing imp were pinching it. Fledgeby, watching him with a twitch in his mean face which did duty there for a smile, looked very like the tormentor who was pinching.

"But I mustn't keep him waiting too long," said Fledgeby, "or he'll revenge it on my unfortunate friend. How's your very clever and agreeable wife? She knows we have broken down?"

"I showed her the letter."

"Very much surprised?" asked Fledgeby.

"I think she would have been more so," answered Lammle, "if there had been more go in *you!*"

"Oh!—She lays it upon me, then?"

"Mr. Fledgeby, I will not have my words misconstrued."

"Don't break out, Lammle," urged Fledgeby, in a sub-missive tone, "because there's no occasion. I only asked a question. Then she don't lay it upon me? To ask another question."

"No, sir."

"Very good," said Fledgeby, plainly seeing that she did. "My compliments to her. Good-bye!"

They shook hands, and Lammle strode out pondering.

Fledgeby saw him into the fog, and, returning to the fire and musing with his face to it, stretched the legs of the rose-coloured Turkish trousers wide apart, and meditatively bent his knees, as if he were going down upon them.

"You have a pair of whiskers, Lammle, which I never liked," murmured Fledgeby, "and which money can't produce; you are boastful of your manners and your conversation; you wanted to pull my nose, and you have let me in for a failure, and your wife says I am the cause of it. I'll bowl you down. I will, though I have no whiskers," here he rubbed the places where they were due, "and no manners, and no conversation!"

Having thus relieved his noble mind, he collected the legs of the Turkish trousers, straightened himself on his knees, and called out to Riah in the next room, "Halloa, you sir!" At sight of the old man re-entering with a gentleness monstrously in contrast with the character he had given him, Mr. Fledgeby was so tickled again, that he exclaimed, laughing, "Good! Good! Upon my soul it is uncommon good!"

"Now, old 'un," proceeded Fledgeby, when he had had his laugh out, "you'll buy up these lots that I mark with my pencil—there's a tick there, and a tick there, and a tick there—and I wager twopence you'll afterwards go on squeezing those Christians like the Jew you are. Now, next you'll want a cheque—or you'll say you want it, though you've capital enough somewhere, if one only knew where, but you'd be peppered and salted and grilled on a gridiron before you'd own to it—and that cheque I'll write."

When he had unlocked a drawer and taken a key from it to open another drawer, in which was another key that opened another drawer, in which was another key that opened another drawer, in which was the cheque book; and when he had written the cheque; and when, reversing the key and drawer process, he had placed his cheque book in safety again; he beckoned the old man, with the folded cheque, to come and take it.

"Old 'un," said Fledgeby, when the Jew had put it in his pocket-book, and was putting that in the breast of his outer garment; "so much at present for my affairs. Now a word about affairs that are not exactly mine. Where is she?"

With his hand not yet withdrawn from the breast of his garment, Riah started and paused.

"Oho!" said Fledgeby. "Didn't expect it! Where have you hidden her?"

Showing that he was taken by surprise, the old man looked at his master with some passing confusion, which the master highly enjoyed.

"Is she in the house I pay rent and taxes for in Saint Mary Axe?" demanded Fledgeby.

"No, sir."

"Is she in your garden up a-top of that house—gone up to be dead, or whatever the game is?" asked Fledgeby.

"No, sir."

"Where is she then?"

Riah bent his eyes upon the ground, as if considering whether he could answer the question without breach of faith, and then silently raised them to Fledgeby's face, as if he could not.

"Come!" said Fledgeby. "I won't press that just now. But I want to know this, and I will know this, mind you. What are you up to?"

The old man, with an apologetic action of his head and hands, as not comprehending the master's meaning, addressed to him a look of mute inquiry.

"You can't be a gallivanting dodger," said Fledgeby. "For you're a regular 'pity the sorrows,' you know—if you *do* know any Christian rhyme—'whose trembling limbs have borne him to'—et cetrer. You're one of the Patriarchs; you're a shaky old card; and you can't be in love with this Lizzie?"

"Oh, sir!" expostulated Riah. "Oh, sir, sir, sir!"

"Then why," retorted Fledgeby, with some slight tinge **of** a blush, "don't you out with your reason for having your spoon in the soup at all?"

"Sir, I will tell you the truth. But (your pardon for the stipulation) it is in sacred confidence; it is strictly upon honour."

"Honour too!" cried Fledgeby, with a mocking lip. "Honour among Jews. Well. Cut away."

"It is upon honour, sir?" the other still stipulated, with respectful firmness.

"Oh, certainly. Honour bright," said Fledgeby.

The old man, never bidden to sit down, stood with an earnest hand laid on the back of the young man's easy chair. The young man sat looking at the fire with a face of listening curiosity, ready to check him off and catch him tripping.

"Cut away," said Fledgeby. "Start with your motive."

"Sir, I have no motive but to help the helpless."

Mr. Fledgeby could only express the feelings to which this incredible statement gave rise in his breast, by a prodigiously long derisive sniff.

"How I came to know, and much to esteem and to respect, this damsel, I mentioned when you saw her in my poor garden on the house-top," said the Jew.

"Did you?" said Fledgeby, distrustfully. "Well, perhaps you did, though."

"The better I knew her, the more interest I felt in her fortunes. They gathered to a crisis. I found her beset by a selfish and ungrateful brother, beset by an unacceptable wooer, beset by the snares of a more powerful lover, beset by the wiles of her own heart."

"She took to one of the chaps then?"

"Sir, it was only natural that she should incline towards him, for he had many and great advantages. But he was not of her station, and to marry her was not in his mind. Perils were closing round her, and the circle was fast darkening, when I—being as you have said, sir, too old and broken

13

to be suspected of any feeling for her but a father's—stepped in, and counselled flight. I said, ' My daughter, there are times of moral danger when the hardest, virtuous resolution to form is flight, and when the most heroic bravery is flight.' She answered, she had had this in her thoughts ; but whither to fly without help she knew not, and there were none to help her. I showed her there was one to help her, and it was I. And she is gone."

" What did you do with her ? " asked Fledgeby, feeling his cheek.

" I placed her," said the old man, " at a distance ; " with a grave, smooth, outward sweep from one another of his two open hands at arm's length ; " at a distance—among certain of our people, where her industry would serve her, and where she could hope to exercise it, unassailed from any quarter."

Fledgeby's eyes had come from the fire to notice the action of his hands when he said " at a distance." Fledgeby now tried (very unsuccessfully) to imitate that action, as he shook his head and said, " Placed her in that direction, did you ? Oh, you circular old dodger ! "

With one hand across his breast and the other on the easy chair, Riah, without justifying himself, waited for further questioning. But, that it was hopeless to question him on that one reserved point, Fledgeby, with his small eyes too near together, saw full well.

" Lizzie," said Fledgeby, looking at the fire again, and then looking up. " Humph, Lizzie. You didn't tell me the other name in your garden a-top of the house. I'll be more communicative with you. The other name's Hexam."

Riah bent his head in assent.

" Look here, you sir," said Fledgeby. " I have a notion I know something of the inveigling chap, the powerful one. Has he anything to do with the law ? "

" Nominally, I believe it his calling."

" I thought so. Name anything like Lightwood ? "

" Sir, not at all like."

"Come, old 'un," said Fledgeby, meeting his eyes with a wink, "say the name."

"Wrayburn."

"By Jupiter!" cried Fledgeby. "That one, is it? I thought it might be the other, but I never dreamt of that one. I shouldn't object to your baulking either of the pair, dodger, for they are both conceited enough; but that one is as cool a customer as ever I met with. Got a beard besides, and presumes upon it. Well done, old 'un! Go on and prosper!"

Brightened by this unexpected commendation, Riah asked were there more instructions for him?

"No," said Fledgeby, "you may toddle now, Judah, and grope about on the orders you have got." Dismissed with those pleasing words, the old man took his broad hat and staff, and left the great presence: more as if he were some superior creature benignantly blessing Mr. Fledgeby, than the poor dependant on whom he set his foot. Left alone, Mr. Fledgeby locked his outer door, and came back to his fire.

"Well done you!" said Fascination to himself. "Slow, you may be; sure, you are!" This he twice or thrice repeated with much complacency, as he again dispersed the legs of the Turkish trousers and bent the knees.

"A tidy shot that, I flatter myself," he then soliloquised. "And a Jew brought down with it! Now, when I heard the story told at Lammle's, I didn't make a jump at Riah. Not a bit of it; I got at him by degrees." Herein he was quite accurate; it being his habit not to jump, or leap, or make an upward spring, at anything in life, but to crawl at everything.

"I got at him," pursued Fledgeby, feeling for his whiskers, "by degrees. If your Lammles or your Lightwoods had got at him anyhow, they would have asked him the question whether he hadn't something to do with that gal's disappearance. I knew a better way of going to work. Having got behind the hedge, and put him in the light, I took a shot at him and brought him down plump. Oh! It don't count for much, being a Jew, in a match against *me!*"

Another dry twist in place of a smile, made his face crooked here.

"As to Christians," proceeded Fledgeby, "look out, fellow-Christians, particularly you that lodge in Queer Street! I have got the run of Queer Street now, and you shall see some games there. To work a lot of power over you and you not know it, knowing as you think yourselves, would be almost worth laying out money upon. But when it comes to squeezing a profit out of you into the bargain, it's something like!"

With this apostrophe Mr. Fledgeby appropriately proceeded to divest himself of his Turkish garments, and invest himself with Christian attire. Pending which operation, and his morning ablutions, and his anointing of himself with the last infallible preparation for the production of luxuriant and glossy hair upon the human countenance (quacks being the only sages he believed in besides usurers), the murky fog closed about him and shut him up in its sooty embrace. If it had never let him out any more, the world would have had no irreparable loss, but could have easily replaced him from its stock on hand.

CHAPTER II

In the evening of this same foggy day when the yellow window-blind of Pubsey and Co. was drawn down upon the day's work, Riah the Jew once more came forth into Saint Mary Axe. But this time he carried no bag, and was not bound on his master's affairs. He passed over London Bridge, and returned to the Middlesex shore by that of Westminster, and so, ever wading through the fog, waded to the doorstep of the dolls' dressmaker.

Miss Wren expected him. He could see her through the window by the light of her low fire—carefully banked up with damp cinders that it might last the longer and waste the less when she went out—sitting waiting for him in her bonnet. His tap at the glass roused her from the musing solitude in which she sat, and she came to the door to open it; aiding her steps with a little crutch-stick.

" Good evening, godmother ! " said Miss Jenny Wren.

The old man laughed, and gave her his arm to lean on.

" Won't you come in and warm yourself, godmother ? " asked Miss Jenny Wren.

" Not if you are ready, Cinderella, my dear."

" Well ! " exclaimed Miss Wren, delighted. " Now you ARE a clever old boy ! If we gave prizes at this establishment (but we only keep blanks), you should have the first silver medal, for taking me up so quick." As she spake thus, Miss Wren removed the key of the house-door from the keyhole and put it in her pocket, and then bustlingly closed the door, and tried it as they both stood on the step. Satisfied that her dwelling was safe, she drew one hand through the old man's arm and prepared to ply her crutch-stick with the other. But the key was an instrument of such gigantic proportions, that before they started Riah proposed to carry it.

"No, no, no! I'll carry it myself," returned Miss Wren. "I'm awfully lop-sided, you know, and stowed down in my pocket it'll trim the ship. To let you into a secret, god-mother, I wear my pocket on my high side, o' purpose."

With that they began their plodding through the fog.

"Yes, it was truly sharp of you, godmother," resumed Miss Wren with great approbation, "to understand me. But, you see, you *are* so like the fairy godmother in the bright little books! You look so unlike the rest of people, and so much as if you had changed yourself into that shape, just this moment, with some benevolent object. Boh!" cried Miss Jenny, putting her face close to the old man's. "I can see your features, godmother, behind the beard."

"Does the fancy go to my changing other objects too, Jenny?"

"Ah! That it does! If you'd only borrow my stick and tap this piece of pavement—this dirty stone that my foot taps —it would start up a coach and six. I say! Let's believe so!"

"With all my heart," replied the good old man.

"And I'll tell you what I must ask you to do, godmother. I must ask you to be so kind as give my child a tap, and change him altogether. Oh, my child has been such a bad, bad child of late! It worries me nearly out of my wits. Not done a stroke of work these ten days. Has had the horrors, too, and fancied that four copper-coloured men in red wanted to throw him into a fiery furnace."

"But that's dangerous, Jenny?"

"Dangerous, godmother? My bad child is always dangerous, more or less. He might "—here the little creature glanced back over her shoulder at the sky—" be setting the

18

house on fire at this present moment. I don't know who would have a child, for my part! It's no use shaking him. I have shaken him till I have made myself giddy. 'Why don't you mind your Commandments and honour your parent, you naughty old boy? I said to him all the time. But he only whimpered and stared at me."

"What shall be changed, after him?" asked Riah in a compassionately playful voice.

" Upon my word, godmother, I am afraid I must be selfish next, and get you to set me right in the back and the legs. It's a little thing to you with your power, godmother, but it's a great deal to poor, weak, aching me."

There was no querulous complaining in the words, but they were not the less touching for that.

" And then?"

" Yes, and then—*you* know, godmother. We'll both jump into the coach and six and go to Lizzie. This reminds me, godmother, to ask you a serious question. You are as wise as wise can be (having been brought up by the fairies), and you can tell me this: Is it better to have had a good thing and lost it, or never to have had it?"

" Explain, goddaughter."

" I feel so much more solitary and helpless without Lizzie now, than I used to feel before I knew her." (Tears were in her eyes as she said so.)

"Some beloved companionship fades out of most lives, my dear," said the Jew,—" that of a wife, and a fair daughter, and a son of promise, has faded out of my own life—but the happiness was."

" Ah!" said Miss Wren thoughtfully, by no means convinced, and chopping the exclamation with that sharp little hatchet of hers; " then I tell you what change I think you had better begin with, godmother. You had better change Is into Was and Was into Is, and keep them so."

" Would that suit your case? Would you not be always in pain then?" asked the old man tenderly.

"Right!" exclaimed Miss Wren with another chop. "You have changed me wiser, godmother.—Not," she added with the quaint hitch of her chin and eyes, "that you need be a very wonderful godmother to do that deed."

Thus conversing, and having crossed Westminster Bridge, they traversed the ground that Riah had lately traversed, and new ground likewise ; for, when they had recrossed the Thames by way of London Bridge, they struck down by the river and held their still foggier course that way.

But previously, as they were going along, Jenny twisted her venerable friend aside to a brilliantly-lighted toy-shop window, and said : "Now look at 'em. All my work !"

This referred to a dazzling semi-circle of dolls in all the colours of the rainbow, who were dressed for presentation at court, for going to balls, for going out driving, for going out on horseback, for going out walking, for going to get married, for going to help other dolls to get married, for all the gay events of life.

"Pretty, pretty, pretty !" said the old man with a clap of his hands. "Most elegant taste."

"Glad you like 'em," returned Miss Wren, loftily. "But the fun is, godmother, how I make the great ladies try my dresses on. Though it's the hardest part of my business, and would be, even if my back were not bad and my legs queer."

He looked at her as not understanding what she said.

"Bless you, godmother," said Miss Wren, "I have to scud about town at all hours. If it was only sitting at my bench, cutting out and sewing, it would be comparatively easy work ; but it's the trying-on by the great ladies that takes it out of me."

"How, the trying-on ?" asked Riah.

"What a mooney godmother you are, after all !" returned Miss Wren. "Look here. There's a Drawing Room, or a grand day in the Park, or a Show, or a Fête, or what you like. Very well. I squeeze among the crowd, and I look about me. When I see a great lady very suitable for my business, I say, 'You'll do, my dear !' and I take particular notice of

Trying on for the Dolls' Dressmaker

her, and run home and cut her out and baste her. Then another day, I come scudding back again to try on, and then I take particular notice of her again. Sometimes she plainly seems to say, 'How that little creature is staring!' and sometimes likes it and sometimes don't, but much more often yes than no. All the time I am only saying to myself, 'I must hollow out a bit here; I must slope away there;' and I am making a perfect slave of her, with making her try on my doll's dress. Evening parties are severer work for me, because there's only a doorway for a full view, and what with hobbling among the wheels of the carriages and the legs of the horses, I fully expect to be run over some night. However, there I have 'em, just the same. When they go bobbing into the hall from the carriage, and catch a glimpse of my little physiognomy poked out from behind a policeman's cape in the rain, I dare say they think I am wondering and admiring with all my eyes and heart, but they little think they're only working for my dolls! There was Lady Belinda Whitrose. I made her do double duty in one night. I said when she came out of the carriage, ' You'll do, my dear!' and I ran straight home and cut her out and basted her. Back I came again, and waited behind the men that called the carriages. Very bad night too. At last ' Lady Belinda Whitrose's carriage! Lady Belinda Whitrose coming down!' And I made her try on—oh! and take pains about it too— before she got seated. That's Lady Belinda hanging up by the waist, much too near the gaslight for a wax one, with her toes turned in."

When they had plodded on for some time nigh the river, Riah asked the way to a certain tavern called the Six Jolly Fellowship Porters. Following the directions he received, they arrived, after two or three puzzled stoppages for consideration, and some uncertain looking about them, at the door of Miss Abbey Potterson's dominions. A peep through the glass portion of the door revealed to them the glories of the bar, and Miss Abbey herself seated in state on her snug throne, reading the newspaper. To whom, with deference, they presented themselves.

Taking her eyes off her newspaper, and pausing with a suspended expression of countenance, as if she must finish the paragraph in hand before undertaking any other business whatever, Miss Abbey demanded, with some slight asperity, "Now then, what's for you?"

"Could we see Miss Potterson?" asked the old man, uncovering his head.

"You not only could, but you can and you do," replied the hostess.

"Might we speak with you, madam?"

By this time Miss Abbey's eyes had possessed themselves of the small figure of Miss Jenny Wren. For the closer observation of which Miss Abbey laid aside her newspaper, rose, and looked over the half-door of the bar. The crutch-stick seemed to entreat for its owner leave to come in and rest by the fire; so Miss Abbey opened the half-door, and said, as though replying to the crutch-stick: "Yes, come in and rest by the fire."

"My name is Riah," said the old man, with courteous action, "and my avocation is in London city. This, my young companion——"

"Stop a bit," interposed Miss Wren. "I'll give the lady my card." She produced it from her pocket with an air, after struggling with the gigantic door-key which had got upon the top of it and kept it down. Miss Abbey, with manifest tokens of astonishment, took the diminutive document, and found it to run concisely thus:—

Miss JENNY WREN,

DOLLS' DRESSMAKER.

———

Dolls attended at their own residences.

"Lud!" exclaimed Miss Potterson, staring. And dropped the card.

"We take the liberty of coming, my young companion and I, madam," said Riah, "on behalf of Lizzie Hexam."

Miss Potterson was stooping to loosen the bonnet-strings of the dolls' dressmaker. She looked round rather angrily, and said: "Lizzie Hexam is a very proud young woman."

"She would be so proud," returned Riah, dexterously, "to stand well in your good opinion, that before she quitted London for——"

"For where, in the name of the Cape of Good Hope?" asked Miss Potterson, as though supposing her to have emigrated.

"For the country," was the cautious answer,—"she made us promise to come and show you a paper, which she left in our hands for that special purpose. I am an unserviceable friend of hers, who began to know her after her departure from this neighbourhood. She has been for some time living with my young companion, and has been a helpful and a comfortable friend to her. Much needed, madam," he added, in a lower voice. "Believe me; if you knew all, much needed."

"I can believe that," said Miss Abbey, with a softening glance at the little creature.

"And if it's proud to have a heart that never hardens, and a temper that never tires, and a touch that never hurts," Miss Jenny struck in, flushed, "she is proud. And if it's not, she is NOT."

Her set purpose of contradicting Miss Abbey point blank, was so far from offending that dread authority, as to elicit a gracious smile. "You do right, child," said Miss Abbey, "to speak well of those who deserve well of you."

"Right or wrong," muttered Miss Wren, inaudibly, with a visible hitch of her chin, "I mean to do it, and you may make up your mind to *that*, old lady."

"Here is the paper, madam," said the Jew, delivering into

Miss Potterson's hands the original document drawn up by Rokesmith, and signed by Riderhood. "Will you please to read it?"

"But first of all," said Miss Abbey, "—did you ever taste shrub, child?"

Miss Wren shook her head.

"Should you like to?"

"Should if it's good," returned Miss Wren.

"You shall try. And, if you find it good, I'll mix some for you with hot water. Put your poor little feet on the fender. It's a cold, cold night, and the fog clings so." As Miss Abbey helped her to turn her chair, her loosened bonnet dropped on the floor. "Why, what lovely hair!" cried Miss Abbey. "And enough to make wigs for all the dolls in the world. What a quantity!"

"Call *that* a quantity?" returned Miss Wren. "Poof! What do you say to the rest of it?" As she spoke, she untied a band, and the golden stream fell over herself and over the chair, and flowed down to the ground. Miss Abbey's admiration seemed to increase her perplexity. She beckoned the Jew towards her, as she reached down the shrub-bottle from its niche, and whispered:

"Child, or woman?"

"Child in years," was the answer; "woman in self-reliance and trial."

"You are talking about Me, good people," thought Miss Jenny, sitting in her golden bower, warming her feet. "I can't hear what you say, but *I* know your tricks and your manners!"

The shrub, when tasted from a spoon, perfectly harmonising with Miss Jenny's palate, a judicious amount was mixed by Miss Potterson's skilful hands, whereof Riah too partook. After this preliminary, Miss Abbey read the document; and, as often as she raised her eyebrows in so doing, the watchful Miss Jenny accompanied the action with an expressive and emphatic sip of the shrub and water.

"As far as this goes," said Miss Abbey Potterson, when she had read it several times, and thought about it, "it proves (what didn't much need proving) that Rogue Riderhood is a villain. I have my doubts whether he is not the villain who solely did the deed; but I have no expectation of those doubts ever being cleared up now. I believe I did Lizzie's father wrong, but never Lizzie's self; because when things were at the worst I trusted her, had perfect confidence in her, and tried to persuade her to come to me for a refuge. I am very sorry to have done a man wrong, particularly when it can't be undone. Be kind enough to let Lizzie know what I say; not forgetting that if she will come to the Porters, after all, bygones being bygones, she will find a home at the Porters, and a friend at the Porters. She knows Miss Abbey of old, remind her, and she knows what-like the home, and what-like the friend, is likely to turn out. I am generally short and sweet—or short and sour, according as it may be and as opinions vary—" remarked Miss Abbey, "and that's about all I have got to say, and enough too."

But before the shrub and water was sipped out, Miss Abbey bethought herself that she would like to keep a copy of the paper by her. "It's not long, sir," said she to Riah, "and perhaps you wouldn't mind just jotting it down." The old man willingly put on his spectacles, and, standing at the little desk in the corner where Miss Abbey filed her receipts and kept her sample phials (customers' scores were interdicted by the strict administration of the Porters), wrote out the copy in a fair round character. As he stood there, doing his methodical penmanship, his ancient scribe-like figure intent upon the work, and the little dolls' dressmaker sitting in her golden bower before the fire, Miss Abbey had her doubts whether she had not dreamed those two rare figures into the bar of the Six Jolly Fellowships, and might not wake with a nod next moment and find them gone.

Miss Abbey had twice made the experiment of shutting

her eyes and opening them again, still finding the figures there, when, dream-like, a confused hubbub arose in the public room. As she started up, and they all three looked at one another, it became a noise of clamouring voices and of the stir of feet; then all the windows were heard to be hastily thrown up, and shouts and cries came floating into the house from the river. A moment more, and Bob Gliddery came clattering along the passage, with the noise of all the nails in his boots condensed into every separate nail.

"What is it?" asked Miss Abbey.

"It's summut run down in the fog, ma'am," answered Bob. "There's ever so many people in the river."

"Tell 'em to put on all the kettles!" cried Miss Abbey. "See that the boiler's full. Get a bath out. Hang some blankets to the fire. Heat some stone bottles. Have your senses about you, you girls down-stairs, and use 'em."

While Miss Abbey partly delivered these directions to Bob—whom she seized by the hair, and whose head she knocked against the wall, as a general injunction to vigilance and presence of mind—and partly hailed the kitchen with them—the company in the public room, jostling one another, rushed out to the causeway, and the outer noise increased.

"Come and look," said Miss Abbey to her visitors. They all three hurried to the vacated public room, and passed by one of the windows into the wooden verandah overhanging the river.

"Does anybody down there know what has happened?" demanded Miss Abbey, in her voice of authority.

"It's a steamer, Miss Abbey," cried one blurred figure in the fog.

"It always *is* a steamer, Miss Abbey," cried another.

"Them's her lights, Miss Abbey, wot you see a-blinking yonder," cried another.

"She's a-blowing off her steam, Miss Abbey, and that's what makes the fog and the noise worse, don't you see?" exclaimed another.

RUN DOWN IN THE FOG

Boats were putting off, torches were lighting up, people were rushing tumultuously to the water's edge. Some man fell in with a splash, and was pulled out again with a roar of laughter. The drags were called for. A cry for the life-buoy passed from mouth to mouth. It was impossible to make out what was going on upon the river, for every boat that put off sculled into the fog and was lost to view at a boat's length. Nothing was clear but that the unpopular steamer was assailed with reproaches on all sides. She was the Murderer, bound for Gallows Bay; she was the Man-slaughterer, bound for Penal Settlement; her captain ought to be tried for his life; her crew ran down men in row-boats with a relish; she mashed up Thames lightermen with her paddles; she fired property with her funnels; she always was, and she always would be, wreaking destruction upon some-body or something, after the manner of all her kind. The whole bulk of the fog teemed with such taunts, uttered in tones of universal hoarseness. All the while, the steamer's lights moved spectrally a very little, as she lay-to, waiting the upshot of whatever accident had happened. Now, she began burning blue-lights. These made a luminous patch about her, as if she had set the fog on fire, and in the patch—the cries changing their note, and becoming more fitful and more excited—shadows of men and boats could be seen moving, while voices shouted: "There!" "There again!" "A couple more strokes a-head!" "Hurrah!" "Look out!" "Hold on!" "Haul in!" and the like. Lastly, with a few tumbling clots of blue fire, the night closed in dark again, the wheels of the steamer were heard revolving, and her lights glided smoothly away in the direction of the sea.

It appeared to Miss Abbey and her two companions that a considerable time had been thus occupied. There was now as eager a set towards the shore beneath the house as there had been from it; and it was only on the first boat of the rush coming in that it was known what had occurred.

"If that's Tom Tootle," Miss Abbey made proclamation, in her most commanding tones, "let him instantly come underneath here."

The submissive Tom complied, attended by a crowd.

"What is it, Tootle?" demanded Miss Abbey.

"It's a foreign steamer, Miss, run down a wherry."

"How many in the wherry?"

"One man, Miss Abbey."

"Found?"

"Yes. He's been under water a long time, Miss; but they've grappled up the body."

"Let 'em bring it here. You, Bob Gliddery, shut the house-door and stand by it on the inside, and don't you open till I tell you. Any police down there?"

"Here, Miss Abbey," was the official rejoinder.

"After they have brought the body in, keep the crowd out, will you? And help Bob Gliddery to shut 'em out."

"All right, Miss Abbey."

The autocratic landlady withdrew into the house with Riah and Miss Jenny, and disposed those forces, one on either side of her, within the half-door of the bar, as behind a breastwork.

"You two stand close here," said Miss Abbey, "and you'll come to no hurt, and see it brought in. Bob, you stand by the door."

That sentinel, smartly giving his rolled shirt-sleeves an extra and a final tuck on his shoulders, obeyed.

Sound of advancing voices, sound of advancing steps. Shuffle and talk without. Momentary pause. Two peculiarly blunt knocks or pokes at the door, as if the dead man arriving on his back were striking at it with the soles of his motionless feet.

"That's the stretcher, or the shutter, whichever of the two they are carrying," said Miss Abbey, with experienced ear. "Open, you Bob!"

Door opened. Heavy tread of laden men. A halt. A

28

rush. Stoppage of rush. Door shut. Baffled hoots from the vexed souls of disappointed outsiders.

" Come on, men ! " said Miss Abbey ; for so potent was she with her subjects that even then the bearers awaited her permission. " First floor."

The entry being low, and the staircase being low, they so took up the burden they had set down, as to carry that low. The recumbent figure, in passing, lay hardly as high as the half-door.

Miss Abbey started back at sight of it. " Why, good God ! " said she, turning to her two companions, " that's the very man who made the declaration we have just had in our hands. That's Riderhood ! "

CHAPTER III

In sooth, it is Riderhood and no other, or it is the outer husk and shell of Riderhood and no other, that is borne into Miss Abbey's first-floor bedroom. Supple to twist and turn as the Rogue has ever been, he is sufficiently rigid now ; and not without much shuffling of attendant feet, and tilting of his bier this way and that way, and peril even of his sliding off it and being tumbled in a heap over the balustrades, can he be got up-stairs.

" Fetch a doctor," quoth Miss Abbey. And then, " Fetch his daughter." On both of which errands, quick messengers depart.

The doctor-seeking messenger meets the doctor half-way, coming under convoy of police. Doctor examines the dank carcase, and pronounces, not hopefully, that it is worth while trying to reanimate the same. All the best means are at once in action, and everybody present lends a hand, and a heart and soul. No one has the least regard for the man : with them all, he has been an object of avoidance, suspicion, and aversion ; but the spark of life within him is curiously separable from himself now, and they have a deep interest in it, probably because it *is* life, and they are living and must die.

In answer to the doctor's inquiry how did it happen, and was any one to blame, Tom Tootle gives in his verdict, unavoidable

30

accident and no one to blame but the sufferer. "He was slinking about in his boat," says Tom, "which slinking were, not to speak ill of the dead, the manner of the man, when he come right athwart the steamer's bows and she cut him in two." Mr. Tootle is so far figurative, touching the dismemberment, as that he means the boat, and not the man. For, the man lies whole before them.

Captain Joey, the bottle-nosed regular customer in the glazed hat, is a pupil of the much-respected old school, and (having insinuated himself into the chamber, in the execution of the important service of carrying the drowned man's neckkerchief) favours the doctor with a sagacious old-scholastic suggestion that the body should be hung up by the heels, "sim'lar," says Captain Joey, "to mutton in a butcher's shop," and should then, as a particularly choice manœuvre for promoting easy respiration, be rolled upon casks. These scraps of the wisdom of the Captain's ancestors are received with such speechless indignation by Miss Abbey, that she instantly seizes the Captain by the collar, and without a single word ejects him, not presuming to remonstrate, from the scene.

There then remain, to assist the doctor and Tom, only those three other regular customers, Bob Glamour, William Williams, and Jonathan (family name of the latter, if any, unknown to mankind), who are quite enough. Miss Abbey having looked in to make sure that nothing is wanted, descends to the bar, and there awaits the result, with the gentle Jew and Miss Jenny Wren.

If you are not gone for good, Mr. Riderhood, it would be something to know where you are hiding at present. This flabby lump of mortality that we work so hard at with such patient perseverance, yields no sign of you. If you are gone for good, Rogue, it is very solemn, and if you are coming back, it is hardly less so. Nay, in the suspense and mystery of the latter question, involving that of where you may be now, there is a solemnity even added to that of death, making

31

us who are in attendance alike afraid to look on you and to look off you, and making those below start at the least sound of a creaking plank in the floor.

Stay! Did that eyelid tremble? So the doctor, breathing low, and closely watching, asks himself.

No.

Did that nostril twitch?

No.

This artificial respiration ceasing, do I feel any faint flutter under my hand upon the chest?

No.

Over and over again No. No. But try over and over again, nevertheless.

See! A token of life! An indubitable token of life! The spark may smoulder and go out, or it may glow and expand, but see! The four rough fellows seeing, shed tears. Neither Riderhood in this world, nor Riderhood in the other, could draw tears from them; but a striving human soul between the two can do it easily.

He is struggling to come back. Now he is almost here, now he is far away again. Now he is struggling harder to get back. And yet—like us all, when we swoon—like us all, every day of our lives when we wake—he is instinctively unwilling to be restored to the consciousness of this existence, and would be left dormant, if he could.

Bob Gliddery returns with Pleasant Riderhood, who was out when sought for, and hard to find. She has a shawl over her head, and her first action, when she takes it off weeping, and curtseys to Miss Abbey, is to wind her hair up.

"Thank you, Miss Abbey, for having father here."

"I am bound to say, girl, I didn't know who it was," returns Miss Abbey; "but I hope it would have been pretty much the same if I had known."

Poor Pleasant, fortified with a sip of brandy, is ushered into the first-floor chamber. She could not express much sentiment about her father if she were called upon to pronounce his funeral oration, but she has a greater tenderness for him than he ever had for her, and crying bitterly when she sees him stretched unconscious, asks the doctor with clasped hands: "Is there no hope, sir? Oh, poor father! Is poor father dead?"

To which the doctor, on one knee beside the body, busy and watchful, only rejoins without looking round: "Now, my girl, unless you have the self-command to be perfectly quiet, I cannot allow you to remain in the room."

Pleasant, consequently, wipes her eyes with her back-hair, which is in fresh need of being wound up, and having got it out of the way, watches with terrified interest all that goes on. Her natural woman's aptitude soon renders her able to give a little help. Anticipating the doctor's want of this or that, she quietly has it ready for him, and so by degrees is intrusted with the charge of supporting her father's head upon her arm.

It is something so new to Pleasant to see her father an object of sympathy and interest, to find any one very willing to tolerate his society in this world, not to say pressingly and soothingly entreating him to belong to it, that it gives her a sensation she never experienced before. Some hazy idea that if affairs could remain thus for a long time it would be a respectable change, floats in her mind. Also some vague idea that the old evil is drowned out of him, and that if he should happily come back to resume his occupation of the empty form that lies upon the bed, his spirit will be altered. In which state of mind she kisses the stony lips, and quite believes that the impassive hand she chafes will revive a tender hand, if it revive ever.

Sweet delusion for Pleasant Riderhood. But they minister to him with such extraordinary interest, their anxiety is so keen, their vigilance is so great, their excited joy grows so intense as the signs of life strengthen, that how can she resist it, poor thing! And now he begins to breathe naturally, and he stirs, and the doctor declares him to have come back from that inexplicable journey where he stopped on the dark road, and to be here.

Tom Tootle, who is nearest to the doctor when he says this, grasps the doctor fervently by the hand. Bob Glamour, William Williams, and Jonathan of the no surname, all shake hands with one another round, and with the doctor too. Bob Glamour blows his nose, and Jonathan of the no surname is moved to do likewise, but lacking a pocket handkerchief, abandons that outlet for his emotion. Pleasant sheds tears deserving her own name, and her sweet delusion is at its height.

There is intelligence in his eyes. He wants to ask a question. He wonders where he is. Tell him.

" Father, you were run down on the river, and are at Miss Abbey Potterson's."

He stares at his daughter, stares all around him, closes his eyes, and lies slumbering on her arm.

The short-lived delusion begins to fade. The low, bad, unimpressible face is coming up from the depths of the river, or what other depths, to the surface again. As he grows warm, the doctor and the four men cool. As his lineaments soften with life, their faces and their hearts harden to him.

" He will do now," says the doctor, washing his hands, and looking at the patient with growing disfavour.

" Many a better man," moralizes Tom Tootle, with a gloomy shake of the head, " ain't had his luck."

" It's to be hoped he'll make a better use of his life," says Bob Glamour, " than I expect he will."

" Or than he done afore ! " adds William Williams.

" But no, not he ! " says Jonathan of the no surname, clinching the quartette.

They speak in a low tone because of his daughter, but she sees that they have all drawn off, and that they stand in a group at the other end of the room, shunning him. It would be too much to suspect them of being sorry that he didn't die when he had done so much towards it, but they clearly

34

Rogue Riderhood's Recovery

wish that they had had a better subject to bestow their pains on. Intelligence is conveyed to Miss Abbey in the bar, who reappears on the scene, and contemplates from a distance, holding whispered discourse with the doctor. The spark of life was deeply interesting while it was in abeyance, but now that it has got established in Mr. Riderhood, there appears to be a general desire that circumstances had admitted of its being developed in anybody else, rather than that gentleman.

" However," says Miss Abbey, cheering them up, " you have done your duty like good and true men, and you had better come down and take something at the expense of the Porters."

This they all do, leaving the daughter watching the father. To whom, in their absence, Bob Gliddery presents himself.

" His gills look rum ; don't they ? " says Bob, after inspecting the patient.

Pleasant faintly nods.

" His gills 'll look rummer when he wakes ; won't they ? " says Bob.

Pleasant hopes not. Why ?

" When he finds himself here, you know," Bob explains. " 'Cause Miss Abbey forbid him the house and ordered him out of it. But what you may call the Fates ordered him into it again. Which is rumness : ain't it ? "

" He wouldn't have come here of his own accord," returns poor Pleasant, with an effort at a little pride.

" No," retorts Bob. " Nor he wouldn't have been let in if he had."

The short delusion is quite dispelled now. As plainly as she sees on her arm the old father, unimproved, Pleasant sees that everybody there will cut him when he recovers consciousness. " I'll take him away ever so soon as I can," thinks Pleasant with a sigh ; " he's best at home."

Presently they all return, and wait for him to become conscious that they will all be glad to get rid of him. Some clothes are got together for him to wear, his own being

35

saturated with water, and his present dress being composed of blankets.

Becoming more and more uncomfortable, as though the prevalent dislike were finding him out somewhere in his sleep and expressing itself to him, the patient at last opens his eyes wide, and is assisted by his daughter to sit up in bed.

" Well, Riderhood," says the doctor, " how do you feel ? "

He replies gruffly, " Nothing to boast on." Having, in fact, returned to life in an uncommonly sulky state.

" I don't mean to preach ; but I hope," says the doctor, gravely shaking his head, " that this escape may have a good effect upon you, Riderhood."

The patient's discontented growl of a reply is not intelligible ; his daughter, however, could interpret, if she would, that what he says is he " don't want no Poll Parroting."

Mr. Riderhood next demands his shirt ; and draws it on over his head (with his daughter's help) exactly as if he had just had a Fight.

" Warn't it a steamer ? " he pauses to ask her.

" Yes, father."

" I'll have the law on her, bust her ! and make her pay for it."

He then buttons his linen very moodily, twice or thrice stopping to examine his arms and hands, as if to see what punishment he has received in the Fight. He then doggedly demands his other garments, and slowly gets them on, with an appearance of great malevolence towards his late opponent and all the spectators. He has an impression that his nose is bleeding, and several times draws the back of his hand across it, and looks for the result, in a pugilistic manner, greatly strengthening that incongruous resemblance.

" Where's my fur cap ? " he asks in a surly voice, when he has shuffled his clothes on.

" In the river," somebody rejoins.

" And warn't there no honest man to pick it up ? O'

course there was though, and to cut off with it arterwards. You are a rare lot, all on you."

Thus, Mr. Riderhood: taking from the hands of his daughter, with special ill-will, a lent cap, and grumbling as he pulls it down over his ears. Then, getting on his unsteady legs, leaning heavily upon her, and growling " Hold still, can't you? What! You must be a staggering next, must you?" he takes his departure out of the ring in which he has had that little turn-up with Death.

CHAPTER IV

Mr. and Mrs. Wilfer had seen a full quarter of a hundred more anniversaries of their wedding-day than Mr. and Mrs. Lammle had seen of theirs, but they still celebrated the occasion in the bosom of their family. Not that these celebrations ever resulted in anything particularly agreeable, or that the family was ever disappointed by that circumstance on account of having looked forward to the return of the auspicious day with sanguine anticipations of enjoyment. It was kept morally, rather as a Fast than a Feast, enabling Mrs. Wilfer to hold a sombre darkling state, which exhibited that impressive woman in her choicest colours.

The noble lady's condition on these delightful occasions was one compounded of heroic endurance and heroic forgiveness. Lurid indications of the better marriages she might have made, shone athwart the awful gloom of her composure, and fitfully revealed the cherub as a little monster unaccountably favoured by Heaven, who had possessed himself of a blessing for which many of his superiors had sued and contended in vain. So firmly had this his position towards his treasure become established, that when the anniversary arrived, it always found him in an apologetic state. It is not impossible that his modest penitence may have even gone the length of sometimes severely reproving him for that he ever took the liberty of making so exalted a character his wife.

38

As for the children of the union, their experience of these festivals had been sufficiently uncomfortable to lead them annually to wish, when out of their tenderest years, either that Ma had married somebody else instead of much-teased Pa, or that Pa had married somebody else instead of Ma. When there came to be but two sisters left at home, the daring mind of Bella on the next of these occasions scaled the height of wondering with droll vexation, " what on earth Pa ever could have seen in Ma, to induce him to make such a little fool of himself as to ask her to have him."

The revolving year now bringing the day round in its orderly sequence, Bella arrived in the Boffin chariot to assist at the celebration. It was the family custom when the day recurred, to sacrifice a pair of fowls on the altar of Hymen ; and Bella had sent a note beforehand, to intimate that she would bring the votive offering with her. So, Bella and the fowls, by the united energies of two horses, two men, four wheels, and a plum-pudding carriage dog with as uncomfortable a collar on as if he had been George the Fourth, were deposited at the door of the parental dwelling. They were there received by Mrs. Wilfer in person, whose dignity on this, as on most special occasions, was heightened by a mysterious toothache.

" I shall not require the carriage at night," said Bella. " I shall walk back."

The male domestic of Mrs. Boffin touched his hat, and in the act of departure had an awful glare bestowed upon him by Mrs. Wilfer, intended to carry deep into his audacious soul the assurance that, whatever his private suspicions might be, male domestics in livery were no rarity there.

" Well, dear Ma," said Bella, " and how do you do ? "

" I am as well, Bella," replied Mrs. Wilfer, " as can be expected."

" Dear me, Ma," said Bella, " you talk as if one was just born ! "

" That's exactly what Ma has been doing," interposed

Lavvy, over the maternal shoulder, "ever since we got up this morning. It's all very well to laugh, Bella, but anything more exasperating it is impossible to conceive."

Mrs. Wilfer, with a look too full of majesty to be accompanied by any words, attended both her daughters to the kitchen, where the sacrifice was to be prepared.

"Mr. Rokesmith," said she, resignedly, "has been so polite as to place his sitting-room at our disposal to-day. You will therefore, Bella, be entertained in the humble abode of your parents, so far in accordance with your present style of living, that there will be a drawing-room for your reception as well as a dining-room. Your papa invited Mr. Rokesmith to partake of our lowly fare. In excusing himself on account of a particular engagement, he offered the use of his apartment."

Bella happened to know that he had no engagement out of his own room at Mr. Boffin's, but she approved of his staying away. "We should only have put one another out of countenance," she thought, "and we do that quite often enough as it is."

Yet she had sufficient curiosity about his room, to run up to it with the least possible delay, and make a close inspection of its contents. It was tastefully though economically furnished, and very neatly arranged. There were shelves and stands of books, English, French, and Italian; and in a portfolio on the writing-table there were sheets upon sheets of memoranda and calculations in figures, evidently referring to the Boffin property. On that table also, carefully backed with canvas, varnished, mounted, and rolled like a map, was the placard descriptive of the murdered man who had come from afar to be her husband. She shrank from this ghostly surprise, and felt quite frightened as she rolled and tied it up again. Peeping about here and there, she came upon a print, a graceful head of a pretty woman, elegantly framed, hanging in the corner by the easy chair. "Oh, indeed, sir!" said Bella, after stopping to ruminate before it. "Oh, indeed, sir! I fancy I can guess whom you think *that's* like. But I'll tell you what it's much more like—your impudence!" Having said which she decamped: not solely because she was offended, but because there was nothing else to look at.

"Now, Ma," said Bella, reappearing in the kitchen with some remains of a blush, "you and Lavvy think magnificent me fit for nothing, but I intend to prove the contrary. I mean to be Cook to-day."

"Hold!" rejoined her majestic mother. "I cannot permit it. Cook, in that dress!"

"As for my dress, Ma," returned Bella, merrily searching in a dresser-drawer, "I mean to apron it and towel it all over the front; and as to permission, I mean to do without."

"*You* cook?" said Mrs. Wilfer. "*You* who never cooked when you were at home?"

"Yes, Ma," returned Bella; "that is precisely the state of the case."

She girded herself with a white apron, and busily with knots and pins contrived a bib to it, coming close and tight under her chin, as if it had caught her round the neck to kiss her. Over this bib her dimples looked delightful, and under it her pretty figure not less so. "Now, Ma," said Bella, pushing back her hair from her temples with both hands, "what's first?"

"First," returned Mrs. Wilfer solemnly, "if you persist in what I cannot but regard as conduct utterly incompatible with the equipage in which you arrived—— "

("Which I do, Ma.")

"First, then, you put the fowls down to the fire."

"To—be—sure!" cried Bella; "and flour them, and twirl them round, and there they go!" sending them spinning at a great rate. "What's next, Ma?"

"Next," said Mrs. Wilfer with a wave of her gloves, expressive of abdication under protest from the culinary throne, "I would recommend examination of the bacon in the saucepan on the fire, and also of the potatoes by the application of a fork. Preparation of the greens will further become necessary if you persist in this unseemly demeanour."

" As of course I do, Ma."

Persisting, Bella gave her attention to one thing and forgot the other, and gave her attention to the other and forgot the third, and remembering the third was distracted by the fourth, and made amends whenever she went wrong by giving the unfortunate fowls an extra spin, which made their chance of ever getting cooked exceedingly doubtful. But it was pleasant cookery too. Meantime Miss Lavinia, oscillating between the kitchen and the opposite room, prepared the dining-table in the latter chamber. This office she (always doing her household spiriting with unwillingness) performed in a startling series of whisks and bumps ; laying the table-cloth as if she were raising the wind, putting down the glasses and salt-cellars as if she were knocking at the door, and clashing the knives and forks in a skirmishing manner suggestive of hand-to-hand conflict.

" Look at Ma," whispered Lavinia to Bella when this was done, and they stood over the roasting fowls. " If one was the most dutiful child in existence (of course on the whole one hopes one is), isn't she enough to make one want to poke her with something wooden, sitting there bolt upright in the corner ? "

" Only suppose," returned Bella, " that poor Pa was to sit bolt upright in another corner."

" My dear, he couldn't do it," said Lavvy. " Pa would loll directly. But indeed I do not believe there ever was any human creature who could keep so bolt upright as Ma, or put such an amount of aggravation into one back ! What's the matter, Ma ? Ain't you well, Ma ? "

" Doubtless I am very well," returned Mrs. Wilfer, turning her eyes upon her youngest born, with scornful fortitude. " What should be the matter with Me ? "

" You don't seem very brisk, Ma," retorted Lavvy the bold.

" Brisk ? " repeated her parent. " Brisk ? Whence the low

42

expression, Lavinia? If I am uncomplaining, if I am silently contented with my lot, let that suffice for my family."

"Well, Ma," returned Lavvy, "since you will force it out of me, I must respectfully take leave to say that your family are no doubt under the greatest obligations to you for having an annual toothache on your wedding-day, and that it's very disinterested in you, and an immense blessing to them. Still, on the whole, it is possible to be too boastful even of that boon."

"You incarnation of sauciness," said Mrs. Wilfer, "do you speak like that to me? On this day of all days in the year? Pray do you know what would have become of you, if I had not bestowed my hand upon R. W., your father, on this day?"

"No, Ma," replied Lavvy, "I really do not; and, with the greatest respect for your abilities and information, I very much doubt if you do either."

Whether or no the sharp vigour of this sally on a weak point of Mrs. Wilfer's entrenchments might have routed that heroine for the time, is rendered uncertain by the arrival of a flag of truce in the person of Mr. George Sampson : bidden to the feast as a friend of the family, whose affections were now understood to be in course of transference from Bella to Lavinia, and whom Lavinia kept—possibly in remembrance of his bad taste in having overlooked her in the first instance— under a course of stinging discipline.

"I congratulate you, Mrs. Wilfer," said Mr. George Sampson, who had meditated this neat address while coming along, "on the day." Mrs. Wilfer thanked him with a magnanimous sigh, and again became an unresisting prey to that inscrutable toothache.

"I am surprised," said Mr. Sampson feebly, "that Miss Bella condescends to cook."

Here Miss Lavinia descended on the ill-starred young gentleman with a crushing supposition that at all events it was no business of his. This disposed of Mr. Sampson in a melancholy retirement of spirit, until the cherub arrived, whose amazement at the lovely woman's occupation was great.

However, she persisted in dishing the dinner as well as cooking it, and then sat down, bibless and apronless, to partake of it as an illustrious guest: Mrs. Wilfer first responding to her husband's cheerful " For what we are about to receive— " with a sepulchral Amen, calculated to cast a damp upon the stoutest appetite.

" But what," said Bella, as she watched the carving of the fowls, " makes them pink inside, I wonder, Pa! Is it the breed ? "

" No, I don't think it's the breed, my dear," returned Pa. " I rather think it is because they are not done."

" They ought to be," said Bella.

" Yes, I'm aware they ought to be, my dear," rejoined her father, " but they—ain't."

So, the gridiron was put in requisition, and the good-tempered cherub, who was often as un-cherubically employed in his own family as if he had been in the employment of some of the Old Masters, undertook to grill the fowls. Indeed, except in respect of staring about him (a branch of the public service to which the pictorial cherub is much addicted), this domestic cherub discharged as many odd functions as his prototype; with the difference, say, that he performed with a blacking-brush on the family's boots, instead of performing on enormous wind instruments and double-basses, and that he conducted himself with cheerful alacrity to much useful purpose, instead of foreshortening himself in the air with the vaguest intentions.

Bella helped him with his supplemental cookery, and made him very happy, but put him in mortal terror too by asking him when they sat down at table again, how he supposed they cooked fowls at the Greenwich dinners, and whether he believed they really were such pleasant dinners as people said ? His secret winks and nods of remonstrance, in reply, made the mischievous Bella laugh until she choked, and then Lavinia was obliged to slap her on the back, and then she laughed the more.

But her mother was a fine corrective at the other end of the table; to whom her father, in the innocence of his good fellowship, at intervals appealed with: " My dear, I am afraid you are not enjoying yourself ? "

" Why so, R. W. ? " she would sonorously reply.

" Because, my dear, you seem a little out of sorts."

" Not at all," would be the rejoinder, in exactly the same tone.

" Would you take a merry-thought, my dear ? "

" Thank you. I will take whatever you please, R. W."

" Well, but, my dear, do you like it ? "

" I like it as well as I like anything, R. W." The stately woman would then, with a meritorious appearance of devoting herself to the general good, pursue her dinner as if she were feeding somebody else on high public grounds.

Bella had brought dessert and two bottles of wine, thus shedding unprecedented splendour on the occasion. Mrs. Wilfer did the honours of the first glass by proclaiming: " R. W., I drink to you."

" Thank you, my dear. And I to you."

" Pa and Ma ! " said Bella.

" Permit me," Mrs. Wilfer interposed, with outstretched glove. " No. I think not. I drank to your Pa. If, however, you insist on including me, I can in gratitude offer no objection."

" Why, Lor, Ma," interposed Lavvy the bold, " isn't it the day that made you and Pa one and the same ? I have no patience."

" By whatever other circumstances the day may be marked, it is not the day, Lavinia, on which I will allow a child of mine to pounce upon me. I beg—nay, command !—that you will not pounce. R. W., it is appropriate to recall that it is for you to command and for me to obey. It is your house,

and you are master at your own table. Both our healths!"
Drinking the toast with tremendous stiffness.

"I really am a little afraid, my dear," hinted the cherub
meekly, "that you are not enjoying yourself?"

"On the contrary," returned Mrs. Wilfer, "quite so. Why
should I not?"

"I thought, my dear, that perhaps your face might——"

"My face might be a martyrdom, but what would that
import, or who should know it if I smiled?"

And she did smile; manifestly freezing the blood of Mr.
George Sampson by so doing. For that young gentleman,
catching her smiling eye, was so very much appalled by its
expression as to cast about in his thoughts concerning what
he had done to bring it down upon himself.

"The mind naturally falls," said Mrs. Wilfer, "shall I
say into a reverie, or shall I say into a retrospect? on a day
like this."

Lavvy, sitting with defiantly folded arms, replied (but
not audibly), "For goodness' sake say whichever of the two
you like best, Ma, and get it over."

"The mind," pursued Mrs. Wilfer in an oratorical manner,
"naturally reverts to Papa and Mamma—I here allude to
my parents—at a period before the earliest dawn of this day.
I was considered tall; perhaps I was. Papa and Mamma
were unquestionably tall. I have rarely seen a finer woman
than my mother; never than my father."

The irrepressible Lavvy remarked aloud, "Whatever grandpapa was, he wasn't a female."

"Your grandpapa," retorted Mrs. Wilfer, with an awful
look, and in an awful tone, "was what I describe him to
have been, and would have struck any of his grandchildren
to the earth who presumed to question it. It was one of
mamma's cherished hopes that I should become united to a
tall member of society. It may have been a weakness, but
if so, it was equally the weakness, I believe, of King Frederick
of Prussia." These remarks being offered to Mr. George

Sampson, who had not the courage to come out for single combat, but lurked with his chest under the table and his eyes cast down, Mrs. Wilfer proceeded, in a voice of increasing sternness and impressiveness, until she should force that skulker to give himself up. "Mamma would appear to have had an indefinable foreboding of what afterwards happened, for she would frequently urge upon me, 'Not a little man. Promise me, my child, not a little man. Never, never, never marry a little man!' Papa also would remark to me (he possessed extraordinary humour), 'that a family of whales must not ally themselves with sprats.' His company was eagerly sought, as may be supposed, by the wits of the day, and our house was their continual resort. I have known as many as three copper-plate engravers exchanging the most exquisite sallies and retorts there, at one time." (Here Mr. Sampson delivered himself captive, and said, with an uneasy movement on his chair, that three was a large number, and it must have been highly entertaining.) "Among the most prominent members of that distinguished circle, was a gentleman measuring six feet four in height. *He* was *not* an engraver." (Here Mr. Sampson said, with no reason whatever, Of course not.) "This gentleman was so obliging as to honour me with attentions which I could not fail to understand." (Here Mr. Sampson murmured that when it came to that, you could always tell.) "I immediately announced to both my parents that those attentions were misplaced, and that I could not favour his suit. They inquired was he too tall? I replied it was not the stature, but the intellect was too lofty. At our house, I said, the tone was too brilliant, the pressure was too high, to be maintained by me, a mere woman, in every-day domestic life. I well remember mamma's clasping her hands, and exclaiming, 'This will end in a little man!'" (Here Mr. Sampson glanced at his host and shook his head with despondency.) "She afterwards went so far as to predict that it would end in a little man whose mind would be below the average, but that was in what I may denominate a paroxysm of maternal disappointment. Within a month," said Mrs. Wilfer, deepening her voice, as if she were relating a terrible ghost story, "within a month, I first saw R. W., my husband. Within a year I married him. It is natural for the mind to recall these dark coincidences on the present day."

Mr. Sampson, at length released from the custody of Mrs. Wilfer's eye, now drew a long breath and made the original and striking remark, that there was no accounting for these sort of presentiments. R. W. scratched his head and looked apologetically all round the table until he came to his wife, when observing her as it were shrouded in a more sombre veil than before, he once more hinted, "My dear, I am really afraid you are not altogether enjoying yourself?" To which she once more replied, "On the contrary, R. W. Quite so."

The wretched Mr. Sampson's position at this agreeable entertainment was truly pitiable. For, not only was he exposed defenceless to the harangues of Mrs. Wilfer, but he received the utmost contumely at the hands of Lavinia; who, partly to show Bella that she (Lavinia) could do what she liked with him, and partly to pay him off for still obviously admiring Bella's beauty, led him the life of a dog. Illuminated on the one hand by the stately graces of Mrs. Wilfer's oratory, and shadowed on the other by the checks and frowns of the young lady to whom he had devoted himself in his destitution, the sufferings of this young gentleman were distressing to witness. If his mind for the moment reeled under them, it may be urged, in extenuation of its weakness, that it was constitutionally a knock-kneed mind, and never very strong upon its legs.

The rosy hours were thus beguiled until it was time for Bella to have Pa's escort back. The dimples duly tied up in the bonnet-strings and the leave-taking done, they got out into the air, and the cherub drew a long breath as if he found it refreshing.

"Well, dear Pa," said Bella, "the anniversary may be considered over."

"Yes, my dear," returned the cherub, "there's another of 'em gone."

Bella drew his arm closer through hers as they walked along, and gave it a number of consolatory pats. "Thank you, my dear," he said, as if she had spoken, "I am all right, my dear. Well, and how do you get on, Bella?"

"I am not at all improved, Pa."

"Ain't you really though?"

"No, Pa. On the contrary, I am worse."

"Lor!" said the cherub.

"I am worse, Pa. I make so many calculations how much a year I must have when I marry, and what is the least I can manage to do with, that I am beginning to get wrinkles over my nose. Did you notice any wrinkles over my nose this evening, Pa?"

Pa laughing at this, Bella gave him two or three shakes.

"You won't laugh, sir, when you see your lovely woman turning haggard. You had better be prepared in time, I can tell you. I shall not be able to keep my greediness for money out of my eyes long, and when you see it there you'll be sorry, and serve you right for not being warned in time. Now, sir, we entered into a bond of confidence. Have you anything to impart?"

"I thought it was you who was to impart, my love."

"Oh! did you indeed, sir? Then why didn't you ask me, the moment we came out? The confidences of lovely women are not to be slighted. However, I forgive you this once, and look here, Pa; that's "—Bella laid the little forefinger of her right glove on her lip, and then laid it on her father's lip—"that's a kiss for you. And now I am going seriously to tell you—let me see how many—four secrets. Mind! Serious, grave, weighty secrets. Strictly between ourselves."

"Number one, my dear?" said her father, settling her arm comfortably and confidentially.

"Number one," said Bella, "will electrify you, Pa. Who do you think has"—she was confused here in spite of her merry way of beginning—"has made an offer to me?"

Pa looked in her face, and looked at the ground, and looked in her face again, and declared he could never guess.

"Mr. Rokesmith."

"You don't tell me so, my dear."

"Mis—ter Roke—smith, Pa," said Bella, separating the syllables for emphasis. "What do you say to *that*?"

Pa answered quietly with the counter-question, "What did *you* say to that, my love?"

"I said No," returned Bella sharply. "Of course."

"Yes. Of course," said her father, meditating.

"And I told him why I thought it a betrayal of trust on his part, and an affront to me," said Bella.

"Yes. To be sure. I am astonished indeed. I wonder he committed himself without seeing more of his way first. Now I think of it, I suspect he always has admired you though, my dear."

"A hackney coachman may admire me," remarked Bella, with a touch of her mother's loftiness.

"It's highly probable, my love. Number two, my dear?"

"Number two, Pa, is much to the same purpose, though not so preposterous. Mr. Lightwood would propose to me, if I would let him."

"Then I understand, my dear, that you don't intend to let him?"

Bella again saying, with her former emphasis, "Why, of course not!" her father felt himself bound to echo, "Of course not."

"I don't care for him," said Bella.

"That's enough," her father interposed.

"No, Pa, it's *not* enough," rejoined Bella, giving him another shake or two. "Haven't I told you what a mercenary little wretch I am? It only becomes enough when he has no money, and no clients, and no expectations, and no anything but debts."

"Hah!" said the cherub, a little depressed. "Number three, my dear?"

"Number three, Pa, is a better thing. A generous thing, a noble thing, a delightful thing. Mrs. Boffin has herself told me, as a secret, with her own kind lips—and truer lips never opened or closed in this life, I am sure—that they wish to see me well married; and that when I marry with their consent they will portion me most handsomely." Here the grateful girl burst out crying very heartily.

"Don't cry, my darling," said her father, with his hand to his eyes; "it's excusable in me to be a little overcome when I find that my dear favourite child is, after all disappointments, to be so provided for and so raised in the world; but don't *you* cry, don't *you* cry. I am very thankful. I congratulate you with all my heart, my dear." The good, soft little fellow, drying his eyes here, Bella put her arms round his neck and tenderly kissed him on the high-road, passionately telling him he was the best of fathers and the best of friends, and that on her wedding-morning she would go down on her knees to him and beg his pardon for having ever teased him, or seemed insensible to the worth of such a patient, sympathetic, genial, fresh young heart. At every one of her adjectives she redoubled her kisses, and finally kissed his hat off, and then laughed immoderately when the wind took it and he ran after it.

When he had recovered his hat and his breath, and they were going on again once more, said her father then: "Number four, my dear?"

Bella's countenance fell in the midst of her mirth. "After all, perhaps I had better put off number four, Pa. Let me try once more, if for never so short a time, to hope that it may not really be so."

The change in her strengthened the cherub's interest in number four, and he said quietly: "May not be so, my dear? May not be how, my dear?"

Bella looked at him pensively, and shook her head.

"And yet I know right well it is so, Pa. I know it only too well."

"My love," returned her father, "you make me quite uncomfortable. Have you said No to anybody else, my dear?"

"No, Pa."

"Yes to anybody?" he suggested, lifting up his eyebrows.

"No, Pa."

"Is there anybody else who would take his chance between Yes and No, if you would let him, my dear?"

"Not that I know of, Pa."

"There can't be somebody who won't take his chance when you want him to?" said the cherub, as a last resource.

"Why, of course not, Pa," said Bella, giving him another shake or two.

"No, of course not," he assented. "Bella, my dear, I am afraid I must either have no sleep to-night, or I must press for number four."

"Oh, Pa, there is no good in number four! I am so sorry for it, I am so unwilling to believe it, I have tried so earnestly not to see it, that it is very hard to tell, even to you. But Mr. Boffin is being spoilt by prosperity, and is changing every day."

"My dear Bella, I hope and trust not."

"I have hoped and trusted not too, Pa; but every day he changes for the worse and for the worse. Not to me—he is always much the same to me—but to others about him. Before my eyes he grows suspicious, capricious, hard, tyrannical, unjust. If ever a good man were ruined by good fortune, it is my benefactor. And yet, Pa, think how terrible the fascination of money is! I see this, and hate this, and dread this, and don't know but that money might make a much worse change in me. And yet I have money always in my thoughts and my desires; and the whole life I place before myself is money, money, money, and what money can make of life!"

CHAPTER V

WERE Bella Wilfer's bright and ready little wits at fault, or was the Golden Dustman passing through the furnace of proof and coming out dross? Ill news travels fast. We shall know full soon.

On that very night of her return from the Happy Return, something chanced which Bella closely followed with her eyes and ears. There was an apartment at the side of the Boffin mansion, known as Mr. Boffin's room. Far less grand than the rest of the house, it was far more comfortable, being pervaded by a certain air of homely snugness, which upholstering despotism had banished to that spot when it inexorably set its face against Mr. Boffin's appeals for mercy in behalf of any other chamber. Thus, although a room of modest situation—for its windows gave on Silas Wegg's old corner—and of no pretensions to velvet, satin, or gilding, it had got itself established in a domestic position analogous to that of an easy dressing-gown or pair of slippers; and whenever the family wanted to enjoy a particularly pleasant fireside evening, they enjoyed it, as an institution that must be, in Mr. Boffin's room.

Mr. and Mrs. Boffin were reported sitting in this room, when Bella got back. Entering it, she found the Secretary there too; in official attendance it would appear, for he was standing with some papers in his hand by a table with shaded candles on it, at which Mr. Boffin was seated thrown back in his easy chair.

" You are busy, sir," said Bella, hesitating at the door.

" Not at all, my dear, not at all. You're one of ourselves. We never make company of you. Come in, come in. Here's the old lady in her usual place."

Mrs. Boffin adding her nod and a smile of welcome to Mr. Boffin's words, Bella took her book to a chair in the fireside corner, by Mrs. Boffin's work-table. Mr. Boffin's station was on the opposite side.

" Now, Rokesmith," said the Golden Dustman, so sharply rapping the table to bespeak his attention as Bella turned the leaves of her book, that she started; " where were we ? "

" You were saying, sir," returned the Secretary, with an air of some reluctance and a glance towards those others who were present, " that you considered the time had come for fixing my salary."

" Don't be above calling it wages, man," said Mr. Boffin, testily. " What the deuce ! I never talked of *my* salary when I was in service."

" My wages," said the Secretary, correcting himself.

" Rokesmith, you are not proud, I hope ? " observed Mr. Boffin, eyeing him askance.

" I hope not, sir."

" Because I never was, when I was poor," said Mr. Boffin. " Poverty and pride don't go at all well together. Mind that. How can they go well together ? Why it stands to reason. A man being poor, has nothing to be proud of. It's nonsense."

With a slight inclination of his head, and a look of some surprise, the Secretary seemed to assent by forming the syllables of the word " nonsense " on his lips.

" Now, concerning these same wages," said Mr. Boffin. " Sit down."

The Secretary sat down.

" Why didn't you sit down before ? " asked Mr. Boffin,

distrustfully. "I hope that wasn't pride? But about these wages. Now, I've gone into the matter, and I say two hundred a year. What do you think of it? Do you think it's enough?"

"Thank you. It is a fair proposal."

"I don't say, you know," Mr. Boffin stipulated, "but what it may be more than enough. And I'll tell you why, Rokesmith. A man of property, like me, is bound to consider the market-price. At first I didn't enter into that as much as I might have done; but I've got acquainted with other men of property since, and I've got acquainted with the duties of property. I mustn't go putting the market-price up, because money may happen not to be an object with me. A sheep is worth so much in the market, and I ought to give it and no more. A secretary is worth so much in the market, and I ought to give it and no more. However, I don't mind stretching a point with you."

"Mr. Boffin, you are very good," replied the Secretary, with an effort.

"Then we put the figure," said Mr. Boffin, "at two hundred a year. Then the figure's disposed of. Now, there must be no misunderstanding regarding what I buy for two hundred a year. If I pay for a sheep, I buy it out and out. Similarly, if I pay for a secretary, I buy *him* out and out."

"In other words, you purchase my whole time?"

"Certainly I do. Look here," said Mr. Boffin, "it ain't that I want to occupy your whole time; you can take up a book for a minute or two when you've nothing better to do, though I think you'll a'most always find something useful to do. But I want to keep you in attendance. It's convenient to have you at all times ready on the premises. Therefore, betwixt your breakfast and your supper,—on the premises I expect to find you."

The Secretary bowed.

"In bygone days, when I was in service myself," said Mr.

Boffin, "I couldn't go cutting about at my will and pleasure, and you won't expect to go cutting about at your will and pleasure. You've rather got into a habit of that, lately; but perhaps it was for want of a right specification betwixt us. Now, let there be a right specification betwixt us, and let it be this. If you want leave, ask for it."

Again the Secretary bowed. His manner was uneasy and astonished, and showed a sense of humiliation.

"I'll have a bell," said Mr. Boffin, "hung from this room to yours, and when I want you I'll touch it. I don't call to mind that I have anything more to say at the present moment."

The Secretary rose, gathered up his papers, and withdrew. Bella's eyes followed him to the door, lighted on Mr. Boffin complacently thrown back in his easy chair, and drooped over her book.

"I have let that chap, that young man of mine," said Mr. Boffin, taking a trot up and down the room, "get above his work. It won't do. I must have him down a peg. A man of property owes a duty to other men of property, and must look sharp after his inferiors."

Bella felt that Mrs. Boffin was not comfortable, and that the eyes of that good creature sought to discover from her face what attention she had given to this discourse, and what impression it had made upon her. For which reason Bella's eyes drooped more engrossedly over her book, and she turned the page with an air of profound absorption in it.

"Noddy," said Mrs. Boffin, after thoughtfully pausing in her work.

"My dear," returned the Golden Dustman, stopping short in his trot.

"Excuse my putting it to you, Noddy, but now really! Haven't you been a little strict with Mr. Rokesmith to-night? Haven't you been a little—just a little little—not quite like your old self?"

"Why, old woman, I hope so," returned Mr. Boffin, cheerfully, if not boastfully.

" Hope so, deary ? "

" Our old selves wouldn't do here, old lady. Haven't you found that out yet ? Our old selves would be fit for nothing here but to be robbed and imposed upon. Our old selves weren't people of fortune ; our new selves are ; it's a great difference."

" Ah ! " said Mrs. Boffin, pausing in her work again, softly to draw a long breath and to look at the fire. " A great difference."

" And we must be up to the difference," pursued her husband ; " we must be equal to the change ; that's what we must be. We've got to hold our own now, against everybody (for everybody's hand is stretched out to be dipped into our pockets), and we have got to recollect that money makes money, as well as makes everything else."

" Mentioning recollecting," said Mrs. Boffin, with her work abandoned, her eyes upon the fire, and her chin upon her hand, " do you recollect, Noddy, how you said to Mr. Rokesmith when he first came to see us at the Bower, and you engaged him—how you said to him that if it had pleased Heaven to send John Harmon to his fortune safe, we could have been content with the one Mound which was our legacy, and should never have wanted the rest ? "

" Ay, I remember, old lady. But we hadn't tried what it was to have the rest then. Our new shoes had come home, but we hadn't put 'em on. We're wearing 'em now, we're wearing 'em, and must step out accordingly."

Mrs. Boffin took up her work again, and plied her needle in silence.

" As to Rokesmith, that young man of mine," said Mr. Boffin, dropping his voice and glancing towards the door with an apprehension of being overheard by some eavesdropper there, " it's the same with him as with the footmen. I have found out that you must either scrunch them, or let them scrunch you. If you ain't imperious with 'em, they won't believe in your being any better than themselves, if as good, after the stories (lies mostly) that they have heard of your beginnings. There's nothing betwixt stiffening yourselves up, and throwing yourself away : take my word for that, old lady."

Bella ventured for a moment to look stealthily towards him under her eyelashes, and she saw a dark cloud of suspicion, covetousness, and conceit, overshadowing the once open face.

" Hows'ever," said he, " this isn't entertaining to Miss Bella. Is it, Bella ? "

A deceiving Bella she was, to look at him with that pensively abstracted air, as if her mind were full of her book, and she had not heard a single word !

" Hah ! Better employed than to attend to it," said Mr. Boffin. " That's right, that's right. Especially as you have no call to be told how to value yourself, my dear."

Colouring a little under this compliment, Bella returned, " I hope, sir, you don't think me vain ? "

" Not a bit, my dear," said Mr. Boffin. " But I think it's very creditable in you, at your age, to be so well up with the pace of the world, and to know what to go in for. You are right. Go in for money, my love. Money's the article. You'll make money of your good looks, and of the money Mrs. Boffin and me will have the pleasure of settling upon you, and you'll live and die rich. That's the state to live and die in ! " said Mr. Boffin, in an unctuous manner. " R—r—rich ! "

There was an expression of distress in Mrs. Boffin's face, as, after watching her husband's, she turned to their adopted girl, and said : " Don't mind him, Bella, my dear."

" Eh ? " cried Mr. Boffin. " What ! Not mind him ? "

" I don't mean that," said Mrs. Boffin, with a worried look, " but I mean, don't believe him to be anything but good and generous, Bella, because he is the best of men. No, I must say that much, Noddy. You are always the best of men."

She made the declaration as if he were objecting to it : which assuredly he was not in any way.

" And as to you, my dear Bella," said Mrs. Boffin, still with that distressed expression, " he is so much attached to you, whatever he says, that your own father has not a truer interest in you and can hardly like you better than he does."

"Says too!" cried Mr. Boffin. "Whatever he says! Why, I say so, openly. Give me a kiss, my dear child, in saying Good Night, and let me confirm what my old lady tells you. I am very fond of you, my dear, and I am entirely of your mind, and you and I will take care that you shall be rich. These good looks of yours (which you have some right to be vain of, my dear, though you are not, you know) are worth money, and you shall make money of 'em. The money you will have, will be worth money, and you shall make money of that too. There's a golden ball at your feet. Good Night, my dear."

Somehow, Bella was not so well pleased with this assurance and this prospect as she might have been. Somehow, when she put her arms round Mrs. Boffin's neck and said Good Night, she derived a sense of unworthiness from the still anxious face of that good woman and her obvious wish to excuse her husband. "Why, what need to excuse him?" thought Bella, sitting down in her own room. "What he said was very sensible, I am sure, and very true, I am sure. It is only what I often say to myself. Don't I like it then? No, I don't like it, and, though he is my liberal benefactor, I disparage him for it. Then pray," said Bella, sternly putting the question to herself in the looking-glass as usual, "what do you mean by this, you inconsistent little Beast?"

The looking-glass preserving a discreet ministerial silence when thus called upon for explanation, Bella went to bed with a weariness upon her spirit which was more than the weariness of want of sleep. And again in the morning, she looked for the cloud, and for the deepening of the cloud, upon the Golden Dustman's face.

She had begun by this time to be his frequent companion in his morning strolls about the streets, and it was at this time that he made her a party to his engaging in a curious pursuit. Having been hard at work in one dull enclosure all his life, he had a child's delight in looking at shops. It had been one of the first novelties and pleasures of his freedom, and was equally the delight of his wife. For many years their only walks in London had been taken on Sundays when the shops were shut ; and when every day in the week became their holiday, they derived an enjoyment from the variety and fancy and beauty of the display in the windows, which seemed incapable of exhaustion. As if the principal streets were a great Theatre and the play were childishly new to them, Mr. and Mrs. Boffin, from the beginning of Bella's intimacy in their house, had been constantly in the front row, charmed with all they saw, and applauding vigorously. But now Mr. Boffin's interest began to centre in book-shops ; and more than that—for that of itself would not have been much—in one exceptional kind of book.

"Look in here, my dear," Mr. Boffin would say, checking Bella's arm at a bookseller's window ; "you can read at sight, and your eyes are as sharp as they're bright. Now, look well about you, my dear, and tell me if you see any book about a Miser."

If Bella saw such a book, Mr. Boffin would instantly dart in and buy it. And still, if they had not found it, they would seek out another book-shop, and Mr. Boffin would say, "Now, look well all round, my dear, for a Life of a Miser, or any book of that sort; any Lives of odd characters who may have been Misers."

Bella, thus directed, would examine the window with the greatest attention, while Mr. Boffin would examine her face. The moment she pointed out any book as being entitled Lives of eccentric personages, Anecdotes of strange characters, Records of remarkable individuals, or anything to that purpose, Mr. Boffin's countenance would light up, and he would instantly dart in and buy it. Size, price, quality, were of no account. Any book that seemed to promise a chance of miserly biography, Mr. Boffin purchased without a moment's delay and carried home. Happening to be informed

Bibliomania of the Golden Dustman

by a bookseller that a portion of the Annual Register was devoted to " Characters," Mr. Boffin at once bought a whole set of that ingenious compilation, and began to carry it home piecemeal, confiding a volume to Bella, and bearing three himself. The completion of this labour occupied them about a fortnight. When the task was done, Mr. Boffin, with his appetite for Misers whetted instead of satiated, began to look out again.

It very soon became unnecessary to tell Bella what to look for, and an understanding was established between her and Mr. Boffin that she was always to look for Lives of Misers. Morning after morning they roamed about the town together, pursuing this singular research. Miserly literature not being abundant, the proportion of failures to successes may have been as a hundred to one ; still Mr. Boffin, never wearied, remained as avaricious for misers as he had been at the first onset. It was curious that Bella never saw the books about the house, nor did she ever hear from Mr. Boffin one word of reference to their contents. He seemed to save up his Misers as they had saved up their money. As they had been greedy for it, and secret about it, and had hidden it, so he was greedy for them, and secret about them, and hid them. But beyond all doubt it was to be noticed, and was by Bella very clearly noticed, that, as he pursued the acquisition of those dismal records with the ardour of Don Quixote for his books of chivalry, he began to spend his money with a more sparing hand. And often when he came out of a shop with some new account of one of those wretched lunatics, she would almost shrink from the sly dry chuckle with which he would take her arm again and trot away. It did not appear that Mrs. Boffin knew of this taste. He made no allusion to it, except in the morning walks when he and Bella were always alone; and Bella, partly under the impression that he took her into his confidence by implication, and partly in remembrance of Mrs. Boffin's anxious face that night, held the same reserve.

While these occurrences were in progress, Mrs. Lammle made
the discovery that Bella had a fascinating influence over her.
The Lammles, originally presented by the dear Veneerings,
visited the Boffins on all grand occasions, and Mrs. Lammle
had not previously found this out; but now the knowledge
came upon her all at once. It was a most extraordinary
thing (she said to Mrs. Boffin); she was foolishly susceptible
of the power of beauty, but it wasn't altogether that; she
never had been able to resist a natural grace of manner, but
it wasn't altogether that; it was more than that, and there
was no name for the indescribable extent and degree to
which she was captivated by this charming girl.

This charming girl having the words repeated to her by
Mrs. Boffin (who was proud of her being admired, and would
have done anything to give her pleasure), naturally recognised
in Mrs. Lammle a woman of penetration and taste. Responding to the sentiments, by being very gracious to Mrs.
Lammle, she gave that lady the means of so improving her
opportunity, as that the captivation became reciprocal, though
always wearing an appearance of greater sobriety on Bella's
part than on the enthusiastic Sophronia's. Howbeit, they
were so much together that, for a time, the Boffin chariot
held Mrs. Lammle oftener than Mrs. Boffin: a preference of
which the latter worthy soul was not in the least jealous,
placidly remarking, " Mrs. Lammle is a younger companion
for her than I am, and Lor! she's more fashionable."

But between Bella Wilfer and Georgiana Podsnap there
was this one difference, among many others, that Bella was
in no danger of being captivated by Alfred. She distrusted
and disliked him. Indeed, her perception was so quick, and
her observation so sharp, that after all she mistrusted his
wife too, though with her giddy vanity and wilfulness she
squeezed the mistrust away into a corner of her mind, and
blocked it up there.

Mrs. Lammle took the friendliest interest in Bella's making
a good match. Mrs. Lammle said, in a sportive way, she

really must show her beautiful Bella what kind of wealthy creatures she and Alfred had on hand, who would as one man fall at her feet enslaved. Fitting occasion made, Mrs. Lammle accordingly produced the most passable of those feverish, boastful, and indefinably loose gentlemen who were always lounging in and out of the City on questions of the Bourse and Greek and Spanish and India and Mexican and par and premium and discount and three-quarters and seven-eighths. Who, in their agreeable manner, did homage to Bella as if she were a compound of fine girl, thorough-bred horse, well-built drag, and remarkable pipe. But without the least effect, though even Mr. Fledgeby's attractions were cast into the scale.

"I fear, Bella dear," said Mrs. Lammle one day in the chariot, "that you will be very hard to please."

"I don't expect to be pleased, dear," said Bella, with a languid turn of her eyes.

"Truly, my love," returned Sophronia, shaking her head, and smiling her best smile, "it would not be very easy to find a man worthy of your attractions."

"The question is not a man, my dear," said Bella, coolly, "but an establishment."

"My love," returned Mrs. Lammle, "your prudence amazes me—where *did* you study life so well?—you are right. In such a case as yours, the object is a fitting establishment. You could not descend to an inadequate one from Mr. Boffin's house, and even if your beauty alone could not command it, it is to be assumed that Mr. and Mrs. Boffin will—— "

"Oh! they have already," Bella interposed.

"No! Have they really?"

A little vexed by a suspicion that she had spoken precipitately, and withal a little defiant of her own vexation, Bella determined not to retreat.

"That is to say," she explained, "they have told me they mean to portion me as their adopted child, if you mean that. But don't mention it."

63

"Mention it!" replied Mrs. Lammle, as if she were full of awakened feeling at the suggestion of such an impossibility. "Men-tion it!"

"I don't mind telling you, Mrs. Lammle——" Bella began again.

"My love, say Sophronia, or I must not say Bella."

With a little short, petulant "Oh!" Bella complied. "Oh!—Sophronia then—I don't mind telling you, Sophronia, that I am convinced I have no heart as people call it; and that I think that sort of thing is nonsense."

"Brave girl!" murmured Mrs. Lammle.

"And so," pursued Bella, "as to seeking to please myself, I don't; except in the one respect I have mentioned. I am indifferent otherwise."

"But you can't help pleasing, Bella," said Mrs. Lammle, rallying her with an arch look and her best smile, "you can't help making a proud and an admiring husband. You may not care to please yourself, and you may not care to please him, but you are not a free agent as to pleasing : you are forced to do that, in spite of yourself, my dear ; so it may be a question whether you may not as well please yourself too, if you can."

Now, the very grossness of this flattery put Bella upon proving that she actually did please in spite of herself. She had a misgiving that she was doing wrong—though she had an indistinct foreshadowing that some harm might come of it thereafter, she little thought what consequences it would really bring about—but she went on with her confidence.

"Don't talk of pleasing in spite of one's self, dear," said Bella. "I have had enough of that."

"Ay ?" cried Mrs. Lammle. "Am I already corroborated, Bella ?"

"Never mind, Sophronia, we will not speak of it any more. Don't ask me about it."

This plainly meaning Do ask me about it, Mrs. Lammle did as she was requested.

"Tell me, Bella. Come, my dear. What provoking burr has been inconveniently attracted to the charming skirts, and with difficulty shaken off?"

"Provoking indeed," said Bella, "and no burr to boast of! But don't ask me."

"Shall I guess?"

"You would never guess. What would you say to our Secretary?"

"My dear! The hermit Secretary, who creeps up and down the back stairs, and is never seen?"

"I don't know about his creeping up and down the back stairs," said Bella, rather contemptuously, "further than knowing that he does no such thing; and as to his never being seen, I should be content never to have seen him, though he is quite as visible as you are. But I pleased *him* (for my sins), and he had the presumption to tell me so."

"The man never made a declaration to you, my dear Bella?"

"Are you sure of that, Sophronia?" said Bella. "*I* am not. In fact, I am sure of the contrary."

"The man must be mad," said Mrs. Lammle, with a kind of resignation.

"He appeared to be in his senses," returned Bella, tossing her head, "and he had plenty to say for himself. I told him my opinion of his declaration and his conduct, and dismissed him. Of course this has all been very inconvenient to me, and very disagreeable. It has remained a secret, however. That word reminds me to observe, Sophronia, that I have glided on into telling you the secret, and that I rely upon you never to mention it."

"Mention it!" repeated Mrs. Lammle with her former feeling. "Men-tion it!"

This time Sophronia was so much in earnest that she found it necessary to bend forward in the carriage and give Bella a kiss. A Judas order of kiss; for she thought, while she yet pressed Bella's hand after giving it, "Upon your own showing,

65

you vain, heartless girl, puffed up by the doting folly of
a dustman, I need have no relenting towards *you*. If my
husband, who sends me here, should form any schemes for
making *you* a victim, I should certainly not cross him again."
In those very same moments, Bella was thinking, " Why am
I always at war with myself? Why have I told, as if upon
compulsion, what I knew all along I ought to have withheld?
Why am I making a friend of this woman beside me, in
spite of the whispers against her that I hear in my heart?"

As usual, there was no answer in the looking-glass when
she got home and referred these questions to it. Perhaps if
she had consulted some better oracle, the result might have
been more satisfactory; but she did not, and all things con-
sequent marched the march before them.

On one point connected with the watch she kept on Mr.
Boffin, she felt very inquisitive, and that was the question
whether the Secretary watched him too, and followed the sure
and steady change in him, as she did? Her very limited
intercourse with Mr. Rokesmith rendered this hard to find
out. Their communication now at no time extended beyond
the preservation of commonplace appearances before Mr. and
Mrs. Boffin; and if Bella and the Secretary were ever left
alone together by any chance, he immediately withdrew.
She consulted his face when she could do so covertly, as she
worked or read, and could make nothing of it. He looked
subdued; but he had acquired a strong command of feature,
and, whenever Mr. Boffin spoke to him in Bella's presence, or
whatever revelation of himself Mr. Boffin made, the Secretary's
face changed no more than a wall. A slightly knitted brow,
that expressed nothing but an almost mechanical attention,
and a compression of the mouth, that might have been a
guard against a scornful smile—these she saw from morning
to night, from day to day, from week to week, monotonous,
unvarying, set, as in a piece of sculpture.

The worst of the matter was, that it thus fell out insensibly
—and most provokingly, as Bella complained to herself, in

her impetuous little manner—that her observation of Mr Boffin involved a continual observation of Mr. Rokesmith.

"Won't *that* extract a look from him?"—"Can it be possible *that* makes no impression on him?" Such questions Bella would propose to herself, often as many times in a day as there were hours in it. Impossible to know. Always the same fixed face.

"Can he be so base as to sell his very nature for two hundred a year?" Bella would think. And then, "But why not? It's a mere question of price with others besides him. I suppose I would sell mine, if I could get enough for it." And so she would come round again to the war with herself.

A kind of illegibility, though a different kind, stole over Mr. Boffin's face. Its old simplicity of expression got masked by a certain craftiness that assimilated even his good-humour to itself. His very smile was cunning, as if he had been studying smiles among the portraits of his misers. Saving an occasional burst of impatience, or coarse assertion of his mastery, his good-humour remained to him, but it had now a sordid alloy of distrust; and though his eyes should twinkle and all his face should laugh, he would sit holding himself in his own arms, as if he had an inclination to hoard himself up, and must always grudgingly stand on the defensive.

What with taking heed of these two faces, and what with feeling conscious that the stealthy occupation must set some mark on her own, Bella soon began to think that there was not a candid or a natural face among them all but Mrs. Boffin's. None the less because it was far less radiant than of yore, faithfully reflecting in its anxiety and regret every line of change in the Golden Dustman's.

"Rokesmith," said Mr. Boffin one evening when they were all in his room again, and he and the Secretary had been going over some accounts, "I am spending too much money. Or leastways, you are spending too much for me."

"You are rich, sir,"

"I am not," said Mr. Boffin.

The sharpness of the retort was next to telling the Secretary that he lied. But it brought no change of expression into the set face.

"I tell you I am not rich," repeated Mr. Boffin, "and I won't have it."

"You are not rich, sir?" repeated the Secretary, in measured words.

"Well," returned Mr. Boffin, "if I am, that's my business. I am not going to spend at this rate, to please you, or anybody. You wouldn't like it, if it was your money."

"Even in that impossible case, sir, I——"

"Hold your tongue!" said Mr. Boffin. "You oughtn't to like it in any case. There! I didn't mean to be rude, but you put me out so, and after all I'm master. I didn't intend to tell you to hold your tongue. I beg your pardon. Don't hold your tongue. Only, don't contradict. Did you ever come across the life of Mr. Elwes?" referring to his favourite subject at last.

"The miser?"

"Ah, people called him a miser. People are always calling other people something. Did you ever read about him?"

"I think so."

"He never owned to being rich, and yet he might have bought me twice over. Did you ever hear of Daniel Dancer?"

"Another miser? Yes."

"He was a good 'un," said Mr. Boffin, "and he had a sister worthy of him. They never called themselves rich neither. If they *had* called themselves rich, most likely they wouldn't have been so."

"They lived and died very miserably. Did they not, sir?"

"No, I don't know that they did," said Mr. Boffin, curtly.

"Then they are not the Misers I mean. Those abject wretches——"

"Don't call names, Rokesmith," said Mr. Boffin.

"——That exemplary brother and sister—lived and died in the foulest and filthiest degradation."

"They pleased themselves," said Mr. Boffin, "and I suppose they could have done no more if they had spent their money. But however, I ain't going to fling mine away. Keep the expenses down. The fact is, you ain't enough here, Rokesmith. It wants constant attention in the littlest things. Some of us will be dying in a workhouse next."

"As the persons you have cited," quietly remarked the Secretary, "thought they would, if I remember, sir?"

"And very creditable in 'em too," said Mr. Boffin. "Very independent in 'em! But never mind them just now. Have you given notice to quit your lodgings?"

"Under your direction, I have, sir."

"Then I tell you what," said Mr. Boffin; "pay the quarter's rent—pay the quarter's rent, it'll be the cheapest thing in the end—and come here at once, so that you may be always on the spot, day and night, and keep the expenses down. You'll charge the quarter's rent to me, and we must try and save it somewhere. You've got some lovely furniture; haven't you?"

"The furniture in my rooms is my own."

"Then we shan't have to buy any for you. In case you was to think it," said Mr. Boffin, with a look of peculiar shrewdness, "so honourably independent in you as to make it a relief to your mind to make that furniture over to me in the light of a set-off against the quarter's rent, why ease your mind, ease your mind. I don't ask it, but I won't stand in your way if you should consider it due to yourself. As to your room, choose any empty room at the top of the house."

"Any empty room will do for me," said the Secretary.

"You can take your pick," said Mr. Boffin, "and it will be as good as eight or ten shillings a week added to your income. I won't deduct for it; I look to you to make it up handsomely by keeping the expenses down. Now, if you'll show a light, I'll come to your office-room and dispose of a letter or two."

On that clear, generous face of Mrs. Boffin's, Bella had seen such traces of a pang at the heart while this dialogue was being held, that she had not the courage to turn her eyes to it when they were left alone. Feigning to be intent on her embroidery, she sat plying her needle until her busy hand was stopped by Mrs. Boffin's hand being lightly laid upon it. Yielding to the touch, she felt her hand carried to the good soul's lips, and felt a tear fall on it.

"Oh, my loved husband!" said Mrs. Boffin. "This is hard to see and hear. But, my dear Bella, believe me that in spite of all the change in him, he is the best of men."

He came back, at the moment when Bella had taken the hand comfortingly between her own.

"Eh?" said he, mistrustfully looking in at the door. "What's she telling you?"

"She's only praising you, sir," said Bella.

"Praising me? You are sure? Not blaming me for standing on my own defence against a crew of plunderers, who would suck me dry by driblets? Not blaming me for getting a little hoard together?"

He came up to them, and his wife folded her hands upon his shoulder, and shook her head as she laid it on her hands.

"There, there, there!" urged Mr. Boffin, not unkindly. "Don't take on, old lady."

"But I can't bear to see you so, my dear."

"Nonsense! Recollect we are not our old selves. Recollect, we must scrunch or be scrunched. Recollect, we must hold our own. Recollect, money makes money. Don't you be uneasy, Bella, my child; don't you be doubtful. The more I save, the more you shall have."

Bella thought it was well for his wife that she was musing with her affectionate face on his shoulder; for there was a cunning light in his eyes as he said all this, which seemed to cast a disagreeable illumination on the change in him, and make it morally uglier.

CHAPTER VI

It had come to pass that Mr. Silas Wegg now rarely attended the minion of fortune and the worm of the hour, at his (the worm's and minion's) own house, but lay under general instructions to await him within a certain margin of hours at the Bower. Mr. Wegg took this arrangement in great dudgeon, because the appointed hours were evening hours, and those he considered precious to the progress of the friendly move. But it was quite in character, he bitterly remarked to Mr. Venus, that the upstart who had trampled on those eminent creatures, Miss Elizabeth, Master George, Aunt Jane, and Uncle Parker, should oppress his literary man.

The Roman Empire having worked out its destruction, Mr. Boffin next appeared in a cab with Rollin's Ancient History, which valuable work being found to possess lethargic properties, broke down, at about the period when the whole of the army of Alexander the Macedonian (at that time about forty thousand strong) burst into tears simultaneously, on his being taken with a shivering fit after bathing. The Wars of the Jews likewise languishing under Mr. Wegg's generalship, Mr. Boffin arrived in another cab with Plutarch: whose Lives he found in the sequel extremely entertaining, though he hoped Plutarch might not expect him to believe them all. What to believe, in the course of his reading, was

71

Mr. Boffin's chief literary difficulty indeed; for some time he was divided in his mind between half, all, or none; at length, when he decided, as a moderate man, to compound with half, the question still remained, which half? And that stumbling-block he never got over.

One evening, when Silas Wegg had grown accustomed to the arrival of his patron in a cab, accompanied by some profane historian charged with unutterable names of incomprehensible peoples, of impossible descent, waging wars any number of years and syllables long, and carrying illimitable hosts and riches about, with the greatest ease, beyond the confines of geography—one evening the usual time passed by, and no patron appeared. After half an hour's grace, Mr. Wegg proceeded to the outer gate, and there executed a whistle, conveying to Mr. Venus, if perchance within hearing, the tidings of his being at home and disengaged. Forth from the shelter of a neighbouring wall, Mr. Venus then emerged.

" Brother in arms," said Mr. Wegg, in excellent spirits, " welcome ! "

In return, Mr. Venus gave him a rather dry good evening.

" Walk in, brother," said Silas, clapping him on the shoulder, " and take your seat in my chimney corner; for what says the ballad?

> 'No malice to dread, sir,
> And no falsehood to fear,
> But truth to delight me, Mr. Venus,
> And I forgot what to cheer.
> Li toddle dee om dee.
> And something to guide,
> My ain fireside, sir,
> My ain fireside.' "

With this quotation (depending for its neatness rather on the spirit than the words), Mr. Wegg conducted his guest to his hearth.

" And you come, brother," said Mr. Wegg, in a hospitable glow, " you come like I don't know what—exactly like it—I shouldn't know you from it—shedding a halo all around you."

" What kind of halo? " asked Mr. Venus.

72

" 'Ope, sir," replied Silas. " That's *your* halo."

Mr. Venus appeared doubtful on the point, and looked rather discontentedly at the fire.

" We'll devote the evening, brother," exclaimed Wegg, " to prosecute our friendly move. And arterwards, crushing a flowing wine-cup—which I allude to brewing rum and water —we'll pledge one another. For what says the Poet?

> 'And you needn't, Mr. Venus, be your black bottle,
> For surely I'll be mine,
> And we'll take a glass with a slice of lemon in it to which you're partial,
> For auld lang syne.' "

This flow of quotation and hospitality in Wegg indicated his observation of some little querulousness on the part of Venus.

" Why, as to the friendly move," observed the last-named gentleman, rubbing his knees peevishly, " one of my objections to it is, that it *don't* move."

" Rome, brother," returned Wegg: " a city which (it may not be generally known) originated in twins and a wolf, and ended in Imperial marble, wasn't built in a day."

" Did I say it was ? " asked Venus.

" No, you did not, brother. Well inquired."

" But I do say," proceeded Venus, " that I am taken from among my trophies of anatomy, am called upon to exchange my human warious for mere coal-ashes warious, and nothing comes of it. I think I must give up."

" No, sir ! " remonstrated Wegg, enthusiastically. " No, sir !

> 'Charge, Chester, charge,
> On, Mr. Venus, on!'

Never say die, sir ! A man of your mark ! "

" It's not so much saying it that I object to," returned Mr. Venus, " as doing it. And having got to do it whether or no, I can't afford to waste my time on groping for nothing in cinders."

" But think how little time you have given to the move, sir, after all," urged Wegg. " Add the evenings so occupied together, and what do they come to? And you, sir, harmonizer with myself in opinions, views, and feelings, you with the patience to fit together on wires the whole framework of society —I allude to the human skelinton—you to give in so soon!"

"I don't like it," returned Mr. Venus moodily, as he put his head between his knees and stuck up his dusty hair. "And there's no encouragement to go on."

"Not them Mounds without," said Mr. Wegg, extending his right hand with an air of solemn reasoning, "encouragement? Not them Mounds now looking down upon us?"

"They're too big," grumbled Venus. "What's a scratch here and a scrape there, a poke in this place and a dig in the other, to them? Besides: what have we found?"

"What *have* we found?" cried Wegg, delighted to be able to acquiesce. "Ah! There I grant you, comrade. Nothing. But on the contrary, comrade, what *may* we find? There you'll grant me. Anything."

"I don't like it," pettishly returned Venus as before. "I came into it without enough consideration. And besides again. Isn't your own Mr. Boffin well acquainted with the Mounds? And wasn't he well acquainted with the deceased and his ways? And has he ever showed any expectation of finding anything?"

At that moment wheels were heard.

"Now, I should be loth," said Mr. Wegg, with an air of patient injury, "to think so ill of him as to suppose him capable of coming at this time of night. And yet it sounds like him."

A ring at the yard bell.

"It *is* him," said Mr. Wegg, "and he *is* capable of it. I am sorry, because I could have wished to keep up a little lingering fragment of respect for him."

Here Mr. Boffin was heard lustily calling at the yard gate, "Halloa! Wegg! Halloa!"

"Keep your seat, Mr. Venus," said Wegg. "He may not stop." And then called out, "Halloa, sir! Halloa! I'm with you directly, sir! Half a minute, Mr. Boffin. Coming, sir, as fast as my leg will bring me!" And so with a show of much cheerful alacrity stumped out to the gate with a light, and there, through the window of a cab, descried Mr. Boffin inside, blocked up with books.

"Here! lend a hand, Wegg," said Mr. Boffin excitedly, "I can't get out till the way is cleared for me. This is the Annual Register, Wegg, in a cabful of wollumes. Do you know him?"

"Know the Animal Register, sir?" returned the Impostor, who had caught the name imperfectly. "For a trifling wager, I think I could find any Animal in him, blindfold, Mr. Boffin."

"And here's Kirby's Wonderful Museum," said Mr. Boffin, "and Caulfield's Characters, and Wilson's. Such Characters, Wegg, such Characters! I must have one or two of the best of 'em to-night. It's amazing what places they used to put the guineas in, wrapped up in rags. Catch hold of that pile of wollumes, Wegg, or it'll bulge out and burst into the mud. Is there any one about, to help?"

"There's a friend of mine, sir, that had the intention of spending the evening with me when I gave you up—much against my will—for the night."

"Call him out," cried Mr. Boffin in a bustle; "get him to bear a hand. Don't drop that one under your arm. It's Dancer. Him and his sister made pies of a dead sheep they found when they were out a-walking. Where's your friend? Oh, here's your friend. Would you be so good as help Wegg and myself with these books? But don't take Jemmy Taylor of Southwark, nor yet Jemmy Wood of Gloucester. These are the two Jemmys. I'll carry them myself."

Not ceasing to talk and bustle, in a state of great excitement, Mr. Boffin directed the removal and arrangement of the books, appearing to be in some sort beside himself until they were all deposited on the floor, and the cab was dismissed.

"There!" said Mr. Boffin, gloating over them. "There they

are, like the four-and-twenty fiddlers—all of a row. Get on your spectacles, Wegg; I know where to find the best of 'em, and we'll have a taste at once of what we have got before us. What's your friend's name?"

Mr. Wegg presented his friend as Mr. Venus.

"Eh?" cried Mr. Boffin, catching at the name. "Of Clerkenwell?"

"Of Clerkenwell, sir," said Mr. Venus.

"Why, I've heard of you," cried Mr. Boffin. "I heard of you in the old man's time. You knew him. Did you ever buy anything of him?" With piercing eagerness.

"No, sir," returned Venus.

"But he showed you things; didn't he?"

Mr. Venus, with a glance at his friend, replied in the affirmative.

"What did he show you?" asked Mr. Boffin, putting his hands behind him, and eagerly advancing his head. "Did he show you boxes, little cabinets, pocket-books, parcels, anything locked or sealed, anything tied up?"

Mr. Venus shook his head.

"Are you a judge of china?"

Mr. Venus again shook his head.

"Because if he had ever showed you a teapot, I should be glad to know of it," said Mr. Boffin. And then, with his right hand at his lips, repeated thoughtfully, "A Teapot, a Teapot," and glanced over the books on the floor, as if he knew there was something interesting connected with a teapot somewhere among them.

Mr. Wegg and Mr. Venus looked at one another wonderingly: and Mr. Wegg, in fitting on his spectacles, opened his eyes wide, over their rims, and tapped the side of his nose: as an admonition to Venus to keep himself generally wide awake.

"A Teapot," repeated Mr. Boffin, continuing to muse and survey the books; "a Teapot, a Teapot. Are you ready, Wegg?"

"I am at your service, sir," replied that gentleman, taking his usual seat on the usual settle, and poking his wooden leg under the table before it. "Mr. Venus, would you make yourself useful, and take a seat beside me, sir, for the conveniency of snuffing the candles?"

Venus complying with the invitation while it was yet being given, Silas pegged at him with his wooden leg to call his particular attention to Mr. Boffin standing musing before the fire, in the space between the two settles.

"Hem! Ahem!" coughed Mr. Wegg to attract his employer's attention. "Would you wish to commence with an Animal, sir—from the Register?"

"No," said Mr. Boffin, "no, Wegg." With that, producing a little book from his breast-pocket, he handed it with great care to the literary gentleman, and inquired, "What do you call that, Wegg?"

"This, sir," replied Silas, adjusting his spectacles, and referring to the title-page, "is Merryweather's Lives and Anecdotes of Misers. Mr. Venus, would you make yourself useful and draw the candles a little nearer, sir?" This to have a special opportunity of bestowing a stare upon his comrade.

"Which of 'em have you got in that lot?" asked Mr. Boffin. "Can you find out pretty easy?"

"Well, sir," replied Silas, turning to the table of contents and slowly fluttering the leaves of the book, "I should say they must be pretty well all here, sir; here's a large assortment, sir; my eye catches John Overs, sir, John Little, sir, Dick Jarrel, John Elwes, the Reverend Mr. Jones of Blewbury, Vulture Hopkins, Daniel Dancer——"

"Give us Dancer, Wegg," said Mr. Boffin.

With another stare at his comrade, Silas sought and found the place.

"Page a hundred and nine, Mr. Boffin. Chapter eight. Contents of chapter, 'His birth and estate. His garments and outward appearance. Miss Dancer and her feminine graces. The Miser's Mansion. The finding of a treasure. The Story of the Mutton Pies. A Miser's Idea of Death. Bob, the Miser's cur. Griffiths and his Master. How to turn a penny. A substitute for a Fire. The Advantages of keeping a Snuff-box. The Miser dies without a Shirt. The Treasures of a Dunghill——'"

" Eh ? What's that ? " demanded Mr. Boffin.

" 'The Treasures,' sir," repeated Silas, reading very distinctly, " ' of a Dunghill.' Mr. Venus, sir, would you obleege with the snuffers ? " This, to secure attention to his adding with his lips only, " Mounds ! "

Mr. Boffin drew an armchair into the space where he stood, and said, seating himself and slyly rubbing his hands :

" Give us Dancer."

Mr. Wegg pursued the biography of that eminent man through its various phases of avarice and dirt, through Miss Dancer's death on a sick regimen of cold dumpling, and through Mr. Dancer's keeping his rags together with a hay-band, and warming his dinner by sitting upon it, down to the consolatory incident of his dying naked in a sack. After which he read on as follows :

" 'The house, or rather the heap of ruins, in which Mr. Dancer lived, and which at his death devolved to the right of Captain Holmes, was a most miserable, decayed building, for it had not been repaired for more than half a century."

(Here Mr. Wegg eyed his comrade and the room in which they sat : which had not been repaired for a long time.)

" 'But though poor in external structure, the ruinous fabric was very rich in the interior. It took many weeks to explore its whole contents, and Captain Holmes found it a very agreeable task to dive into the miser's secret hoards.'"

(Here Mr. Wegg repeated 'secret hoards,' and pegged his comrade again.)

" 'One of Mr. Dancer's richest escretoires was found to be a dungheap in the cowhouse; a sum but little short of two thousand five hundred pounds was contained in this rich piece of manure ; and in an old jacket, carefully tied, and strongly nailed down to the manger, in bank notes and gold were found five hundred pounds more.'"

(Here Mr. Wegg's wooden leg started forward under the table, and slowly elevated itself as he read on.)

"'Several bowls were discovered filled with guineas and half-guineas; and at different times on searching the corners of the house they found various parcels of bank notes. Some were crammed into the crevices of the wall;'"

(Here Mr. Venus looked at the wall.)

"'Bundles were hid under the cushions and covers of the chairs;'"

(Here Mr. Venus looked under himself on the settle.)

"'Some were reposing snugly at the back of the drawers; and notes amounting to six hundred pounds were found neatly doubled up in the inside of an old teapot. In the stable the Captain found jugs full of old dollars and shillings. The chimney was not left unsearched, and paid very well for the trouble; for in nineteen different holes, all filled with soot, were found various sums of money, amounting together to more than two hundred pounds.'"

On the way to this crisis Mr. Wegg's wooden leg had gradually elevated itself more and more, and he had nudged Mr. Venus with his opposite elbow deeper and deeper, until at length the preservation of his balance became incompatible with the two actions, and he now dropped over sideways upon that gentleman, squeezing him against the settle's edge. Nor did either of the two, for some few seconds, make any effort to recover himself; both remaining in a kind of pecuniary swoon.

But the sight of Mr. Boffin sitting in the armchair hugging himself, with his eyes upon the fire, acted as a restorative. Counterfeiting a sneeze to cover their movements, Mr. Wegg, with a spasmodic "Tish-ho!" pulled himself and Mr. Venus up in a masterly manner.

"Let's have some more," said Mr. Boffin, hungrily.

".John Elwes is the next, sir. Is it your pleasure to take John Elwes?"

" Ah !" said Mr. Boffin. " Let's hear what John did."

He did not appear to have hidden anything, so went off rather flatly. But an exemplary lady named Wilcocks, who had stowed away gold and silver in a pickle-pot in a clock-case, a canister-full of treasure in a hole under her stairs, and a quantity of money in an old rat-trap, revived the interest. To her succeeded another lady, claiming to be a pauper, whose wealth was found wrapped up in little scraps of paper and old rag. To her, another lady, applewoman by trade, who had saved a fortune of ten thousand pounds and hidden it " here and there, in cracks and corners, behind bricks and under the flooring." To her, a French gentleman, who had crammed up his chimney, rather to the detriment of its drawing powers, " a leather valise, containing twenty-thousand francs, gold coins, and a large quantity of precious stones," as discovered by a chimney-sweep after his death. By these steps Mr. Wegg arrived at a concluding instance of the human Magpie :

" ' Many years ago, there lived at Cambridge a miserly old couple of the name of Jardine : they had two sons : the father was a perfect miser, and at his death one thousand guineas were discovered secreted in his bed. The two sons grew up as parsimonious as their sire. When about twenty years of age, they commenced business at Cambridge as drapers, and they continued there until their death. The establishment of the Messrs. Jardine was the most dirty of all the shops in Cambridge. Customers seldom went in to purchase, except perhaps out of curiosity. The brothers were most disreputable-looking beings ; for, although surrounded with gay apparel as their staple in trade, they wore the most filthy rags themselves. It is said that they had no bed, and, to save the expense of one, always slept on a bundle of packing-cloths under the counter. In their house-keeping they were penurious in the extreme. A joint of meat did not grace their board for twenty years. Yet when the first of the brothers died, the other, much to his surprise, found large sums of money which had been secreted even from him.'"

"There!" cried Mr. Boffin. "Even from him, you see! There was only two of 'em, and yet one of 'em hid from the other."

Mr. Venus, who since his introduction to the French gentleman had been stooping to peer up the chimney, had his attention recalled by the last sentence, and took the liberty of repeating it.

"Do you like it?" asked Mr. Boffin, turning suddenly.

"I beg your pardon, sir?"

"Do you like what Wegg's been a-reading?"

Mr. Venus answered that he found it extremely interesting.

"Then come again," said Mr. Boffin, "and hear some more. Come when you like; come the day after to-morrow, half an hour sooner. There's plenty more; there's no end to it."

Mr. Venus expressed his acknowledgments and accepted the invitation.

"It's wonderful what's been hid, at one time and another," said Mr. Boffin, ruminating; "truly wonderful."

"Meaning, sir," observed Wegg, with a propitiatory face to draw him out, and with another peg at his friend and brother, "in the way of money?"

"Money," said Mr. Boffin. "Ah! And papers."

Mr. Wegg, in a languid transport, again dropped over on Mr. Venus, and again recovering himself, masked his emotions with a sneeze.

"Tish-ho! Did you say papers too, sir? Been hidden, sir?"

"Hidden and forgot," said Mr. Boffin. "Why the book-seller that sold me the Wonderful Museum—where's the Wonderful Museum?" He was on his knees on the floor in a moment, groping eagerly among the books.

"Can I assist you, sir?" asked Wegg.

"No, I have got it; here it is," said Mr. Boffin, dusting it with the sleeve of his coat. "Wollume four. I know it was the fourth wollume, that the bookseller read it to me out of. Look for it, Wegg."

Silas took the book and turned the leaves.

"Remarkable petrefaction, sir?"

"No, that's not it," said Mr. Boffin. "It can't have been a petrefaction."

"Memoirs of General John Reid, commonly called The Walking Rushlight, sir? With portrait."

"No, nor yet him," said Mr. Boffin.

"Remarkable case of a person who swallowed a crown-piece, sir?"

"To hide it?" asked Mr. Boffin.

"Why, no, sir," replied Wegg, consulting the text, "it appears to have been done by accident. Oh! This next must be it. 'Singular discovery of a will, lost twenty-one years.'"

"That's it!" cried Mr. Boffin. "Read that."

"'A most extraordinary case,'" read Silas Wegg aloud, "'was tried at the last Maryborough assizes in Ireland. It was briefly this. Robert Baldwin, in March 1782, made his will, in which he devised the lands now in question to the children of his youngest son; soon after which his faculties failed him, and he became altogether childish, and died, above eighty years old. The defendant, the eldest son, immediately afterwards gave out that his father had destroyed the will, and no will being found, he entered into possession of the lands in question, and so matters remained for twenty-one years, the whole family during all that time believing that the father had died without a will. But after twenty-one years the defendant's wife died, and he very soon afterwards, at the age of seventy-eight, married a very young woman: which caused some anxiety to his two sons, whose poignant expressions of this feeling so exasperated their father, that he in his resentment executed a will to disinherit his eldest son, and in his fit of anger showed it to his second son, who instantly determined to get at it, and destroy it, in order to preserve the property to his brother. With this view, he broke open his father's desk, where he found— not his father's will which he sought after, but the will of his grandfather, which was then altogether forgotten in the family.'"

"There!" said Mr. Boffin. "See what men put away and forget, or mean to destroy, and don't!" He then added in a slow tone, "As—ton—ish—ing!" And as he rolled his eyes all round the room, Wegg and Venus likewise rolled their eyes all round the room. And then Wegg, singly, fixed his eyes on Mr. Boffin looking at the fire again; as if he had a mind to spring upon him and demand his thoughts or his life.

"However, time's up for to-night," said Mr. Boffin, waving his hand after a silence. "More, the day after to-morrow. Range the books upon the shelves, Wegg. I dare say Mr. Venus will be so kind as to help you."

While speaking, he thrust his hand into the breast of his outer coat, and struggled with some object there that was too large to be got out easily. What was the stupefaction of the friendly movers when this object at last emerging, proved to be a much-dilapidated dark lantern!

Without at all noticing the effect produced by this little instrument, Mr. Boffin stood it on his knee, and, producing a box of matches, deliberately lighted the candle in the lantern, blew out the kindled match, and cast the end into the fire. "I'm going, Wegg," he then announced, "to take a turn about the place and round the yard. I don't want you. Me and this same lantern have taken hundreds— thousands—of such turns in our time together."

"But I couldn't think, sir—not on any account, I couldn't," —Wegg was politely beginning, when Mr. Boffin, who had risen and was going towards the door, stopped:

"I have told you that I don't want you, Wegg.

Wegg looked intelligently thoughtful, as if that had not occurred to his mind until he now brought it to bear on the circumstance. He had nothing for it but to let Mr. Boffin go out and shut the door behind him. But, the instant he was on the other side of it, Wegg clutched Venus with both hands, and said in a choking whisper, as if he were being strangled :

"Mr. Venus, he must be followed, he must be watched, he mustn't be lost sight of for a moment."

"Why mustn't he?" asked Venus, also strangling.

"Comrade, you might have noticed I was a little elewated in spirits when you come in to-night. I've found something."

"What have you found?" asked Venus, clutching him with both hands, so that they stood interlocked like a couple of preposterous gladiators.

"There's no time to tell you now. I think he must have gone to look for it. We must have an eye upon him instantly."

Releasing each other, they crept to the door, opened it softly, and peeped out. It was a cloudy night, and the black shadow of the Mounds made the dark yard darker. "If not a double swindler," whispered Wegg, "why a dark lantern? We could have seen what he was about, if he had carried a light one. Softly, this way."

Cautiously along the path that was bordered by fragments of crockery set in ashes, the two stole after him. They could hear him at his peculiar trot, crushing the loose cinders as he went. "He knows the place by heart," muttered Silas, "and don't need to turn his lantern on, confound him!" But he did turn it on, almost in that same instant, and flashed its light upon the first of the Mounds.

"Is that the spot?" asked Venus in a whisper.

"He's warm," said Silas in the same tone. "He's precious warm. He's close. I think he must be going to look for it. What's that he's got in his hand?"

"A shovel," answered Venus. "And he knows how to use it, remember, fifty times as well as either of us."

"If he looks for it and misses it, partner," suggested Wegg, "what shall we do?"

"First of all, wait till he does," said Venus.

Discreet advice too, for he darkened his lantern again, and the mound turned black. After a few seconds, he turned the light on once more, and was seen standing at the foot of the second mound, slowly raising the lantern little by little until he held it up at arm's length, as if he were examining the condition of the whole surface.

"That can't be the spot too," said Venus.

"No," said Wegg, "he's getting cold."

"It strikes me," whispered Venus, "that he wants to find out whether any one has been groping about there."

"Hush!" returned Wegg, "he's getting colder and colder! —Now he's freezing!"

This exclamation was elicited by his having turned the lantern off again, and on again, and being visible at the foot of the third Mound.

"Why, he's going up it!" said Venus.

"Shovel and all!" said Wegg.

At a nimble trot, as if the shovel over his shoulder stimu-lated him by reviving old associations, Mr. Boffin ascended the "serpentining walk," up the Mound which he had described to Silas Wegg on the occasion of their beginning to decline and fall. On striking into it he turned his lantern off. The two followed him, stooping low, so that their figures might make no mark in relief against the sky when he should turn his lantern on again. Mr. Venus took the lead, towing Mr. Wegg, in order that his refractory leg might be promptly extricated from any pitfalls it should dig for itself. They could just make out that the Golden Dustman stopped to breathe. Of course they stopped too, instantly.

"This is his own Mound," whispered Wegg, as he recovered his wind, "this one."

"Why all three are his own," returned Venus.

"So he thinks; but he's used to call this his own, because it's the one first left to him; the one that was his legacy when it was all he took under the will."

"When he shows his light," said Venus, keeping watch upon his dusky figure all the time, "drop lower and keep closer."

He went on again, and they followed again. Gaining the top of the Mound, he turned on his light—but only partially —and stood it on the ground. A bare lopsided, weather-beaten pole was planted in the ashes there, and had been there many a year. Hard by this pole his lantern stood; lighting a few feet of the lower part of it and a little of the ashy surface around, and then casting off a purposeless little clear trail of light into the air.

"He can never be going to dig up the pole!" whispered Venus as they dropped low and kept close.

"Perhaps it's holler and full of something," whispered Wegg.

He was going to dig, with whatsoever object, for he tucked up his cuffs and spat on his hands, and then went at it like an old digger as he was. He had no design upon the pole, except that he measured a shovel's length from it before beginning, nor was it his purpose to dig deep. Some dozen or so of expert strokes sufficed. Then, he stopped, looked down into the cavity, bent over it, and took out what appeared to be an ordinary case-bottle; one of those squat, high-shouldered, short-necked glass bottles which the Dutch-man is said to keep his Courage in. As soon as he had done this, he turned off his lantern, and they could hear that he was filling up the hole in the dark. The ashes being easily moved by a skilful hand, the spies took this as a hint to make off in good time. Accordingly, Mr. Venus slipped past Mr. Wegg and towed him down. But Mr. Wegg's descent was not accomplished without some personal inconvenience, for his self-willed leg sticking into the ashes about half-way down, and time pressing, Mr. Venus took the liberty of hauling him from his tether by the collar: which occasioned him to make the rest of the journey on his back, with his head enveloped in the skirts of his coat, and his wooden leg coming last, like a drag So flustered was Mr. Wegg by this mode of travelling, that when he was set on the level ground with his intellectual developments uppermost, he was quite unconscious of his bearings, and had not the least idea where his place of residence was to be found, until Mr. Venus shoved him into it. Even then he staggered round and round, weakly staring about him, until Mr. Venus with a hard brush brushed his senses into him and the dust out of him.

Mr. Boffin came down leisurely, for this brushing process had been well accomplished, and Mr. Venus had had time to take his breath, before he reappeared. That he had the bottle somewhere about him could not be doubted; where, was not so clear. He wore a large rough coat, buttoned over, and it might be in any one of half a dozen pockets.

"What's the matter, Wegg?" said Mr. Boffin. "You are as pale as a candle."

Mr. Wegg replied, with literal exactness, that he felt as if he had had a turn.

"Bile," said Mr. Boffin, blowing out the light in the lantern, shutting it up, and stowing it away in the breast of his coat as before. "Are you subject to bile, Wegg?"

Mr. Wegg again replied, with strict adherence to truth, that he didn't think he had ever had a similar sensation in his head, to anything like the same extent

"Physic yourself to-morrow, Wegg," said Mr. Boffin, "to be in order for next night. By-the-bye, this neighbourhood is going to have a loss, Wegg."

"A loss, sir?"

"Going to lose the Mounds."

The friendly movers made such an obvious effort not to look at one another, that they might as well have stared at one another with all their might.

"Have you parted with them, Mr. Boffin?" asked Silas.

"Yes; they're going. Mine's as good as gone already."

"You mean the little one of the three, with the pole atop, sir?"

"Yes," said Mr. Boffin, rubbing his ear in his old way, with that new touch of craftiness added to it. "It has fetched a penny. It'll begin to be carted off to-morrow."

"Have you been out to take leave of your old friend, sir?" asked Silas, jocosely.

"No," said Mr. Boffin. "What the devil put that in your head?"

He was so sudden and rough, that Wegg, who had been hovering closer and closer to his skirts, despatching the back of his hand on exploring expeditions in search of the bottle's surface, retired two or three paces.

"No offence, sir," said Wegg, humbly. "No offence."

Mr. Boffin eyed him as a dog might eye another dog who wanted his bone; and actually retorted with a low growl, as the dog might have retorted.

"Good night," he said, after having sunk into a moody silence, with his hands clasped behind him, and his eyes suspiciously wandering about Wegg.—"No! Stop there. I know the way out, and I want no light."

Avarice, and the evening's legends of avarice, and the inflammatory effect of what he had seen, and perhaps the rush of his ill-conditioned blood to his brain in his descent, wrought Silas Wegg to such a pitch of insatiable appetite, that when the door closed he made a swoop at it and drew Venus along with him.

"He mustn't go," he cried. "We mustn't let him go! He has got that bottle about him. We must have that bottle."

"Why, you wouldn't take it by force?" said Venus, restraining him.

"Wouldn't I? Yes, I would. I'd take it by any force, I'd have it at any price! Are you so afraid of one old man as to let him go, you coward?"

"I am so afraid of you as not to let *you* go," muttered Venus, sturdily clasping him in his arms.

"Did you hear him?" retorted Wegg. "Did you hear

him say that he was resolved to disappoint us? Did you hear him say, you cur, that he was going to have the Mounds cleared off, when no doubt the whole place will be rummaged? If you haven't the spirit of a mouse to defend your rights, I have. Let me go after him."

As in his wildness he was making a strong struggle for it, Mr. Venus deemed it expedient to lift him, throw him, and fall with him; well knowing that, once down, he would not be up again easily with his wooden leg. So they both rolled on the floor, and, as they did so, Mr. Boffin shut the gate.

CHAPTER VII

THE FRIENDLY MOVE TAKES UP A STRONG POSITION.

THE friendly movers sat upright on the floor, panting and
eyeing one another, after Mr. Boffin had slammed the gate
and gone away. In the weak eyes of Venus, and in every
reddish dust-coloured hair in his shock of hair, there was a
marked distrust of Wegg and an alertness to fly at him
on perceiving the smallest occasion. In the hard-grained
face of Wegg, and in his stiff knotty figure (he looked like
a German wooden toy), there was expressed a politic con-
ciliation, which had no spontaneity in it. Both were flushed,
flustered, and rumpled, by the late scuffle; and Wegg, in
coming to the ground, had received a humming knock on
the back of his devoted head, which caused him still to rub
it with an air of having been highly—but disagreeably—
astonished. Each was silent for some time, leaving it to
the other to begin.

"Brother," said Wegg, at length breaking the silence,
"you were right, and I was wrong. I forgot myself."

Mr. Venus knowingly cocked his shock of hair, as rather
thinking Mr. Wegg had remembered himself, in respect of
appearing without any disguise.

"But, comrade," pursued Wegg, "it was never your lot
to know Miss Elizabeth, Master George, Aunt Jane, nor
Uncle Parker."

Mr. Venus admitted that he had never known those

distinguished persons, and added, in effect, that he had never so much as desired the honour of their acquaintance.

"Don't say that, comrade," retorted Wegg: "No, don't say that! Because, without having known them, you never can fully know what it is to be stimulated to frenzy by the sight of the Usurper."

Offering these excusatory words as if they reflected great credit on himself, Mr. Wegg impelled himself with his hands towards a chair in a corner of the room, and there, after a variety of awkward gambols, attained a perpendicular position. Mr. Venus also rose.

"Comrade," said Wegg, "take a seat. Comrade, what a speaking countenance is yours!"

Mr. Venus involuntarily smoothed his countenance, and looked at his hand, as if to see whether any of its speaking properties came off.

"For clearly do I know, mark you," pursued Wegg, pointing his words with his forefinger, "clearly do I know what question your expressive features puts to me."

"What question?" said Venus.

"The question," returned Wegg, with a sort of joyful affability, "why I didn't mention sooner that I had found something. Says your speaking countenance to me: 'Why didn't you communicate that when I first come in this evening? Why did you keep it back till you thought Mr. Boffin had come to look for the article?' Your speaking countenance," said Wegg, "puts it plainer than language. Now, you can't read in my face what answer I give?"

"No, I can't," said Venus.

"I knew it! And why not?" returned Wegg, with the same joyful candour. "Because I lay no claims to a speaking countenance. Because I am well aware of my deficiencies. All men are not gifted alike. But I can answer in words. And in what words? These. I wanted to give you a delightful sap--pur—ize!"

Having thus elongated and emphasised the word Surprise,

91

Mr. Wegg shook his friend and brother by both hands, and then clapped him on both knees, like an affectionate patron who entreated him not to mention so small a service as that which it had been his happy privilege to render.

" Your speaking countenance," said Wegg, " being answered to its satisfaction, only asks then, ' What have you found ?' Why, I hear it say the words ! "

" Well ? " retorted Venus, snappishly, after waiting in vain. " If you hear it say the words, why don't you answer it ? "

" Hear me out ! " said Wegg. " I'm a-going to. Hear me out ! Man and brother, partner in feelings equally with undertakings and actions, I have found a cash-box."

" Where ? "

" —Hear me out ! " said Wegg. (He tried to reserve whatever he could, and, whenever disclosure was forced upon him, broke into a radiant gush of Hear me out.) " On a certain day, sir—— "

" When ? " said Venus, bluntly.

" N—no," returned Wegg, shaking his head at once observantly, thoughtfully, and playfully. " No, sir! That's not your expressive countenance which asks that question. That's your voice ; merely your voice. To proceed. On a certain day, sir, I happened to be walking in the yard—taking my lonely round—for in the words of a friend of my own family, the author of All's Well arranged as a duet:

' Deserted, as you will remember, Mr. Venus, by the waning moon,
  When stars, it will occur to you before I mention it, proclaim night's cheer-
    less noon,
  On tower, fort, or tented ground,
  The sentry walks his lonely round,
  The sentry walks ; '

—under those circumstances, sir, I happened to be walking in the yard early one afternoon, and happened to have an iron rod in my hand, with which I have been sometimes accustomed to beguile the monotony of a literary life, when I struck it against an object not necessary to trouble you by naming—— "

"It *is* necessary. What object?" demanded Venus, in a wrathful tone.

"Hear me out!" said Wegg. "The Pump.—When I struck it against the Pump, and found, not only that the top was loose and opened with a lid, but that something in it rattled. That something, comrade, I discovered to be a small, flat oblong cash-box. Shall I say it was disappintingly light?"

"There were papers in it?" said Venus.

"There your expressive countenance speaks indeed!" cried Wegg. "*A* paper. The box was locked, tied up, and sealed, and on the outside was a parchment label, with the writing, 'MY WILL, JOHN HARMON, TEMPORARILY DEPOSITED HERE.'"

"We must know its contents," said Venus.

"—Hear me out!" cried Wegg. "I said so, and I broke the box open."

"Without coming to me!" exclaimed Venus.

"Exactly so, sir!" returned Wegg, blandly and buoyantly. "I see I take you with me! Hear, hear, hear! Resolved, as your discriminating good sense perceives, that if you was to have a sap—pur—IZE, it should be a complete one! Well, sir. And so, as you have honoured me by anticipating, I examined the document. Regularly executed, regularly witnessed, very short. Inasmuch as he has never made friends, and has ever had a rebellious family, he, John Harmon, gives to Nicodemus Boffin the Little Mound, which is quite enough for him, and gives the whole rest and residue of his property to the Crown."

"The date of the will that has been proved must be looked to," remarked Venus. "It may be later than this one."

"Hear me out!" cried Wegg. "I said so. I paid a shilling (never mind your sixpence of it) to look up that will. Brother, that will is dated months before this will. And now, as a fellow-man, and as a partner in a friendly move," added Wegg, benignantly taking him by both hands again, and clapping

93

him on both knees again, "say, have I completed my labour of love to your perfect satisfaction, and are you sap—pur —IZED?"

Mr. Venus contemplated his fellow-man and partner with doubting eyes, and then rejoined stiffly:

"This is great news indeed, Mr. Wegg. There's no denying it. But I could have wished you had told it me before you got your fright to-night, and I could have wished you had ever asked me as your partner what we were to do, before you thought you were dividing a responsibility."

"—Hear me out!" cried Wegg. "I knew you was a-going to say so. But alone I bore the anxiety, and alone I'll bear the blame!" This with an air of great magnanimity.

"Now," said Venus. "Let's see this will and this box."

"Do I understand, brother," returned Wegg with consider-able reluctance, "that it is your wish to see this will and this —— ?"

Mr. Venus smote the table with his hand.

"—Hear me out!" said Wegg. "Hear me out! I'll go and fetch 'em."

After being some time absent, as if in his covetousness he could hardly make up his mind to produce the treasure to his partner, he returned with an old leathern hat-box, into which he had put the other box, for the better preservation of commonplace appearances, and for the disarming of sus-picion. "But I don't half like opening it here," said Silas in a low voice, looking around: "he might come back, he may not be gone; we don't know what he may be up to, after what we've seen."

"There's something in that," assented Venus. "Come to my place."

Jealous of the custody of the box, and yet fearful of opening it under the existing circumstances, Wegg hesitated. "Come, I tell you," repeated Venus, chafing, "to my place." Not very well seeing his way to a refusal, Mr. Wegg then rejoined in a gush, "—Hear me out!—Certainly." So he locked up the Bower and they set forth: Mr. Venus taking his arm, and keeping it with remarkable tenacity.

They found the usual dim light burning in the window of Mr. Venus's establishment, imperfectly disclosing to the public the usual pair of preserved frogs, sword in hand, with their point of honour still unsettled. Mr. Venus had closed his shop door on coming out, and now opened it with the key and shut it again as soon as they were within ; but not before he had put up and barred the shutters of the shop window. "No one can get in without being let in," said he then, "and we couldn't be more snug than here." So he raked together the yet warm cinders in the rusty grate, and made a fire, and trimmed the candle on the little counter. As the fire cast its flickering gleams here and there upon the dark greasy walls; the Hindoo baby, the African baby, the articulated English baby, the assortment of skulls, and the rest of the collection, came starting to their various stations as if they had all been out, like their master, and were punctual in a general rendezvous to assist at the secret. The French gentleman had grown considerably since Mr. Wegg last saw him, being now accommodated with a pair of legs and a head, though his arms were yet in abeyance. To whomsoever the head had originally belonged, Silas Wegg would have regarded it as a personal favour if he had not cut quite so many teeth.

Silas took his seat in silence on the wooden box before the fire, and Venus dropping into his low chair, produced from among his skeleton hands, his tea-tray and teacups, and put the kettle on. Silas inwardly approved of these preparations, trusting they might end in Mr. Venus's diluting his intellect.

"Now, sir," said Venus, "all is safe and quiet. Let us see this discovery."

With still reluctant hands, and not without several glances towards the skeleton hands, as if he mistrusted that a couple of them might spring forth and clutch the document, Wegg opened the hat-box and revealed the cash-box, opened the cash-box and revealed the will. He held a corner of it tight, while Venus, taking hold of another corner, searchingly and attentively read it.

"Was I correct in my account of it, partner?" said Mr. Wegg, at length.

"Partner, you were," said Mr. Venus.

Mr. Wegg thereupon made an easy, graceful movement, as though he would fold it up; but Mr. Venus held on by his corner.

"No, sir," said Mr. Venus, winking his weak eyes and shaking his head. "No, partner. The question is now brought up, who is going to take care of this. Do you know who is going to take care of this, partner?"

"I am," said Wegg.

"Oh dear no, partner," retorted Venus. "That's a mistake. I am. Now look here, Mr. Wegg. I don't want to have any words with you, and still less do I want to have any anatomical pursuits with you."

"What do you mean?" said Wegg, quickly.

"I mean, partner," replied Venus, slowly, "that it's hardly possible for a man to feel in a more amiable state towards another man than I do towards you at this present moment. But I am on my own ground, I am surrounded by the trophies of my art, and my tools is very handy."

"What do you mean, Mr. Venus?" asked Wegg again.

"I am surrounded, as I have observed," said Mr. Venus, placidly, "by the trophies of my art. They are numerous, my stock of human warious is large, the shop is pretty well crammed, and I don't just now want any more trophies of my art. But I like my art, and I know how to exercise my art."

"No man better," assented Mr. Wegg, with a somewhat staggered air.

"There's the Miscellanies of several human specimens," said Venus, "(though you mightn't think it,) in the box on which you're sitting. There's the Miscellanies of several human

96

specimens in the lovely compo-one behind the door;" with a nod towards the French gentleman. "It still wants a pair of arms. I *don't* say that I'm in any hurry for 'em."

"You must be wandering in your mind, partner," Silas remonstrated.

"You'll excuse me if I wander," returned Venus; "I am sometimes rather subject to it. I like my art, and I know how to exercise my art, and I mean to have the keeping of this document."

"But what has that got to do with your art, partner?" asked Wegg, in an insinuating tone.

Mr. Venus winked his chronically-fatigued eyes both at once, and adjusting the kettle on the fire, remarked to himself, in a hollow voice, "She'll bile in a couple of minutes."

Silas Wegg glanced at the kettle, glanced at the shelves, glanced at the French gentleman behind the door, and shrank a little as he glanced at Mr. Venus winking his red eyes, and feeling in his waistcoat pocket—as for a lancet, say—with his unoccupied hand. He and Venus were necessarily seated close together, as each held a corner of the document, which was but a common sheet of paper.

"Partner," said Wegg, even more insinuatingly than before, "I propose that we cut it in half, and each keep a half."

Venus shook his shock of hair, as he replied, "It wouldn't do to mutilate it, partner. It might seem to be cancelled."

"Partner," said Wegg, after a silence, during which they had contemplated one another, "don't your speaking countenance say that you're a-going to suggest a middle course?"

Venus shook his shock of hair, as he replied, "Partner, you have kept this paper from me once. You shall never keep it from me again. I offer you the box and the label to take care of, but I'll take care of the paper."

Silas hesitated a little longer, and then suddenly releasing his corner, and resuming his buoyant and benignant tone, exclaimed, "What's life without trustfulness! What's a fellow-man without honour! You're welcome to it, partner, in a spirit of trust and confidence."

Continuing to wink his red eyes both together—but in a self-communing way, and without any show of triumph— Mr. Venus folded the paper now left in his hand, and locked it in a drawer behind him, and pocketed the key. He then proposed, "A cup of tea, partner?" To which Mr. Wegg returned, "Thank'ee, partner," and the tea was made and poured out.

"Next," said Venus, blowing at his tea in his saucer, and looking over it at his confidential friend, "comes the question, What's the course to be pursued?"

On this head, Silas Wegg had much to say. Silas had to say That, he would beg to remind his comrade, brother, and partner, of the impressive passages they had read that evening; of the evident parallel in Mr. Boffin's mind between them and the late owner of the Bower, and the present circumstances of the Bower; of the bottle; and of the box. That, the fortunes of his brother and comrade, and of himself, were evidently made, inasmuch as they had but to put their price upon this document, and get that price from the minion of fortune and the worm of the hour: who now appeared to be less of a minion and more of a worm than had been previously supposed. That, he considered it plain that such price was stateable in a single expressive word, and that word was, "Halves!" That, the question then arose when "Halves!" should be called. That, here he had a plan of action to recommend, with a conditional clause. That, the plan of action was that they should lie by with patience; that they should allow the Mounds to be gradually levelled and cleared away, while retaining to themselves their present opportunity of watching the process—which would be, he conceived, to put the trouble and cost of daily digging and delving upon somebody else, while they might nightly turn such complete disturbance of the dust to the account of their own private investigations; and that, when the Mounds were gone, and they had worked those chances for their own joint benefit solely, they should then, and not before, explode on the minion and worm. But here came the conditional clause, and to this he entreated the special attention of his comrade, brother, and partner. It was not to be borne that the minion and worm should carry off any of that property which was now to be regarded as their own property. When he, Mr. Wegg, had seen the minion surreptitiously making off with that bottle, and its precious contents unknown, he had looked upon him in the light of a mere robber, and, as such, would have despoiled him of his ill-gotten gain, but for the judicious interference of his comrade, brother, and partner. Therefore, the conditional clause he proposed was, that, if the minion should return in his late sneaking manner, and if, being closely watched, he should be found to possess himself of anything, no matter what, the sharp sword impending over his head should be instantly shown him, he should be strictly examined as to what he knew or suspected, should be severely handled by them his masters, and should be kept in a state of abject moral bondage and slavery until the time when they should see fit to permit him to purchase his freedom at the price of half his possessions. If, said Mr. Wegg by way of peroration, he had erred in saying only " Halves ! " he trusted to his comrade, brother, and partner not to hesitate to set him right, and to reprove his weakness. It might be more according to the rights of things, to say Two-thirds; it might be more according to the rights of things, to say Three-fourths. On those points he was ever open to correction.

Mr. Venus, having wafted his attention to this discourse over three successive saucers of tea, signified his concurrence in the views advanced. Inspirited hereby, Mr. Wegg extended his right hand, and declared it to be a hand which never yet. Without entering into more minute particulars, Mr. Venus, sticking to his tea, briefly professed his belief, as polite forms required of him, that it *was* a hand which never yet. But contented himself with looking at it, and did not take it to his bosom.

"Brother," said Wegg, when this happy understanding was established, "I should like to ask you something. You remember the night when I first looked in here, and found you floating your powerful mind in tea?"

Still swilling tea, Mr. Venus nodded assent.

"And there you sit, sir," pursued Wegg with an air of thoughtful admiration, "as if you had never left off! There you sit, sir, as if you had an unlimited capacity of assimilating the fragrant article! There you sit, sir, in the midst of your works, looking as if you'd been called upon for Home, Sweet Home, and was obleeging the company!

> 'A exile from home splendour dazzles in vain,
> O give you your lowly Preparations again,
> The birds stuffed so sweetly that can't be expected to come at your call,
> Give you these with the peace of mind dearer than all.
> Home, Home, Home, sweet Home!'

—Be it ever," added Mr. Wegg in prose as he glanced about the shop, "ever so ghastly, all things considered there's no place like it."

"You said you'd like to ask something; but you haven't asked it," remarked Venus, very unsympathetic in manner.

"Your peace of mind," said Wegg, offering condolence, "your peace of mind was in a poor way that night. *How's* it going on? *Is* it looking up at all?"

"She does not wish," replied Mr. Venus with a comical mixture of indignant obstinacy and tender melancholy, "to regard herself, nor yet to be regarded, in that particular light. There's no more to be said."

"Ah, dear me, dear me!" exclaimed Wegg with a sigh, but eyeing him while pretending to keep him company in eyeing the fire, "such is woman! And I remember you said that night, sitting there as I sat here—said that night when your peace of mind was first laid low, that you had taken an interest in these very affairs. Such is coincidence!"

"Her father," rejoined Venus, and then stopped to swallow more tea, "her father was mixed up in them."

"You didn't mention her name, sir, I think?" observed Wegg, pensively. "No, you didn't mention her name that night."

"Pleasant Riderhood."

"In—deed!" cried Wegg. "Pleasant Riderhood. There's something moving in the name. Pleasant. Dear me! Seems to express what she might have been, if she hadn't made that unpleasant remark—and what she ain't, in consequence of having made it. Would it at all pour balm into your wounds, Mr. Venus, to inquire how you came acquainted with her?"

"I was down at the water-side," said Venus, taking another gulp of tea and mournfully winking at the fire—"looking for parrots"—taking another gulp and stopping.

Mr. Wegg hinted, to jog his attention: "You could hardly have been out parrot-shooting, in the British climate, sir?"

"No, no, no," said Venus fretfully. "I was down at the water-side, looking for parrots brought home by sailors, to buy for stuffing."

"Ay, ay, ay, sir!"

"—And looking for a nice pair of rattlesnakes, to articulate for a Museum—when I was doomed to fall in with her and deal with her. It was just at the time of that discovery in the river. Her father had seen the discovery being towed in the river. I made the popularity of the subject a reason for going back to improve the acquaintance, and I have never since been the man I was. My very bones is rendered flabby by brooding over it. If they could be brought to me loose, to sort, I should hardly have the face to claim 'em as mine. To such an extent have I fallen off under it."

Mr. Wegg, less interested than he had been, glanced at one particular shelf in the dark.

"Why, I remember, Mr. Venus," he said in a tone of friendly commiseration " (for I remember every word that falls from you, sir), I remember that you said that night, you had got up there—and then your words was, 'Never mind.'"

"—The parrot that I bought of her," said Venus, with a despondent rise and fall of his eyes. "Yes; there it lies on its side, dried up; except for its plumage, very like myself. I've never had the heart to prepare it, and I never shall have now."

With a disappointed face, Silas mentally consigned this parrot to regions more than tropical, and, seeming for the time to have lost his power of assuming an interest in the woes of Mr. Venus, fell to tightening his wooden leg as a preparation for departure : its gymnastic performances of that evening having severely tried its constitution.

After Silas had left the shop, hat-box in hand, and had left Mr. Venus to lower himself to oblivion-point with the requisite weight of tea, it greatly preyed on his ingenuous mind that he had taken this artist into partnership at all. He bitterly felt that he had over-reached himself in the beginning, by grasping at Mr. Venus's mere straws of hints, now shown to be worthless for his purpose. Casting about for ways and means of dissolving the connection without loss of money, reproaching himself for having been betrayed into an avowal of his secret, and complimenting himself beyond measure on his purely accidental good luck, he beguiled the distance between Clerkenwell and the mansion of the Golden Dustman.

For, Silas Wegg felt it to be quite out of the question that he could lay his head upon his pillow in peace, without first hovering over Mr. Boffin's house in the superior character of its Evil Genius. Power (unless it be the power of intellect or virtue) has ever the greatest attraction for the lowest natures; and the mere defiance of the unconscious house-front, with his power to strip the roof off the inhabiting family like the roof of a house of cards, was a treat which had a charm for Silas Wegg.

As he hovered on the opposite side of the street, exulting, the carriage drove up.

The Evil Genius of the House of Boffin

"There'll shortly be an end of *you*," said Wegg, threatening it with the hat-box. "*Your* varnish is fading."

Mrs. Boffin descended and went in.

"Look out for a fall, my Lady Dustwoman," said Wegg.

Bella lightly descended and ran in after her.

"How brisk we are!" said Wegg. "You won't run so gaily to your old shabby home, my girl. You'll have to go there, though."

A little while, and the Secretary came out.

"I was passed over for you," said Wegg. "But you had better provide yourself with another situation, young man."

Mr. Boffin's shadow passed upon the blinds of three large windows as he trotted down the room, and passed again as he went back.

"Yoop!" cried Wegg. "You're there, are you? Where's the bottle? You would give your bottle for my box, Dustman!"

Having now composed his mind for slumber, he turned homeward. Such was the greed of the fellow, that his mind had shot beyond halves, two-thirds, three-fourths, and gone straight to spoliation of the whole. "Though that wouldn't quite do," he considered, growing cooler as he got away. "That's what would happen to him if he didn't buy us up. We should get nothing by that."

We so judge others by ourselves, that it had never come into his head before, that he might not buy us up, and might prove honest, and prefer to be poor. It caused him a slight tremor as it passed; but a very slight one, for the idle thought was gone directly.

"He's grown too fond of money for that," said Wegg; "he's grown too fond of money." The burden fell into a strain or tune as he stumped along the pavements. All the way home he stumped it out of the rattling streets, *piano* with his own foot, and *forte* with his wooden leg, "He's GROWN too FOND of MONEY for THAT, he's GROWN too FOND of MONEY."

Even next day Silas soothed himself with this melodious strain, when he was called out of bed at daybreak, to set open the yard-gate and admit the train of carts and horses that came to carry off the little Mound. And all day long, as he kept unwinking watch on the slow process which promised to protract itself through many days and weeks, whenever (to save himself from being choked with dust) he patrolled a little cinderous beat he established for the purpose, without taking his eyes from the diggers, he still stumped to the tune: "He's GROWN too FOND of MONEY for THAT, he's GROWN too FOND of MONEY."

CHAPTER VIII

THE END OF A LONG JOURNEY

THE train of carts and horses came and went all day from dawn to nightfall, making little or no daily impression on the heap of ashes, though, as the days passed on, the heap was seen to be slowly melting. My lords and gentlemen and honourable boards, when you, in the course of your dust-shovelling and cinder-raking, have piled up a mountain of pretentious failure, you must off with your honourable coats for the removal of it, and fall to the work with the power of all the queen's horses and all the queen's men, or it will come rushing down and bury us alive.

Yes, verily, my lords and gentlemen and honourable boards, adapting your Catechism to the occasion, and by God's help so you must. For when we have got things to the pass that with an enormous treasure at disposal to relieve the poor, the best of the poor detest our mercies, hide their heads from us, and shame us by starving to death in the midst of us, it is a pass impossible of prosperity, impossible of continuance. It may not be so written in the Gospel according to Podsnappery; you may not " find these words " for the text of a sermon, in the Returns of the Board of Trade; but they have been the truth since the foundations of the universe were laid, and they will be the truth until the foundations of the universe are shaken by the Builder. This boastful handiwork of ours, which fails in its terrors for the professional pauper, the sturdy

105

breaker of windows and the rampant tearer of clothes, strikes with a cruel and a wicked stab at the stricken sufferer, and is a horror to the deserving and unfortunate. We must mend it, lords and gentlemen and honourable boards, or in its own evil hour it will mar every one of us.

Old Betty Higden fared upon her pilgrimage as many ruggedly honest creatures, women and men, fare on their toiling way along the roads of life. Patiently to earn a spare bare living, and quietly to die, untouched by workhouse hands —this was her highest sublunary hope.

Nothing had been heard of her at Mr. Boffin's house since she trudged off. The weather had been hard and the roads had been bad, and her spirit was up. A less staunch spirit might have been subdued by such adverse influences ; but the loan for her little outfit was in no part repaid, and it had gone worse with her than she had foreseen, and she was put upon proving her case and maintaining her independence.

Faithful soul ! When she had spoken to the Secretary of that "deadness that steals over me at times," her fortitude had made too little of it. Oftener and ever oftener, it came stealing over her; darker and ever darker, like the shadow of advancing Death. That the shadow should be deep as it came on, like the shadow of an actual presence, was in accordance with the laws of the physical world, for all the Light that shone on Betty Higden lay beyond Death.

The poor old creature had taken the upward course of the river Thames as her general track ; it was the track in which her last home lay, and of which she had last had local love and knowledge. She had hovered for a little while in the near neighbourhood of her abandoned dwelling, and had sold, and knitted and sold, and gone on. In the pleasant towns of Chertsey, Walton, Kingston, and Staines, her figure came to be quite well known for some short weeks, and then again passed on.

She would take her stand in market-places, where there were such things, on market-days ; at other times, in the busiest (that was seldom very busy) portion of the little quiet High Street; at still other times she would explore the outlying roads for great houses, and would ask leave at the Lodge to pass in with her basket, and would not often get it. But ladies in carriages would frequently make purchases from her trifling stock, and were usually pleased with her bright eyes and her hopeful speech. In these and her clean dress originated a fable that she was well to do in the world : one might say, for her station, rich. As making a comfortable provision for its subject which costs nobody anything, this class of fable has long been popular.

In those pleasant little towns on Thames, you may hear the fall of the water over the weirs, or even, in still weather, the rustle of the rushes; and from the bridge you may see the young river, dimpled like a young child, playfully gliding away among the trees, unpolluted by the defilements that lie in wait for it on its course, and as yet out of hearing of the deep summons of the sea. It were too much to pretend that Betty Higden made out such thoughts; no; but she heard the tender river whispering to many like herself, " Come to me, come to me! When the cruel shame and terror you have so long fled from, most beset you, come to me! I am the Relieving Officer appointed by eternal ordinance to do my work; I am not held in estimation according as I shirk it. My breast is softer than the pauper-nurse's; death in my arms is peacefuller than among the pauper-wards. Come to me!"

There was abundant place for gentler fancies, too, in her untutored mind. Those gentlefolks and their children inside those fine houses, could they think, as they looked out at her, what it was to be really hungry, really cold? Did they feel any of the wonder about her, that she felt about them? Bless the dear laughing children! If they could have seen sick Johnny in her arms, would they have cried for pity? If they could have seen dead Johnny on that little bed, would they have understood it? Bless the dear children for his sake, anyhow! So with the humbler houses in the little street, the inner firelight shining on the panes as the outer twilight darkened. When the families gathered in-doors there, for the night, it was only a foolish fancy to feel as if it were a little hard in them to close the shutter and blacken the flame. So with the lighted shops, and speculations whether their masters and mistresses taking tea in a perspective of back parlour—not so far within but that the flavour of tea and toast came out, mingled with the glow of light, into the street—ate or drank or wore what they sold, with the greater relish because they dealt in it. So with the churchyard on a branch of the solitary way to the night's sleeping-place. "Ah me! The dead and I seem to have it pretty much to ourselves in the dark and in this weather! But so much the better for all who are warmly housed at home." The poor soul envied no one in bitterness, and grudged no one anything.

But the old abhorrence grew stronger on her as she grew weaker, and it found more sustaining food than she did in her wanderings. Now, she would light upon the shameful spectacle of some desolate creature—or some wretched, ragged groups of either sex, or of both sexes, with children among them, huddled together like the smaller vermin, for a little warmth—lingering and lingering on a doorstep, while the appointed evader of the public trust did his dirty office of trying to weary them out and so get rid of them. Now, she would light upon some poor decent person, like herself, going afoot on a pilgrimage of many weary miles to see some worn-out relative or friend who had been charitably clutched off to a great, blank, barren Union House, as far from old home as the County Jail (the remoteness of which is always its worst punishment for small rural offenders), and in its dietary, and in its lodging, and in its tending of the sick, a much more penal establishment. Sometimes she would hear a newspaper read out, and would learn how the Registrar General cast up the units that had within the last week died of want and of exposure to the weather: for which that Recording Angel seemed to have a regular fixed place in his sum, as if they were its halfpence. All such things she would hear discussed, as we, my lords and gentlemen and honourable boards, in our unapproachable magnificence never hear them, and from all such things she would fly with the wings of raging Despair.

This is not to be received as a figure of speech. Old Betty Higden, however tired, however footsore, would start up and be driven away by her awakened horror of falling into the hands of Charity. It is a remarkable Christian improvement, to have made a pursuing Fury of the Good Samaritan; but it was so in this case, and it is a type of many, many, many.

Two incidents united to intensify the old unreasoning abhorrence—granted in a previous place to be unreasoning, because the people always are unreasoning, and invariably make a point of producing all their smoke without fire.

One day she was sitting in a market-place on a bench outside an inn, with her little wares for sale, when the deadness that she strove against came over her so heavily that the scene departed from before her eyes; when it returned, she found herself on the ground, her head supported by some good-natured market-women, and a little crowd about her.

"Are you better now, mother?" asked one of the women. "Do you think you can do nicely now?"

"Have I been ill then?" asked old Betty.

"You have had a faint like," was the answer, "or a fit. It ain't that you've been a-struggling, mother, but you've been stiff and numbed."

"Ah!" said Betty, recovering her memory. "It's the numbness. Yes. It comes over me at times."

Was it gone? the women asked her.

"It's gone now," said Betty. "I shall be stronger than I was afore. Many thanks to ye, my dears, and when you come to be as old as I am, may others do as much for you!"

They assisted her to rise, but she could not stand yet, and they supported her when she sat down again upon the bench.

"My head's a bit light, and my feet are a bit heavy," said old Betty, leaning her face drowsily on the breast of the woman who had spoken before. "They'll both come nat'ral in a minute. There's nothing more the matter."

"Ask her," said some farmers standing by, who had come out from their market-dinner, "who belongs to her."

"Are there any folks belonging to you, mother?" said the woman.

"Yes sure," answered Betty. "I heerd the gentleman say it, but I couldn't answer quick enough. There's plenty belonging to me. Don't ye fear for me, my dear."

"But are any of 'em near here?" said the men's voices; the women's voices chiming in when it was said, and prolonging the strain.

"Quite near enough," said Betty, rousing herself. "Don't ye be afeard for me, neighbours."

"But you are not fit to travel. Where are you going?" was the next compassionate chorus she heard.

"I'm a-going to London, when I've sold out all," said Betty, rising with difficulty. "I've right good friends in London. I want for nothing. I shall come to no harm. Thankye. Don't ye be afeard for me."

A well-meaning bystander, yellow-legginged and purple-faced, said hoarsely over his red comforter, as she rose to her feet, that she "oughtn't to be let to go."

"For the Lord's love don't meddle with me!" cried old Betty, all her fears crowding on her. "I am quite well now, and I must go this minute."

She caught up her basket as she spoke and was making an unsteady rush away from them, when the same bystander checked her with his hand on her sleeve, and urged her to come with him and see the parish-doctor. Strengthening herself by the utmost exercise of her resolution, the poor trembling creature shook him off, almost fiercely, and took to flight. Nor did she feel safe until she had set a mile or two of by-road between herself and the market-place, and had crept into a copse, like a hunted animal, to hide and recover breath. Not until then, for the first time, did she venture to recall how she had looked over her shoulder before turning out of the town, and had seen the sign of the White Lion hanging across the road, and the fluttering market booths, and the old grey church, and the little crowd gazing after her, but not attempting to follow her.

The second frightening incident was this. She had been again as bad, and had been for some days better, and was travelling along by a part of the road where it touched the river, and in wet seasons was so often overflowed by it that there were tall white posts set up to mark the way. A barge was being towed towards her, and she sat down on the bank to rest and watch it. As the tow-rope was slackened by a turn of the stream and dipped into the water, such a confusion stole into her mind, that she thought she saw the forms of her dead children and dead grandchildren peopling the barge, and waving their hands to her in solemn measure ; then as the rope tightened and came up, dropping diamonds, it seemed to vibrate into two parallel ropes and strike her, with a twang, though it was far off. When she looked again there was no barge, no river, no daylight, and a man whom she had never before seen held a candle close to her face.

" Now, Missis," said he ; " where did you come from and where are you going to ? "

The poor soul confusedly asked the counter-question where she was ?

" I am the Lock," said the man.

" The Lock ? "

" I am the Deputy Lock, on job, and this is the Lock-house. (Lock or Deputy Lock, it's all one, while the t'other man's in the hospital.) What's your Parish ? "

"Parish!" She was up from the truckle-bed directly, wildly feeling about her for her basket, and gazing at him in affright.

"You'll be asked the question down town," said the man. "They won't let you be more than a Casual there. They'll pass you on to your settlement, Missis, with all speed. You're not in a state to be let come upon strange parishes 'ceptin as a Casual."

"'Twas the deadness again!" murmured Betty Higden, with her hand to her head.

"It was the deadness, there's not a doubt about it," returned the man. "I should have thought the deadness was a mild word for it, if it had been named to me when we brought you in. Have you got any friends, Missis?"

"The best of friends, Master."

"I should recommend your looking 'em up if you consider 'em game to do anything for you," said the Deputy Lock. "Have you got any money?"

"Just a morsel of money, sir."

"Do you want to keep it?"

"Sure I do!"

"Well, you know," said the Deputy Lock, shrugging his shoulders with his hands in his pockets, and shaking his head in a sulkily ominous manner, "the parish authorities down town will have it out of you, if you go on, you may take your Alfred David."

"Then I'll not go on."

"They'll make you pay, as fur as your money will go," pursued the Deputy, "for your relief as a Casual and for your being passed to your Parish."

"Thank ye kindly, Master, for your warning, thank ye for your shelter, and good-night."

"Stop a bit," said the Deputy, striking in between her and the door. "Why are you all of a shake, and what's your hurry, Missis?"

"Oh, Master, Master," returned Betty Higden, "I've fought

112

against the Parish and fled from it, all my life, and I want to die free of it!"

"I don't know," said the Deputy, with deliberation, "as I ought to let you go. I'm a honest man as gets my living by the sweat of my brow, and I may fall into trouble by letting you go. I've fell into trouble afore now, by George, and I know what it is, and it's made me careful. You might be took with your deadness again, half a mile off—or half of half a quarter for the matter of that—and then it would be asked, Why did that there honest Deputy Lock let her go, instead of putting her safe with the Parish? That's what a man of his character ought to have done, it would be argueyfied," said the Deputy Lock, cunningly harping on the strong string of her terror; "he ought to have handed her over safe to the Parish. That was to be expected of a man of his merits."

As he stood in the doorway, the poor old, careworn, wayworn woman burst into tears, and clasped her hands, as if in a very agony she prayed to him.

"As I've told you, Master, I've the best of friends. This letter will show how true I spoke, and they will be thankful for me."

The Deputy Lock opened the letter with a grave face, which underwent no change as he eyed its contents. But it might have done, if he could have read them.

"What amount of small change, Missis," he said with an abstracted air, after a little meditation, "might you call a morsel of money?"

Hurriedly emptying her pocket, old Betty laid down on the table, a shilling and two sixpenny pieces, and a few pence.

"If I was to let you go instead of handing you over safe to the Parish," said the Deputy, counting the money with his eyes, "might it be your own free wish to leave that there behind you?"

"Take it, Master, take it, and welcome and thankful!"

"I'm a man," said the Deputy, giving her back the letter,

and pocketing the coins, one by one, "as earns his living by
the sweat of his brow;" here he drew his sleeve across his
forehead, as if this particular portion of his humble gains
were the result of sheer hard labour and virtuous industry;
"and I won't stand in your way. Go where you like."

She was gone out of the Lock-house as soon as he gave her
this permission, and her tottering steps were on the road
again. But, afraid to go back and afraid to go forward;
seeing what she fled from, in the sky-glare of the lights of
the little town before her, and leaving a confused horror of
it everywhere behind her, as if she had escaped it in every
stone of every market-place; she struck off by side ways,
among which she got bewildered and lost. That night she
took refuge from the Samaritan in his latest accredited form,
under a farmer's rick; and if—worth thinking of, perhaps,
my fellow-Christians—the Samaritan had in the lonely night
"passed by on the other side," she would have most devoutly
thanked High Heaven for her escape from him.

The morning found her afoot again, but fast declining as
to the clearness of her thoughts, though not as to the steadiness of her purpose. Comprehending that her strength was
quitting her, and that the struggle of her life was almost
ended, she could neither reason out the means of getting back
to her protectors, nor even form the idea. The overmastering
dread, and the proud stubborn resolution it engendered in her
to die undegraded, were the two distinct impressions left in
her failing mind. Supported only by a sense that she was
bent on conquering in her life-long fight, she went on.

The time was come, now, when the wants of this little life
were passing away from her. She could not have swallowed
food, though a table had been spread for her in the next field.
The day was cold and wet, but she scarcely knew it. She
crept on, poor soul, like a criminal afraid of being taken, and
felt little beyond the terror of falling down while it was yet
daylight, and being found alive. She had no fear that she
would live through another night.

Sewn in the breast of her gown, the money to pay for her burial was still intact. If she could wear through the day, and then lie down to die under cover of the darkness, she would die independent. If she were captured previously, the money would be taken from her as a pauper who had no right to it, and she would be carried to the accursed workhouse. Gaining her end, the letter would be found in her breast, along with the money, and the gentlefolks would say when it was given back to them, " She prized it, did old Betty Higden; she was true to it; and while she lived, she would never let it be disgraced by falling into the hands of those that she held in horror." Most illogical, inconsequential, and light-headed, this; but travellers in the valley of the shadow of death are apt to be light-headed; and worn-out old people of low estate have a trick of reasoning as indifferently as they live, and doubtless would appreciate our Poor Law more philosophically on an income of ten thousand a year.

So, keeping to by-ways, and shunning human approach, this troublesome old woman hid herself, and fared on all through the dreary day. Yet so unlike was she to vagrant hiders in general, that sometimes, as the day advanced, there was a bright fire in her eyes, and a quicker beating at her feeble heart, as though she said exultingly, " The Lord will see me through it ! "

By what visionary hands she was led along upon that journey of escape from the Samaritan; by what voices, hushed in the grave, she seemed to be addressed; how she fancied the dead child in her arms again, and times innumerable adjusted her shawl to keep it warm ; what infinite variety of forms of tower and roof and steeple the trees took ; how many furious horsemen rode at her, crying, " There she goes ! Stop ! Stop, Betty Higden ! " and melted away as they came close ; be these things left untold. Faring on and hiding, hiding and faring on, the poor harmless creature, as though she were a Murderess and the whole country were up after her, wore out the day and gained the night.

" Water-meadows, or such like," she had sometimes murmured, on the day's pilgrimage, when she had raised her head and taken any note of the real objects about her. There now arose in the darkness, a great building full of lighted windows. Smoke was issuing from a high chimney in the rear of it, and there was the sound of a water-wheel at the side. Between her and the building lay a piece of water, in which the lighted windows were reflected, and on its nearest margin was a plantation of trees. " I humbly thank the Power and the Glory," said Betty Higden, holding up her withered hands, " that I have come to my journey's end ! "

She crept among the trees to the trunk of a tree whence she could see, beyond some intervening trees and branches, the lighted windows, both in their reality and their reflection in the water. She placed her orderly little basket at her side, and sank upon the ground, supporting herself against the tree. It brought to her mind the foot of the Cross, and she committed herself to Him who died upon it. Her strength held out to enable her to arrange the letter in her breast, so as that it could be seen that she had a paper there. It had held out for this, and it departed when this was done.

" I am safe here," was her last benumbed thought. " When I am found dead at the foot of the Cross, it will be by some of my own sort; some of the working people who work among the lights yonder. I cannot see the lighted windows now, but they are there. I am thankful for all ! "

* * * * * * *

The darkness gone, and a face bending down.

" It cannot be the boofer lady ? "

" I don't understand what you say. Let me wet your lips again with this brandy. I have been away to fetch it. Did you think that I was long gone ? "

It is as the face of a woman, shaded by a quantity of rich dark hair. It is the earnest face of a woman who is young and handsome. But all is over with me on earth, and this must be an Angel.

"Have I been long dead?"

"I don't understand what you say. Let me wet your lips again. I hurried all I could, and brought no one back with me, lest you should die of the shock of strangers."

"Am I not dead?"

"I cannot understand what you say. Your voice is so low and broken that I cannot hear you. Do you hear me?"

"Yes."

"Do you mean yes?"

"Yes."

"I was coming from my work just now, along the path outside (I was up with the night-hands last night), and I heard a groan, and found you lying here."

"What work, deary?"

"Did you ask what work? At the paper-mill."

"Where is it?"

"Your face is turned up to the sky, and you can't see it. It is close by. You can see my face, here, between you and the sky?"

"Yes."

"Dare I lift you?"

"Not yet."

"Not even lift your head to get it on my arm? I will do it by very gentle degrees. You shall hardly feel it."

"Not yet. Paper. Letter."

"This paper in your breast?"

"Bless ye!"

"Let me wet your lips again. Am I to open it. To read it?"

"Bless ye!"

She reads it with surprise, and looks down with a new expression and an added interest on the motionless face she kneels beside.

"I know these names. I have heard them often."

117

"Will you send it, my dear?"

"I cannot understand you. Let me wet your lips again, and your forehead. There. O poor thing, poor thing!" These words through her fast-dropping tears. "What was it that you asked me? Wait till I bring my ear quite close."

"Will you send it, my dear?"

"Will I send it to the writers? Is that your wish? Yes, certainly."

"You'll not give it up to any one but them?"

"No."

"As you must grow old in time, and come to your dying hour, my dear, you'll not give it up to any one but them?"

"No. Most solemnly."

"Never to the Parish?" with a convulsed struggle.

"No. Most solemnly."

"Nor let the Parish touch me, nor yet so much as look at me?" with another struggle.

"No. Faithfully."

A look of thankfulness and triumph lights the worn old face. The eyes, which have been darkly fixed upon the sky, turn with meaning in them towards the compassionate face from which the tears are dropping, and a smile is on the aged lips as they ask:

"What is your name, my dear!"

"My name is Lizzie Hexam."

"I must be sore disfigured Are you afraid to kiss me?"

The answer is, the ready pressure of her lips upon the cold but smiling mouth.

"Bless ye! *Now* lift me, my love."

Lizzie Hexam very softly raised the weather-stained grey head, and lifted her as high as Heaven.

CHAPTER IX

"'WE GIVE THEE HEARTY THANKS FOR THAT IT HATH PLEASED THEE TO DELIVER THIS OUR SISTER OUT OF THE MISERIES OF THIS SINFUL WORLD.'" So read the Reverend Frank Milvey in a not untroubled voice, for his heart misgave him that all was not quite right between us and our sister—or say our sister in Law—Poor Law—and that we sometimes read these words in an awful manner, over our Sister and our Brother too.

And Sloppy—on whom the brave deceased had never turned her back until she ran away from him, knowing that otherwise he would not be separated from her—Sloppy could not in his conscience as yet find the hearty thanks required of it. Selfish in Sloppy, and yet excusable, it may be humbly hoped, because our sister had been more than his mother.

The words were read above the ashes of Betty Higden, in a corner of a churchyard near the river; in a churchyard so obscure that there was nothing in it but grass-mounds, not so much as one single tombstone. It might not be to do an unreasonably great deal for the diggers and hewers, in a registering age, if we ticketed their graves at the common charge; so that a new generation might know which was which: so that the soldier, sailor, emigrant, coming home, should be able to identify the resting-place of father, mother, playmate, or betrothed. For, we turn up our eyes and say that we are all alike in death, and we might turn them down

119

and work the saying out in this world, so far. It would be sentimental, perhaps? But how say ye, my lords and gentlemen and honourable boards, shall we not find good standing-room left for a little sentiment, if we look into our crowds?

Near unto the Reverend Frank Milvey as he read, stood his little wife, John Rokesmith the Secretary, and Bella Wilfer. These, over and above Sloppy, were the mourners at the lowly grave. Not a penny had been added to the money sewn in her dress: what her honest spirit had so long projected, was fulfilled.

"I've took it in my head," said Sloppy, laying it, inconsolable, against the church door, when all was done: "I've took it in my wretched head that I might have sometimes turned a little harder for her, and it cuts me deep to think so now."

The Reverend Frank Milvey, comforting Sloppy, expounded to him how the best of us were more or less remiss in our turnings at our respective Mangles—some of us very much so—and how we were all a halting, failing, feeble, and inconstant crew.

"*She* warn't, sir," said Sloppy, taking this ghostly counsel rather ill, in behalf of his late benefactress. "Let us speak for ourselves, sir. She went through with whatever duty she had to do. She went through with me, she went through with the Minders, she went through with herself, she went through with everything. O Mrs. Higden, Mrs. Higden, you was a woman and a mother and a mangler in a million million!"

With those heartfelt words, Sloppy removed his dejected head from the church door, and took it back to the grave in the corner and laid it down there, and wept alone. "Not a very poor grave," said the Reverend Frank Milvey, brushing his hand across his eyes, "when it has that homely figure on it. Richer, I think, than it could be made by most of the sculpture in Westminster Abbey!"

120

They left him undisturbed, and passed out at the wicket-gate. The water-wheel of the paper-mill was audible there, and seemed to have a softening influence on the bright wintry scene. They had arrived but a little while before, and Lizzie Hexam now told them the little she could add to the letter in which she had enclosed Mr. Rokesmith's letter and had asked for their instructions. This was merely how she had heard the groan, and what had afterwards passed, and how she had obtained leave for the remains to be placed in that sweet, fresh, empty store-room of the mill from which they had just accompanied them to the churchyard, and how the last request had been religiously observed.

"I could not have done it all, or nearly all, of myself," said Lizzie. "I should not have wanted the will; but I should not have had the power, without our managing partner."

"Surely not the Jew who received us?" said Mrs. Milvey.

("My dear," observed her husband, in parenthesis, "why not?")

"The gentleman certainly is a Jew," said Lizzie, "and the lady, his wife, is a Jewess, and I was first brought to their notice by a Jew. But I think there cannot be kinder people in the world."

"But suppose they try to convert you!" suggested Mrs. Milvey, bristling in her good little way, as a clergyman's wife.

"To do what, ma'am?" asked Lizzie, with a modest smile.

"To make you change your religion," said Mrs. Milvey.

Lizzie shook her head, still smiling. "They have never asked me what my religion is. They asked me what my story was, and I told them. They asked me to be industrious and faithful, and I promised to be so. They most willingly and cheerfully do their duty to all of us who are employed here, and we try to do ours to them. Indeed they do much more than their duty to us, for they are wonderfully mindful of us in many ways."

121

"It is easy to see you're a favourite, my dear," said little Mrs. Milvey, not quite pleased.

"It would be very ungrateful in me to say I am not," returned Lizzie, "for I have been already raised to a place of confidence here. But that makes no difference in their following their own religion and leaving all of us to ours. They never talk of theirs to us, and they never talk of ours to us. If I was the last in the mill it would be just the same. They never asked me what religion that poor thing had followed."

"My dear," said Mrs. Milvey, aside to the Reverend Frank, "I wish you would talk to her."

"My dear," said the Reverend Frank, aside to his good little wife. "I think I will leave it to somebody else. The circumstances are hardly favourable. There are plenty of talkers going about, my love, and she will soon find one"

While this discourse was interchanging, both Bella and the Secretary observed Lizzie Hexam with great attention. Brought face to face for the first time with the daughter of his supposed murderer, it was natural that John Harmon should have his own secret reasons for a careful scrutiny of her countenance and manner. Bella knew that Lizzie's father had been falsely accused of the crime which had had so great an influence on her own life and fortunes; and her interest, though it had no secret springs, like that of the Secretary, was equally natural. Both had expected to see something very different from the real Lizzie Hexam, and thus it fell out that she became the unconscious means of bringing them together.

For, when they had walked on with her to the little house in the clean village by the paper-mill, where Lizzie had a lodging with an elderly couple employed in the establishment, and when Mrs. Milvey and Bella had been up to see her room and had come down, the mill bell rang. This called Lizzie away for the time, and left the Secretary and Bella standing rather awkwardly in the small street; Mrs. Milvey being engaged in pursuing the village children, and her investigations whether they were in danger of becoming children of Israel; and the Reverend Frank being engaged—to say the truth—in evading that branch of his spiritual functions, and getting out of sight surreptitiously.

Bella at length said:

"Hadn't we better talk about the commission we have undertaken, Mr. Rokesmith?"

"By all means," said the Secretary.

"I suppose," faltered Bella, "that we *are* both commissioned, or we shouldn't both be here?"

"I suppose so," was the Secretary's answer

"When I proposed to come with Mr. and Mrs. Milvey," said Bella, "Mrs. Boffin urged me to do so, in order that I might give her my small report—it's not worth anything, Mr. Rokesmith, except for its being a woman's—which indeed with you may be a fresh reason for its being worth nothing—of Lizzie Hexam."

"Mr. Boffin," said the Secretary, "directed me to come for the same purpose."

As they spoke they were leaving the little street and emerging on the wooded landscape by the river.

"You think well of her, Mr. Rokesmith?" pursued Bella, conscious of making all the advances.

"I think highly of her"

"I am so glad of that! Something quite refined in her beauty, is there not?"

"Her appearance is very striking."

"There is a shade of sadness upon her that is quite touching. At least I—I am not setting up my own poor opinion, you know, Mr. Rokesmith," said Bella, excusing and explaining herself in a pretty, shy way; "I am consulting you."

"I noticed that sadness. I hope it may not," said the Secretary in a lower voice, "be the result of the false accusation which has been retracted."

When they had passed on a little further without speaking,

Bella, after stealing a glance or two at the Secretary, suddenly said :

"Oh, Mr. Rokesmith, don't be hard with me, don't be stern with me ; be magnanimous ! I want to talk with you on equal terms."

The Secretary as suddenly brightened, and returned : "Upon my honour I had no thought but for you. I forced myself to be constrained, lest you might misinterpret my being more natural. There. It's gone."

"Thank you," said Bella, holding out her little hand. "Forgive me."

"No !" cried the Secretary, eagerly. "Forgive *me !*" For there were tears in her eyes, and they were prettier in his sight (though they smote him on the heart rather reproachfully too) than any other glitter in the world.

When they had walked a little further :

"You were going to speak to me," said the Secretary, with the shadow so long on him quite thrown off and cast away, "about Lizzie Hexam. So was I going to speak to you, if I could have begun."

"Now that you *can* begin, sir," returned Bella, with a look as if she italicised the word by putting one of her dimples under it, "what were you going to say ?"

"You remember, of course, that in her short letter to Mrs. Boffin—short, but containing everything to the purpose—she stipulated that either her name, or else her place of residence, must be kept strictly a secret among us."

Bella nodded Yes.

"It is my duty to find out why she made that stipulation. I have it in charge from Mr. Boffin to discover, and I am very desirous for myself to discover, whether that retracted accusation still leaves any stain upon her. I mean whether it places her at any disadvantage towards any one, even towards herself."

"Yes," said Bella, nodding thoughtfully ; "I understand. That seems wise and considerate."

" You may not have noticed, Miss Wilfer, that she has the same kind of interest in you that you have in her. Just as you are attracted by her beaut—by her appearance and manner, she is attracted by yours."

" I certainly have *not* noticed it," returned Bella, again italicising with the dimple, " and I should have given her credit for——"

The Secretary with a smile held up his hand, so plainly interposing " not for better taste," that Bella's colour deepened over the little piece of coquetry she was checked in.

" And so," resumed the Secretary, " if you would speak with her alone before we go away from here, I feel quite sure that a natural and easy confidence would arise between you. Of course you would not be asked to betray it ; and of course you would not, if you were. But if you do not object to put this question to her—to ascertain for us her own feeling in this one matter—you can do so at a far greater advantage than I or any else could. Mr. Boffin is anxious on the subject. And I am," added the Secretary after a moment, " for a special reason, very anxious."

" I shall be happy, Mr. Rokesmith," returned Bella, " to be of the least use ; for I feel, after the serious scene of to-day, that I am useless enough in this world."

" Don't say that," urged the Secretary.

" Oh, but I mean that," said Bella, raising her eyebrows.

" No one is useless in this world," retorted the Secretary, " who lightens the burden of it for any one else."

" But I assure you I *don't*, Mr. Rokesmith," said Bella, half crying.

" Not for your father ? "

" Dear, loving, self-forgetting, easily-satisfied Pa ! Oh, yes ! He thinks so."

" It is enough if he only thinks so," said the Secretary. " Excuse the interruption : I don't like to hear you depreciate yourself."

" But *you* once depreciated *me*, sir," thought Bella, pouting, "and I hope you may be satisfied with the consequences you brought upon your head!" However, she said nothing to that purpose; she even said something to a different purpose.

"Mr. Rokesmith, it seems so long since we spoke together naturally, that I am embarrassed in approaching another subject. Mr. Boffin. You know I am very grateful to him; don't you? You know I feel a true respect for him, and am bound to him by the strong ties of his own generosity; now don't you?"

"Unquestionably. And also that you are his favourite companion."

"That makes it," said Bella, "so very difficult to speak of him. But—— Does he treat you well?"

"You see how he treats me," the Secretary answered, with a patient and yet proud air.

"Yes, and I see it with pain," said Bella, very energetically.

The Secretary gave her such a radiant look, that if he had thanked her a hundred times, he could not have said as much as the look said.

"I see it with pain," repeated Bella, "and it often makes me miserable. Miserable, because I cannot bear to be supposed to approve of it, or have any indirect share in it. Miserable, because I cannot bear to be forced to admit to myself that Fortune is spoiling Mr. Boffin."

"Miss Wilfer," said the Secretary, with a beaming face, "if you could know with what delight I make the discovery that Fortune is not spoiling *you*, you would know that it more than compensates me for any slight at any other hands."

"Oh, don't speak of *me*," said Bella, giving herself an impatient little slap with her glove. "You don't know me as well as——"

"As you know yourself?" suggested the Secretary, finding that she stopped. "*Do* you know yourself?"

"I know quite enough of myself," said Bella, with a charming air of being inclined to give herself up as a bad

126

job, "and I don't improve upon acquaintance. But Mr. Boffin."

"That Mr. Boffin's manner to me, or consideration for me, is not what it used to be," observed the Secretary, "must be admitted. It is too plain to be denied."

"Are you disposed to deny it, Mr. Rokesmith?" asked Bella, with a look of wonder.

"Ought I not to be glad to do so, if I could: though it were only for my own sake?"

"Truly," returned Bella, "it must try you very much, and—you must please promise me that you won't take ill what I am going to add, Mr. Rokesmith?"

"I promise it with all my heart."

"—And it must sometimes, I should think," said Bella, hesitating, "a little lower you in your own estimation?"

Assenting with a movement of his head, though not at all looking as if he did, the Secretary replied:

"I have very strong reasons, Miss Wilfer, for bearing with the drawbacks of my position in the house we both inhabit. Believe that they are not all mercenary, although I have, through a series of strange fatalities, faded out of my place in life. If what you see with such a gracious and good sympathy is calculated to rouse my pride, there are other considerations (and those you do not see) urging me to quiet endurance. The latter are by far the stronger."

"I think I have noticed, Mr. Rokesmith," said Bella, looking at him with curiosity, as not quite making him out, "that you repress yourself, and force yourself, to act a passive part."

"You are right. I repress myself, and force myself to act a part. It is not in tameness of spirit that I submit. I have a settled purpose."

"And a good one, I hope," said Bella.

"And a good one, I hope," he answered, looking steadily at her.

"Sometimes I have fancied, sir," said Bella, turning away

127

her eyes, "that your great regard for Mrs. Boffin is a very powerful motive with you."

"You are right again; it is. I would do anything for her, bear anything for her. There are no words to express how I esteem that good, good woman."

"As I do too! May I ask you one thing more, Mr. Rokesmith?"

"Anything more."

"Of course you see that she really suffers, when Mr. Boffin shows how he is changing?"

"I see it, every day, as you see it, and am grieved to give her pain."

"To give her pain?" said Bella, repeating the phrase quickly, with her eyebrows raised.

"I am generally the unfortunate cause of it."

"Perhaps she says to you, as she often says to me, that he is the best of men in spite of all."

"I often overhear her, in her honest and beautiful devotion to him, saying so to you," returned the Secretary with the same steady look, "but I cannot assert that she ever says so to me."

Bella met the steady look for a moment with a wistful, musing little look of her own, and then, nodding her pretty head several times, like a dimpled philosopher (of the very best school) who was moralising on Life, heaved a little sigh, and gave up things in general for a bad job, as she had previously been inclined to give up herself.

But, for all that, they had a very pleasant walk. The trees were bare of leaves, and the river was bare of water-lilies; but the sky was not bare of its beautiful blue, and the water reflected it, and a delicious wind ran with the stream, touching the surface crisply. Perhaps the old mirror was never yet made by human hands, which, if all the images it had in its time reflected could pass across its surface again, would fail to reveal some scene of horror or distress. But the great serene mirror of the river seemed as if it might have reproduced all it had ever reflected between those placid banks, and brought nothing to the light save what was peaceful, pastoral, and blooming.

So, they walked, speaking of the newly filled-up grave, and of Johnny, and of many things. So, on their return, they met brisk Mrs. Milvey coming to seek them, with the agreeable intelligence that there was no fear for the village children, there being a Christian school in the village, and no worse Judaical interference with it than to plant its garden. So, they got back to the village as Lizzie Hexam was coming from the paper-mill, and Bella detached herself to speak with her in her own home.

"I am afraid it is a poor room for you," said Lizzie, with a smile of welcome, as she offered the post of honour by the fireside.

"Not so poor as you think, my dear," returned Bella, "if you knew all." Indeed, though attained by some wonderful winding narrow stairs, which seemed to have been erected in a pure white chimney, and though very low in the ceiling, and very rugged in the floor, and rather blinking as to the proportions of its lattice window, it was a pleasanter room than that despised chamber once at home, in which Bella had first bemoaned the miseries of taking lodgers.

The day was closing as the two girls looked at one another by the fireside. The dusky room was lighted by the fire. The grate might have been the old brazier, and the glow might have been the old hollow down by the flare.

"It's quite new to me," said Lizzie, "to be visited by a lady so nearly of my own age, and so pretty as you. It's a pleasure to me to look at you."

"I have nothing left to begin with," returned Bella, blushing, "because I was going to say that it was a pleasure to me to look at you, Lizzie. But we can begin without a beginning, can't we?"

Lizzie took the pretty little hand that was held out in as pretty a little frankness.

"Now, dear," said Bella, drawing her chair a little nearer, and taking Lizzie's arm as if they were going out for a walk, "I am commissioned with something to say, and I dare say I shall say it wrong, but I won't if I can help it. It is in reference to your letter to Mr. and Mrs. Boffin, and this is what it is. Let me see. Oh yes! This is what it is."

With this exordium, Bella set forth that request of Lizzie's touching secrecy, and delicately spoke of that false accusation and its retractation, and asked might she beg to be informed whether it had any bearing, near or remote, on such request. "I feel, my dear," said Bella, quite amazing herself by the business-like manner in which she was getting on, "that the subject must be a painful one to you, but I am mixed up in it also; for—I don't know whether you may know it or suspect it—I am the willed-away girl who was to have been married to the unfortunate gentleman, if he had been pleased to approve of me. So I was dragged into the subject without my consent, and you were dragged into it without your consent, and there is very little to choose between us."

"I had no doubt," said Lizzie, "that you were the Miss Wilfer I have often heard named. Can you tell me who my unknown friend is?"

"Unknown friend, my dear?" said Bella.

"Who caused the charge against poor father to be contradicted, and sent me the written paper."

Bella had never heard of him. Had no notion who he was.

"I should have been glad to thank him," returned Lizzie. "He has done a great deal for me. I must hope that he will let me thank him some day. You asked me has it anything to do——"

"It or the accusation itself," Bella put in.

"Yes. Has either anything to do with my wishing to live quite secret and retired here? No."

As Lizzie Hexam shook her head in giving this reply, and as her glance sought the fire, there was a quiet resolution in her folded hands, not lost on Bella's bright eyes.

130

"Have you lived much alone?" asked Bella.

"Yes. It's nothing new to me. I used to be always alone many hours together, in the day and in the night, when poor father was alive."

"You have a brother, I have been told?"

"I have a brother; but he is not friendly with me. He is a very good boy though, and has raised himself by his industry. I don't complain of him."

As she said it, with her eyes upon the fire-glow, there was an instantaneous escape of distress into her face. Bella seized the moment to touch her hand.

"Lizzie, I wish you would tell me whether you have any friend of your own sex and age."

"I have lived that lonely kind of life, that I have never had one," was the answer.

"Nor I neither," said Bella. "Not that my life has been lonely, for I could have sometimes wished it lonelier, instead of having Ma going on like the Tragic Muse with a face-ache in majestic corners, and Lavvy being spiteful—though, of course, I am very fond of them both. I wish you could make a friend of me, Lizzie. Do you think you could? I have no more of what they call character, my dear, than a canary-bird; but I know I am trustworthy."

The wayward, playful, affectionate nature, giddy for want of the weight of some sustaining purpose, and capricious because it was always fluttering among little things, was yet a captivating one. To Lizzie it was so new, so pretty, at once so womanly and so childish, that it won her completely. And when Bella said again, "Do you think you could, Lizzie?" with her eyebrows raised, her head inquiringly on one side, and an odd doubt about it in her own bosom, Lizzie showed beyond all question that she thought she could.

"Tell me, my dear," said Bella, "what is the matter, and why you live like this."

Lizzie presently began, by way of prelude, "You must

131

have many lovers—" when Bella checked her with a little scream of astonishment.

" My dear, I haven't one ! "

" Not one ? "

" Well ! Perhaps one," said Bella. " I am sure I don't know. I *had* one, but what he may think about it at the present time I can't say. Perhaps I have half a one (of course I don't count that Idiot, George Sampson). However, never mind me. I want to hear about you."

"There is a certain man," said Lizzie, " a passionate and angry man, who says he loves me, and who I must believe does love me. He is the friend of my brother. I shrank from him within myself when my brother first brought him to me ; but the last time I saw him, he terrified me more than I can say." There she stopped.

" Did you come here to escape from him, Lizzie ? "

"I came here immediately after he so alarmed me."

" Are you afraid of him here ? "

"I am not timid generally, but I am always afraid of him. I am afraid to see a newspaper, or to hear a word spoken of what is done in London, lest he should have done some violence."

" Then you are not afraid of him for yourself, dear ? " said Bella, after pondering on the words.

"I should be even that, if I met him about here. I look round for him always as I pass to and fro at night."

" Are you afraid of anything he may do to himself in London, my dear ? "

" No. He might be fierce enough even to do some violence to himself, but I don't think of that."

" Then it would almost seem, dear," said Bella, quaintly, " as if there must be somebody else ? "

Lizzie put her hands before her face for a moment, before replying : " The words are always in my ears, and the blow he struck upon a stone wall as he said them, is always before my eyes. I have tried hard to think it not worth remembering, but I cannot make so little of it. His hand was trickling down with blood as he said to me, 'Then I hope that I may never kill him!'"

Rather startled, Bella made and clasped a girdle of her arms round Lizzie's waist, and then asked quietly, in a soft voice, as they both looked at the fire:

"Kill him! Is this man so jealous, then?"

"Of a gentleman," said Lizzie. "—I hardly know how to tell you—of a gentleman far above me and my way of life, who broke father's death to me, and has shown an interest in me since."

"Does he love you?"

Lizzie shook her head.

"Does he admire you?"

Lizzie ceased to shake her head, and pressed her hand upon her living girdle.

"Is it through his influence that you came here?"

"Oh, no! And of all the world I wouldn't have him know that I am here, or get the least clue where to find me."

"Lizzie, dear! Why?" asked Bella, in amazement at this burst. But then quickly added, reading Lizzie's face: "No. Don't say why. That was a foolish question of mine. I see. I see."

There was silence between them. Lizzie, with a drooping head, glanced down at the glow in the fire where her first fancies had been nursed, and her first escape made from the grim life out of which she had plucked her brother, foreseeing her reward.

"You know all now," she said, raising her eyes to Bella's. "There is nothing left out. This is my reason for living secret here, with the aid of a good old man who is my true friend. For a short part of my life at home with father, I knew of things—don't ask me what—that I set my face against, and tried to better. I don't think I could have done more, then, without letting my hold on father go; but they sometimes lie heavy on my mind. By doing all for the best, I hope I may wear them out."

" And wear out too," said Bella soothingly, " this weakness, Lizzie, in favour of one who is not worthy of it."

" No. I don't want to wear that out," was the flushed reply, " nor do I want to believe, nor do I believe, that he is not worthy of it. What should I gain by that, and how much should I lose ! "

Bella's expressive little eyebrows remonstrated with the fire for some short time before she rejoined :

" Don't think that I press you, Lizzie; but wouldn't you gain in peace, and hope, and even in freedom ? Wouldn't it be better not to live a secret life in hiding, and not to be shut out from your natural and wholesome prospects ? Forgive my asking you, would that be no gain ? "

" Does a woman's heart that—that has that weakness in it which you have spoken of," returned Lizzie, " seek to gain anything ? "

The question was so directly at variance with Bella's views in life, as set forth to her father, that she said internally, " There, you little mercenary wretch ! Do you hear that ? Ain't you ashamed of yourself ? " and unclasped the girdle of her arms, expressly to give herself a penitential poke in the side.

" But you said, Lizzie," observed Bella, returning to her subject when she had administered this chastisement, " that you would lose, besides. Would you mind telling me what you would lose, Lizzie ? "

" I should lose some of the best recollections, best encouragements, and best objects, that I carry through my daily life. I should lose my belief that if I had been his equal, and he had loved me, I should have tried with all my might to make him better and happier, as he would have made me. I should lose almost all the value that I put upon the little learning I have, which is all owing to him, and which I conquered the difficulties of, that he might not think it thrown away upon me. I should lose a kind of picture of him—or of what he might have been, if I had been a lady, and he had loved me—which is always with me, and which I somehow feel that I could not do a mean or a wrong thing before. I should leave off prizing the remembrance that he has done me nothing but good since I have known him, and that he has made a change within me, like—like the change in the grain of these hands, which were coarse, and cracked, and hard, and brown when I rowed on the river with father, and are softened and made supple by this new work as you see them now."

They trembled, but with no weakness, as she showed them.

" Understand me, my dear ; " thus she went on. " I have never dreamed of the possibility of his being anything to me on this earth but the kind of picture that I know I could not make you understand, if the understanding was not in your own breast already. I have no more dreamed of the possibility of *my* being his wife, than he ever has—and words could not be stronger than that. And yet I love him. I love him so much and so dearly, that when I sometimes think my life may be but a weary one, I am proud of it and glad of it. I am proud and glad to suffer something for him, even though it is of no service to him, and he will never know of it or care for it."

Bella sat enchained by the deep, unselfish passion of this girl or woman of her own age, courageously revealing itself in the confidence of her sympathetic perception of its truth. And yet she had never experienced anything like it, or thought of the existence of anything like it.

" It was late upon a wretched night," said Lizzie, " when his eyes first looked at me in my old river-side home, very different from this. His eyes may never look at me again. I would rather that they never did ; I hope that they never may. But I would not have the light of them taken out of my life, for anything my life can give me. I have told you everything now, my dear. If it comes a little strange to me

135

to have parted with it, I am not sorry. I had no thought of ever parting with a single word of it, a moment before you came in ; but you came in, and my mind changed."

Bella kissed her on the cheek, and thanked her warmly for her confidence. " I only wish," said Bella, " I was more deserving of it."

" More deserving of it ? " repeated Lizzie, with an incredulous smile.

" I don't mean in respect of keeping it," said Bella, " because any one should tear me to bits before getting at a syllable of it—though there's no merit in that, for I am naturally as obstinate as a Pig. What I mean is, Lizzie, that I am a mere impertinent piece of conceit, and you shame me."

Lizzie put up the pretty brown hair that came tumbling down, owing to the energy with which Bella shook her head : and she remonstrated while thus engaged, " My dear ! "

" Oh, it's all very well to call me your dear," said Bella, with a pettish whimper, " and I am glad to be called so, though I have slight enough claim to be. But I AM such a nasty little thing ! "

" My dear ! " urged Lizzie again.

" Such a shallow, cold, worldly, Limited little brute ! " said Bella, bringing out her last adjective with culminating force.

" Do you think," inquired Lizzie, with her quiet smile, the hair being now secured, " that I don't know better ? "

" Do you know better, though ? " said Bella. " Do you really believe you know better ? Oh, I should be so glad if you did know better, but I am so very much afraid that I must know best ! "

Lizzie asked her, laughing outright, whether she ever saw her own face or heard her own voice ?

" I suppose so," returned Bella ; " I look in the glass often enough, and I chatter like a Magpie."

" I have seen your face, and heard your voice, at any rate," said Lizzie, " and they have tempted me to say to you—with a certainty of not going wrong—what I thought I should never say to any one. Does that look ill?"

"No, I hope it doesn't," pouted Bella, stopping herself in something between a humoured laugh and a humoured sob.

"I used once to see pictures in the fire," said Lizzie, playfully, "to please my brother. Shall I tell you what I see down there where the fire is glowing?"

They had risen, and were standing on the hearth, the time being come for separating ; each had drawn an arm around the other to take leave.

"Shall I tell you," asked Lizzie, "what I see down there?"

"Limited little b?" suggested Bella, with her eyebrows raised.

"A heart well worth winning, and well won. A heart that, once won, goes through fire and water for the winner, and never changes, and is never daunted."

"Girl's heart?" asked Bella, with accompanying eyebrows.

Lizzie nodded. "And the figure to which it belongs—— "

"Is yours," suggested Bella.

"No. Most clearly and distinctly yours."

So the interview terminated with pleasant words on both sides, and with many reminders on the part of Bella that they were friends, and pledges that she would soon come down into that part of the country again. Therewith Lizzie returned to her occupation, and Bella ran over to the little inn to rejoin her company.

"You look rather serious, Miss Wilfer," was the Secretary's first remark.

"I feel rather serious," returned Miss Wilfer.

She had nothing else to tell him but that Lizzie Hexam's secret had no reference whatever to the cruel charge, or its withdrawal. Oh yes, though! said Bella : she might as well mention one other thing ; Lizzie was very desirous to thank her unknown friend who had sent her the written retractation. Was she indeed? observed the Secretary. Ah! Bella asked him, had he any notion who that unknown friend might be? He had no notion whatever.

They were on the borders of Oxfordshire, so far had poor old Betty Higden strayed. They were to return by the train presently, and, the station being near at hand, the Rev. Frank and Mrs. Frank, and Sloppy and Bella and the Secretary, set out to walk to it. Few rustic paths are wide enough for five, and Bella and the Secretary dropped behind.

"Can you believe, Mr. Rokesmith," said Bella, "that I feel as if whole years had passed since I went into Lizzie Hexam's cottage?"

"We have crowded a good deal into the day," he returned, "and you were much affected in the churchyard. You are over-tired."

"No, I am not at all tired. I have not quite expressed what I mean. I don't mean that I feel as if a great space of time had gone by, but that I feel as if much had happened —to myself, you know."

"For good, I hope?"

"I hope so," said Bella.

"You are cold; I felt you tremble. Pray let me put this wrapper of mine about you. May I fold it over this shoulder without injuring your dress? Now, it will be too heavy and too long. Let me carry this end over my arm, as you have no arm to give me."

Yes, she had, though. How she got it out in her muffled state, Heaven knows; but she got it out somehow—there it was—and slipped it through the Secretary's.

"I have had a long and interesting talk with Lizzie, Mr. Rokesmith, and she gave me her full confidence."

"She could not withhold it," said the Secretary.

"I wonder how you come," said Bella, stopping short as she glanced at him, "to say to me just what she said about it!"

"I infer that it must be because I feel just as she felt about it."

"And how was that, do you mean to say, sir?" asked Bella, moving again.

"That if you were inclined to win her confidence—anybody's confidence—you were sure to do it."

The railway, at this point, knowingly shutting a green eye and opening a red one, they had to run for it. As Bella could not run easily so wrapped up, the Secretary had to help her. When she took her opposite place in the carriage corner, the brightness in her face was so charming to behold, that on her exclaiming, "What beautiful stars and what a glorious night!" the Secretary said "Yes," but seemed to prefer to see the night and the stars in the light of her lovely little countenance, to looking out of window.

O boofer lady, fascinating boofer lady! If I were but legally executor of Johnny's will! If I had but the right to pay your legacy and to take your receipt!—Something to this purpose surely mingled with the blast of the train as it cleared the stations, all knowingly shutting up their green eyes and opening their red ones when they prepared to let the boofer lady pass.

CHAPTER X

" AND SO, Miss Wren," said Mr. Eugene Wrayburn, " I cannot persuade you to dress me a doll ? "

" No," replied Miss Wren, snappishly ; "if you want one, go and buy one at the shop."

" And my charming young goddaughter," said Mr. Wrayburn, plaintively, " down in Hertfordshire—— "

(" Humbugshire you mean, I think," interposed Miss Wren.)

" —is to be put upon the cold footing of the general public, and is to derive no advantage from my private acquaintance with the Court Dressmaker ? "

" If it's any advantage to your charming godchild—and oh, a precious godfather she has got ! " replied Miss Wren, pricking at him in the air with her needle, " to be informed that the Court Dressmaker knows your tricks and your manners, you may tell her so by post, and with my compliments."

Miss Wren was busy at her work by candle-light, and Mr. Wrayburn, half amused and half vexed, and all idle and shiftless, stood by her bench looking on. Miss Wren's troublesome child was in the corner in deep disgrace, and exhibiting great wretchedness in the shivering stage of prostration from drink.

" Ugh, you disgraceful boy ! " exclaimed Miss Wren, attracted by the sound of his chattering teeth, " I wish they'd all drop down your throat and play at dice in your stomach ! Boh, wicked child ! Bee-baa, black sheep ! "

140

MR. DOLLS IN DISGRACE

On her accompanying each of these reproaches with a threatening stamp of the foot, the wretched creature protested with a whine.

" Pay five shillings for you indeed ! " Miss Wren proceeded ; " how many hours do you suppose it costs me to earn five shillings, you infamous boy ?—Don't cry like that, or I'll throw a doll at you. Pay five shillings fine for you indeed. Fine in more ways than one, I think ! I'd give the dustman five shillings to carry you off in the dust cart."

" No, no," pleaded the absurd creature. " Please ! "

" He's enough to break his mother's heart, is this boy," said Miss Wren, half appealing to Eugene. " I wish I had never brought him up. He'd be sharper than a serpent's tooth, if he wasn't as dull as ditch water. Look at him. There's a pretty object for a parent's eyes ! "

Assuredly, in his worse than swinish state (for swine at least fatten on their guzzling, and make themselves good to eat), he was a pretty object for any eyes.

" A muddling and a swipey old child," said Miss Wren, rating him with great severity, " fit for nothing but to be preserved in the liquor that destroys him, and put in a great glass bottle as a sight for other swipey children of his own pattern,—if he has no consideration for his liver, has he none for his mother ? "

" Yes. Deration, oh don't ! " cried the subject of these angry remarks.

" Oh don't and oh don't," pursued Miss Wren. " It's oh do and oh do. And why do you ? "

" Won't do so any more. Won't indeed. Pray ! "

" There ! " said Miss Wren, covering her eyes with her hand. " I can't bear to look at you. Go up-stairs and get me my bonnet and shawl. Make yourself useful in some way, bad boy, and let me have your room instead of your company, for one half-minute."

Obeying her, he shambled out, and Eugene Wrayburn saw the tears exude from between the little creature's fingers as she kept her hand before her eyes. He was sorry, but his sympathy did not move his carelessness to do anything but feel sorry.

"I'm going to the Italian Opera to try on," said Miss Wren, taking away her hand after a little while, and laughing satirically to hide that she had been crying; "I must see your back before I go, Mr. Wrayburn. Let me first tell you, once for all, that it's of no use your paying visits to me. You wouldn't get what you want of me, no, not if you brought pincers with you to tear it out."

"Are you so obstinate on the subject of a doll's dress for my godchild?"

"Ah!" returned Miss Wren with a hitch of her chin, "I am so obstinate. And of course it's on the subject of a doll's dress —or *ad*dress—whichever you like. Get along and give it up!"

Her degraded charge had come back, and was standing behind her with the bonnet and shawl.

"Give 'em to me and get back into your corner, you naughty old thing!" said Miss Wren, as she turned and espied him. "No, no, I won't have your help. Go into your corner, this minute!"

The miserable man, feebly rubbing the back of his faltering hands downwards from the wrists, shuffled on to his post of disgrace; but not without a curious glance at Eugene in passing him, accompanied with what seemed as if it might have been an action of his elbow, if any action of any limb or joint he had would have answered truly to his will. Taking no more particular notice of him than instinctively falling away from the disagreeable contact, Eugene, with a lazy compliment or so to Miss Wren, begged leave to light his cigar and departed.

"Now, you prodigal old son," said Jenny, shaking her head and her emphatic little forefinger at her burden, "you sit there till I come back. You dare to move out of your corner for a single instant while I'm gone, and I'll know the reason why."

142

With this admonition, she blew her work candles out, leaving him to the light of the fire, and, taking her big door-key in her pocket and her crutch-stick in her hand, marched off.

Eugene lounged slowly towards the Temple, smoking his cigar, but saw no more of the dolls' dressmaker, through the accident of their taking opposite sides of the street. He lounged along moodily, and stopped at Charing Cross to look about him, with as little interest in the crowd as any man might take, and was lounging on again, when a most unexpected object caught his eyes. No less an object than Jenny Wren's bad boy trying to make up his mind to cross the road.

A more ridiculous and feeble spectacle than this tottering wretch making unsteady sallies into the roadway, and as often staggering back again, oppressed by terrors of vehicles that were a long way off or were nowhere, the streets could not have shown. Over and over again, when the course was perfectly clear, he set out, got half-way, described a loop, turned, and went back again, when he might have crossed and re-crossed half-a-dozen times. Then, he would stand shivering on the edge of the pavement, looking up the street and looking down, while scores of people jostled him, and crossed, and went on. Stimulated in course of time by the sight of so many successes, he would make another sally, make another loop, would all but have his foot on the opposite pavement, would see or imagine something coming, and would stagger back again. There, he would stand making spasmodic preparations as if for a great leap, and at last would decide on a start at precisely the wrong moment, and would be roared at by drivers, and would shrink back once more, and stand in the old spot shivering, with the whole of the proceedings to go through again.

"It strikes me," remarked Eugene coolly, after watching him for some minutes, "that my friend is likely to be rather behind time if he has any appointment on hand." With which remark he strolled on, and took no further thought of him.

Lightwood was at home when he got to the Chambers, and had dined alone there. Eugene drew a chair to the fire by which he was having his wine and reading the evening paper, and brought a glass, and filled it for good fellowship's sake.

"My dear Mortimer, you are the express picture of contented industry, reposing (on credit) after the virtuous labours of the day."

"My dear Eugene, you are the express picture of discontented idleness not reposing at all. Where have you been?"

"I have been," replied Wrayburn, "—about town. I have turned up at the present juncture, with the intention of consulting my highly intelligent and respected solicitor on the position of my affairs."

"Your highly intelligent and respected solicitor is of opinion that your affairs are in a bad way, Eugene."

"Though whether," said Eugene thoughtfully, "that can be intelligently said, now, of the affairs of a client who has nothing to lose and who cannot possibly be made to pay, may be open to question."

"You have fallen into the hands of the Jews, Eugene."

"My dear boy," returned the debtor, very composedly taking up his glass, "having previously fallen into the hands of some of the Christians, I can bear it with philosophy."

"I have had an interview to-day, Eugene, with a Jew, who seems determined to press us hard. Quite a Shylock, and quite a Patriarch. A picturesque grey-headed and grey-bearded old Jew, in a shovel-hat and gaberdine."

"Not," said Eugene, pausing in setting down his glass, "surely not my worthy friend Mr. Aaron?"

"He calls himself Mr. Riah."

"By-the-bye," said Eugene, "it comes into my mind that —no doubt with an instinctive desire to receive him into the bosom of our Church—*I* gave him the name of Aaron!"

144

"Eugene, Eugene," returned Lightwood, "you are more ridiculous than usual. Say what you mean."

"Merely, my dear fellow, that I have the honour and pleasure of a speaking acquaintance with such a Patriarch as you describe, and that I address him as Mr. Aaron, because it appears to me Hebraic, expressive, appropriate, and complimentary. Notwithstanding which strong reasons for its being his name, it may not be his name."

"I believe you are the absurdest man on the face of the earth," said Lightwood, laughing.

"Not at all, I assure you. Did he mention that he knew me?"

"He did not. He only said of you that he expected to be paid by you."

"Which looks," remarked Eugene with much gravity, "like *not* knowing me. I hope it may not be my worthy friend Mr. Aaron, for, to tell you the truth, Mortimer, I doubt he may have a prepossession against me. I strongly suspect him of having had a hand in spiriting away Lizzie."

"Everything," returned Lightwood impatiently, "seems, by a fatality, to bring us round to Lizzie. 'About town' meant about Lizzie, just now, Eugene."

"My solicitor, do you know," observed Eugene, turning round to the furniture, "is a man of infinite discernment."

"Did it not, Eugene?"

"Yes, it did, Mortimer."

"And yet, Eugene, you know you do not really care for her."

Eugene Wrayburn rose, and put his hands in his pockets, and stood with a foot on the fender, indolently rocking his body and looking at the fire. After a prolonged pause, he replied: "I don't know that. I must ask you not to say that, as if we took it for granted."

"But if you do care for her, so much the more should you leave her to herself."

Having again paused as before, Eugene said: "I don't

know that, either. But tell me. Did you ever see me take so much trouble about anything, as about this disappearance of hers? I ask, for information."

"My dear Eugene, I wish I ever had!"

"Then you have not? Just so. You confirm my own impression. Does that look as if I cared for her? I ask, for information."

"I asked *you* for information, Eugene," said Mortimer, reproachfully.

"Dear boy, I know it, but I can't give it. I thirst for information. What do I mean? If my taking so much trouble to recover her does not mean that I care for her, what does it mean? 'If Peter Piper picked a peck of pickled pepper, where's the peck,' &c.?"

Though he said this gaily, he said it with a perplexed and inquisitive face, as if he actually did not know what to make of himself. "Look on to the end—" Lightwood was beginning to remonstrate, when he caught at the words:

"Ah! See now! That's exactly what I am incapable of doing. How very acute you are, Mortimer, in finding my weak place! When we were at school together, I got up my lessons at the last moment, day by day and bit by bit; now we are out in life together, I get up my lessons in the same way. In the present task I have not got beyond this: —I am bent on finding Lizzie, and I mean to find her, and I will take any means of finding her that offer themselves. Fair means or foul means, are all alike to me. I ask you— for information—what does that mean? When I have found her I may ask you—also for information—what do I mean now? But it would be premature in this stage, and it's not the character of my mind."

Lightwood was shaking his head over the air with which his friend held forth thus—an air so whimsically open and argumentative as almost to deprive what he said of the appearance of evasion—when a shuffling was heard at the outer door, and then an undecided knock, as though some

146

hand were groping for the knocker. "The frolicsome youth of the neighbourhood," said Eugene, "whom I should be delighted to pitch from this elevation into the churchyard below, without any intermediate ceremonies, have probably turned the lamp out. I am on duty to-night, and will see to the door."

His friend had barely had time to recall the unprecedented gleam of determination with which he had spoken of finding this girl, and which had faded out of him with the breath of the spoken words, when Eugene came back, ushering in a most disgraceful shadow of a man, shaking from head to foot, and clothed in shabby grease and smear.

"This interesting gentleman," said Eugene, "is the son—the occasionally rather trying son, for he has his failings—of a lady of my acquaintance. My dear Mortimer—Mr. Dolls." Eugene had no idea what his name was, knowing the little dressmaker's to be assumed, but presented him with easy confidence under the first appellation that his associations suggested.

"I gather, my dear Mortimer," pursued Eugene, as Lightwood stared at the obscene visitor, "from the manner of Mr. Dolls—which is occasionally complicated—that he desires to make some communication to me. I have mentioned to Mr. Dolls that you and I are on terms of confidence, and have requested Mr. Dolls to develop his views here."

The wretched object being much embarrassed by holding what remained of his hat, Eugene airily tossed it to the door, and put him down in a chair.

"It will be necessary, I think," he observed, "to wind up Mr. Dolls, before anything to any mortal purpose can be got out of him. Brandy, Mr. Dolls, or—— ?"

"Threepenn'orth Rum," said Mr. Dolls.

A judiciously small quantity of the spirit was given him in a wine-glass, and he began to convey it to his mouth, with all kinds of falterings and gyrations on the road.

"The nerves of Mr. Dolls," remarked Eugene to Lightwood,

"are considerably unstrung. And I deem it on the whole expedient to fumigate Mr. Dolls."

He took the shovel from the grate, sprinkled a few live ashes on it, and from a box on the chimney-piece took a few pastilles, which he set upon them; then, with great composure, began placidly waving the shovel in front of Mr. Dolls, to cut him off from his company.

"Lord bless my soul, Eugene!" cried Lightwood, laughing again, "what a mad fellow you are! Why does this creature come to see you?"

"We shall hear," said Wrayburn, very observant of his face withal. "Now then. Speak out. Don't be afraid. State your business, Dolls."

"Mist Wrayburn!" said the visitor, thickly and huskily. "—'*Tis* Mist Wrayburn, ain't?" With a stupid stare.

"Of course it is. Look at me. What do you want?"

Mr. Dolls collapsed in his chair, and faintly said "Threepenn'orth Rum."

"Will you do me the favour, my dear Mortimer, to wind up Mr. Dolls again?" said Eugene. "I am occupied with the fumigation."

A similar quantity was poured into his glass, and he got it to his lips by similar circuitous ways. Having drunk it, Mr. Dolls, with an evident fear of running down again unless he made haste, proceeded to business.

"Mist Wrayburn. Tried to nudge you, but you wouldn't. You want that drection. You want t'know where she lives. *Do* you, Mist Wrayburn?"

With a glance at his friend, Eugene replied to the question sternly, "I do."

"I am er man," said Mr. Dolls, trying to smite himself on the breast, but bringing his hand to bear upon the vicinity of his eye, "er do it. I am er man er do it."

"What are you the man to do?" demanded Eugene, still sternly.

"Er give up that drection."

148

Three-penn'orth Rum

" Have you got it ? "

With a most laborious attempt at pride and dignity, Mr. Dolls rolled his head for some time, awakening the highest expectations, and then answered, as if it were the happiest point that could possibly be expected of him : " No."

" What do you mean then ? "

Mr. Dolls, collapsing in the drowsiest manner after his late intellectual triumph, replied : " Threepenn'orth Rum."

" Wind him up again, my dear Mortimer," said Wrayburn ; " wind him up again."

" Eugene, Eugene," urged Lightwood in a low voice, as he complied, " can you stoop to the use of such an instrument as this ? "

" I said," was the reply, made with that former gleam of determination, " that I would find her out by any means, fair or foul. These are foul, and I'll take them—if I am not first tempted to break the head of Mr. Dolls with the fumigator. Can you get the direction ? Do you mean that ? Speak ! If that's what you have come for, say how much you want."

" Ten shillings—Threepenn'orths Rum," said Mr. Dolls.

" You shall have it."

" Fifteen shillings—Threepenn'orths Rum," said Mr. Dolls, making an attempt to stiffen himself.

" You shall have it. Stop at that. How will you get the direction you talk of ? "

" I am er man," said Mr. Dolls, with majesty, " er get it, sir."

" How will you get it, I ask you ? "

" I am ill-used vidual," said Mr. Dolls. " Blown up morning t'night. Called names. She makes Mint money, sir, and never stands Threepenn'orth Rum."

" Get on," rejoined Eugene, tapping his palsied head with the fire-shovel, as it sank on his breast. " What comes next?"

Making a dignified attempt to gather himself together, but, as it were, dropping half-a-dozen pieces of himself while he tried in vain to pick up one, Mr. Dolls, swaying his head from side to side, regarded his questioner with what he supposed to be a haughty smile and a scornful glance.

"She looks upon me as mere child, sir. I am NOT mere child, sir. Man. Man talent. Lerrers pass betwixt 'em. Postman lerrers. Easy for man talent er get drection, as get his own drection."

" Get it then," said Eugene; adding very heartily under his breath, " —You Brute ! Get it, and bring it here to me, and earn the money for sixty threepenn'orths of rum, and drink them all, one a top of another, and drink yourself dead with all possible expedition." The latter clauses of these special instructions he addressed to the fire, as he gave it back the ashes he had taken from it, and replaced the shovel.

Mr. Dolls now struck out the highly unexpected discovery that he had been insulted by Lightwood, and stated his desire to " have it out with him " on the spot, and defied him to come on, upon the liberal terms of a sovereign to a half-penny. Mr. Dolls then fell a-crying, and then exhibited a tendency to fall asleep. This last manifestation as by far the most alarming, by reason of its threatening his prolonged stay on the premises, necessitated vigorous measures. Eugene picked up his worn-out hat with the tongs, clapped it on his head, and, taking him by the collar—all this at arm's length— conducted him down-stairs and out of the precincts into Fleet Street. There, he turned his face westward, and left him.

When he got back, Lightwood was standing over the fire, brooding in a sufficiently low-spirited manner.

" I'll wash my hands of Mr. Dolls—physically— " said Eugene, " and be with you again directly, Mortimer."

" I would much prefer," retorted Mortimer, " your washing your hands of Mr. Dolls, morally, Eugene."

" So would I," said Eugene; " but you see, dear boy, I can't do without him."

In a minute or two he resumed his chair, as perfectly

unconcerned as usual, and rallied his friend on having so narrowly escaped the prowess of their muscular visitor.

"I can't be amused on this theme," said Mortimer, restlessly. "You can make almost any theme amusing to me, Eugene, but not this."

"Well!" cried Eugene, "I am a little ashamed of it myself, and therefore let us change the subject."

"It is so deplorably underhanded," said Mortimer. "It is so unworthy of you, this setting on of such a shameful scout."

"We have changed the subject!" exclaimed Eugene, airily. "We have found a new one in that word, scout. Don't be like Patience on a mantel-piece frowning at Dolls, but sit down, and I'll tell you something that you really will find amusing. Take a cigar. Look at this of mine. I light it— draw one puff—breathe the smoke out—there it goes—it's Dolls!—it's gone, and being gone, you are a man again."

"Your subject," said Mortimer, after lighting a cigar, and comforting himself with a whiff or two, "was scouts, Eugene."

"Exactly. Isn't it droll that I never go out after dark, but I find myself attended, always by one scout, and often by two?"

Lightwood took his cigar from his lips in surprise, and looked at his friend, as if with a latent suspicion that there must be a jest or hidden meaning in his words.

"On my honour, no," said Wrayburn, answering the look and smiling carelessly; "I don't wonder at your supposing so, but on my honour, no. I say what I mean. I never go out after dark, but I find myself in the ludicrous situation of being followed and observed at a distance, always by one scout, and often by two."

"Are you sure, Eugene?"

"Sure? My dear boy, they are always the same."

"But there's no process out against you. The Jews only threaten. They have done nothing. Besides, they know where to find you, and I represent you. Why take the trouble ? "

" Observe the legal mind ! " remarked Eugene, turning round to the furniture again, with an air of indolent rapture. " Observe the dyer's hand, assimilating itself to what it works in,—or would work in, if anybody would give it anything to do. Respected solicitor, it's not that. The schoolmaster's abroad."

" The schoolmaster ? "

" Ay ! Sometimes the schoolmaster and the pupil are both abroad. Why, how soon you rust in my absence ! You don't understand yet ? Those fellows who were here one night. They are the scouts I speak of as doing me the honour to attend me after dark."

" How long has this been going on ? " asked Lightwood, opposing a serious face to the laugh of his friend.

" I apprehend it has been going on ever since a certain person went off. Probably, it had been going on some little time before I noticed it ; which would bring it to about that time."

" Do you think they suppose you to have inveigled her away ? "

" My dear Mortimer, you know the absorbing nature of my professional occupations ; I really have not had leisure to think about it."

" Have you asked them what they want ? Have you objected ? "

" Why should I ask them what they want, dear fellow, when I am indifferent what they want ? Why should I express objection, when I don't object ? "

" You are in your most reckless mood. But you called the situation just now, a ludicrous one ; and most men object to that, even those who are utterly indifferent to everything else."

" You charm me, Mortimer, with your reading of my weaknesses. (By-the-bye, that very word, Reading, in its critical use, always charms me. An actress's Reading of a chamber-maid, a dancer's Reading of a hornpipe, a singer's Reading of a song, a mariner-painter's Reading of the sea, the kettle-drum's Reading of an Instrumental passage, are phrases ever youthful and delightful.) I was mentioning your perception of my weaknesses. I own to the weakness of objecting to occupy a ludicrous position, and therefore I transfer the position to the scouts."

" I wish, Eugene, you would speak a little more soberly and plainly, if it were only out of consideration for my feeling less at ease than you do."

" Then soberly and plainly, Mortimer, I goad the school-master to madness. I make the schoolmaster so ridiculous, and so aware of being made ridiculous, that I see him chafe and fret at every pore when we cross one another. The amiable occupation has been the solace of my life, since I was baulked in the manner unnecessary to recall. I have derived inexpressible comfort from it. I do it thus : I stroll out after dark, stroll a little way, look in at a window and furtively look out for the schoolmaster. Sooner or later, I perceive the schoolmaster on the watch ; sometimes accompanied by his hopeful pupil ; oftener pupil-less. Having made sure of his watching me, I tempt him on, all over London. One night I go east, another night north, in a few nights I go all round the compass. Sometimes, I walk ; sometimes, I proceed in cabs, draining the pocket of the schoolmaster, who then follows in cabs. I study and get up abstruse No Thoroughfares in the course of the day. With Venetian mystery I seek those No Thoroughfares at night, glide into them by means of dark courts, tempt the schoolmaster to follow, turn suddenly, and catch him before he can retreat. Then we face one another, and I pass him as unaware of his existence, and he undergoes grinding torments. Similarly, I walk at a great pace down a short street, rapidly turn the corner, and, getting out of his view, as rapidly turn back. I catch him coming on post, again pass him as unaware of his existence, and again he undergoes grinding torments. Night after night his disappointment is acute, but hope springs eternal in the scholastic breast, and he follows me again to-morrow. Thus I enjoy the pleasures of the chase, and derive great benefit from the healthful exercise. When I do not enjoy the pleasures of the chase, for anything I know he watches at the Temple Gate all night."

"This is an extraordinary story," observed Lightwood, who had heard it out with serious attention. "I don't like it."

"You are a little hipped, dear fellow," said Eugene ; "you have been too sedentary. Come and enjoy the pleasures of the chase."

"Do you mean that you believe he is watching now?"

"I have not the slightest doubt he is."

"Have you seen him to-night?"

"I forgot to look for him when I was last out," returned Eugene, with the calmest indifference ; "but I dare say he was there. Come! Be a British sportsman, and enjoy the pleasures of the chase. It will do you good."

Lightwood hesitated ; but, yielding to his curiosity, rose.

"Bravo!" cried Eugene, rising too. "Or, if Yoicks would be in better keeping, consider that I said Yoicks. Look to your feet, Mortimer, for we shall try your boots. When you are ready I am—need I say with a Hey Ho Chivy, and likewise with a Hark Forward, Hark Forward, Tantivy?"

"Will nothing make you serious?" said Mortimer, laughing through his gravity.

"I am always serious, but just now I am a little excited by the glorious fact that a southerly wind and a cloudy sky proclaim a hunting evening. Ready? So. We turn out the lamp and shut the door, and take the field."

As the two friends passed out of the Temple into the public street, Eugene demanded with a show of courteous patronage in which direction Mortimer would like the run to be? "There is a rather difficult country about Bethnal Green," said Eugene, "and we have not taken in that

direction lately. What is your opinion of Bethnal Green?"
Mortimer assented to Bethnal Green, and they turned east-
ward. "Now, when we come to St. Paul's churchyard,"
pursued Eugene, "we'll loiter artfully, and I'll show you
the schoolmaster." But, they both saw him, before they got
there; alone, and stealing after them in the shadow of the
houses, on the opposite side of the way.

"Get your wind," said Eugene, "for I am off directly.
Does it occur to you that the boys of Merry England will
begin to deteriorate in an educational light, if this lasts long?
The schoolmaster can't attend to me and the boys too. Got
your wind? I am off!"

At what a rate he went, to breathe the schoolmaster; and
how he then lounged and loitered, to put his patience to
another kind of wear; what preposterous ways he took, with
no other object on earth than to disappoint and punish him;
and how he wore him out by every piece of ingenuity that
his eccentric humour could devise; all this Lightwood noted,
with a feeling of astonishment that so careless a man could
be so wary, and that so idle a man could take so much
trouble. At last, far on in the third hour of the pleasures
of the chase, when he had brought the poor dogging wretch
round again into the City, he twisted Mortimer up a few
dark entries, twisted him into a little square court, twisted
him sharp round again, and they almost ran against Bradley
Headstone.

"And you see, as I was saying, Mortimer," remarked
Eugene aloud, with the utmost coolness, as though there
were no one within hearing but themselves; "and you see,
as I was saying—undergoing grinding torments."

It was not too strong a phrase for the occasion. Looking
like the hunted, and not the hunter, baffled, worn, with the
exhaustion of deferred hope and consuming hate and anger
in his face, white-lipped, wild-eyed, draggle-haired, seamed
with jealousy and anger, and torturing himself with the
conviction that he showed it all and they exulted in it, he

went by them in the dark, like a haggard head suspended in the air: so completely did the force of his expression cancel his figure.

Mortimer Lightwood was not an extraordinarily impressible man, but this face impressed him. He spoke of it more than once on the remainder of the way home, and more than once when they got home.

They had been a-bed in their respective rooms two or three hours, when Eugene was partly awakened by hearing a footstep going about, and was fully awakened by seeing Lightwood standing at his bedside.

"Nothing wrong, Mortimer?"

"No."

"What fancy takes you, then, for walking about in the night?"

"I am horribly wakeful."

"How comes that about, I wonder?"

"Eugene, I cannot lose sight of that fellow's face."

"Odd," said Eugene, with a light laugh, "*I* can." And turned over, and fell asleep again.

CHAPTER XI

THERE was no sleep for Bradley Headstone on that night when Eugene Wrayburn turned so easily in his bed; there was no sleep for little Miss Peecher. Bradley consumed the lonely hours, and consumed himself, in haunting the spot where his careless rival lay a-dreaming; little Miss Peecher wore them away in listening for the return home of the master of her heart, and in sorrowfully presaging that much was amiss with him. Yet more was amiss with him than Miss Peecher's simply arranged little work-box of thoughts, fitted with no gloomy and dark recesses, could hold. For, the state of the man was murderous.

The state of the man was murderous, and he knew it. More; he irritated it, with a kind of perverse pleasure akin to that which a sick man sometimes has in irritating a wound upon his body. Tied up all day with his disciplined show upon him, subdued to the performance of his routine of educational tricks, encircled by a gabbling crowd, he broke loose at night like an ill-tamed wild animal. Under his daily restraint, it was his compensation, not his trouble, to give a glance towards his state at night, and to the freedom of its being indulged. If great criminals told the truth—which, being great criminals, they do not—they would very rarely tell of their struggles against the crime. Their struggles are towards it. They buffet with opposing waves, to gain the bloody shore, not to recede from it. This man perfectly comprehended that he hated his rival with his strongest and worst forces, and that if he tracked him to Lizzie Hexam, his so doing would never serve himself with her, or serve her. All his pains were taken, to the end that he might incense himself with the sight of the detested figure in her company and favour, in her place of concealment. And he knew as well what act of his would follow if he did, as he knew that his mother had borne him. Granted, that he may not have held it necessary to make express mention to himself of the one familiar truth any more than of the other.

He knew equally well that he fed his wrath and hatred, and that he accumulated provocation and self-justification, by being made the nightly sport of the reckless and insolent Eugene. Knowing all this, and still always going on with infinite endurance, pains, and perseverance, could his dark soul doubt whither he went?

Baffled, exasperated, and weary, he lingered opposite the Temple gate when it closed on Wrayburn and Lightwood, debating with himself should he go home for that time or should he watch longer. Possessed in his jealousy by the fixed idea that Wrayburn was in the secret, if it were not altogether of his contriving, Bradley was as confident of getting the better of him at last by sullenly sticking to him, as he would have been—and often had been—of mastering any piece of study in the way of his vocation, by the like slow persistent process. A man of rapid passions and sluggish intelligence, it had served him often, and should serve him again.

The suspicion crossed him as he rested in a doorway with his eyes upon the Temple gate, that perhaps she was even concealed in that set of Chambers. It would furnish another reason for Wrayburn's purposeless walks, and it might be. He thought of it and thought of it, until he resolved to steal up the stairs, if the gate-keeper would let him through, and listen. So, the haggard head suspended in the air flitted across the road, like the spectre of one of the many heads erst hoisted upon neighbouring Temple Bar, and stopped before the watchman.

The watchman looked at it, and asked : " Who for ? "

" Mr. Wrayburn."

" It's very late."

" He came back with Mr. Lightwood, I know, near upon two hours ago. But if he has gone to bed, I'll put a paper in his letter-box. I am expected."

The watchman said no more, but opened the gate, though rather doubtfully. Seeing, however, that the visitor went straight and fast in the right direction, he seemed satisfied.

The haggard head floated up the dark staircase, and softly descended nearer to the floor outside the outer door of the chambers. The doors of the rooms within appeared to be standing open. There were rays of candlelight from one of them, and there was the sound of a footstep going about. There were two voices. The words they uttered were not distinguishable, but they were both the voices of men. In a few moments the voices were silent, and there was no sound of footstep, and the inner light went out. If Lightwood could have seen the face which kept him awake, staring and listening in the darkness outside the door as he spoke of it, he might have been less disposed to sleep through the remainder of the night.

" Not there," said Bradley, " but she might have been." The head arose to its former height from the ground, floated down the staircase again, and passed on to the gate. A man was standing there in parley with the watchman.

" Oh ! " said the watchman. " Here he is ! "

Perceiving himself to be the antecedent, Bradley looked from the watchman to the man.

" This man is leaving a letter for Mr. Lightwood," the watchman explained, showing it in his hand; " and I was mentioning that a person had just gone up to Mr. Lightwood's chambers. It might be the same business perhaps ? "

159

"No," said Bradley, glancing at the man, who was a stranger to him.

"No," the man assented in a surly way; "my letter—it's wrote by my daughter, but it's mine—it's about my business, and my business ain't nobody else's business."

As Bradley passed out of the gate with an undecided foot, he heard it shut behind him, and heard the footstep of the man coming after him.

"'Scuse me," said the man, who appeared to have been drinking, and rather stumbled at him than touched him, to attract his attention; "but might you be acquainted with the T'other Governor?"

"With whom?" asked Bradley.

"With," returned the man, pointing backward over his right shoulder with his right thumb, "the T'other Governor?"

"I don't know what you mean."

"Why look here," hooking his proposition on his left-hand fingers with the forefinger of his right. "There's two Governors, ain't there? One and one, two—Lawyer Lightwood, my first finger, he's one, ain't he? Well; might you be acquainted with my middle finger, the T'other?"

"I know quite as much of him," said Bradley, with a frown and a distant look before him, "as I want to know."

"Hooroar!" cried the man. "Hooroar, T'other T'other Governor. Hooroar T'otherest Governor! I am of your way of thinkin'."

"Don't make such a noise at this dead hour of the night. What are you talking about?"

"Look here, T'otherest Governor," replied the man, becoming hoarsely confidential. "The T'other Governor he's always joked his jokes agin me, owing, as I believe, to my being a honest man as gets my living by the sweat of my brow. Which he ain't, and he don't."

"What is that to me?"

"T'otherest Governor," returned the man in a tone of injured innocence, "if you don't care to hear no more, don't hear no more. You begun it. You said, and likewise showed pretty plain, as you warn't by no means friendly to him. But I don't seek to force my company nor yet my opinions on no man. I am a honest man, that's what I am. Put me in the dock anywhere—I don't care where—and I says, 'My Lord, I am a honest man.' Put me in the witness-box anywhere—I don't care where—and I says the same to his lordship, and I kisses the book. I don't kiss my coat-cuff; I kisses the book."

It was not so much in deference to these strong testimonials to character, as in his restless casting about for any way or help towards the discovery on which he was concentrated, that Bradley Headstone replied : " You needn't take offence. I didn't mean to stop you. You were too loud in the open street ; that was all."

" T'otherest Governor," replied Mr. Riderhood, mollified and mysterious, " I know wot it is to be loud, and I know wot it is to be soft. Nat'rally I do. It would be a wonder if I did not, being by the Chris'en name of Roger, which took it arter my own father, which took it from his own father, though which of our fam'ly fust took it nat'ral I will not in any ways mislead you by undertakin' to say. And wishing that your elth may be better than your looks, which your inside must be bad indeed if it's on the footing of your out."

Startled by the implication that his face revealed too much of his mind, Bradley made an effort to clear his brow. It might be worth knowing what this strange man's business was with Lightwood, or Wrayburn, or both, at such an unseasonable hour. He set himself to find out, for the man might prove to be a messenger between those two.

" You call at the Temple late," he remarked with a lumbering show of ease.

" Wish I may die," cried Mr. Riderhood, with a hoarse laugh, " if I warn't a-goin' to say the self-same words to you, T'otherest Governor ! "

161

"It chanced so with me," said Bradley, looking discon-
certedly about him.

"And it chanced so with me," said Riderhood. "But I
don't mind telling you how. Why should I mind telling
you? I'm a Deputy Lock-keeper up the river, and I was
off duty yes'day, and I shall be on to-morrow."

"Yes?"

"Yes, and I come to London to look arter my private
affairs. My private affairs is to get appinted to the Lock as
reg'lar keeper at fust hand, and to have the law of a Busted
B'low-Bridge steamer which drownded of me. I ain't a-goin'
to be drownded and not paid for it!"

Bradley looked at him, as though he were claiming to be
a Ghost.

"The Steamer," said Mr. Riderhood, obstinately, "run me
down and drownded of me. Interference on the part of other
parties brought me round; but I never asked 'em to bring me
round, nor yet the steamer never asked 'em to it. I mean to
be paid for the life as the steamer took."

"Was that your business at Mr. Lightwood's chambers in
the middle of the night?" asked Bradley, eyeing him with
distrust.

"That, and to get a writing to be fust-hand Lock-keeper.
A recommendation in writing being looked for, who else
ought to give it to me? As I says in the letter in my
daughter's hand, with my mark put to it to make it good in
law, Who but you, Lawyer Lightwood, ought to hand over
this here stifficate, and who but you ought to go in for
damages on my account agin the Steamer? For (as I says
under my mark) I have had trouble enough along of you and
your friend. If you, Lawyer Lightwood, had backed me good
and true, and if the T'other Governor had took me down
correct (I says under my mark), I should have been worth
money at the present time, instead of having a barge-load of
bad names chucked at me, and being forced to eat my words,
which is a unsatisfying sort of food, wotever a man's appetite!"

162

And when you mention the middle of the night, T'otherest Governor," growled Mr. Riderhood, winding up his monotonous summary of his wrongs, " throw your eye on this here bundle under my arm, and bear in mind that I'm a walking back to my Lock, and that the Temple laid upon my line of road."

Bradley Headstone's face had changed during this latter recital, and he had observed the speaker with a more sustained attention.

" Do you know," said he, after a pause, during which they walked on side by side, " that I believe I could tell you your name, if I tried ? "

" Prove your opinion," was the answer, accompanied with a stop and a stare. " Try."

" Your name is Riderhood."

" I'm blest if it ain't," returned that gentleman. " But I don't know your'n."

" That's quite another thing," said Bradley. " I never supposed you did."

As Bradley walked on meditating, the Rogue walked on at his side muttering. The purport of the muttering was : " that Rogue Riderhood, by George ! seemed to be made public property on, now, and that every man seemed to think himself free to handle his name as if it was a Street Pump." The purport of the meditating was : " Here is an instrument, Can I use it ? "

They had walked along the Strand, and into Pall Mall, and had turned up-hill towards Hyde Park Corner; Bradley Headstone waiting on the pace and lead of Riderhood, and leaving him to indicate the course. So slow were the schoolmaster's thoughts, and so indistinct his purposes when they were but tributary to the one absorbing purpose—or rather when, like dark trees under a stormy sky, they only lined the long vista at the end of which he saw those two figures of Wrayburn and Lizzie on which his eyes were fixed—that at least a good half-mile was traversed before he spoke again. Even then, it was only to ask :

"Where is your Lock?"

"Twenty mile and odd—call it five-and-twenty mile and odd, if you like—up stream," was the sullen reply.

"How is it called?"

"Plashwater Weir Mill Lock."

"Suppose I was to offer you five shillings; what then?"

"Why, then, I'd take it," said Mr. Riderhood.

The schoolmaster put his hand in his pocket, and produced two half-crowns, and placed them in Mr. Riderhood's palm; who stopped at a convenient doorstep to ring them both, before acknowledging their receipt.

"There's one thing about you, T'otherest Governor," said Riderhood, faring on again, "as looks well and goes fur. You're a ready-money man. Now;" when he had carefully pocketed the coins on that side of himself which was furthest from his new friend; "what's this for?"

"For you."

"Why, o' course I know *that*," said Riderhood, as arguing something that was self-evident. "O' course I know very well as no man in his right senses would suppose as anythink would make me give it up agin when I'd once got it. But what do you want for it?"

"I don't know that I want anything for it. Or if I do want anything for it, I don't know what it is." Bradley gave this answer in a stolid, vacant, and self-communing manner, which Mr. Riderhood found very extraordinary.

"You have no goodwill towards this Wrayburn," said Bradley, coming to the name in a reluctant and forced way, as if he were dragged to it.

"No."

"Neither have I."

Riderhood nodded, and asked: "Is it for that?"

"It's as much for that as anything else. It's something to be agreed with, on a subject that occupies so much of one's thoughts."

"It don't agree with *you*," returned Mr. Riderhood, bluntly.

" No ! It don't, T'otherest Governor, and it's no use a-lookin' as if you wanted to make out that it did. I tell you it rankles in you. It rankles in you, rusts in you, and pisons you."

" Say that it does so," returned Bradley, with quivering lips ; " is there no cause for it ? "

" Cause enough, I'll bet a pound ! " cried Mr. Riderhood.

" Haven't you yourself declared that the fellow has heaped provocation, insults, and affronts on you, or something to that effect ? He has done the same by me. He is made of venomous insults and affronts, from the crown of his head to the sole of his foot. Are you so hopeful or so stupid, as not to know that he and the other will treat your application with contempt, and light their cigars with it ? "

" I shouldn't wonder if they did, by George," said Riderhood, turning angry.

" If they did ! They will. Let me ask you a question. I know something more than your name about you ; I knew something about Gaffer Hexam. When did you last set eyes upon his daughter ? "

" When did I last set eyes upon his daughter, T'otherest Governor ? " repeated Mr. Riderhood, growing intentionally slower of comprehension as the other quickened in his speech.

" Yes. Not to speak to her. To see her—anywhere ? "

The Rogue had got the clue he wanted, though he held it with a clumsy hand. Looking perplexedly at the passionate face, as if he were trying to work out a sum in his mind, he slowly answered : " I ain't set eyes upon her—never once—not since the day of Gaffer's death."

" You know her well, by sight ? "

" I should think I did ! No one better."

" And you know him as well ? "

" Who's him ? " asked Riderhood, taking off his hat and rubbing his forehead, as he directed a dull look at his questioner.

"Curse the name! Is it so agreeable to you that you want to hear it again?"

"Oh! *Him!*" said Riderhood, who had craftily worked the schoolmaster into this corner, that he might again take note of his face under its evil possession. "I'd know *him* among a thousand."

"Did you——" Bradley tried to ask it quietly; but, do what he might with his voice, he could not subdue his face; —"did you ever see them together?"

(The Rogue had got the clue in both hands now.)

"I see 'em together, T'otherest Governor, on the very day when Gaffer was towed ashore."

Bradley could have hidden a reserved piece of information from the sharp eyes of a whole inquisitive class, but he could not veil from the eyes of the ignorant Riderhood the withheld question next in his breast. "You shall put it plain if you want it answered," thought the Rogue doggedly; "I ain't a-going a wolunteering."

"Well! was he insolent to her too?" asked Bradley after a struggle. "Or did he make a show of being kind to her?"

"He made a show of being most uncommon kind to her," said Riderhood. "By George! now I——"

His flying off at a tangent was indisputably natural. Bradley looked at him for the reason.

"Now I think of it," said Mr. Riderhood, evasively, for he was substituting those words for "Now I see you so jealous," which was the phrase really in his mind; "p'r'aps he went and took me down wrong, a purpose, on account o' being sweet upon her!"

The baseness of confirming him in this suspicion or pretence of one (for he could not have really entertained it), was a line's breadth beyond the mark the schoolmaster had reached. The baseness of communing and intriguing with the fellow who would have set that stain upon her, and upon her brother too, was attained. The line's breadth further, lay beyond. He made no reply, but walked on with a lowering face.

What he might gain by this acquaintance, he could not work out in his slow and cumbrous thoughts. The man had an injury against the object of his hatred, and that was something; though it was less than he supposed, for there dwelt in the man no such deadly rage and resentment as burned in his own breast. The man knew her, and might, by a fortunate chance, see her, or hear of her; that was something, as enlisting one pair of eyes and ears the more. The man was a bad man, and willing enough to be in his pay. That was something, for his own state and purpose were as bad as bad could be, and he seemed to derive a vague support from the possession of a congenial instrument, though it might never be used.

Suddenly he stood still, and asked Riderhood point-blank if he knew where she was? Clearly, he did not know. He asked Riderhood if he would be willing, in case any intelligence of her, or of Wrayburn as seeking her or associating with her, should fall in his way, to communicate it if it were paid for? He would be very willing indeed. He was " agin 'em both," he said with an oath, and for why? 'Cause they had both stood betwixt him and his getting his living by the sweat of his brow.

" It will not be long then," said Bradley Headstone, after some more discourse to this effect, " before we see one another again. Here is the country road, and here is the day. Both have come upon me by surprise."

" But, T'otherest Governor," urged Mr. Riderhood, " I don't know where to find you."

" It is of no consequence. I know where to find you, and I'll come to your Lock."

" But, T'otherest Governor," urged Mr. Riderhood again, " no luck never come yet of a dry acquaintance. Let's wet it in a mouthful of rum and milk, T'otherest Governor."

Bradley assenting, went with him into an early public-house, haunted by unsavoury smells of musty hay and stale straw, where returning carts, farmers' men, gaunt dogs, fowls of a beery breed, and certain human night-birds fluttering home to roost, were solacing themselves after their several manners; and where not one of the night-birds hovering about the sloppy bar failed to discern at a glance in the passion-wasted night-bird with respectable feathers, the worst night-bird of all.

An inspiration of affection for a half-drunken carter going his way led to Mr. Riderhood's being elevated on a high heap of baskets on a waggon, and pursuing his journey recumbent on his back with his head on his bundle. Bradley then turned to retrace his steps, and by-and-by struck off through little-traversed ways, and by-and-by reached school and home. Up came the sun to find him washed and brushed, methodically dressed in decent black coat and waistcoat, decent formal black tie, and pepper and salt pantaloons, with his decent silver watch in its pocket, and its decent hair-guard round his neck : a scholastic huntsman clad for the field, with his fresh pack yelping and barking around him.

Yet more really bewitched than the miserable creatures of the much-lamented times, who accused themselves of im-possibilities under a contagion of horror and the strongly suggestive influences of Torture, he had been ridden hard by Evil Spirits in the night that was newly gone. He had been spurred and whipped and heavily sweated. If a record of the sport had usurped the places of peaceful texts from Scripture on the wall, the most advanced of the scholars might have taken fright and run away from the master.

CHAPTER XII

Up came the sun, streaming all over London, and in its glorious impartiality even condescending to make prismatic sparkles in the whiskers of Mr. Alfred Lammle as he sat at breakfast. In need of some brightening from without was Mr. Alfred Lammle, for he had the air of being dull enough within, and looked grievously discontented.

Mrs. Alfred Lammle faced her lord. The happy pair of swindlers, with the comfortable tie between them that each had swindled the other, sat moodily observant of the table-cloth. Things looked so gloomy in the breakfast-room, albeit on the sunny side of Sackville Street, that any of the family tradespeople glancing through the blinds might have taken the hint to send in his account and press for it. But this, indeed, most of the family tradespeople had already done, without the hint.

" It seems to me," said Mrs. Lammle, " that you have had no money at all ever since we have been married."

" What seems to you," said Mr. Lammle, " to have been the case, may possibly have been the case. It doesn't matter."

Was it the speciality of Mr. and Mrs. Lammle, or does it ever obtain with other loving couples ? In these matrimonial dialogues they never addressed each other, but always some invisible presence that appeared to take a station about midway between them. Perhaps the skeleton in the cupboard comes out to be talked to, on such domestic occasions?

"I have never seen any money in the house," said Mrs. Lammle to the skeleton, "except my own annuity. That I swear."

"You needn't take the trouble of swearing," said Mr. Lammle to the skeleton; "once more, it doesn't matter. You never turned your annuity to so good an account."

"Good an account! In what way?" asked Mrs. Lammle.

"In the way of getting credit, and living well," said Mr. Lammle.

Perhaps the skeleton laughed scornfully on being intrusted with this question and this answer; certainly Mrs. Lammle did, and Mr. Lammle did.

"And what is to happen next?" asked Mrs. Lammle of the skeleton.

"Smash is to happen next," said Mr. Lammle to the same authority.

After this, Mrs. Lammle looked disdainfully at the skeleton —but without carrying the look on to Mr. Lammle—and drooped her eyes. After that, Mr. Lammle did exactly the same thing, and drooped *his* eyes. A servant then entering with toast, the skeleton retired into the closet, and shut itself up.

"Sophronia," said Mr. Lammle, when the servant had withdrawn. And then, very much louder: "Sophronia!"

"Well?"

"Attend to me, if you please." He eyed her sternly until she did attend, and then went on. "I want to take counsel with you. Come, come; no more trifling. You know our league and covenant. We are to work together for our joint interest, and you are as knowing a hand as I am. We shouldn't be together if you were not. What's to be done? We are hemmed into a corner. What shall we do?"

"Have you no scheme on foot that will bring in any-thing?"

Mr. Lammle plunged into his whiskers for reflection, and came out hopeless: "No; as adventurers we are obliged to play rash games for chances of high winnings, and there has been a run of luck against us."

She was resuming, "Have you nothing——" when he stopped her.

"We, Sophronia. We, we, we."

"Have we nothing to sell?"

"Deuce a bit. I have given a Jew a bill of sale on this furniture, and he could take it to-morrow, to-day, now. He would have taken it before now, I believe, but for Fledgeby."

"What has Fledgeby to do with him?"

"Knew him. Cautioned me against him before I got into his claws. Couldn't persuade him then, in behalf of some-body else."

"Do you mean that Fledgeby has at all softened him towards you?"

"Us, Sophronia. Us, us, us."

"Towards us?"

"I mean that the Jew has not yet done what he might have done, and that Fledgeby takes the credit of having got him to hold his hand."

"Do you believe Fledgeby?"

"Sophronia, I never believe anybody. I never have, my dear, since I believed you. But it looks like it."

Having given her this back-handed reminder of her mutinous observations to the skeleton, Mr. Lammle rose from table—perhaps, the better to conceal a smile, and a white dint or two about his nose—and took a turn on the carpet and came to the hearthrug.

"If we could have packed the brute off with Georgiana;—but however; that's spilled milk."

As Lammle, standing gathering up the skirts of his dressing-gown with his back to the fire, said this, looking down at his wife, she turned pale and looked down at the ground. With a sense of disloyalty upon her, and perhaps with a sense of personal danger—for she was afraid of him—even afraid of his hand and afraid of his foot, though he had never done her violence—she hastened to put herself right in his eyes.

" If we could borrow money, Alfred——"

" Beg money, borrow money, or steal money. It would be all one to us, Sophronia," her husband struck in.

" —Then, we could weather this ? "

" No doubt. To offer another original and undeniable remark, Sophronia, two and two make four."

But, seeing that she was turning something in her mind, he gathered up the skirts of his dressing-gown again, and, tucking them under one arm, and collecting his ample whiskers in his other hand, kept his eye upon her silently.

" It is natural, Alfred," she said, looking up with some timidity into his face, " to think in such an emergency of the richest people we know, and the simplest."

" Just so, Sophronia."

" The Boffins."

" Just so, Sophronia."

" Is there nothing to be done with them ? "

" What is there to be done with them, Sophronia ? "

She cast about in her thoughts again, and he kept his eyes upon her as before.

" Of course, I have repeatedly thought of the Boffins, Sophronia," he resumed, after a fruitless silence, " but I have seen my way to nothing. They are well guarded. That infernal Secretary stands between them and—people of merit."

" If he could be got rid of ? " said she, brightening a little, after more casting about.

" Take time, Sophronia," observed her watchful husband, in a patronising manner.

" If working him out of the way could be presented in the light of a service to Mr. Boffin ? "

" Take time, Sophronia."

" We have remarked lately, Alfred, that the old man is turning very suspicious and distrustful."

" Miserly too, my dear; which is far the most unpromising for us. Nevertheless, take time, Sophronia, take time."

She took time, and then said :

" Suppose we should address ourselves to that tendency in him of which we have made ourselves quite sure. Suppose my conscience—— "

" And we know what a conscience it is, my soul. Yes ? "

" Suppose my conscience should not allow me to keep to myself any longer what that upstart girl told me of the Secretary's having made a declaration to her. Suppose my conscience should oblige me to repeat it to Mr. Boffin."

" I rather like that," said Lammle.

" Suppose I so repeated it to Mr. Boffin, as to insinuate that my sensitive delicacy and honour—— "

" Very good words, Sophronia."

" —As to insinuate that *our* sensitive delicacy and honour," she resumed, with a bitter stress upon the phrase, " would not allow us to be silent parties to so mercenary and designing a speculation on the Secretary's part, and so gross a breach of faith towards his confiding employer. Suppose I had imparted my virtuous uneasiness to my excellent husband, and he had said, in his integrity, 'Sophronia, you must immediately disclose this to Mr. Boffin.'"

" Once more, Sophronia," observed Lammle, changing the leg on which he stood, " I rather like that."

" You remarked that he is well guarded," she pursued. " I think so too. But if this should lead to his discharging his Secretary, there would be a weak place made."

" Go on expounding, Sophronia. I begin to like this very much."

" Having, in our unimpeachable rectitude, done him the service of opening his eyes to the treachery of the person he trusted, we shall have established a claim upon him and a confidence with him. Whether it can be made much of, or

173

little of, we must wait—because we can't help it—to see.
Probably we shall make the most of it that is to be made."

" Probably," said Lammle.

" Do you think it impossible," she asked, in the same cold
plotting way, " that you might replace the Secretary ? "

" Not impossible, Sophronia. It might be brought about.
At any rate it might be skilfully led up to."

She nodded her understanding of the hint, as she looked
at the fire. " Mr. Lammle," she said, musingly : not without
a slight ironical touch; " Mr. Lammle would be so delighted
to do anything in his power. Mr. Lammle, himself a man
of business as well as a capitalist. Mr. Lammle, accustomed
to be intrusted with the most delicate affairs. Mr. Lammle,
who has managed my own little fortune so admirably, but
who, to be sure, began to make his reputation with the
advantage of being a man of property, above temptation,
and beyond suspicion.

Mr. Lammle smiled, and even patted her on the head. In
his sinister relish of the scheme, as he stood above her,
making it the subject of his cogitations, he seemed to have
twice as much nose on his face as he had ever had in his life.

He stood pondering, and she sat looking at the dusty fire
without moving, for some time. But, the moment he began
to speak again, she looked up with a wince and attended to
him, as if that double-dealing of hers had been in her mind,
and the fear were revived in her of his hand or his foot.

" It appears to me, Sophronia, that you have omitted one
branch of the subject. Perhaps not, for women understand
women. We might oust the girl herself ? "

Mrs. Lammle shook her head. " She has an immensely
strong hold upon them both, Alfred. Not to be compared
with that of a paid secretary."

" But the dear child," said Lammle, with a crooked smile,
" ought to have been open with her benefactor and benefactress. The darling love ought to have reposed unbounded
confidence in her benefactor and benefactress."

174

Sophronia shook her head again.

"Well! Women understand women," said her husband, rather disappointed. "I don't press it. It might be the making of our fortune to make a clean sweep of them both. With me to manage the property, and my wife to manage the people—Whew!"

Again shaking her head, she returned: "They will never quarrel with the girl. They will never punish the girl. We must accept the girl, rely upon it."

"Well!" cried Lammle, shrugging his shoulders, "so be it: only always remember that we don't want her."

"Now, the sole remaining question is," said Mrs. Lammle, "when shall I begin?"

"You cannot begin too soon, Sophronia. As I have told you, the condition of our affairs is desperate, and may be blown upon at any moment."

"I must secure Mr. Boffin alone, Alfred. If his wife was present, she would throw oil upon the waters. I know I should fail to move him to an angry outburst, if his wife was there. And as to the girl herself—as I am going to betray her confidence, she is equally out of the question."

"It wouldn't do to write for an appointment?" said Lammle.

"No, certainly not. They would wonder among themselves why I wrote, and I want to have him wholly unprepared."

"Call, and ask to see him alone?" suggested Lammle.

"I would rather not do that either. Leave it to me. Spare me the little carriage for to-day, and for to-morrow (if I don't succeed to-day), and I'll lie in wait for him."

It was barely settled when a manly form was seen to pass the windows and heard to knock and ring. "Here's Fledgeby," said Lammle. "He admires you, and has a high opinion of you. I'll be out. Coax him to use his influence with the Jew. His name is Riah, of the house of Pubsey and Co." Adding these words under his breath, lest he should be audible in the erect ears of Mr. Fledgeby, through two keyhcles and the hall, Lammle, making signals of discretion to his servant, went softly up-stairs.

"Mr. Fledgeby," said Mrs. Lammle, giving him a very gracious reception, "so glad to see you! My poor dear Alfred, who is greatly worried just now about his affairs, went out rather early. Dear Mr. Fledgeby, do sit down."

Dear Mr. Fledgeby did sit down, and satisfied himself (or, judging from the expression of his countenance, *dis*satisfied himself) that nothing new had occurred in the way of whisker-sprout since he came round the corner from the Albany.

"Dear Mr. Fledgeby, it was needless to mention to you that my poor dear Alfred is much worried about his affairs at present, for he has told me what a comfort you are to him in his temporary difficulties, and what a great service you have rendered him."

"Oh!" said Mr. Fledgeby.

"Yes," said Mrs. Lammle.

"I didn't know," remarked Mr. Fledgeby, trying a new part of his chair, "but that Lammle might be reserved about his affairs."

"Not to me," said Mrs. Lammle, with deep feeling.

"Oh, indeed?" said Fledgeby.

"Not to me, dear Mr. Fledgeby. I am his wife."

"Yes. I—I always understood so," said Mr. Fledgeby.

"And as the wife of Alfred, may I, dear Mr. Fledgeby, wholly without his authority or knowledge, as I am sure your discernment will perceive, entreat you to continue that great service, and once more use your well-earned influence with Mr. Riah for a little more indulgence? The name I have heard Alfred mention, tossing in his dreams, *is* Riah; is it not?"

"The name of the Creditor is Riah," said Mr. Fledgeby, with a rather uncompromising accent on his noun-substantive. "Saint Mary Axe. Pubsey and Co."

"Oh, yes!" exclaimed Mrs. Lammle, clasping her hands with a certain gushing wildness. "Pubsey and Co.!"

176

Mr. Fledgeby departs on his Errand of Mercy

"The pleading of the feminine——" Mr. Fledgeby began, and there stuck so long for a word to get on with, that Mrs. Lammle offered him sweetly, "Heart?"

"No," said Mr. Fledgeby, "Gender—is ever what a man is bound to listen to, and I wish it rested with myself. But this Riah is a nasty one, Mrs. Lammle; he really is."

"Not if *you* speak to him, dear Mr. Fledgeby."

"Upon my soul and body he is!" said Fledgeby.

"Try. Try once more, dearest Mr. Fledgeby. What is there you cannot do, if you will?"

"Thank you," said Fledgeby, "you're very complimentary to say so. I don't mind trying him again, at your request. But of course I can't answer for the consequences. Riah is a tough subject, and when he says he'll do a thing, he'll do it."

"Exactly so," cried Mrs. Lammle, "and when he says to you he'll wait, he'll wait."

("She is a devilish clever woman," thought Fledgeby. "I didn't see that opening, but she spies it out and cuts into it as soon as it's made.")

"In point of fact, dear Mr. Fledgeby," Mrs. Lammle went on in a very interesting manner, "not to affect concealment of Alfred's hopes, to you who are so much his friend, there is a distant break in his horizon."

This figure of speech seemed rather mysterious to Fascination Fledgeby, who said, "There's a what in his—eh?"

"Alfred, dear Mr. Fledgeby, discussed with me this very morning before he went out, some prospects he has, which might entirely change the aspect of his present troubles."

"Really?" said Fledgeby.

"O yes!" Here Mrs. Lammle brought her handkerchief into play. "And you know, dear Mr. Fledgeby—you who study the human heart, and study the world—what an affliction it would be to lose position and to lose credit, when ability to tide over a very short time might save all appearances."

"Oh!" said Fledgeby. "Then you think, Mrs. Lammle,

that if Lammle got time, he wouldn't burst up?—To use an expression," Mr. Fledgeby apologetically explained, " which is adopted in the Money Market."

" Indeed, yes. Truly, truly, yes ! "

" That makes all the difference," said Fledgeby. " I'll make a point of seeing Riah at once."

" Blessings on you, dearest Mr. Fledgeby ! "

" Not at all," said Fledgeby. She gave him her hand. " The hand," said Mr. Fledgeby, " of a lovely and superior-minded female is ever the repayment of a—— "

" Noble action ! " said Mrs. Lammle, extremely anxious to get rid of him.

" It wasn't what I was going to say," returned Fledgeby, who never would, under any circumstances, accept a suggested expression, " but you're very complimentary. May I imprint a—a one—upon it? Good morning ! "

" I may depend upon your promptitude, dearest Mr. Fledgeby ? "

Said Fledgeby, looking back at the door and respectfully kissing his hand, " You may depend upon it."

In fact, Mr. Fledgeby sped on his errand of mercy through the streets, at so brisk a rate that his feet might have been winged by all the good spirits that wait on Generosity. They might have taken up their station in his breast, too, for he was blithe and merry. There was quite a fresh trill in his voice, when, arriving at the counting-house in St. Mary Axe, and finding it for the moment empty, he trolled forth at the foot of the staircase: " Now, Judah, what are you up to there ? "

The old man appeared, with his accustomed deference.

' Halloa ! " said Fledgeby, falling back, with a wink. " You mean mischief, Jerusalem ! "

The old man raised his eyes inquiringly.

" Yes, you do," said Fledgeby. " Oh, you sinner ! Oh, you dodger ! What ! You're going to act upon that bill of sale at Lammle's, are you ? Nothing will turn you, won't it ? You won't be put off for another single minute, won't you ? "

Ordered to immediate action by the master's tone and look, the old man took up his hat from the little counter where it lay.

" You have been told that he might pull through it, if you didn't go in to win, Wide-Awake ; have you ? " said Fledgeby. " And it's not your game that he should pull through it ; ain't it ? You having got security, and there being enough to pay you ? Oh, you Jew ! "

The old man stood irresolute and uncertain for a moment, as if there might be further instructions for him in reserve.

" Do I go, sir ? " he at length asked in a low voice.

" Asks me if he is going ? " exclaimed Fledgeby. " Asks me, as if he didn't know his own purpose ! Asks me, as if he hadn't got his hat on ready ! Asks me, as if his sharp old eye—why, it cuts like a knife—wasn't looking at his walking-stick by the door ! "

" Do I go, sir ? "

" Do you go ? " sneered Fledgeby. " Yes, you do go. Toddle, Judah ! "

CHAPTER XIII

FASCINATION FLEDGEBY, left alone in the counting-house, strolled about with his hat on one side, whistling, and investigating the drawers, and prying here and there for any small evidences of his being cheated, but could find none. "Not his merit that he don't cheat me," was Mr. Fledgeby's commentary delivered with a wink, "but my precaution." He then with a lazy grandeur asserted his rights as Lord of Pubsey and Co. by poking his cane at the stools and boxes, and spitting in the fireplace, and so loitered royally to the window and looked out into the narrow street, with his small eyes just peering over the top of Pubsey and Co.'s blind. As a blind in more senses than one, it reminded him that he was alone in the counting-house, with the front door open. He was moving away to shut it, lest he should be injudiciously identified with the establishment, when he was stopped by some one coming to the door.

This some one was the dolls' dressmaker, with a little basket on her arm, and her crutch stick in her hand. Her keen eyes had espied Mr. Fledgeby before Mr. Fledgeby had espied her, and he was paralysed in his purpose of shutting her out, not so much by her approaching the door, as by her favouring him with a shower of nods, the instant he saw her. This advantage she improved by hobbling up the steps with such despatch that before Mr. Fledgeby could take measures for her finding nobody at home, she was face to face with him in the counting-house.

" Hope I see you well, sir," said Miss Wren. " Mr. Riah in ? "

Fledgeby had dropped into a chair, in the attitude of one waiting wearily. " I suppose he will be back soon," he replied ; " he has cut out and left me expecting him back, in an odd way. Haven't I seen you before ? "

" Once before—if you had your eyesight," replied Miss Wren ; the conditional clause in an under-tone.

" When you were carrying on some games up at the top of the house. I remember. How's your friend ? "

" I have more friends than one, sir, I hope," replied Miss Wren. " Which friend ? "

" Never mind," said Mr. Fledgeby, shutting up one eye, " any of your friends, all your friends. Are they pretty tolerable ? "

Somewhat confounded, Miss Wren parried the pleasantry, and sat down in a corner behind the door, with her basket in her lap. By-and-by, she said, breaking a long and patient silence :

" I beg your pardon, sir, but I am used to find Mr. Riah at this time, and so I generally come at this time. I only want to buy my poor little two shillings' worth of waste. Perhaps you'll kindly let me have it, and I'll trot off to my work."

" *I* let you have it ? " said Fledgeby, turning his head towards her ; for he had been sitting blinking at the light, and feeling his cheek. " Why, you don't really suppose that I have anything to do with the place, or the business ; do you ? "

" Suppose ? " exclaimed Miss Wren. " He said, that day, you were the master ! "

" The old cock in black said ? Riah said ? Why, he'd say anything."

" Well ; but you said so too," returned Miss Wren. " Or

at least you took on like the master, and didn't contradict him."

"One of his dodges," said Mr. Fledgeby, with a cool and contemptuous shrug. "He's made of dodges. He said to me, 'Come up to the top of the house, sir, and I'll show you a handsome girl. But I shall call you the master.' So I went up to the top of the house and he showed me the handsome girl (very well worth looking at she was), and I was called the master. I don't know why. I dare say he don't. He loves a dodge for its own sake; being," added Mr. Fledgeby, after casting about for an expressive phrase, "the dodgerest of all the dodgers."

"Oh, my head!" cried the dolls' dressmaker, holding it with both her hands, as if it were cracking. "You can't mean what you say."

"I can, my little woman," retorted Fledgeby, "and I do, I assure you."

This repudiation was not only an act of deliberate policy on Fledgeby's part, in case of his being surprised by any other caller, but was also a retort upon Miss Wren for her over-sharpness, and a pleasant instance of his humour as regarded the old Jew. "He has got a bad name as an old Jew, and he is paid for the use of it, and I'll have my money's worth out of him." This was Fledgeby's habitual reflection in the way of business, and it was sharpened just now by the old man's presuming to have a secret from him: though of the secret itself, as annoying somebody else whom he disliked, he by no means disapproved.

Miss Wren with a fallen countenance sat behind the door looking thoughtfully at the ground, and the long and patient silence had again set in for some time, when the expression of Mr. Fledgeby's face betokened that through the upper portion of the door, which was of glass, he saw some one faltering on the brink of the counting-house. Presently there was a rustle and a tap, and then some more rustling and another tap. Fledgeby taking no notice, the door was at length softly opened, and the dried face of a mild little elderly gentleman looked in.

"Mr. Riah?" said this visitor, very politely.

"I am waiting for him, sir," returned Mr. Fledgeby. "He went out and left me here. I expect him back every minute. Perhaps you had better take a chair."

The gentleman took a chair, and put his hand to his forehead, as if he were in a melancholy frame of mind. Mr. Fledgeby eyed him aside, and seemed to relish his attitude.

"A fine day, sir," remarked Fledgeby.

The little dried gentleman was so occupied with his own depressed reflections that he did not notice the remark until the sound of Mr. Fledgeby's voice had died out of the counting-house. Then he started and said: "I beg your pardon, sir. I fear you spoke to me?"

"I said," remarked Fledgeby, a little louder than before, "it was a fine day."

"I beg your pardon. I beg your pardon. Yes."

Again the little dried gentleman put his hand to his forehead, and again Mr. Fledgeby seemed to enjoy his doing it. When the gentleman changed his attitude with a sigh, Fledgeby spake with a grin.

"Mr. Twemlow, I think?"

The dried gentleman seemed much surprised.

"Had the pleasure of dining with you at Lammle's," said Fledgeby. "Even have the honour of being a connection of yours. An unexpected sort of place this to meet in; but one never knows, when one gets into the City, what people one may knock up against. I hope you have your health, and are enjoying yourself."

There might have been a touch of impertinence in the last words: on the other hand, it might have been but the native grace of Mr. Fledgeby's manner. Mr. Fledgeby sat on a stool with a foot on the rail of another stool, and his hat on. Mr. Twemlow had uncovered on looking in at the door, and remained so.

Now the conscientious Twemlow, knowing what he had done to thwart the gracious Fledgeby, was particularly disconcerted by this encounter. He was as ill at ease as a gentleman well could be. He felt himself bound to conduct himself stiffly towards Fledgeby, and he made him a distant bow. Fledgeby made his small eyes smaller in taking special note of his manner. The dolls' dressmaker sat in her corner behind the door, with her eyes on the ground and her hands folded on her basket, holding her crutch stick between them, and appearing to take no heed of anything,

"He's a long time," muttered Mr. Fledgeby, looking at his watch. "What time may you make it, Mr. Twemlow?"

Mr. Twemlow made it ten minutes past twelve, sir.

"As near as a toucher," assented Fledgeby. "I hope, Mr. Twemlow, your business here may be of a more agreeable character than mine."

"Thank you, sir," said Mr. Twemlow.

Fledgeby again made his small eyes smaller, as he glanced with great complacency at Twemlow, who was timorously tapping the table with a folded letter.

"What I know of Mr. Riah," said Fledgeby, with a very disparaging utterance of his name, "leads me to believe that this is about the shop for disagreeable business. I have always found him the bitingest and tightest screw in London."

Mr. Twemlow acknowledged the remark with a little distant bow. It evidently made him nervous.

"So much so," pursued Fledgeby, "that if it wasn't to be true to a friend, nobody should catch me waiting here a single minute. But if you have friends in adversity, stand by them. That's what I say and act up to."

The equitable Twemlow felt that this sentiment, irrespective of the utterer, demanded his cordial assent. "You are very right, sir," he rejoined with spirit. "You indicate the generous and manly course."

"Glad to have your approbation," returned Fledgeby. "It's

a coincidence, Mr. Twemlow;" here he descended from his perch, and sauntered towards him; "that the friends I am standing by to-day are the friends at whose house I met you! The Lammles. She's a very taking and agreeable woman?"

Conscience smote the gentle Twemlow pale. "Yes," he said. "She is."

"And when she appealed to me this morning, to come and try what I could do to pacify their creditor, this Mr. Riah—that I certainly have gained some little influence with in transacting business for another friend, but nothing like so much as she supposes—and when a woman like that spoke to me as her dearest Mr. Fledgeby, and shed tears—why what could I do, you know?"

Twemlow gasped "Nothing but come."

"Nothing but come. And so I came. But why," said Fledgeby, putting his hands in his pockets and counterfeiting deep meditation, "why Riah should have started up, when I told him that the Lammles entreated him to hold over a Bill of Sale he has on all their effects; and why he should have cut out, saying he would be back directly; and why he should have left me here alone so long; I cannot understand."

The chivalrous Twemlow, Knight of the Simple Heart, was not in a condition to offer any suggestion. He was too penitent, too remorseful. For the first time in his life he had done an under-handed action, and he had done wrong. He had secretly interposed against this confiding young man, for no better real reason than because the young man's ways were not his ways.

But, the confiding young man proceeded to heap coals of fire on his sensitive head.

"I beg your pardon, Mr. Twemlow; you see I am acquainted with the nature of the affairs that are transacted here. Is there anything I can do for you here? You have always been brought up as a gentleman, and never as a man of business;" another touch of possible impertinence in this place; "and perhaps you are but a poor man of business. What else is to be expected?"

"I am even a poorer man of business than I am a man, sir," returned Twemlow, "and I could hardly express my deficiency in a stronger way. I really do not so much as clearly understand my position in the matter on which I am brought here. But there are reasons which make me very delicate of accepting your assistance. I am greatly, greatly, disinclined to profit by it. I don't deserve it."

Good childish creature! Condemned to a passage through the world by such narrow little dimly-lighted ways, and picking up so few specks or spots on the road!

"Perhaps," said Fledgeby, "you may be a little proud of entering on the topic—having been brought up as a gentleman."

"It's not that, sir," returned Twemlow, "it's not that. I hope I distinguish between true pride and false pride."

"I have no pride at all, myself," said Fledgeby, "and perhaps I don't cut things so fine as to know one from t'other. But I know this is a place where even a man of business needs his wits about him; and if mine can be of any use to you here, you're welcome to them."

"You are very good," said Twemlow, faltering. "But I am most unwilling——"

"I don't, you know," proceeded Fledgeby, with an ill-favoured glance, "entertain the vanity of supposing that my wits could be of any use to you in society, but they might be here. You cultivate society and society cultivates you, but Mr. Riah's not society. In society, Mr. Riah is kept dark; eh, Mr. Twemlow?"

Twemlow, much disturbed, and with his hand fluttering about his forehead, replied: "Quite true."

The confiding young man besought him to state his case. The innocent Twemlow expecting Fledgeby to be astounded by what he should unfold, and not for an instant conceiving the possibility of its happening every day, but treating of it

186

as a terrible phenomenon occurring in the course of ages, related how that he had had a deceased friend, a married civil officer with a family, who had wanted money for change of place on change of post, and how he, Twemlow, had "given him his name," with the usual, but in the eyes of Twemlow almost incredible result that he had been left to repay what he had never had. How, in the course of years, he had reduced the principal by trifling sums, "having," said Twemlow, "always to observe great economy, being in the enjoyment of a fixed income limited in extent, and that depending on the munificence of a certain nobleman," and had always pinched the full interest out of himself with punctual pinches. How he had come, in course of time, to look upon this one only debt of his life as a regular quarterly drawback, and no worse, when "his name" had some way fallen into the possession of Mr. Riah, who had sent him notice to redeem it by paying up in full, in one plump sum, or take tremendous consequences. This, with hazy remembrances of how he had been carried to some office to "confess judgment" (as he recollected the phrase), and how he had been carried to another office where his life was assured for somebody not wholly unconnected with the sherry trade whom he remembered by the remarkable circumstance that he had a Straduarius violin to dispose of, and also a Madonna, formed the sum and substance of Mr. Twemlow's narrative. Through which stalked the shadow of the awful Snigsworth, eyed afar off by money-lenders as Security in the Mist, and menacing Twemlow with his baronial truncheon.

To all, Mr. Fledgeby listened with the modest gravity becoming a confiding young man who knew it all beforehand, and, when it was finished, seriously shook his head. "I don't like, Mr. Twemlow," said Fledgeby, "I don't like Riah's calling in the principal. If he's determined to call it in, it must come."

"But supposing, sir," said Twemlow, downcast. "that it can't come?"

"Then," retorted Fledgeby, "you must go, you know."

"Where?" asked Twemlow, faintly.

"To prison," returned Fledgeby. Whereat Mr. Twemlow leaned his innocent head upon his hand, and moaned a little moan of distress and disgrace.

"However," said Fledgeby, appearing to pluck up his spirits, "we'll hope it's not so bad as that comes to. If you'll allow me, I'll mention to Mr. Riah, when he comes in, who you are, and I'll tell him you're my friend, and I'll say my say for you, instead of your saying it for yourself; I may be able to do it in a more business-like way. You won't consider it a liberty?"

"I thank you again and again, sir," said Twemlow. "I am strong, strongly disinclined to avail myself of your generosity, though my helplessness yields. For I cannot but feel that I—to put it in the mildest form of speech—that I have done nothing to deserve it."

"Where *can* he be?" muttered Fledgeby, referring to his watch again. "What *can* he have gone out for? Did you ever see him, Mr. Twemlow?"

"Never."

"He is a thorough Jew to look at, but he is a more thorough Jew to deal with. He's worse when he's quiet. If he's quiet, I shall take it as a very bad sign. Keep your eye upon him when he comes in, and, if he's quiet, don't be hopeful. Here he is!—He looks quiet."

With these words, which had the effect of causing the harmless Twemlow painful agitation, Mr. Fledgeby withdrew to his former post, and the old man entered the counting-house.

"Why, Mr. Riah," said Fledgeby, "I thought you were lost!"

The old man, glancing at the stranger, stood stock-still. He perceived that his master was leading up to the orders he was to take, and he waited to understand them.

"I really thought," repeated Fledgeby, slowly, "that you

were lost, Mr. Riah. Why, now I look at you—but no, you can't have done it ; no, you can't have done it !"

Hat in hand, the old man lifted his head, and looked distressfully at Fledgeby as seeking to know what new moral burden he was to bear.

" You can't have rushed out to get the start of everybody else, and put in that bill of sale at Lammle's ? " said Fledgeby. "Say you haven't, Mr. Riah."

" Sir, I have," replied the old man in a low voice.

" Oh, my eye !" cried Fledgeby. "Tut, tut, tut! Dear, dear, dear ! Well ! I knew you were a hard customer, Mr. Riah, but I never thought you were as hard as that."

" Sir," said the old man, with great uneasiness, "I do as I am directed. I am not the principal here. I am but the agent of a superior, and I have no choice, no power."

" Don't say so," returned Fledgeby, secretly exultant as the old man stretched out his hands, with a shrinking action of defending himself against the sharp construction of the two observers. "Don't play the tune of the trade, Mr. Riah. You've a right to get in your debts, if you're determined to do it, but don't pretend what every one in your line regularly pretends. At least, don't do it to me. Why should you, Mr. Riah ? You know I know all about you."

The old man clasped the skirt of his long coat with his disengaged hand, and directed a wistful look at Fledgeby.

" And don't," said Fledgeby, " don't, I entreat you as a favour, Mr. Riah, be so devilish meek, for I know what'll follow if you are. Look here, Mr. Riah. This gentleman is Mr. Twemlow."

The Jew turned to him and bowed. That poor lamb bowed in return ; polite, and terrified.

" I have made such a failure," proceeded Fledgeby, " in trying to do anything with you for my friend Lammle, that I've hardly a hope of doing anything with you for my friend (and connection indeed) Mr. Twemlow. But I do think that if you would do a favour for anybody, you would for me, and

I won't fail for want of trying, and I've passed my promise to Mr. Twemlow besides. Now, Mr. Riah, here is Mr. Twemlow. Always good for his interest, always coming up to time, always paying his little way. Now, why should you press Mr. Twemlow? You can't have any spite against Mr. Twemlow! Why not be easy with Mr. Twemlow?'

The old man looked into Fledgeby's little eyes for any sign of leave to be easy with Mr. Twemlow; but there was no sign in them.

"Mr. Twemlow is no connection of yours, Mr. Riah," said Fledgeby; "you can't want to be even with him for having through life gone in for a gentleman and hung on to his Family. If Mr. Twemlow has a contempt for business, what can it matter to you?"

"But pardon me," interposed the gentle victim, "I have not. I should consider it presumption."

"There, Mr. Riah!" said Fledgeby; "isn't that handsomely said? Come! Make terms with me for Mr. Twemlow."

The old man looked again for any sign of permission to spare the poor little gentleman. No. Mr. Fledgeby meant him to be racked.

"I am very sorry, Mr. Twemlow," said Riah, "I have my instructions. I am invested with no authority for diverging from them. The money must be paid."

"In full and slap down, do you mean, Mr. Riah?" asked Fledgeby, to make things quite explicit.

"In full, sir, and at once," was Riah's answer.

Mr. Fledgeby shook his head deploringly at Twemlow, and mutely expressed in reference to the venerable figure standing before him with eyes upon the ground: "What a Monster of an Israelite this is!"

"Mr. Riah," said Fledgeby.

The old man lifted up his eyes once more to the little eyes in Mr. Fledgeby's head, with some reviving hope that the sign might be coming yet.

"Mr. Riah, it's of no use my holding back the fact.

There's a certain great party in the background in Mr. Twemlow's case, and you know it."

" I know it," the old man admitted.

" Now, I'll put it as a plain point of business, Mr. Riah. Are you fully determined (as a plain point of business) either to have that said great party's security, or that said great party's money ? "

" Fully determined," answered Riah, as he read his master's face, and learnt the book.

" Not at all caring for, and indeed as it seems to me rather enjoying," said Fledgeby, with peculiar unction, " the precious kick-up and row that will come off between Mr. Twemlow and the said great party ? "

This required no answer, and received none. Poor Mr. Twemlow, who had betrayed the keenest mental terrors since his noble kinsman loomed in the perspective, rose with a sigh to take his departure. " I thank you very much, sir," he said, offering Fledgeby his feverish hand. " You have done me an unmerited service. Thank you, thank you ! "

" Don't mention it," answered Fledgeby. " It's a failure so far, but I'll stay behind, and take another touch at Mr. Riah."

" Do not deceive yourself, Mr. Twemlow," said the Jew, then addressing him directly for the first time. " There is no hope for you. You must expect no leniency here. You must pay in full, and you cannot pay too promptly, or you will be put to heavy charges. Trust nothing to me, sir. Money, money, money." When he had said these words in an emphatic manner, he acknowledged Mr. Twemlow's still polite motion of his head, and that amiable little worthy took his departure in the lowest spirits.

Fascination Fledgeby was in such a merry vein when the counting-house was cleared of him, that he had nothing for it but to go to the window, and lean his arms on the frame of the blind, and have his silent laugh out, with his back to his subordinate. When he turned round again with a composed countenance, his subordinate still stood in the same place, and the dolls' dressmaker sat behind the door with a look of horror.

"Halloa!" cried Mr. Fledgeby, "you're forgetting this young lady, Mr. Riah, and she has been waiting long enough too. Sell her her waste, please, and give her good measure if you can make up your mind to do the liberal thing for once."

He looked on for a time, as the Jew filled her little basket with such scraps as she was used to buy ; but, his merry vein coming on again, he was obliged to turn round to the window once more, and lean his arms on the blind.

"There, my Cinderella dear," said the old man in a whisper, and with a worn-out look, "the basket's full now. Bless you ! And get you gone !"

"Don't call me your Cinderella dear," returned Miss Wren. "Oh, you cruel godmother !"

She shook that emphatic little forefinger of hers in his face at parting, as earnestly and reproachfully as she had ever shaken it at her grim old child at home.

"You are not the godmother at all !" said she. "You are the Wolf in the Forest, the wicked Wolf! And if ever my dear Lizzie is sold and betrayed, I shall know who sold and betrayed her ! "

CHAPTER XIV

MR. WEGG PREPARES A GRINDSTONE FOR MR. BOFFIN'S NOSE

HAVING assisted at a few more expositions of the lives of Misers, Mr. Venus became almost indispensable to the evenings at the Bower. The circumstance of having another listener to the wonders unfolded by Wegg, or, as it were, another calculator to cast up the guineas found in teapots, chimneys, racks and mangers, and other such banks of deposit, seemed greatly to heighten Mr. Boffin's enjoyment; while Silas Wegg, for his part, though of a jealous temperament which might under ordinary circumstances have resented the anatomist's getting into favour, was so very anxious to keep his eye on that gentleman—lest, being too much left to himself, he should be tempted to play any tricks with the precious document in his keeping—that he never lost an opportunity of commending him to Mr. Boffin's notice as a third party whose company was much to be desired. Another friendly demonstration towards him Mr. Wegg now regularly gratified. After each sitting was over, and the patron had departed, Mr. Wegg invariably saw Mr. Venus home. To be sure, he as invariably requested to be refreshed with a sight of the paper in which he was a joint proprietor; but he never failed to remark that it was the great pleasure he derived from Mr. Venus's improving society which had insensibly lured him round to Clerkenwell again, and that, finding himself once more attracted to the spot by the social powers of Mr. V., he would beg leave to go through that little incidental procedure, as a matter of form. "For well I know, sir," Mr. Wegg would add, "that a man of your delicate mind would wish to be checked off whenever the opportunity arises, and it is not for me to baulk your feelings."

A certain rustiness in Mr. Venus, which never became so lubricated by the oil of Mr. Wegg but that he turned under the screw in a creaking and stiff manner, was very noticeable at about this period. While assisting at the literary evenings, he even went so far, on two or three occasions, as to correct Mr. Wegg when he grossly mispronounced a word, or made nonsense of a passage; insomuch that Mr. Wegg took to surveying his course in the day, and to making arrangements for getting round rocks at night instead of running straight upon them. Of the slightest anatomical reference he became particularly shy, and, if he saw a bone ahead, would go any distance out of his way rather than mention it by name.

The adverse destinies ordained that one evening Mr. Wegg's labouring bark became beset by polysyllables, and embarrassed among a perfect archipelago of hard words. It being necessary to take soundings every minute, and to feel the way with the greatest caution, Mr. Wegg's attention was fully employed. Advantage was taken of this dilemma by Mr. Venus, to pass a scrap of paper into Mr. Boffin's hand, and lay his finger on his own lip.

When Mr. Boffin got home at night he found that the paper contained Mr. Venus's card and these words: "Should be glad to be honoured with a call respecting business of your own, about dusk on an early evening."

The very next evening saw Mr. Boffin peeping in at the preserved frogs in Mr. Venus's shop-window, and saw Mr. Venus espying Mr. Boffin with the readiness of one on the alert, and beckoning that gentleman into his interior. Responding, Mr. Boffin was invited to seat himself on the box of human miscellanies before the fire, and did so, looking round the place with admiring eyes. The fire being low and fitful, and the dusk gloomy, the whole stock seemed to be winking and blinking with both eyes, as Mr. Venus did. The French gentleman, though he had no eyes, was not at all behind-hand, but appeared, as the flame rose and fell, to open and shut his no eyes, with the regularity of the glass-eyed dogs and ducks and birds. The big-headed babies were equally obliging in lending their grotesque aid to the general effect.

"You see, Mr. Venus, I've lost no time," said Mr. Boffin. "Here I am."

"Here you are, sir," assented Mr. Venus.

"I don't like secrecy," pursued Mr. Boffin—"at least, not in a general way I don't—but I dare say you'll show me good reason for being secret so far."

"I think I shall, sir," returned Venus.

"Good," said Mr. Boffin. "You don't expect Wegg, I take it for granted?"

"No, sir. I expect no one but the present company."

Mr. Boffin glanced about him, as accepting under that inclusive denomination the French gentleman and the circle in which he didn't move, and repeated, "The present company."

"Sir," said Mr. Venus, "before entering upon business, I shall have to ask you for your word and honour that we are in confidence."

"Let's wait a bit and understand what the expression means," answered Mr. Boffin. "In confidence for how long? In confidence for ever and a day?"

"I take the hint, sir," said Venus; "you think you might consider the business, when you came to know it, to be of a nature incompatible with confidence on your part?"

"I might," said Mr. Boffin, with a cautious look.

"True, sir. Well, sir," observed Venus, after clutching at his dusty hair, to brighten his ideas, "let us put it another way. I open the business with you, relying upon your honour not to do anything in it, and not to mention me in it, without my knowledge."

"That sounds fair," said Mr. Boffin. "I agree to that."

"I have your word and honour, sir?"

"My good fellow," retorted Mr. Boffin, "you have my word; and how you can have that, without my honour too, I don't know. I've sorted a lot of dust in my time, but I never knew the two things go into separate heaps."

This remark seemed rather to abash Mr. Venus. He hesitated, and said, "Very true, sir;" and again, "Very true, sir," before resuming the thread of his discourse.

"Mr. Boffin, if I confess to you that I fell into a proposal of which you were the subject, and of which you oughtn't to have been the subject, you will allow me to mention, and will please take into favourable consideration, that I was in a crushed state of mind at the time."

The Golden Dustman, with his hands folded on the top of his stout stick, with his chin resting upon them, and with something leering and whimsical in his eyes, gave a nod and said, "Quite so, Venus."

"That proposal, sir, was a conspiring breach of your confidence, to such an extent, that I ought at once to have made it known to you. But I didn't, Mr. Boffin, and I fell into it."

Without moving eye or finger, Mr. Boffin gave another nod, and placidly repeated, "Quite so, Venus."

"Not that I was ever hearty in it, sir," the penitent anatomist went on, "or that I ever viewed myself with anything but reproach for having turned out of the paths of science into the paths of——" he was going to say "villainy," but, unwilling to press too hard upon himself, substituted with great emphasis—"Weggery."

Placid and whimsical of look as ever, Mr. Boffin answered: "Quite so, Venus."

"And now, sir," said Venus, "having prepared your mind in the rough, I will articulate the details." With which brief professional exordium, he entered on the history of the friendly move, and truly recounted it. One might have thought that it would have extracted some show of surprise or anger, or other emotion, from Mr. Boffin, but it extracted nothing beyond his former comment: " Quite so, Venus."

" I have astonished you, sir, I believe?" said Mr. Venus, pausing dubiously.

Mr. Boffin simply answered as aforesaid: "Quite so, Venus."

By this time the astonishment was all on the other side. It did not, however, so continue. For, when Venus passed to Wegg's discovery, and from that to their having both seen Mr. Boffin dig up the Dutch bottle, that gentleman changed colour, changed his attitude, became extremely restless, and ended (when Venus ended) by being in a state of manifest anxiety, trepidation, and confusion.

" Now, sir," said Venus, finishing off; "you best know what was in that Dutch bottle, and why you dug it up and took it away. I don't pretend to know anything more about it than I saw. All I know is this : I am proud of my calling after all (though it has been attended by one dreadful drawback which has told upon my heart, and almost equally upon my skeleton), and I mean to live by my calling. Putting the same meaning into other words, I do not mean to turn a single dishonest penny by this affair. As the best amends I can make you for having ever gone into it, I make known to you, as a warning, what Wegg has found out. My opinion is, that Wegg is not to be silenced at a modest price, and I build that opinion on his beginning to dispose of your property the moment he knew his power. Whether it's worth your while to silence him at any price, you will decide for yourself, and take your measures accordingly. As far as I am concerned, I have no price. If I am ever called upon for the truth, I tell it, but I want to do no more than I have now done and ended."

" Thank'ee, Venus !" said Mr. Boffin, with a hearty grip of his hand ; " thank'ee, Venus, thank'ee, Venus !" And then walked up and down the little shop in great agitation.

"But look here, Venus," he by-and-by resumed, nervously sitting down again; "if I have to buy Wegg up, I shan't buy him any cheaper for your being out of it. Instead of his having half the money—it was to have been half, I suppose? Share and share alike?"

"It was to have been half, sir," answered Venus.

"Instead of that, he'll now have all. I shall pay the same, if not more. For you tell me he's an unconscionable dog, a ravenous rascal."

"He is," said Venus.

"Don't you think, Venus," insinuated Mr. Boffin, after looking at the fire for awhile—"don't you feel as if—you might like to pretend to be in it till Wegg was bought up, and then ease your mind by handing over to me what you had made believe to pocket?"

"No, I don't, sir," returned Venus, very positively.

"Not to make amends?" insinuated Mr. Boffin.

"No, sir. It seems to me, after maturely thinking it over, that the best amends for having got out of the square is to get back into the square."

"Humph!" mused Mr. Boffin. "When you say the square, you mean——"

"I mean," said Venus, stoutly and shortly, "the right."

"It appears to me," said Mr. Boffin, grumbling over the fire in an injured manner, "that the right is with me, if it's anywhere. I have much more right to the old man's money than the Crown can ever have. What was the Crown to him except the King's Taxes? Whereas, me and my wife, we was all in all to him."

Mr. Venus, with his head upon his hands, rendered melancholy by the contemplation of Mr. Boffin's avarice, only murmured to steep himself in the luxury of that frame of mind: "She did not wish so to regard herself, nor yet to be so regarded."

"And how am I to live," asked Mr. Boffin piteously, "if I'm to be going buying fellows up out of the little that

I've got? And how am I to set about it? When am I to get my money ready? When am I to make a bid? You haven't told me when he threatens to drop down upon me."

Venus explained under what conditions, and with what views, the dropping down upon Mr. Boffin was held over until the Mounds should be cleared away. Mr. Boffin listened attentively. "I suppose," said he, with a gleam of hope, "there's no doubt about the genuineness and date of this confounded will?"

"None whatever," said Mr. Venus.

"Where might it be deposited at present?" asked Mr. Boffin, in a wheedling tone.

"It's in my possession, sir."

"Is it?" he cried, with great eagerness. "Now, for any liberal sum of money that could be agreed upon, Venus, would you put it in the fire?"

"No, sir, I wouldn't," interrupted Mr Venus.

"Nor pass it over to me?"

"That would be the same thing. No, sir," said Mr. Venus.

The Golden Dustman seemed about to pursue these questions, when a stumping noise was heard outside, coming towards the door. "Hush! here's Wegg!" said Venus. "Get behind the young alligator in the corner, Mr. Boffin, and judge him for yourself. I won't light a candle till he's gone: there'll only be the glow of the fire; Wegg's well acquainted with the alligator, and he won't take particular notice of him. Draw your legs in, Mr. Boffin; at present I see a pair of shoes at the end of his tail. Get your head well behind his smile, Mr. Boffin, and you'll lie comfortable there; you'll find plenty of room behind his smile. He's a little dusty, but he's very like you in tone. Are you right, sir?"

Mr. Boffin had but whispered an affirmative response, when Wegg came stumping in. "Partner," said that gentleman in a sprightly manner, "how's yourself?"

"Tolerable," returned Mr. Venus. "Not much to boast of."

"In-deed!" said Wegg: "sorry, partner, that you're not picking up faster, but your soul's too large for your body, sir; that's where it is. And how's our stock in trade, partner? Safe bind, safe find, partner? Is that about it?"

"Do you wish to see it?" asked Venus.

"If you please, partner," said Wegg, rubbing his hands. "I wish to see it jintly with yourself. Or, in similar words to some that was set to music some time back:

> 'I wish you to see it with your eyes,
> And I will pledge with mine.'"

Turning his back and turning a key, Mr. Venus produced the document, holding on by his usual corner. Mr. Wegg, holding on by the opposite corner, sat down on the seat so lately vacated by Mr. Boffin, and looked it over. "All right, sir," he slowly and unwillingly admitted, in his reluctance to loose his hold, "all right!" And greedily watched his partner as he turned his back again, and turned his key again.

"There's nothing new, I suppose?" said Venus, resuming his low chair behind the counter.

"Yes, there is, sir," replied Wegg; "there was something new this morning. That foxey old grasper and griper——"

"Mr. Boffin?" inquired Venus, with a glance towards the alligator's yard or two of smile.

"Mister be blowed!" cried Wegg, yielding to his honest indignation. "Boffin. Dusty Boffin. That foxey old grunter and grinder, sir, turns into the yard this morning, to meddle with our property, a menial tool of his own, a young man by the name of Sloppy. Ecod, when I say to him, 'What do you want here, young man? This is a private yard,' he pulls out a paper from Boffin's other blackguard, the one I was passed over for. 'This is to authorise Sloppy to overlook the carting and to watch the work.' That's pretty strong, I think, Mr. Venus?"

"Remember he doesn't know yet of our claim on the property," suggested Venus.

"Then he must have a hint of it," said Wegg, "and a strong one that'll jog his terrors a bit. Give him an inch, and he'll take an ell. Let him alone this time, and what'll he do with our property next? I tell you what, Mr. Venus; it comes to this; I must be overbearing with Boffin, or I shall fly into several pieces. I can't contain myself when I look at him. Every time I see him putting his hand in his pocket, I see him putting it into my pocket. Every time I hear him jingling his money, I hear him taking liberties with my money. Flesh and blood can't bear it. No," said Mr. Wegg, greatly exasperated, "and I'll go further. A wooden leg can't bear it!"

"But, Mr. Wegg," urged Venus, "it was your own idea that he should not be exploded upon, till the Mounds were carted away."

"But it was likewise my idea, Mr. Venus," retorted Wegg, "that if he came sneaking and sniffing about the property, he should be threatened, given to understand that he has no right to it, and be made our slave. Wasn't that my idea, Mr. Venus?"

"It certainly was, Mr. Wegg."

"It certainly was, as you say, partner," assented Wegg, put into a better humour by the ready admission. "Very well. I consider his planting one of his menial tools in the yard, an act of sneaking and sniffing. And his nose shall be put to the grindstone for it."

"It was not your fault, Mr. Wegg, I must admit," said Venus, "that he got off with the Dutch bottle that night."

"As you handsomely say again, partner! No, it was not my fault. I'd have had that bottle out of him. Was it to be borne that he should come, like a thief in the dark, digging among stuff that was far more ours than his (seeing that we could deprive him of every grain of it, if he didn't buy us at our own figure), and carrying off treasure from its bowels? No, it was not to be borne. And for that, too, his nose shall be put to the grindstone."

"How do you propose to do it, Mr. Wegg?"

"To put his nose to the grindstone? I propose," returned that estimable man, "to insult him openly. And if, looking into this eye of mine, he dares to offer a word in answer, to retort upon him before he can take his breath, 'Add another word to that, you dusty old dog, and you're a beggar.'"

"Suppose he says nothing, Mr. Wegg?"

"Then," replied Wegg, "we shall have come to an understanding with very little trouble, and I'll break him and drive him, Mr. Venus. I'll put him in harness, and I'll bear him up tight, and I'll break him and drive him. The harder the old Dust is driven, sir, the higher he'll pay. And I mean to be paid high, Mr. Venus, I promise you."

"You speak quite revengefully, Mr. Wegg."

"Revengefully, sir? Is it for him that I have declined and falled, night after night? Is it for his pleasure that I've waited at home of an evening, like a set of skittles, to be set up and knocked over, set up and knocked over, by whatever balls—or books—he chose to bring against me? Why, I'm a hundred times the man he is, sir; five hundred times!"

Perhaps it was with the malicious intent of urging him on to his worst that Mr. Venus looked as if he doubted that.

"What? Was it outside the house at present ockypied, to its disgrace, by that minion of fortune and worm of the hour," said Wegg, falling back upon his strongest terms of reprobation, and slapping the counter, "that I, Silas Wegg, five hundred times the man he ever was, sat in all weathers, waiting for a errand or a customer? Was it outside that very house as I first set eyes upon him, rolling in the lap of luxury, when I was a selling halfpenny ballads there for a living? And am I to grovel in the dust for *him* to walk over? No!"

There was a grin upon the ghastly countenance of the

Mr. Wegg prepares a Grindstone for Mr. Boffin's Nose

French gentleman under the influence of the firelight, as if he were computing how many thousand slanderers and traitors array themselves against the fortunate, on premises exactly answering to those of Mr. Wegg. One might have fancied that the big-headed babies were toppling over with their hydrocephalic attempts to reckon up the children of men who transform their benefactors into their injurers by the same process. The yard or two of smile on the part of the alligator might have been invested with the meaning, "All about this was quite familiar knowledge down in the depths of the slime, ages ago."

"But," said Wegg, possibly with some slight perception to the foregoing effect, "your speaking countenance remarks, Mr. Venus, that I'm duller and savager than usual. Perhaps I *have* allowed myself to brood too much. Begone, dull Care! 'Tis gone, sir. I've looked in upon you, and empire resumes her sway. For, as the song says—subject to your correction, sir—

> When the heart of a man is depressed with cares,
> The mist is dispelled if Venus appears.
> Like the notes of a fiddle, you sweetly, sir, sweetly,
> Raises our spirits and charms our ears.'

Good-night, sir."

"I shall have a word or two to say to you, Mr. Wegg, before long," remarked Venus, "respecting my share in the project we've been speaking of."

"My time, sir," returned Wegg, "is yours. In the meanwhile let it be fully understood that I shall not neglect bringing the grindstone to bear, nor yet bringing Dusty Boffin's nose to it. His nose once brought to it, shall be held to it by these hands, Mr. Venus, till the sparks flies out in showers."

With this agreeable promise Wegg stumped out, and shut the shop-door after him. "Wait till I light a candle, Mr. Boffin," said Venus, "and you'll come out more comfortable." So, he lighting a candle and holding it up at arm's length,

Mr. Boffin disengaged himself from behind the alligator's smile, with an expression of countenance so very downcast that it not only appeared as if the alligator had the whole of the joke to himself, but further as if it had been conceived and executed at Mr. Boffin's expense.

"That's a treacherous fellow," said Mr. Boffin, dusting his arms and legs as he came forth, the alligator having been but musty company. "That's a dreadful fellow."

"The alligator, sir?" said Venus.

"No, Venus, no. The Serpent."

"You'll have the goodness to notice, Mr. Boffin," remarked Venus, "that I said nothing to him about my going out of the affair altogether, because I didn't wish to take you anyways by surprise. But I can't be too soon out of it for my satisfaction, Mr. Boffin, and I now put it to you when it will suit your views for me to retire?"

"Thank'ee, Venus, thank'ee, Venus; but I don't know what to say," returned Mr. Boffin. "I don't know what to do. He'll drop down on me any way. He seems fully determined to drop down; don't he?"

Mr. Venus opined that such was clearly his intention.

"You might be a sort of protection for me, if you remained in it," said Mr. Boffin; "you might stand betwixt him and me, and take the edge off him. Don't you feel as if you could make a show of remaining in it, Venus, till I had time to turn myself round?"

Venus naturally inquired how long Mr. Boffin thought it might take him to turn himself round?

"I am sure I don't know," was the answer, given quite at a loss. "Everything is so at sixes and sevens. If I had never come into the property, I shouldn't have minded. But being in it, it would be very trying to be turned out; now, don't you acknowledge that it would, Venus?"

Mr. Venus preferred, he said, to leave Mr. Boffin to arrive at his own conclusions on that delicate question.

"I am sure I don't know what to do," said Mr. Boffin.

204

"If I ask advice of any one else, it's only letting in another person to be bought out, and then I shall be ruined that way, and might as well have given up the property and gone slap to the workhouse. If I was to take advice of my young man, Rokesmith, I should have to buy *him* out. Sooner or later, of course, he'd drop down upon me, like Wegg. I was brought into the world to be dropped down upon, it appears to me."

Mr. Venus listened to these lamentations in silence, while Mr. Boffin jogged to and fro, holding his pockets as if he had a pain in them.

"After all, you haven't said what you mean to do yourself, Venus. When you do go out of it, how do you mean to go?"

Venus replied that as Wegg had found the document and handed it to him, it was his intention to hand it back to Wegg, with the declaration that he himself would have nothing to say to it, or do with it, and that Wegg must act as he chose, and take the consequences.

"And then he drops down with his whole weight upon me!" cried Mr. Boffin, ruefully. "I'd sooner be dropped upon by you than by him, or even by you jintly, than by him alone!"

Mr. Venus could only repeat that it was his fixed intention to betake himself to the paths of science, and to walk in the same all the days of his life; not dropping down upon his fellow-creatures until they were deceased, and then only to articulate them to the best of his humble ability.

"How long could you be persuaded to keep up the appearance of remaining in it?" asked Mr. Boffin, retiring on his other idea. "Could you be got to do so till the Mounds are gone?"

No. That would protract the mental uneasiness of Mr. Venus too long, he said.

"Not if I was to show you reason now?" demanded Mr. Boffin; "not if I was to show you good and sufficient reason?"

If by good and sufficient reason Mr. Boffin meant honest

205

and unimpeachable reason, that might weigh with Mr. Venus against his personal wishes and convenience. But he must add that he saw no opening to the possibility of such reason being shown him.

"Come and see me, Venus," said Mr. Boffin, "at my house."

"Is the reason there, sir?" asked Mr. Venus, with an incredulous smile and blink.

"It may be, or may not be," said Mr. Boffin, "just as you view it. But in the meantime don't go out of the matter. Look here. Do this. Give me your word that you won't take any steps with Wegg, without my knowledge, just as I have given you my word that I won't without yours."

"Done, Mr. Boffin!" said Venus, after a brief consideration.

"Thank'ee, Venus, thank'ee, Venus! Done!"

"When shall I come to see you, Mr. Boffin?"

"When you like. The sooner the better. I must be going now. Good-night, Venus."

"Good-night, sir."

"And good-night to the rest of the present company," said Mr. Boffin, glancing round the shop. "They make a queer show, Venus, and I should like to be better acquainted with them some day. Good-night, Venus, good-night! Thank'ee, Venus, thank'ee, Venus!" With that he jogged out into the street, and jogged upon his homeward way.

"Now, I wonder," he meditated as he went along, nursing his stick, "whether it can be, that Venus is setting himself to get the better of Wegg? Whether it can be, that he means, when I have bought Wegg out, to have me all to himself and to pick me clean to the bones?"

It was a cunning and suspicious idea, quite in the way of his school of Misers, and he looked very cunning and suspicious as he went jogging through the streets. More than once or twice, more than twice or thrice, say half-a-dozen times, he took his stick from the arm on which he nursed it, and hit a straight sharp rap at the air with its head.

Possibly the wooden countenance of Mr. Silas Wegg was incorporeally before him at those moments, for he hit with intense satisfaction.

He was within a few streets of his own house, when a little private carriage, coming in the contrary direction, passed him, turned round, and passed him again. It was a little carriage of eccentric movement, for again he heard it stop behind him and turn round, and again he saw it pass him. Then it stopped, and then went on, out of sight. But, not far out of sight, for, when he came to the corner of his own street, there it stood again.

There was a lady's face at the window as he came up with this carriage, and he was passing it when the lady softly called to him by his name.

"I beg your pardon, Ma'am?" said Mr. Boffin, coming to a stop.

"It is Mrs. Lammle," said the lady.

Mr. Boffin went up to the window and hoped Mrs. Lammle was well.

"Not very well, dear Mr. Boffin; I have fluttered myself by being—perhaps foolishly—uneasy and anxious. I have been waiting for you some time. Can I speak to you?"

Mr. Boffin proposed that Mrs. Lammle should drive on to his house, a few hundred yards further.

"I would rather not, Mr. Boffin, unless you particularly wish it. I feel the difficulty and delicacy of the matter so much that I would rather avoid speaking to you at your own home. You must think this very strange?"

Mr. Boffin said no, but meant yes.

"It is because I am so grateful for the good opinion of all my friends, and am so touched by it, that I cannot bear to run the risk of forfeiting it in any case, even in the cause of duty. I have asked my husband (my dear Alfred, Mr. Boffin) whether it *is* the cause of duty, and he has most emphatically said Yes. I wish I had asked him sooner. It would have spared me much distress."

("Can this be more dropping down upon me!" thought Mr. Boffin, quite bewildered.)

"It was Alfred who sent me to you, Mr. Boffin. Alfred said, 'Don't come back, Sophronia, until you have seen Mr. Boffin, and told him all. Whatever he may think of it, he ought certainly to know it.' Would you mind coming into the carriage?"

Mr. Boffin answered, "Not at all," and took his seat at Mrs. Lammle's side.

"Drive slowly anywhere," Mrs. Lammle called to her coachman, "and don't let the carriage rattle."

"It *must* be more dropping down, I think," said Mr. Boffin to himself. "What next?"

CHAPTER XV

THE breakfast table at Mr. Boffin's was usually a very pleasant one, and was always presided over by Bella. As though he began each new day in his healthy natural character, and some waking hours were necessary to his relapse into the corrupting influences of his wealth, the face and the demeanour of the Golden Dustman were generally unclouded at that meal. It would have been easy to believe then, that there was no change in him. It was as the day went on that the clouds gathered, and the brightness of the morning became obscured. One might have said that the shadows of avarice and distrust lengthened as his own shadow lengthened, and that the night closed around him gradually.

But, one morning long afterwards to be remembered, it was black midnight with the Golden Dustman when he first appeared. His altered character had never been so grossly marked. His bearing towards his Secretary was so charged with insolent distrust and arrogance, that the latter rose and left the table before breakfast was half done. The look he directed at the Secretary's retiring figure was so cunningly malignant, that Bella would have sat astounded and indignant, even though he had not gone the length of secretly threatening Rokesmith with his clenched fist as he closed the door. This unlucky morning, of all mornings in the year, was the morning next after Mr. Boffin's interview with Mrs. Lammle in her little carriage.

Bella looked to Mrs. Boffin's face for comment on, or explanation of, this stormy humour in her husband, but none was there. An anxious and a distressed observation of her own face was all she could read in it. When they were left alone together—which was not until noon, for Mr. Boffin sat long in his easy-chair, by turns jogging up and down the breakfast-room, clenching his fist and muttering— Bella, in consternation, asked her what had happened, what was wrong? "I am forbidden to speak to you about it, Bella dear; I mustn't tell you," was all the answer she could get. And still, whenever, in her wonder and dismay, she raised her eyes to Mrs. Boffin's face, she saw in it the same anxious and distressed observation of her own.

Oppressed by her sense that trouble was impending, and lost in speculations why Mrs. Boffin should look at her as if she had any part in it, Bella found the day long and dreary. It was far on in the afternoon when, she being in her own room, a servant brought her a message from Mr. Boffin begging her to come to his.

Mrs. Boffin was there, seated on a sofa, and Mr. Boffin was jogging up and down. On seeing Bella he stopped, beckoned her to him, and drew her arm through his. "Don't be alarmed, my dear," he said, gently; "I am not angry with you. Why you actually tremble! Don't be alarmed, Bella, my dear. I'll see you righted."

"See me righted?' thought Bella. And then repeated aloud in a tone of astonishment: "See me righted, sir?"

"Ay, ay!" said Mr. Boffin. "See you righted. Send Mr. Rokesmith here, you sir."

Bella would have been lost in perplexity if there had been pause enough; but the servant found Mr. Rokesmith near at hand, and he almost immediately presented himself.

"Shut the door, sir!" said Mr. Boffin. "I have got something to say to you which I fancy you'll not be pleased to hear."

"I am sorry to reply, Mr. Boffin," returned the Secretary,

as, having closed the door, he turned and faced him, "that I think that very likely."

"What do you mean?" blustered Mr. Boffin.

"I mean that it has become no novelty to me to hear from your lips what I would rather not hear."

"Oh! Perhaps we shall change that," said Mr. Boffin, with a threatening roll of his head.

"I hope so," returned the Secretary. He was quiet and respectful; but stood, as Bella thought (and was glad to think), on his manhood too.

"Now, sir," said Mr. Boffin, "look at this young lady on my arm."

Bella involuntarily raising her eyes, when this sudden reference was made to herself, met those of Mr. Rokesmith. He was pale and seemed agitated. Then her eyes passed on to Mrs. Boffin's, and she met the look again. In a flash it enlightened her, and she began to understand what she had done.

"I say to you, sir," Mr. Boffin repeated, "look at this young lady on my arm."

"I do so," returned the Secretary.

As his glance rested again on Bella for a moment, she thought there was reproach in it. But it is possible that the reproach was within herself.

"How dare you, sir," said Mr. Boffin, "tamper, unknown to me, with this young lady? How dare you come out of your station, and your place in my house, to pester this young lady with your impudent addresses?"

"I must decline to answer questions," said the Secretary, "that are so offensively asked."

"You decline to answer?" retorted Mr. Boffin. "You decline to answer, do you? Then I'll tell you what it is, Rokesmith; I'll answer for you. There are two sides in this matter, and I'll take 'em separately. The first side is, sheer Insolence. That's the first side."

The Secretary smiled with some bitterness, as though he would have said, "So I see and hear."

"It was sheer Insolence in you, I tell you," said Mr. Boffin, "even to think of this young lady. This young lady was far above *you*. This young lady was no match for *you*. This young lady was lying in wait (as she was qualified to do) for money, and you had no money."

Bella hung her head and seemed to shrink a little from Mr. Boffin's protecting arm.

"What are you, I should like to know," pursued Mr. Boffin, "that you were to have the audacity to follow up this young lady? This young lady was looking about the market for a good bid; she wasn't in it to be snapped up by fellows that had no money to lay out; nothing to buy with."

"Oh, Mr. Boffin! Mrs. Boffin, pray say something for me!" murmured Bella, disengaging her arm, and covering her face with her hands.

"Old lady," said Mr. Boffin, anticipating his wife, "you hold your tongue. Bella, my dear, don't you let yourself be put out. I'll right you."

"But you don't, you don't right me!" exclaimed Bella, with great emphasis. "You wrong me, wrong me!"

"Don't you be put out, my dear," complacently retorted Mr. Boffin. "I'll bring this young man to book. Now, you Rokesmith! You can't decline to hear, you know, as ll as to answer. You hear me tell you that the first side of your conduct was Insolence—Insolence and Presumption. Answer me one thing, if you can. Didn't this young lady tell you so herself?"

"Did I, Mr. Rokesmith?" asked Bella with her face still covered. "O say, Mr. Rokesmith! Did I?"

"Don't be distressed, Miss Wilfer; it matters very little now."

"Ah! You can't deny it, though!" said Mr. Boffin, with a knowing shake of his head.

"But I have asked him to forgive me since," cried Bella; "and I would ask him to forgive me now again, upon my knees, if it would spare him!"

Here Mrs. Boffin broke out a-crying.

"Old lady," said Mr. Boffin, "stop that noise!. Tender-hearted in you, Miss Bella; but I mean to have it out right through with this young man, having got him into a corner. Now, you Rokesmith. I tell you that's one side of your conduct—Insolence and Presumption. Now, I'm a-coming to the other, which is much worse. This was a speculation of yours."

"I indignantly deny it."

"It's of no use your denying it; it doesn't signify a bit whether you deny it or not; I've got a head on my shoulders, and it ain't a baby's. What!" said Mr. Boffin, gathering himself together in his most suspicious attitude, and wrink-ling his face into a very map of curves and corners. "Don't I know what grabs are made at a man with money? If I didn't keep my eyes open, and my pockets buttoned, shouldn't I be brought to the workhouse before I knew where I was? Wasn't the experience of Dancer, and Elwes, and Hopkins, and Blewbury Jones, and ever so many more of 'em, similar to mine? Didn't everybody want to make grabs at what they'd got, and bring 'em to poverty and ruin? Weren't they forced to hide everything belonging to 'em, for fear it should be snatched from 'em? Of course they was. I shall be told next that they didn't know human natur!"

"They! Poor creatures," murmured the Secretary.

"What do you say?" asked Mr. Boffin, snapping at him. "However, you needn't be at the trouble of repeating it, for it ain't worth hearing, and won't go down with _me_. I'm a-going to unfold your plan, before this young lady; I'm a-going to show this young lady the second view of you; and nothing you can say will stave it off. (Now, attend here, Bella, my dear.) Rokesmith, you're a needy chap. You're a chap that I pick up in the street. Are you, or ain't you?"

"Go on, Mr. Boffin; don't appeal to me."

"Not appeal to _you_," retorted Mr. Boffin as if he hadn't done so. "No, I should hope not! Appealing to _you_ would

213

be rather a rum course. As I was saying, you're a needy chap that I pick up in the street. You come and ask me in the street to take you for a Secretary, and I take you. Very good."

"Very bad," murmured the Secretary.

"What do you say?" asked Mr. Boffin, snapping at him again.

He returned no answer. Mr. Boffin, after eyeing him with a comical look of discomfited curiosity, was fain to begin afresh.

"This Rokesmith is a needy young man that I take for my Secretary out of the open street. This Rokesmith gets acquainted with my affairs, and gets to know that I mean to settle a sum of money on this young lady. 'Oho!' says this Rokesmith;" here Mr. Boffin clapped a finger against his nose, and tapped it several times with a sneaking air, as embodying Rokesmith confidentially confabulating with his own nose; "'This will be a good haul; I'll go in for this!' And so this Rokesmith, greedy and hungering, begins a-creeping on his hands and knees towards the money. Not so bad a speculation either: for if this young lady had had less spirit, or had had less sense, through being at all in the romantic line, by George he might have worked it out and made it pay! But fortunately she was too many for him, and a pretty figure he cuts now he is exposed. There he stands!" said Mr. Boffin, addressing Rokesmith himself with ridiculous inconsistency. "Look at him!"

"Your unfortunate suspicions, Mr. Boffin——" began the Secretary.

"Precious unfortunate for *you*, I can tell you," said Mr. Boffin.

"——are not to be combated by any one, and I address myself to no such hopeless task. But I will say a word upon the truth."

"Yah! Much you care about the truth," said Mr. Boffin, with a snap of his fingers.

"Noddy! My dear love!" expostulated his wife.

"Old lady," returned Mr. Boffin, "you keep still. I say to this Rokesmith here, much he cares about the truth. I tell him again, much he cares about the truth."

"Our connection being at an end, Mr. Boffin," said the Secretary, "it can be of very little moment to me what you say."

"Oh! You are knowing enough," retorted Mr. Boffin, with a sly look, "to have found out that our connection's at an end, eh? But you can't get beforehand with me. Look at this in my hand. This is your pay, on your discharge. You can only follow suit. You can't deprive me of the lead. Let's have no pretending that you discharge yourself. I discharge you."

"So that I go," remarked the Secretary, waving the point aside with his hand, "it is all one to me."

"Is it?" said Mr. Boffin. "But it's two to me, let me tell you. Allowing a fellow that's found out to discharge himself, is one thing; discharging him for insolence and presumption, and likewise for designs upon his master's money, is another. One and one's two; not one. (Old lady, don't you cut in. You keep still.)"

"Have you said all you wish to say to me?" demanded the Secretary.

"I don't know whether I have or not." answered Mr. Boffin. "It depends."

"Perhaps you will consider whether there are any other strong expressions that you would like to bestow upon me?"

"I'll consider that," said Mr. Boffin, obstinately, "at my convenience, and not at yours. You want the last word. It may not be suitable to let you have it."

"Noddy! My dear, dear Noddy! You sound so hard." cried poor Mrs. Boffin, not to be quite repressed.

"Old lady," said her husband, but without harshness, "if you cut in when requested not, I'll get a pillow and carry

215

you out of the room upon it. What do you want to say, you Rokesmith?"

"To you, Mr. Boffin, nothing. But to Miss Wilfer and to your good kind wife, a word."

"Out with it then," replied Mr. Boffin, "and cut it short, for we've had enough of you."

"I have borne," said the Secretary, in a low voice, "with my false position here, that I might not be separated from Miss Wilfer. To be near her, has been a recompense to me from day to day, even for the undeserved treatment I have had here, and for the degraded aspect in which she has often seen me. Since Miss Wilfer rejected me, I have never again urged my suit, to the best of my belief, with a spoken syllable or a look. But I have never changed in my devotion to her, except—if she will forgive my saying so—that it is deeper than it was, and better founded."

"Now, mark this chap's saying Miss Wilfer, when he means £ s. d.!" cried Mr. Boffin, with a cunning wink. "Now, mark this chap's making Miss Wilfer stand for Pounds, Shillings, and Pence!"

"My feeling for Miss Wilfer," pursued the Secretary, without deigning to notice him, "is not one to be ashamed of. I avow it. I love her. Let me go where I may when I presently leave this house, I shall go into a blank life, leaving her."

"Leaving £ s. d. behind me," said Mr. Boffin, by way of commentary, with another wink.

"That I am incapable," the Secretary went on, still without heeding him, "of a mercenary project, or a mercenary thought, in connection with Miss Wilfer, is nothing meritorious in me, because any prize that I could put before my fancy would sink into insignificance beside her. If the greatest wealth or the highest rank were hers, it would only be important in my sight as removing her still further from me, and making me more hopeless, if that could be. Say," remarked the Secretary, looking full at his late master, "say

216

that with a word she could strip Mr. Boffin of his fortune and take possession of it, she would be of no greater worth in my eyes than she is."

"What do you think by this time, old lady," asked Mr. Boffin, turning to his wife in a bantering tone, "about this Rokesmith here, and his caring for the truth? You needn't say what you think, my dear, because I don't want you to cut in, but you can think it all the same. As to taking possession of my property, I warrant you he wouldn't do that himself if he could."

"No," returned the Secretary, with another full look.

"Ha, ha, ha!" laughed Mr. Boffin. "There's nothing like a good 'un while you *are* about it."

"I have been for a moment," said the Secretary, turning from him and falling into his former manner, "diverted from the little I have to say. My interest in Miss Wilfer began when I first saw her; even began when I had only heard of her. It was, in fact, the cause of my throwing myself in Mr. Boffin's way, and entering his service. Miss Wilfer has never known this until now. I mention it now, only as a corroboration (though I hope it may be needless) of my being free from the sordid design attributed to me."

"Now, this is a very artful dodge," said Mr. Boffin, with a deep look. "This is a longer-headed schemer than I thought him. See how patiently and methodically he goes to work. He gets to know about me and my property, and about this young lady, and her share in poor young John's story, and he puts this and that together, and he says to himself, 'I'll get in with Boffin, and I'll get in with this young lady, and I'll work 'em both at the same time, and I'll bring my pigs to market somewhere.' I hear him say it, bless you! Why, I look at him, now, and I see him say it."

Mr. Boffin pointed at the culprit, as it were in the act, and hugged himself in his great penetration.

"But luckily he hadn't to deal with the people he supposed,

Bella, my dear!" said Mr. Boffin. "No! Luckily he had to deal with you, and with me, and with Daniel and Miss Dancer, and with Elwes, and with Vulture Hopkins, and with Blewbury Jones and all the rest of us, one down t'other come on. And he's beat; that's what he is; regularly beat. He thought to squeeze money out of us, and he has done for himself instead, Bella, my dear!"

Bella my dear made no response, gave no sign of acquiescence. When she had first covered her face she had sunk upon a chair with her hands resting on the back of it, and had never moved since. There was a short silence at this point, and Mrs. Boffin softly rose as if to go to her. But Mr. Boffin stopped her with a gesture, and she obediently sat down again and stayed where she was.

"There's your pay, Mr. Rokesmith," said the Golden Dustman, jerking the folded scrap of paper he had in his hand towards his late Secretary. "I dare say you can stoop to pick it up, after what you have stooped to here."

"I have stooped to nothing but this," Rokesmith answered as he took it from the ground; "and this is mine, for I have earned it by the hardest of hard labour."

"You're a pretty quick packer, I hope," said Mr. Boffin; "because the sooner you are gone, bag and baggage, the better for all parties."

"You need have no fear of my lingering."

"There's just one thing, though," said Mr. Boffin, "that I should like to ask you before we come to a good riddance, if it was only to show this young lady how conceited you schemers are, in thinking that nobody finds out how you contradict yourselves."

"Ask me anything you wish to ask," returned Rokesmith, "but use the expedition that you recommend."

"You pretend to have a mighty admiration for this young lady?" said Mr. Boffin, laying his hand protectingly on Bella's head without looking down at her.

"I do not pretend."

218

"Oh! Well. You *have* a mighty admiration for this young lady—since you are so particular?"

"Yes."

"How do you reconcile that, with this young lady's being a weak-spirited, improvident idiot, not knowing what was due to herself, flinging up her money to the church-weathercocks, and racing off at a splitting pace for the workhouse?"

"I don't understand you."

"Don't you? Or won't you? What else could you have made this young lady out to be, if she had listened to such addresses as yours?"

"What else, if I had been so happy as to win her affections and possess her heart?"

"Win her affections," retorted Mr. Boffin, with ineffable contempt, "and possess her heart! Mew says the cat, Quack-quack says the duck, Bow-wow-wow says the dog! Win her affections and possess her heart! Mew, Quack-quack, Bow-wow!"

John Rokesmith stared at him in his outburst, as if with some faint idea that he had gone mad.

"What is due to this young lady," said Mr. Boffin, "is Money, and this young lady right well knows it."

"You slander the young lady."

"*You* slander the young lady; you with your affections and hearts and trumpery," returned Mr. Boffin. "It's of a piece with the rest of your behaviour. I heard of these doings of yours only last night, or you should have heard of 'em from me, sooner, take your oath of it. I heard of 'em from a lady with as good a headpiece as the best, and she knows this young lady, and I know this young lady, and we all three know that it's Money she makes a stand for—money, money, money—and that you and your affections and hearts are a Lie, sir!"

"Mrs. Boffin," said Rokesmith, quietly turning to her, "for your delicate and unvarying kindness I thank you with the warmest gratitude. Good-bye! Miss Wilfer, good-bye!"

219

"And now, my dear," said Mr. Boffin, laying his hand on Bella's head again, "you may begin to make yourself quite comfortable, and I hope you feel that you've been righted."

But Bella was so far from appearing to feel it, that she shrank from his hand and from the chair, and, starting up in an incoherent passion of tears, and stretching out her arms, cried, "Oh, Mr. Rokesmith, before you go, if you could but make me poor again! Oh! Make me poor again, Somebody, I beg and pray, or my heart will break if this goes on! Pa, dear, make me poor again and take me home! I was bad enough there, but I have been so much worse here. Don't give me money, Mr. Boffin, I won't have money. Keep it away from me, and only let me speak to good little Pa, and lay my head upon his shoulder, and tell him all my griefs. Nobody else can understand me, nobody else can comfort me, nobody else knows how unworthy I am, and yet can love me like a little child. I am better with Pa than any one—more innocent, more sorry, more glad!" So, crying out in a wild way that she could not bear this, Bella dropped her head on Mrs. Boffin's ready breast.

John Rokesmith from his place in the room, and Mr. Boffin from his, looked on at her in silence until she was silent herself. Then Mr. Boffin observed in a soothing and comfortable tone, "There, my dear, there; you are righted now, and it's *all* right. I don't wonder, I'm sure, at your being a little flurried by having a scene with this fellow, but it's all over, my dear, and you're righted, and it's—and it's *all* right!" Which Mr. Boffin repeated with a highly satisfied air of completeness and finality.

"I hate you!" cried Bella, turning suddenly upon him, with a stamp of her little foot—"at least, I can't hate you, but I don't like you!"

"Hul—lo!" exclaimed Mr. Boffin in an amazed under-tone.

"You're a scolding, unjust, abusive, aggravating, bad old creature!" cried Bella. "I am angry with my ungrateful

self for calling you names; but you are, you are; you know
you are!"

Mr. Boffin stared here, and stared there, as misdoubting
that he must be in some sort of fit.

"I have heard you with shame," said Bella. "With shame
for myself, and with shame for you. You ought to be above
the base tale-bearing of a time-serving woman; but you are
above nothing now."

Mr. Boffin, seeming to become convinced that this was a
fit, rolled his eyes and loosened his neckcloth.

"When I came here, I respected you and honoured you,
and I soon loved you," cried Bella. "And now I can't bear
the sight of you. At least, I don't know that I ought to go
so far as that—only you're a—you're a Monster!" Having
shot this bolt out with a great expenditure of force, Bella
hysterically laughed and cried together.

"The best wish I can wish you is," said Bella, returning
to the charge, "that you had not one single farthing in the
world. If any true friend and well-wisher could make you a
bankrupt you would be a Duck; but as a man of property
you are a Demon!"

After despatching this second bolt with a still greater
expenditure of force, Bella laughed and cried still more.

"Mr. Rokesmith, pray stay one moment. Pray hear one
word from me before you go! I am deeply sorry for the
reproaches you have borne on my account. Out of the depths
of my heart I earnestly and truly beg your pardon."

As she stepped towards him, he met her. As she gave
him her hand, he put it to his lips, and said, "God bless
you!" No laughing was mixed with Bella's crying then; her
tears were pure and fervent.

"There is not an ungenerous word that I have heard
addressed to you—heard with scorn and indignation, Mr.
Rokesmith—but it has wounded me far more than you, for I
have deserved it, and you never have. Mr. Rokesmith, it is
to me you owe this perverted account of what passed between

221

us that night. I parted with the secret, even while I was angry with myself for doing so. It was very bad in me, but indeed it was not wicked. I did it in a moment of conceit and folly—one of my many such moments—one of my many such hours—years. As I am punished for it severely, try to forgive it!"

"I do with all my soul."

"Thank you. Oh, thank you! Don't part from me till I have said one other word, to do you justice. The only fault you can be truly charged with, in having spoken to me as you did that night—with how much delicacy and how much forbearance no one but I can know or be grateful to you for —is that you laid yourself open to be slighted by a worldly shallow girl whose head was turned, and who was quite unable to rise to the worth of what you offered her. Mr. Rokesmith, that girl has often seen herself in a pitiful and poor light since, but never in as pitiful and poor a light as now, when the mean tone in which she answered you—sordid and vain girl that she was—has been echoed in her ears by Mr. Boffin."

He kissed her hand again.

"Mr. Boffin's speeches were detestable to me, shocking to me," said Bella, startling that gentleman with another stamp of her little foot. "It is quite true that there was a time, and very lately, when I deserved to be so 'righted,' Mr. Rokesmith; but I hope that I shall never deserve it again!"

He once more put her hand to his lips, and then relinquished it, and left the room. Bella was hurrying back to the chair in which she had hidden her face so long, when, catching sight of Mrs. Boffin by the way, she stopped at her. "He is gone," sobbed Bella, indignantly, despairingly, in fifty ways at once, with her arms round Mrs. Boffin's neck. "He has been most shamefully abused, and most unjustly and most basely driven away, and I am the cause of it!"

All this time Mr. Boffin had been rolling his eyes over

his loosened neckerchief, as if his fit were still upon him. Appearing now to think that he was coming to, he stared straight before him for a while, tied his neckerchief again, took several long inspirations, swallowed several times, and ultimately exclaimed with a deep sigh, as if he felt himself on the whole better: "Well!"

No word, good or bad, did Mrs. Boffin say; but she tenderly took care of Bella, and glanced at her husband as if for orders. Mr. Boffin, without imparting any, took his seat on a chair over against them, and there sat leaning forward, with a fixed countenance, his legs apart, a hand on each knee, and his elbows squared, until Bella should dry her eyes and raise her head, which in the fulness of time she did.

"I must go home," said Bella, rising hurriedly. "I am very grateful to you for all you have done for me, but I can't stay here."

"My darling girl!" remonstrated Mrs. Boffin.

"No, I can't stay here," said Bella; "I can't indeed.—Ugh! you vicious old thing!" (This to Mr. Boffin.)

"Don't be rash, my love." urged Mrs. Boffin. "Think well of what you do."

"Yes, you had better think well," said Mr. Boffin.

"I shall never more think well of *you*," cried Bella, cutting him short, with intense defiance in her expressive little eyebrows, and championship of the late Secretary in every dimple. "No! Never again! Your money has changed you to marble. You are a hard-hearted Miser. You are worse than Dancer, worse than Hopkins, worse than Blackberry Jones, worse than any of the wretches. And more!" proceeded Bella, breaking into tears again, " you were wholly undeserving of the Gentleman you have lost."

"Why, you don't mean to say, Miss Bella," the Golden Dustman slowly remonstrated, "that you set up Rokesmith against me?"

"I do!" said Bella. "He is worth a Million of you."

223

Very pretty she looked, though very angry, as she made herself as tall as she possibly could (which was not extremely tall), and utterly renounced her patron with a lofty toss of her rich brown head.

" I would rather he thought well of me," said Bella, " though he swept the street for bread, than that you did, though you splashed the mud upon him from the wheels of a chariot of pure gold.—There ! "

" Well I'm sure ! " cried Mr. Boffin, staring.

" And for a long time past, when you have thought you set yourself above him, I have only seen you under his feet," said Bella—" There ! And throughout I saw in him the master, and I saw in you the man—There ! And when you used him shamefully, I took his part and loved him—There ! I boast of it ! " After which strong avowal Bella underwent reaction, and cried to any extent, with her face on the back of her chair.

" Now, look here," said Mr. Boffin, as soon as he could find an opening for breaking the silence and striking in. " Give me your attention, Bella. I am not angry."

" I *am !* " said Bella.

" I say," resumed the Golden Dustman, " I am not angry, and I mean kindly to you, and I want to overlook this. So you'll stay where you are, and we'll agree to say no more about it."

" No, I can't stay here," cried Bella, rising hurriedly again ; " I can't think of staying here. I must go home for good."

" Now, don't be silly," Mr. Boffin reasoned. " Don't do what you can't undo ; don't do what you're sure to be sorry for."

" I shall never be sorry for it," said Bella ; " and I should always be sorry, and should every minute of my life despise myself, if I remained here after what has happened."

" At least, Bella," argued Mr. Boffin, " let there be no mistake about it. Look before you leap, you know. Stay where you are, and all's well, and all's as it was to be. Go away, and you can never come back."

"I know that I can never come back, and that's what I mean," said Bella.

"You mustn't expect," Mr. Boffin pursued, "that I'm a-going to settle money on you, if you leave us like this, because I am not. No, Bella! Be careful! Not one brass farthing."

"Expect!" said Bella, haughtily. "Do you think that any power on earth could make me take it, if you did, sir?"

But there was Mrs. Boffin to part from, and, in the full flush of her dignity, the impressible little soul collapsed again. Down upon her knees before that good woman, she rocked herself upon her breast, and cried, and sobbed, and folded her in her arms with all her might.

"You're a dear, a dear, the best of dears!" cried Bella. "You're the best of human creatures. I can never be thankful enough to you, and can never forget you. If I should live to be blind and deaf, I know I shall see and hear you, in my fancy, to the last of my dim old days!"

Mrs. Boffin wept most heartily, and embraced her with all fondness; but said not one single word except that she was her dear girl. She said that often enough, to be sure, for she said it over and over again; but not one word else.

Bella broke from her at length, and was going weeping out of the room, when in her own little queer affectionate way, she half relented towards Mr. Boffin.

"I am very glad," sobbed Bella, "that I called you names, sir, because you richly deserved it. But I am very sorry that I called you names, because you used to be so different. Say good-bye!"

"Good-bye," said Mr. Boffin, shortly.

"If I knew which of your hands was the least spoilt, I would ask you to let me touch it," said Bella, "for the last time. But not because I repent of what I have said to you. For I don't. It's true!"

"Try the left hand," said Mr. Boffin, holding it out in a stolid manner; "it's the least used."

"You have been wonderfully good and kind to me," said Bella, "and I kiss it for that. You have been as bad as bad could be to Mr. Rokesmith, and I throw it away for that. Thank you for myself, and good-bye!"

"Good-bye," said Mr. Boffin as before.

Bella caught him round the neck and kissed him, and ran out for ever.

She ran up-stairs, and sat down on the floor in her own room and cried abundantly. But the day was declining and she had no time to lose. She opened all the places where she kept her dresses; selected only those she had brought with her, leaving all the rest; and made a great misshapen bundle of them to be sent for afterwards.

"I won't take one of the others," said Bella, tying the knots of the bundle very tight, in the severity of her resolution. "I'll leave all the presents behind, and begin again entirely on my own account." That the resolution might be thoroughly carried into practice, she even changed the dress she wore for that in which she had come to the grand mansion. Even the bonnet she put on was the bonnet that had mounted into the Boffin chariot at Holloway.

"Now, I am complete," said Bella. "It's a little trying, but I have steeped my eyes in cold water, and I won't cry any more. You have been a pleasant room to me, dear room. Adieu! We shall never see each other again."

With a parting kiss of her fingers to it she softly closed the door, and went with a light foot down the great staircase, pausing and listening as she went, that she might meet none of the household. No one chanced to be about, and she got down to the hall in quiet. The door of the late Secretary's room stood open. She peeped in as she passed, and divined from the emptiness of his table, and the general appearance of things, that he was already gone. Softly opening the great hall door, and softly closing it upon herself, she turned and kissed it on the outside—insensible old combination of wood and iron that it was!—before she ran away from the house at a swift pace.

"That was well done!" panted Bella, slackening in the next street, and subsiding into a walk. "If I had left myself any breath to cry with, I should have cried again. Now poor dear, darling little Pa, you are going to see your lovely woman unexpectedly."

CHAPTER XVI.

The City looked unpromising enough, as Bella made her way along its gritty streets. Most of its money-mills were slackening sail, or had left off grinding for the day. The master-millers had already departed, and the journeymen were departing. There was a jaded aspect on the business lanes and courts, and the very pavements had a weary appearance, confused by the tread of a million of feet. There must be hours of night to temper down the day's distraction of so feverish a place. As yet, the worry of the newly-stopped whirling and grinding on the part of the money-mills seemed to linger in the air, and the quiet was more like the prostration of a spent giant than the repose of one who was renewing his strength.

If Bella thought, as she glanced at the mighty Bank, how agreeable it would be to have an hour's gardening there, with a bright copper shovel, among the money, still she was not in an avaricious vein. Much improved in that respect, and with certain half-formed images which had little gold in their composition, dancing before her bright eyes, she arrived in the drug-flavoured region of Mincing Lane, with the sensation of having just opened a drawer in a chemist's shop.

The counting-house of Chicksey, Veneering, and Stobbles was pointed out by an elderly female accustomed to the care of offices, who dropped upon Bella out of a public-house, wiping her mouth, and accounted for its humidity on natural principles well known to the physical sciences, by explaining that she had looked in at the door to see what o'clock it was. The counting-house was a wall-eyed ground-floor by a dark gateway, and Bella was considering, as she approached it, could there be any precedent in the City for her going in and asking for R. Wilfer, when whom should she see, sitting at one of the windows with the plate-glass sash raised, but R. Wilfer himself, preparing to take a slight refection.

On approaching nearer, Bella discerned that the refection had the appearance of a small cottage-loaf and a pennyworth of milk. Simultaneously with this discovery on her part, her father discovered her, and invoked the echoes of Mincing Lane to exclaim " My gracious, me!"

He then came cherubically flying out without a hat, and embraced her, and handed her in. "For it's after hours and I am all alone, my dear," he explained, "and am having—as I sometimes do, when they are all gone—a quiet tea."

Looking round the office, as if her father were a captive and this his cell, Bella hugged him and choked him to her heart's content.

"I never was so surprised, my dear," said her father. "I couldn't believe my eyes. Upon my life, I thought they had taken to lying! The idea of your coming down the Lane yourself! Why didn't you send the footman down the Lane, my dear?"

"I have brought no footman with me, Pa."

"Oh, indeed! But you have brought the elegant turn-out, my love?"

"No, Pa."

"You never can have walked, my dear?"

"Yes, I have, Pa."

He looked so very much astonished, that Bella could not make up her mind to break it to him just yet.

"The consequence is, Pa, that your lovely woman feels a little faint, and would very much like to share your tea."

The cottage-loaf and the pennyworth of milk had been set forth on a sheet of paper on the window-seat. The cherubic pocket-knife, with the first bit of the loaf still on its point, lay beside them where it had been hastily thrown down. Bella took the bit off, and put it in her mouth. " My dear child," said her father, " the idea of your partaking of such lowly fare ! But, at least, you must have your own loaf and your own penn'orth. One moment, my dear. The Dairy is just over the way and round the corner."

Regardless of Bella's dissuasions he ran out, and quickly returned with the new supply. "My dear child," he said, as he spread it on another piece of paper before her, " the idea of a splendid—— ! " and then looked at her figure, and stopped short.

" What's the matter, Pa ? "

" —of a splendid female," he resumed, more slowly, " putting up with such accommodation as the present !—Is that a new dress you have on, my dear ? "

" No, Pa, an old one. Don't you remember it ? "

" Why, I *thought* I remembered it, my dear ! "

" You should, for you bought it, Pa."

" Yes, I *thought* I bought it, my dear ! " said the cherub, giving himself a little shake, as if to rouse his faculties.

" And have you grown so fickle that you don't like your own taste, Pa, dear ? "

" Well, my love," he returned, swallowing a bit of the cottage-loaf with considerable effort, for it seemed to stick by the way : " I should have thought it was hardly sufficiently splendid for existing circumstances."

" And so, Pa," said Bella, moving coaxingly to his side, instead of remaining opposite, " you sometimes have a quiet tea here all alone ? I am not in the tea's way, if I draw my arm over your shoulder like this, Pa ? "

" Yes, my dear, and no, my dear. Yes to the first question, and certainly Not to the second. Respecting the quiet tea, my dear, why you see the occupations of the day

are sometimes a little wearing; and if there's nothing interposed between the day and your mother, why *she* is sometimes
a little wearing too."

" I know, Pa."

" Yes, my dear. So sometimes I put a quiet tea at the
window here, with a little quiet contemplation of the Lane
(which comes soothing), between the day, and domestic——"

" Bliss," suggested Bella, sorrowfully.

" And domestic Bliss," said her father, quite contented to
accept the phrase.

Bella kissed him. " And it is in this dark, dingy place of
captivity, poor dear, that you pass all the hours of your life
when you are not at home ? "

" Not at home, or not on the road there, or on the road
here, my love. Yes. You see that little desk in the
corner ? "

" In the dark corner, furthest both from the light and from
the fireplace ? The shabbiest desk of all the desks ? "

" Now, does it really strike you in that point of view, my
dear ? " said her father, surveying it artistically with his head
on one side : " that's mine. That's called Rumty's Perch."

" Whose Perch ? " asked Bella, with great indignation.

" Rumty's. You see, being rather high and up two steps
they call it a Perch. And they call *me* Rumty."

" How dare they ! " exclaimed Bella.

" They're playful, Bella, my dear ; they're playful. They're
more or less younger than I am, and they're playful. What
does it matter? It might be Surly, or Sulky, or fifty
disagreeable things that I really shouldn't like to be considered. But Rumty ! Lor, why not Rumty ? "

To inflict a heavy disappointment on this sweet nature,
which had been, through all her caprices, the object of her
recognition, love, and admiration from infancy, Bella felt to
be the hardest task of her hard day. " I should have done
better," she thought, " to tell him at first ; I should have
done better to tell him just now, when he had some slight

misgiving; he is quite happy again, and I shall make him wretched."

He was falling back on his loaf and milk, with the pleasantest composure, and Bella, stealing her arm a little closer about him, and at the same time sticking up his hair with an irresistible propensity to play with him, founded on the habit of her whole life, had prepared herself to say: "Pa, dear, don't be cast down, but I must tell you something disagreeable!" when he interrupted her in an unlooked-for manner.

"My gracious me!" he exclaimed, invoking the Mincing Lane echoes as before. "This is very extraordinary!"

"What is, Pa?"

"Why here's Mr. Rokesmith now!"

"No, no, Pa, no," cried Bella, greatly flurried. "Surely not."

"Yes, there is! Look here!"

Sooth to say, Mr. Rokesmith not only passed the window, but came into the counting-house. And not only came into the counting-house, but, finding himself alone there with Bella and her father, rushed at Bella and caught her in his arms, with the rapturous words, "My dear, dear girl; my gallant, generous, disinterested, courageous, noble girl!" And not only that even (which one might have thought astonishment enough for one dose), but Bella, after hanging her head for a moment, lifted it up and laid it on his breast, as if that were her head's chosen and lasting resting-place!

"I knew you would come to him, and I followed you," said Rokesmith. "My love, my life! You ARE mine?"

To which Bella responded, "Yes, I AM yours if you think me worth taking!" And after that, seemed to shrink to next to nothing in the clasp of his arms, partly because it was such a strong one on his part, and partly because there was such a yielding to it on hers.

The cherub, whose hair would have done for itself, under the influence of this amazing spectacle, what Bella had just now done for it, staggered back into the window-seat from which he had risen, and surveyed the pair with his eyes dilated to their utmost.

" But we must think of dear Pa," said Bella; " I haven't told dear Pa ; let us speak to Pa." Upon which they turned to do so.

" I wish first, my dear," remarked the cherub faintly, " that you'd have the kindness to sprinkle me with a little milk, for I feel as if I was—Going."

In fact, the good little fellow had become alarmingly limp, and his senses seemed to be rapidly escaping, from the knees upward. Bella sprinkled him with kisses instead of milk, but gave him a little of that article to drink ; and he gradually revived under her caressing care.

" We'll break it to you gently, dearest Pa," said Bella.

" My dear," returned the cherub, looking at them both, " you broke so much in the first—Gush, if I may so express myself —that I think I am equal to a good large breakage now."

" Mr. Wilfer," said John Rokesmith, excitedly and joyfully, " Bella takes me, though I have no fortune, even no present occupation ; nothing but what I can get in the life before us. Bella takes me ! "

" Yes, I should rather have inferred, my dear sir," returned the cherub feebly, " that Bella took you, from what I have within these few minutes remarked."

" You don't know, Pa," said Bella, " how ill I have used him ! "

" You don't know, sir," said Rokesmith, " what a heart she has ! "

" You don't know, Pa," said Bella, " what a shocking creature I was growing, when he saved me from myself ! "

" You don't know, sir," said Rokesmith, " what a sacrifice she has made for me ! "

" My dear Bella," replied the cherub, still pathetically scared, " and my dear John Rokesmith, if you will allow me so to call you—— "

"Yes, do, Pa, do!" urged Bella. "*I* allow you, and my will is his law. Isn't it—dear John Rokesmith?"

There was an engaging shyness in Bella, coupled with an engaging tenderness of love and confidence and pride, in thus first calling him by name, which made it quite excusable in John Rokesmith to do what he did. What he did was, once more to give to her the appearance of vanishing as aforesaid.

"I think, my dears," observed the cherub, "that if you could make it convenient to sit one on one side of me, and the other on the other, we should get on rather more consecutively, and make things rather plainer. John Rokesmith mentioned, a while ago, that he had no present occupation."

"None," said Rokesmith.

"No, Pa, none," said Bella.

"From which I argue," proceeded the cherub, "that he has left Mr. Boffin?"

"Yes, Pa. And so——"

"Stop a bit, my dear. I wish to lead up to it by degrees. And that Mr. Boffin has not treated him well?"

"Has treated him most shamefully, dear Pa!" cried Bella, with a flashing face.

"Of which," pursued the cherub, enjoining patience with his hand, "a certain mercenary young person distantly related to myself could not approve? Am I leading up to it right?"

"Could not approve, sweet Pa," said Bella, with a tearful laugh and a joyful kiss.

"Upon which," pursued the cherub, "the certain mercenary young person distantly related to myself, having previously observed and mentioned to myself that prosperity was spoiling Mr. Boffin, felt that she must not sell her sense of what was right and what was wrong, and what was true and what was false, and what was just and what was unjust, for any price that could be paid to her by any one alive? Am I leading up to it right?"

With another tearful laugh, Bella joyfully kissed him again.

"And therefore—and therefore," the cherub went on in a

glowing voice, as Bella's hand stole gradually up his waist-coat to his neck, "this mercenary young person distantly related to myself refused the price, took off the splendid fashions that were part of it, put on the comparatively poor dress that I had last given her, and trusting to my supporting her in what was right, came straight to me. Have I led up to it?"

Bella's hand was round his neck by this time, and her face was on it.

"The mercenary young person distantly related to myself," said her good father, "did well! The mercenary young person distantly related to myself did not trust to me in vain! I admire this mercenary young person distantly related to my-self, more in this dress than if she had come to me in China silks, Cashmere shawls, and Golconda diamonds. I love this young person dearly. I say to the man of this young person's heart, out of my heart and with all of it, 'My blessing on this engagement betwixt you, and she brings you a good fortune when she brings you the poverty she has accepted for your sake and the honest truth's!'"

The staunch little man's voice failed him as he gave John Rokesmith his hand, and he was silent, bending his face low over his daughter. But, not for long. He soon looked up, saying in a sprightly tone:

"And now, my dear child, if you think you can entertain John Rokesmith for a minute and a half, I'll run over to the Dairy, and fetch *him* a cottage-loaf and a drink of milk, that we may all have tea together."

It was, as Bella gaily said, like the supper provided for the three nursery hobgoblins at their house in the forest, without their thunderous low growlings of the alarming discovery, "Somebody's been drinking *my* milk!" It was a delicious repast; by far the most delicious that Bella, or John Rokesmith, or even R. Wilfer, had ever made. The uncongenial oddity of its surroundings, with the two brass knobs of the iron safe of Chicksey, Veneering, and Stobbles staring from a corner, like the eyes of some dull dragon, only made it the more delightful.

"To think," said the cherub, looking round the office with unspeakable enjoyment, "that anything of a tender nature should come off here, is what tickles me. To think that ever I should have seen my Bella folded in the arms of her future husband *here*, you know!"

It was not until the cottage-loaves and the milk had for some time disappeared, and the foreshadowings of night were creeping over Mincing Lane, that the cherub by degrees became a little nervous, and said to Bella, as he cleared his throat:

"Hem!—Have you thought at all about your mother, my dear?"

"Yes, Pa."

"And your sister Lavvy, for instance, my dear?"

"Yes, Pa. I think we had better not enter into particulars at home. I think it will be quite enough to say that I had a difference with Mr. Boffin, and have left for good."

"John Rokesmith being acquainted with your Ma, my love," said her father, after some slight hesitation, "I need have no delicacy in hinting before him that you may perhaps find your Ma a little wearing."

"A little, patient Pa?" said Bella with a tuneful laugh: the tunefuller for being so loving in its tone.

"Well! We'll say, strictly in confidence among ourselves, wearing; we won't qualify it," the cherub stoutly admitted. "And your sister's temper is wearing."

"I don't mind, Pa."

"And you must prepare yourself, you know, my precious," said her father, with much gentleness, "for our looking very poor and meagre at home, and being at the best but very uncomfortable, after Mr. Boffin's house."

"I don't mind, Pa. I could bear much harder trials—— for John."

The closing words were not so softly and blushingly said

236

but that John heard them, and showed that he heard them by again assisting Bella to another of those mysterious disappearances.

"Well!" said the cherub gaily, and not expressing disapproval, "when you—when you come back from retirement, my love, and reappear on the surface, I think it will be time to lock up and go."

If the counting-house of Chicksey, Veneering, and Stobbles had ever been shut up by three happier people, glad as most people were to shut it up, they must have been superlatively happy indeed. But first Bella mounted upon Rumty's Perch, and said, "Show me what you do here all day long, dear Pa. Do you write like this?" laying her round cheek upon her plump left arm, and losing sight of her pen in waves of hair, in a highly unbusiness-like manner. Though John Rokesmith seemed to like it.

So, the three hobgoblins, having effaced all traces of their feast, and swept up the crumbs, came out of Mincing Lane to walk to Holloway; and if two of the hobgoblins didn't wish the distance twice as long as it was, the third hobgoblin was much mistaken. Indeed, that modest spirit deemed himself so much in the way of their deep enjoyment of the journey, that he apologetically remarked: "I think, my dears, I'll take the lead on the other side of the road, and seem not to belong to you." Which he did, cherubically strewing the path with smiles, in the absence of flowers.

It was almost ten o'clock when they stopped within view of Wilfer Castle; and then, the spot being quiet and deserted, Bella began a series of disappearances which threatened to last all night.

"I think, John," the cherub hinted at last, "that if you can spare me the young person distantly related to myself, I'll take her in."

"I can't spare her," answered John, "but I must lend her to you.—My Darling!" A word of magic which caused Bella instantly to disappear again.

"Now, dearest Pa," said Bella, when she became visible, "put your hand in mine, and we'll run home as fast as ever we can run, and get it over. Now, Pa. Once!——"

"My dear," the cherub faltered, with something of a craven air, "I was going to observe that if your mother——"

"You mustn't hang back, sir, to gain time," cried Bella, putting out her right foot; "do you see that, sir? That's the mark; come up to the mark, sir. Once! Twice! Three times and away, Pa!" Off she skimmed, bearing the cherub along, nor ever stopped, nor suffered him to stop, until she had pulled at the bell. "Now, dear Pa," said Bella, taking him by both ears as if he were a pitcher, and conveying his face to her rosy lips, "we are in for it!"

Miss Lavvy came out to open the gate, waited on by that attentive cavalier and friend of the family, Mr. George Sampson. "Why, it's never Bella!" exclaimed Miss Lavvy, starting back at the sight. And then bawled, "Ma! Here's Bella!"

This produced, before they could get into the house, Mrs. Wilfer. Who, standing in the portal, received them with ghostly gloom, and all her other appliances of ceremony.

"My child is welcome, though unlooked for," said she, at the time presenting her cheek as if it were a cool slate for visitors to enrol themselves upon. "You too, R. W., are welcome, though late. Does the male domestic of Mrs. Boffin hear me there?" This deep-toned inquiry was cast forth into the night, for response from the menial in question.

"There is no one waiting, Ma dear," said Bella.

"There is no one waiting?" repeated Mrs. Wilfer, in majestic accents.

"No, Ma dear."

A dignified shiver pervaded Mrs. Wilfer's shoulders and gloves, as who should say, "An Enigma!" and then she marched at the head of the procession to the family keeping-room, where she observed:

238

"Unless, R. W.:" who started on being solemnly turned upon: "you have taken the precaution of making some addition to our frugal supper on your way home, it will prove but a distasteful one to Bella. Cold neck of mutton and a lettuce can ill compete with the luxuries of Mr. Boffin's board."

"Pray don't talk like that, Ma dear," said Bella; "Mr. Boffin's board is nothing to me."

But, here Miss Lavinia, who had been intently eyeing Bella's bonnet, struck in with "Why, Bella!"

"Yes, Lavvy, I know."

The Irrepressible lowered her eyes to Bella's dress, and stooped to look at it, exclaiming again: "Why, Bella!"

"Yes, Lavvy, I know what I have got on. I was going to tell Ma when you interrupted. I have left Mr. Boffin's house for good, Ma, and I have come home again."

Mrs. Wilfer spake no word, but, having glared at her offspring for a minute or two in an awful silence, retired into her corner of state backward, and sat down: like a frozen article on sale in a Russian market.

"In short, dear Ma," said Bella, taking off the depreciated bonnet and shaking out her hair, "I have had a very serious difference with Mr. Boffin on the subject of his treatment of a member of his household, and it's a final difference, and there's an end of all."

"And I am bound to tell you, my dear," added R. W., submissively, "that Bella has acted in a truly brave spirit, and with a truly right feeling. And therefore I hope, my dear, you'll not allow yourself to be greatly disappointed."

"George!" said Miss Lavvy, in a sepulchral, warning voice, founded on her mother's: "George Sampson, speak! What did I tell you about those Boffins?"

Mr. Sampson perceiving his frail bark to be labouring among shoals and breakers, thought it safest not to refer back to any particular thing that he had been told, lest he should refer back to the wrong thing. With admirable seamanship he got his bark into deep water by murmuring, "Yes indeed."

"Yes! I told George Sampson, as George Sampson tells you," said Miss Lavvy, "that those hateful Boffins would pick a quarrel with Bella, as soon as her novelty had worn off. Have they done it, or have they not? Was I right, or was I wrong? And what do you say to us, Bella, of your Boffins now?"

"Lavvy and Ma," said Bella, "I say of Mr. and Mrs. Boffin what I always have said; and I always shall say of them what I always have said. But nothing will induce me to quarrel with any one to-night. I hope you are not sorry to see me, Ma dear," kissing her; "and I hope you are not sorry to see me, Lavvy," kissing her too; "and as I notice the lettuce Ma mentioned, on the table, I'll make the salad."

Bella playfully setting herself about the task, Mrs. Wilfer's impressive countenance followed her with glaring eyes, presenting a combination of the once popular sign of the Saracen's Head, with a piece of Dutch clockwork, and suggesting to an imaginative mind that from the composition of the salad, her daughter might prudently omit the vinegar. But no word issued from the majestic matron's lips. And this was more terrific to her husband (as perhaps she knew) than any flow of eloquence with which she could have edified the company.

"Now, Ma dear," said Bella, in due course, "the salad's ready, and it's past supper-time."

Mrs. Wilfer rose, but remained speechless. "George!" said Miss Lavinia in her voice of warning, "Ma's chair!" Mr. Sampson flew to the excellent lady's back, and followed her up close, chair in hand, as she stalked to the banquet. Arrived at the table, she took her rigid seat, after favouring Mr. Sampson with a glare for himself, which caused the young gentleman to retire to his place in much confusion.

The cherub not presuming to address so tremendous an object, transacted her supper through the agency of a third

person, as "Mutton to your Ma, Bella, my dear;" and
"Lavvy, I dare say your Ma would take some lettuce if
you were to put it on her plate." Mrs. Wilfer's manner
of receiving those viands was marked by petrified absence of
mind; in which state, likewise, she partook of them, occasionally laying down her knife and fork, as saying within her
own spirit, "What is this I am doing?" and glaring at one
or other of the party, as if in indignant search of information.
A magnetic result of such glaring was, that the person glared
at could not by any means successfully pretend to be ignorant
of the fact: so that a bystander, without beholding Mrs.
Wilfer at all, must have known at whom she was glaring, by
seeing her refracted from the countenance of the beglared one.

Miss Lavinia was extremely affable to Mr. Sampson on
this special occasion, and took the opportunity of informing
her sister why.

"It was not worth troubling you about, Bella, when you
were in a sphere so far removed from your family as to
make it a matter in which you could be expected to take
very little interest," said Lavinia with a toss of her chin;
"but George Sampson is paying his addresses to me."

Bella was glad to hear it. Mr. Sampson became thoughtfully red, and felt called upon to encircle Miss Lavinia's waist
with his arm; but encountering a large pin in the young
lady's belt, scarified a finger, uttered a sharp exclamation,
and attracted the lightning of Mrs. Wilfer's glare.

"George is getting on very well," said Miss Lavinia—
which might not have been supposed at the moment—"and
I dare say we shall be married one of these days. I didn't
care to mention it when you were with your Bof——" here
Miss Lavinia checked herself in a bounce, and added more
placidly, "when you were with Mr. and Mrs. Boffin; but
now I think it sisterly to name the circumstance."

"Thank you, Lavvy dear. I congratulate you."

"Thank you, Bella. The truth is, George and I did
discuss whether I should tell you; but I said to George that

241

you wouldn't be much interested in so paltry an affair, and that it was far more likely you would rather detach yourself from us altogether, than have him added to the rest of us."

"That was a 'mistake, dear Lavvy," said Bella.

"It turns out to be," replied Miss Lavinia; "but circumstances have changed, you know, my dear. George is in a new situation, and his prospects are very good indeed. I should not have had the courage to tell you so yesterday, when you would have thought his prospects poor, and not worth notice; but I feel quite bold to-night."

"When did you begin to feel timid, Lavvy?" inquired Bella, with a smile.

"I didn't say that I ever felt timid, Bella," replied the Irrepressible. "But perhaps I might have said, if I had not been restrained by delicacy towards a sister's feelings, that I have for some time felt independent; too independent, my dear, to subject myself to have my intended match (you'll prick yourself again, George) looked down upon. It is not that I could have blamed you for looking down upon it, when you were looking up to a rich and great match, Bella; it is only that I was independent."

Whether the Irrepressible felt slighted by Bella's declaration that she would not quarrel, or whether her spitefulness was evoked by Bella's return to the sphere of Mr. George Sampson's courtship, or whether it was a necessary fillip to her spirits that she should come into collision with somebody on the present occasion,—anyhow she made a dash at her stately parent now, with the greatest impetuosity.

"Ma. pray don't sit staring at me in that intensely aggravating manner! If you see a black on my nose, tell me so; if you don't, leave me alone."

"Do you address Me in those words?" said Mrs. Wilfer. "Do you presume?"

"Don't talk about presuming, Ma, for goodness' sake. A girl who is old enough to be engaged, is quite old enough to object to be stared at as if she was a Clock."

"Audacious one!" said Mrs. Wilfer. "Your grandmamma, if so addressed by one of her daughters, at any age, would have insisted on her retiring to a dark apartment."

"My grandmamma," returned Lavvy, folding her arms and leaning back in her chair, "wouldn't have sat staring people out of countenance, I think."

"She would!" said Mrs. Wilfer.

"Then it's a pity she didn't know better," said Lavvy. "And if my grandmamma wasn't in her dotage when she took to insisting on people's retiring to dark apartments, she ought to have been. A pretty exhibition my grandmamma must have made of herself! I wonder whether she ever insisted on people's retiring into the ball of St. Paul's; and if she did, how she got them there!"

"Silence!" proclaimed Mrs. Wilfer. "I command silence!"

"I have not the slightest intention of being silent, Ma," returned Lavinia, coolly, "but quite the contrary. I am not going to be eyed as if *I* had come from the Boffins, and sit silent under it. I am not going to have George Sampson eyed as if *he* had come from the Boffins, and sit silent under it. If Pa thinks proper to be eyed as if *he* had come from the Boffins also, well and good. I don't choose to. And I won't."

Lavinia's engineering having made this crooked opening at Bella, Mrs. Wilfer strode into it.

"You rebellious spirit! You mutinous child! Tell me this, Lavinia. If, in violation of your mother's sentiments, you had condescended to allow yourself to be patronised by the Boffins, and if you had come from those halls of slavery——"

"That's mere nonsense, Ma," said Lavinia.

"How!" exclaimed Mrs. Wilfer, with sublime severity.

"Halls of slavery, Ma, is mere stuff and nonsense," returned the unmoved Irrepressible.

"I say, presumptuous child, if you had come from the neighbourhood of Portland Place, bending under the yoke of patronage, and attended by its domestics in glittering garb

243

to visit me, do you think my deep-seated feelings could have been expressed in looks?"

"All I think about it is," returned Lavinia, "that I should wish them expressed to the right person."

"And if," pursued her mother, "if, making light of my warnings that the face of Mrs. Boffin alone was a face teeming with evil, you had clung to Mrs. Boffin instead of to me, and had, after all, come home rejected by Mrs. Boffin, trampled under foot by Mrs. Boffin, and cast out by Mrs. Boffin, do you think my feelings could have been expressed in looks?"

Lavinia was about replying to her honoured parent that she might as well have dispensed with her looks altogether then, when Bella rose and said, "Good-night, dear Ma. I have had a tiring day, and I'll go to bed." This broke up the agreeable party. Mr. George Sampson shortly afterwards took his leave, accompanied by Miss Lavinia with a candle as far as the hall, and without a candle as far as the garden gate; Mrs. Wilfer, washing her hands of the Boffins, went to bed after the manner of Lady Macbeth; and R. W. was left alone among the dilapidations of the supper table, in a melancholy attitude.

But, a light footstep aroused him from his meditations, and it was Bella's. Her pretty hair was hanging all about her, and she had tripped down softly, brush in hand, and barefoot, to say good-night to him.

"My dear, you most unquestionably *are* a lovely woman," said the cherub, taking up a tress in his hand.

"Look here, sir," said Bella; "when your lovely woman marries, you shall have that piece if you like, and she'll make you a chain of it. Would you prize that remembrance of the dear creature?"

"Yes, my precious."

"Then you shall have it if you're good, sir. I am very, very sorry, dearest Pa, to have brought home all this trouble."

The Lovely Woman has her Fortune told

"My pet," returned her father, in the simplest good faith, "don't make yourself uneasy about that. It really is not worth mentioning, because things at home would have taken pretty much the same turn any way. If your mother and sister don't find one subject to get at times a little wearing on, they find another. We're never out of a wearing subject, my dear, I assure you. I am afraid you find your old room with Lavvy dreadfully inconvenient, Bella?"

"No, I don't, Pa; I don't mind. Why don't I mind, do you think, Pa?"

"Well, my child, you used to complain of it when it wasn't such a contrast as it must be now. Upon my word, I can only answer, because you are so much improved."

"No, Pa. Because I am so thankful and so happy!"

Here she choked him until her long hair made him sneeze, and then she laughed until she made him laugh, and then she choked him again that they might not be overheard.

"Listen, sir," said Bella. "Your lovely woman was told her fortune to-night on her way home. It won't be a large fortune, because if the lovely woman's Intended gets a certain appointment that he hopes to get soon, she will marry on a hundred and fifty pounds a-year. But that's at first, and even if it should never be more, the lovely woman will make it quite enough. But that's not all, sir. In the fortune there's a certain fair man—a little man, the fortune-teller said—who, it seems, will always find himself near the lovely woman, and will always have kept, expressly for him, such a peaceful corner in the lovely woman's little house as never was. Tell me the name of that man, sir."

"Is he a Knave in the pack of cards?" inquired the cherub, with a twinkle in his eyes.

"Yes!" cried Bella, in high glee, choking him again. "He's the Knave of Wilfers! Dear Pa, the lovely woman means to look forward to this fortune that has been told for her so delightfully, and to cause it to make her a much better lovely woman than she ever has been yet. What the little fair man is expected to do, sir, is to look forward to it also, by saying to himself when he is in danger of being over-worried, ' I see land at last!'"

"I see land at last!" repeated her father.

"There's a dear Knave of Wilfers!" exclaimed Bella; then putting out her small, white, bare foot, "That's the mark, sir. Come to the mark. Put your boot against it. We keep to it together, mind! Now, sir, you may kiss the lovely woman before she runs away, so thankful and so happy. O yes, fair little man, so thankful and so happy!"

CHAPTER XVII

A SOCIAL CHORUS

AMAZEMENT sits enthroned upon the countenances of Mr. and Mrs. Alfred Lammle's circle of acquaintance, when the disposal of their first-class furniture and effects (including a Billiard Table in capital letters), " by auction under a bill of sale," is publicly announced on a waving hearthrug in Sackville Street. But nobody is half so much amazed as Hamilton Veneering, Esquire, M.P. for Pocket Breaches, who instantly begins to find out that the Lammles are the only people ever entered on his soul's register who are *not* the oldest and dearest friends he has in the world. Mrs. Veneering, W.M.P. for Pocket Breaches, like a faithful wife, shares her husband's discovery and inexpressible astonishment. Perhaps the Veneerings twain may deem the last unutterable feeling particularly due to their reputation, by reason that once upon a time some of the longer heads in the City are whispered to have shaken themselves, when Veneering's extensive dealings and great wealth were mentioned. But it is certain that neither Mr. nor Mrs. Veneering can find words to wonder in, and it becomes necessary that they give to the oldest and dearest friends they have in the world, a wondering dinner.

For it is by this time noticeable that, whatever befalls, the Veneerings must give a dinner upon it. Lady Tippins lives in a chronic state of invitation to dine with the Veneerings, and in a chronic state of inflammation arising from the dinners. Boots and Brewer go about in cabs, with no other intelligible

247

business on earth than to beat up people to come and dine with the Veneerings. Veneering pervades the legislative lobbies, intent upon entrapping his fellow-legislators to dinner. Mrs. Veneering dined with five-and-twenty bran-new faces over-night; calls upon them all to-day; sends them every one a dinner-card to-morrow, for the week after next; before that dinner is digested, calls upon their brothers and sisters, their sons and daughters, their nephews and nieces, their aunts and uncles and cousins, and invites them all to dinner. And still, as at first, howsoever the dining circle widens, it is to be observed that all the diners are consistent in appearing to go to the Veneerings', not to dine with Mr. and Mrs. Veneering (which would seem to be the last thing in their minds), but to dine with one another.

Perhaps, after all,—who knows?—Veneering may find this dining, though expensive, remunerative in the sense that it makes champions. Mr. Podsnap, as a representative man, is not alone in caring very particularly for his own dignity, if not for that of his acquaintances, and therefore in angrily supporting the acquaintances who have taken out his Permit, lest, in their being lessened, he should be. The gold and silver camels, and the ice-pails, and the rest of the Veneering table decorations, make a brilliant show, and when I, Podsnap, casually remark elsewhere that I dined last Monday with a gorgeous caravan of camels, I find it personally offensive to have it hinted to me that they are broken-kneed camels, or camels labouring under suspicion of any sort. "I don't display camels myself, I am above them : I am a more solid man ; but these camels have basked in the light of my countenance, and how dare you, sir, insinuate to me that I have irradiated any but unimpeachable camels?"

The camels are polishing up in the Analytical's pantry for the dinner of wonderment on the occasion of the Lammles going to pieces, and Mr. Twemlow feels a little queer on the sofa at his lodgings over the stable-yard in Duke Street, Saint James's, in consequence of having taken two advertised

pills at about mid-day, on the faith of the printed represen-
tation accompanying the box (price one and a penny half-
penny, government stamp included), that the same " will
be found highly salutary as a precautionary measure in connection with the pleasures of the table." To whom, while
sickly with the fancy of an insoluble pill sticking in his
gullet, and also with the sensation of a deposit of warm gum
languidly wandering within him a little lower down, a servant
enters with an announcement that a lady wishes to speak
with him.

" A lady," says Twemlow, pluming his ruffled feathers.
" Ask the favour of the lady's name."

The lady's name is Lammle. The lady will not detain
Mr. Twemlow longer than a very few minutes. The lady is
sure that Mr. Twemlow will do her the kindness to see her
on being told that she particularly desires a short interview.
The lady has no doubt whatever of Mr. Twemlow's compliance
when he hears her name. Has begged the servant to be particular not to mistake her name. Would have sent in a card,
but has none.

" Show the lady in." Lady shown in, comes in.

Mr. Twemlow's little rooms are modestly furnished, in an
old-fashioned manner (rather like the housekeeper's room at
Snigsworthy Park), and would be bare of mere ornament,
were it not for a full-length engraving of the sublime Snigsworth over the chimney-piece, snorting at a Corinthian
column, with an enormous roll of paper at his feet, and a
heavy curtain going to tumble down on his head ; those
accessories being understood to represent the noble lord as
somehow in the act of saving his country.

" Pray take a seat, Mrs. Lammle." Mrs. Lammle takes a
seat and opens the conversation.

" I have no doubt, Mr. Twemlow, that you have heard of
a reverse of fortune having befallen us. Of course you have
heard of it, for no kind of news travels so fast—among one's
friends especially."

249

Mindful of the wondering dinner, Twemlow, with a little twinge, admits the imputation.

"Probably it will not," says Mrs. Lammle, with a certain hardened manner upon her, that makes Twemlow shrink, "have surprised you so much as some others, after what passed between us at the house which is now turned out at windows. I have taken the liberty of calling upon you, Mr. Twemlow, to add a sort of postscript to what I said that day."

Mr. Twemlow's dry and hollow cheeks become more dry and hollow at the prospect of some new complication.

"Really," says the uneasy little gentleman, "really, Mrs. Lammle, I should take it as a favour if you could excuse me from any further confidence. It has ever been one of the objects of my life—which, unfortunately, has not had many objects—to be inoffensive, and to keep out of cabals and interferences."

Mrs. Lammle, by far the more observant of the two, scarcely finds it necessary to look at Twemlow while he speaks, so easily does she read him.

"My postscript—to retain the term I have used"—says Mrs. Lammle, fixing her eyes on his face, to enforce what she says herself—"coincides exactly with what you say, Mr. Twemlow. So far from troubling you with any new confidence, I merely wish to remind you what the old one was. So far from asking you for interference, I merely wish to claim your strict neutrality."

Twemlow going on to reply, she rests her eyes again, knowing her ears to be quite enough for the contents of so weak a vessel.

"I can, I suppose," says Twemlow, nervously, "offer no reasonable objection to hearing anything that you do me the honour to wish to say to me under those heads. But if I may, with all possible delicacy and politeness, entreat you not to range beyond them, I—I beg to do so."

"Sir," says Mrs. Lammle, raising her eyes to his face again, and quite daunting him with her hardened manner, "I imparted to you a certain piece of knowledge, to be imparted again, as you thought best, to a certain person."

"Which I did," says Twemlow.

"And for doing which, I thank you; though, indeed, I scarcely know why I turned traitress to my husband in the matter, for the girl is a poor little fool. I was a poor little fool once myself; I can find no better reason." Seeing the effect she produces on him by her indifferent laugh and cold look, she keeps her eyes upon him as she proceeds. "Mr. Twemlow, if you should chance to see my husband, or to see me, or to see both of us, in the favour or confidence of any one else—whether of our common acquaintance or not, is of no consequence—you have no right to use against us the knowledge I intrusted you with, for one special purpose which has been accomplished. This is what I came to say. It is not a stipulation; to a gentleman it is simply a reminder."

Twemlow sits murmuring to himself with his hand to his forehead.

"It is so plain a case," Mrs. Lammle goes on, "as between me (from the first relying on your honour) and you, that I will not waste another word upon it." She looks steadily at Mr. Twemlow, until, with a shrug, he makes her a little one-sided bow, as though saying, "Yes, I think you have a right to rely upon me," and then she moistens her lips, and shows a sense of relief.

"I trust I have kept the promise I made through your servant, that I would detain you a very few minutes. I need trouble you no longer, Mr. Twemlow."

"Stay!" says Twemlow, rising as she rises. "Pardon me a moment. I should never have sought you out, madam, to say what I am going to say, but since you have sought me out and are here, I will throw it off my mind. Was it quite consistent, in candour, with our taking that resolution against Mr. Fledgeby, that you should afterwards address Mr. Fledgeby as your dear and confidential friend, and entreat a favour of Mr. Fledgeby? Always supposing that you did; I assert no knowledge of my own on the subject; it has been represented to me that you did."

"Then he told you?" retorts Mrs. Lammle, who again has saved her eyes while listening, and uses them with strong effect while speaking.

"Yes."

"It is strange that he should have told you the truth," says Mrs. Lammle, seriously pondering. "Pray where did a circumstance so very extraordinary happen?"

Twemlow hesitates. He is shorter than the lady as well as weaker, and as she stands above him with her hardened manner, and her well-used eyes, he finds himself at such a disadvantage that he would like to be of the opposite sex.

"May I ask where it happened, Mr. Twemlow? In strict confidence?"

"I must confess," says the mild little gentleman, coming to his answer by degrees, "that I felt some compunctions when Mr. Fledgeby mentioned it. I must admit that I could not regard myself in an agreeable light. More particularly, as Mr. Fledgeby did, with great civility, which I could not feel that I deserved from him, render me the same service that you had entreated him to render you."

It is a part of the true nobility of the poor gentleman's soul to say this last sentence. "Otherwise," he has reflected, "I shall assume the superior position of having no difficulties of my own, while I know of hers. Which would be mean, very mean."

"Was Mr. Fledgeby's advocacy as effectual in your case as in ours?" Mrs. Lammle demands.

"As *in*effectual."

"Can you make up your mind to tell me where you saw Mr. Fledgeby, Mr. Twemlow?"

"I beg your pardon. I fully intended to have done so. The reservation was not intentional. I encountered Mr.

Fledgeby, quite by accident, on the spot.—By the expression, on the spot, I mean at Mr. Riah's in Saint Mary Axe."

"Have you the misfortune to be in Mr. Riah's hands then?"

"Unfortunately, madam," returns Twemlow, "the one money-obligation to which I stand committed, the one debt of my life (but it is a just debt; pray observe that I don't dispute it), has fallen into Mr. Riah's hands."

"Mr. Twemlow," says Mrs. Lammle, fixing his eyes with hers: which he would prevent her doing if he could, but he can't; "it has fallen into Mr. Fledgeby's hands. Mr. Riah is his mask. It has fallen into Mr. Fledgeby's hands. Let me tell you that, for your guidance. The information may be of use to you, if only to prevent your credulity, in judging another man's truthfulness by your own, from being imposed upon."

"Impossible!" cries Twemlow, standing aghast. "How do you know it?"

"I scarcely know how I know it. The whole train of circumstances seemed to take fire at once, and show it to me."

"Oh! Then you have no proof."

"It is very strange," says Mrs. Lammle, coldly and boldly, and with some disdain, "how like men are to one another in some things, though their characters are as different as can be! No two men can have less affinity between them, one would say, than Mr. Twemlow and my husband. Yet my husband replies to me 'You have no proof,' and Mr. Twemlow replies to me with the very same words!"

"But why, madam?" Twemlow ventures gently to argue. "Consider why the very same words? Because they state the fact. Because you *have* no proof."

"Men are very wise in their way," quoth Mrs. Lammle, glancing haughtily at the Snigsworth portrait, and shaking out her dress before departing; "but they have wisdom to learn. My husband, who is not over-confiding, ingenuous,

253

or inexperienced, sees this plain thing no more than Mr. Twemlow does—because there is no proof. Yet I believe five women out of six, in my place, would see it as clearly as I do. However, I will never rest (if only in remembrance of Mr. Fledgeby's having kissed my hand) until my husband does see it. And you will do well for yourself to see it from this time forth, Mr. Twemlow, though I *can* give you no proof."

As she moves towards the door, Mr. Twemlow, attending on her, expresses his soothing hope that the condition of Mr. Lammle's affairs is not irretrievable.

"I don't know," Mrs. Lammle answers, stopping, and sketching out the pattern of the paper on the wall with the point of her parasol; "it depends. There may be an opening for him dawning now, or there may be none. We shall soon find out. If none, we are bankrupt here, and must go abroad, I suppose."

Mr. Twemlow, in his good-natured desire to make the best of it, remarks that there are pleasant lives abroad.

"Yes," returns Mrs. Lammle, still sketching on the wall, "but I doubt whether billiard-playing, card-playing, and so forth, for the means to live under suspicion at a dirty table-d'hôte, is one of them."

It is much for Mr. Lammle, Twemlow politely intimates (though greatly shocked) to have one always beside him who is attached to him in all his fortunes, and whose restraining influence will prevent him from courses that would be discreditable and ruinous. As he says it, Mrs. Lammle leaves off sketching, and looks at him.

"Restraining influence, Mr. Twemlow? We must eat and drink, and dress, and have a roof over our heads. Always beside him and attached in all his fortunes? Not much to boast of in that; what can a woman at my age do? My husband and I deceived one another when we married; we must bear the consequences of the deception—that is to say, bear one another, and bear the burden of scheming together for to-day's dinner and to-morrow's breakfast—till death divorces us."

With those words, she walks out into Duke Street, Saint James's. Mr. Twemlow returning to his sofa, lays down his aching head on its slippery little horse-hair bolster, with a strong internal conviction that a painful interview is not the kind of thing to be taken after the dinner pills which are so highly salutary in connection with the pleasures of the table.

But, six o'clock in the evening finds the worthy little gentleman getting better, and also getting himself into his obsolete little silk stockings and pumps, for the wondering dinner at the Veneerings'. At seven o'clock in the evening finds him trotting out into Duke Street to trot to the corner and save a sixpence in coach-hire.

Tippins the divine has dined herself into such a condition by this time, that a morbid mind might desire her, for a blessed change, to sup at last, and turn into bed. Such a mind has Mr. Eugene Wrayburn, whom Twemlow finds contemplating Tippins with the moodiest of visages, while that playful creature rallies him on being so long overdue at the woolsack. Skittish is Tippins with Mortimer Lightwood too, and has raps to give him with her fan for having been best man at the nuptials of these deceiving what's-their-names who have gone to pieces. Though, indeed, the fan is generally lively, and taps away at the men in all directions, with something of a grisly sound suggestive of the clattering of Lady Tippins's bones.

A new race of intimate friends has sprung up at Veneering's since he went into Parliament for the public good, to whom Mrs. Veneering is very attentive. These friends, like astronomical distances, are only to be spoken of in the very largest figures. Boots says that one of them is a Contractor who (it has been calculated) gives employment, directly and indirectly, to five hundred thousand men. Brewer says that another of them is a Chairman, in such request at so many

Boards, so far apart, that he never travels less by railway than three thousand miles a week. Buffer says that another of them hadn't a sixpence eighteen months ago, and, through the brilliancy of his genius in getting those shares issued at eighty-five, and buying them all up with no money and selling them at par for cash, has now three hundred and seventy-five thousand pounds—Buffer particularly insisting on the odd seventy-five, and declining to take a farthing less. With Buffer, Boots, and Brewer, Lady Tippins is eminently facetious on the subject of these Fathers of the Scrip-Church: surveying them through her eye-glass, and inquiring whether Boots and Brewer and Buffer think they will make her fortune if she makes love to them? with other pleasantries of that nature. Veneering, in his different way, is much occupied with the Fathers too, piously retiring with them into the conservatory, from which retreat the word "Committee" is occasionally heard, and where the Fathers instruct Veneering how he must leave the valley of the piano on his left, take the level of the mantel-piece, cross by an open cutting at the candelabra, seize the carrying traffic at the console, and cut up the opposition root and branch at the window curtains.

Mr. and Mrs. Podsnap are of the company, and the Fathers descry in Mrs. Podsnap a fine woman. She is consigned to a Father—Boots's Father, who employs five hundred thousand men—and is brought to anchor on Veneering's left; thus affording opportunity to the sportive Tippins on his right (he, as usual, being mere vacant space), to entreat to be told something about those loves of Navvies, and whether they do really live on raw beefsteaks, and drink porter out of their barrows. But, in spite of such little skirmishes it is felt that this was to be a wondering dinner, and that the wondering must not be neglected. Accordingly, Brewer, as the man who has the greatest reputation to sustain, becomes the interpreter of the general instinct.

"I took," says Brewer in a favourable pause, "a cab this morning, and I rattled off to that Sale."

Boots (devoured by envy) says, "So did I."

Buffer says, "So did I;" but can find nobody to care whether he did or not.

"And what was it like?" inquires Veneering.

"I assure you," replies Brewer, looking about for anybody else to address his answer to, and giving the preference to Lightwood; "I assure you, the things were going for a song. Handsome things enough, but fetching nothing."

"So I heard this afternoon," says Lightwood.

Brewer begs to know now, would it be fair to ask a professional man how—on—earth—these—people—ever—did—come—*to*—such—*a*—total smash? (Brewer's divisions being for emphasis.)

Lightwood replies that he was consulted certainly, but could give no opinion which would pay off the Bill of Sale, and therefore violates no confidence in supposing that it came of their living beyond their means.

"But how," says Veneering, "CAN people do that!"

Hah! That is felt on all hands to be a shot in the bull's-eye. How CAN people do that! The Analytical Chemist going round with champagne, looks very much as if *he* could give them a pretty good idea how people did that, if he had a mind.

"How," says Mrs. Veneering, laying down her fork to press her aquiline hands together at the tips of the fingers, and addressing the Father who travels the three thousand miles per week: "how a mother can look at her baby, and know that she lives beyond her husband's means, I cannot imagine."

Eugene suggests that Mrs. Lammle, not being a mother, had no baby to look at.

"True," says Mrs. Veneering, "but the principle is the same."

Boots is clear that the principle is the same. So is Buffer. It is the unfortunate destiny of Buffer to damage a cause by espousing it. The rest of the company have meekly yielded to the proposition that the principle is the same, until Buffer says it is; when instantly a general murmur arises that the principle is not the same.

"But I don't understand," says the Father of the three hundred and seventy-five thousand pounds, " —if these people spoken of, occupied the position of being in society—they were in society?"

Veneering is bound to confess that they dined here, and were even married from here.

"Then I don't understand," pursues the Father, "how even their living beyond their means could bring them to what has been termed a total smash. Because there is always such a thing as an adjustment of affairs, in the case of people of any standing at all."

Eugene (who would seem to be in a gloomy state of suggestiveness) suggests, "Suppose you have no means and live beyond them?"

This is too insolvent a state of things for the Father to entertain. It is too insolvent a state of things for any one with any self-respect to entertain, and is universally scouted. But it is so amazing how any people can have come to a total smash. that everybody feels bound to account for it specially. One of the Fathers says, "Gaming table." Another of the Fathers says, "Speculated without knowing that speculation is a science." Boots says, "Horses." Lady Tippins says to her fan, "Two establishments." Mr. Podsnap saying nothing, is referred to for his opinion; which he delivers as follows; much flushed and extremely angry:

"Don't ask me. I desire to take no part in the discussion of these people's affairs. I abhor the subject. It is an odious subject, an offensive subject, a subject that makes me sick, and I—— " And with his favourite right-arm flourish which sweeps away everything and settles it for ever, Mr. Podsnap sweeps these inconveniently unexplainable wretches, who have lived beyond their means and gone to total smash, off the face of the universe.

Eugene, leaning back in his chair, is observing Mr. Podsnap

with an irreverent face, and may be about to offer a new suggestion, when the Analytical is beheld in collision with the Coachman; the Coachman manifesting a purpose of coming at the company with a silver salver, as though intent upon making a collection for his wife and family; the Analytical cutting him off at the sideboard. The superior stateliness, if not the superior generalship, of the Analytical, prevails over a man who is as nothing off the box; and the Coachman, yielding up his salver, retires defeated.

Then, the Analytical, perusing a scrap of paper lying on the salver, with the air of a literary Censor, adjusts it, takes his time about going to the table with it, and presents it to Mr. Eugene Wrayburn. Whereupon the pleasant Tippins says aloud, "The Lord Chancellor has resigned!"

With distracting coolness and slowness—for he knows the curiosity of the Charmer to be always devouring—Eugene makes a pretence of getting out an eye-glass, polishing it, and reading the paper with difficulty, long after he has seen what is written on it. What is written on it in wet ink, is:

"Young Blight."

"Waiting?" says Eugene over his shoulder, in confidence with the Analytical.

"Waiting," returns the Analytical, in responsive confidence.

Eugene looks "Excuse me," towards Mrs. Veneering, goes out, and finds Young Blight, Mortimer's clerk, at the hall-door.

"You told me to bring him, sir, to wherever you was, if he come while you was out and I was in," says that discreet young gentleman, standing on tiptoe to whisper; "and I've brought him."

"Sharp boy. Where is he?" asks Eugene.

"He's in a cab, sir, at the door. I thought it best not to show him, you see, if it could be helped; for he's a shaking all over, like"—Blight's simile is perhaps inspired by the surrounding dishes of sweets—"like Glue Monge."

"Sharp boy again," returns Eugene. "I'll go to him."

Goes out straightway, and, leisurely leaning his arms on the open window of a cab in waiting, looks in at Mr. Dolls who has brought his own atmosphere with him, and would seem from its odour to have brought it, for convenience of carriage, in a rum-cask.

"Now, Dolls, wake up!"

"Mist Wrayburn? Drection! Fifteen shillings!"

After carefully reading the dingy scrap of paper handed to him, and as carefully tucking it into his waistcoat pocket, Eugene tells out the money; beginning incautiously by telling the first shilling into Mr. Dolls's hand, which instantly jerks it out of window; and ending by telling the fifteen shillings on the seat.

"Give him a ride back to Charing Cross, sharp boy, and there get rid of him."

Returning to the dining-room, and pausing for an instant behind the screen at the door, Eugene overhears, above the hum and clatter, the fair Tippins saying: "I am dying to ask him what he was called out for!"

"Are you?" mutters Eugene; "then perhaps if you can't ask him, you'll die. So I'll be a benefactor to society, and go. A stroll and a cigar, and I can think this over. Think this over." Thus, with a thoughtful face, he finds his hat and cloak, unseen of the Analytical, and goes his way.

BOOK IV

A TURNING

CHAPTER I

SETTING TRAPS

PLASHWATER Weir-Mill Lock looked tranquil and pretty on an evening in the summer time. A soft air stirred the leaves of the fresh green trees, and passed like a smooth shadow over the river, and like a smoother shadow over the yielding grass. The voice of the falling water, like the voices of the sea and the wind, was an outer memory to a contemplative listener; but not particularly so to Mr. Riderhood, who sat on one of the blunt wooden levers of his lock-gates, dozing. Wine must be got into a butt by some agency before it can be drawn out: and the wine of sentiment never having been got into Mr. Riderhood by any agency, nothing in nature tapped him.

As the Rogue sat, ever and again nodding himself off his balance, his recovery was always attended by an angry stare and growl, as if, in the absence of any one else, he had aggressive inclinations towards himself. In one of these starts the cry of "Lock, ho! Lock!" prevented his relapse into a doze. Shaking himself as he got up, like the surly brute he was, he gave his growl a responsive twist at the end, and turned his face down-stream to see who hailed.

It was an amateur sculler, well up to his work though taking it easily, in so light a boat that the Rogue remarked : " A little less on you, and you'd a'most ha' been a Wagerbut ; " then went to work at his windlass handles and sluices, to let the sculler in. As the latter stood in his boat, holding on by the boat-hook to the woodwork at the lock-side, waiting for the gates to open, Rogue Riderhood recognised his " T'other governor," Mr. Eugene Wrayburn ; who was, however, too indifferent or too much engaged to recognise him.

The creaking lock-gates opened slowly, and the light boat passed in as soon as there was room enough, and the creaking lock-gates closed upon it, and it floated low down in the dock between the two sets of gates, until the water should rise and the second gates should open and let it out. When Riderhood had run to his second windlass and turned it, and while he leaned against the lever of that gate to help it to swing open presently, he noticed, lying to rest under the green hedge by the towing-path astern of the Lock, a Bargeman.

The water rose and rose as the sluice poured in, dispersing the scum which had formed behind the lumbering gates, and sending the boat up, so that the sculler gradually rose like an apparition against the light from the bargeman's point of view. Riderhood observed that the bargeman rose too, leaning on his arm, and seemed to have his eyes fastened on the rising figure.

But, there was the toll to be taken, as the gates were now complaining and opening. The T'other governor tossed it ashore, twisted in a piece of paper, and as he did so, knew his man.

" Ay, ay ? It's you, is it, honest friend ? " said Eugene, seating himself preparatory to resuming his sculls. " You got the place then ? "

" I got the place, and no thanks to you for it, nor yet none to Lawyer Lightwood," gruffly answered Riderhood.

" We saved our recommendation, honest fellow," said

Eugene, "for the next candidate—the one who will offer himself when you are transported or hanged. Don't be long about it; will you be so good?"

So imperturbable was the air with which he gravely bent to his work that Riderhood remained staring at him, without having found a retort, until he had rowed past a line of wooden objects by the weir, which showed like huge teetotums standing at rest in the water, and was almost hidden by the drooping boughs on the left bank, as he rowed away, keeping out of the opposing current. It being then too late to retort with any effect—if that could ever have been done—the honest man confined himself to cursing and growling in a grim under-tone. Having then got his gates shut, he crossed back by his plank Lock-bridge to the towing-path side of the river.

If, in so doing, he took another glance at the bargeman, he did it by stealth. He cast himself on the grass by the Lock side, in an indolent way, with his back in that direction, and, having gathered a few blades, fell to chewing them. The dip of Eugene Wrayburn's sculls had become hardly audible in his ears when the bargeman passed him, putting the utmost width that he could between them, and keeping under the hedge. Then Riderhood sat up and took a long look at his figure, and then cried: "Hi—i—i! Lock, ho! Lock! Plashwater Weir-Mill Lock!"

The bargeman stopped, and looked back.

"Plashwater Weir-Mill Lock, T'otherest gov—er—nor—or —or—or!" cried Mr. Riderhood, with his hands to his mouth.

The bargeman turned back. Approaching nearer and nearer, the bargeman became Bradley Headstone, in rough water-side second-hand clothing.

"Wish I may die," said Riderhood, smiting his right leg, and laughing, as he sat on the grass, "if you ain't ha' been a imitating me, T'otherest governor! Never thought myself so good-looking afore!"

Truly, Bradley Headstone had taken careful note of the honest man's dress in the course of that night-walk they had had together. He must have committed it to memory, and slowly got it by heart. It was exactly reproduced in the dress he now wore. And whereas, in his own schoolmaster clothes, he usually looked as if they were the clothes of some other man, he now looked, in the clothes of some other man, or men, as if they were his own.

"*This* your Lock?" said Bradley, whose surprise had a genuine air; "they told me, where I last inquired, it was the third I should come to. This is only the second."

"It's my belief, governor," returned Riderhood, with a wink and shake of his head, "that you've dropped one in your counting. It ain't Locks as *you*'ve been giving your mind to. No, no!"

As he expressively jerked his pointing finger in the direction the boat had taken, a flush of impatience mounted into Bradley's face, and he looked anxiously up the river.

"It ain't Locks as *you*'ve been a-reckoning up," said Riderhood, when the schoolmaster's eyes came back again. "No, no!"

"What other calculations do you suppose I have been occupied with? Mathematics?"

"I never heerd it called that. It's a long word for it. Hows'ever, p'raps you call it so," said Riderhood, stubbornly chewing his grass.

"It. What?"

"I'll say them, instead of it, if you like," was the coolly growled reply. "It's safer talk too."

"What do you mean that I should understand by them?"

"Spites, affronts, offences giv' and took, deadly aggrawations, such like," answered Riderhood.

Do what Bradley Headstone would, he could not keep that former flush of impatience out of his face, or so master his eyes as to prevent their again looking anxiously up the river.

"Ha ha! Don't be afeerd, T'otherest," said Riderhood. "The T'other's got to make way agin the stream, and he takes it easy. You can soon come up with him. But wot's the good of saying that to you! *You* know how fur you could have outwalked him betwixt anywheres about where he lost the tide—say Richmond—and this, if you had had a mind to it."

"You think I have been following him?" said Bradley.

"I KNOW you have," said Riderhood.

"Well! I have, I have," Bradley admitted. "But," with another anxious look up the river, "he may land."

"Easy you! He won't be lost if he does land," said Riderhood. "He must leave his boat behind him. He can't make a bundle or a parcel on it, and carry it ashore with him under his arm."

"He was speaking to you just now," said Bradley, kneeling on one knee on the grass beside the Lock-keeper. "What did he say?"

"Cheek," said Riderhood.

"What?"

"Cheek," repeated Riderhood, with an angry oath; "cheek is what he said. He can't say nothing but cheek. I'd ha' liked to plump down aboard of him, neck and crop, with a heavy jump, and sunk him."

Bradley turned away his haggard face for a few moments, and then said, tearing up a tuft of grass:

"Damn him!"

"Hooroar!" cried Riderhood. "Does you credit. Hooroar! I cry chorus to the T'otherest."

"What turn," said Bradley, with an effort at self-repression that forced him to wipe his face, "did his insolence take to-day?"

"It took the turn," answered Riderhood, with sullen ferocity, "of hoping as I was getting ready to be hanged."

"Let him look to that," cried Bradley. "Let him look to that! It will be bad for him when men he has injured, and

265

at whom he has jeered, are thinking of getting hanged. Let *him* get ready for *his* fate, when that comes about. There was more meaning in what he said than he knew of, or he wouldn't have had brains enough to say it. Let him look to it; let him look to it! When men he has wronged, and on whom he has bestowed his insolence, are getting ready to be hanged, there is a death-bell ringing. And not for them."

Riderhood, looking fixedly at him, gradually arose from his recumbent posture while the schoolmaster said these words with the utmost concentration of rage and hatred. So, when the words were all spoken, he too kneeled on one knee on the grass, and the two men looked at one another.

"Oh!" said Riderhood, very deliberately spitting out the grass he had been chewing. "Then I make out, T'otherest, as he is a-going to her?"

"He left London," answered Bradley, "yesterday. I have hardly a doubt, this time, that at last he is going to her."

"You ain't sure, then?"

"I am as sure here," said Bradley, with a clutch at the breast of his coarse shirt, "as if it was written there;" with a blow or a stab at the sky.

"Ah! But judging from the looks on you," retorted Riderhood, completely ridding himself of his grass, and drawing his sleeve across his mouth, "you've made ekally sure afore, and have got disapinted. It has told upon you."

"Listen," said Bradley, in a low voice, bending forward to lay his hand upon the Lock-keeper's shoulder. "These are my holidays."

"Are they, by George!" muttered Riderhood, with his eyes on the passion-wasted face. "Your working-days must be stiff 'uns, if these is your holidays."

"And I have never left him," pursued Bradley, waving the interruption aside with an impatient hand, "since they began. And I never will leave him now, till I have seen him with her."

"And when you have seen him with her?" said Riderhood.

" —I'll come back to you."

Riderhood stiffened the knee on which he had been resting, got up, and looked gloomily at his new friend. After a few moments they walked side by side in the direction the boat had taken, as if by tacit consent; Bradley pressing forward, and Riderhood holding back; Bradley getting out his neat prim purse into his hand (a present made him by penny subscription among his pupils), and Riderhood unfolding his arms to smear his coat-cuff across his mouth with a thoughtful air.

" I have a pound for you," said Bradley.

" You've two," said Riderhood.

Bradley held a sovereign between his fingers. Slouching at his side with his eyes upon the towing-path, Riderhood held his left hand open, with a certain slight drawing action towards himself. Bradley dipped in his purse for another sovereign, and two chinked in Riderhood's hand, the drawing action of which, promptly strengthening, drew them home to his pocket.

" Now, I must follow him," said Bradley Headstone. " He takes this river-road—the fool!—to confuse observation, or divert attention, if not solely to baffle me. But he must have the power of making himself invisible before he can shake Me off."

Riderhood stopped. " If you don't get disapinted agin, T'otherest, maybe you'll put up at the Lock-house when you come back ? "

" I will."

Riderhood nodded, and the figure of the bargeman went its way along the soft turf by the side of the towing-path, keeping near the hedge and moving quickly. They had turned a point from which a long stretch of river was visible. A stranger to the scene might have been certain that here and there along the line of hedge a figure stood, watching the bargeman, and waiting for him to come up. So he himself had often believed at first, until his eyes became used

267

to the posts, bearing the dagger that slew Wat Tyler, in the City of London shield.

Within Mr. Riderhood's knowledge all daggers were as one. Even to Bradley Headstone, who could have told to the letter without book all about Wat Tyler, Lord Mayor Walworth, and the King, that it is dutiful for youth to know, there was but one subject living in the world for every sharp destructive instrument that summer evening. So Riderhood looking after him as he went, and he with his furtive hand laid upon the dagger as he passed it, and his eyes upon the boat, were much upon a par.

The boat went on, under the arching trees, and over their tranquil shadows in the water. The bargeman skulking on the opposite bank of the stream, went on after it. Sparkles of light showed Riderhood when and where the rower dipped his blades, until, even as he stood idly watching, the sun went down and the landscape was dyed red. And then the red had the appearance of fading out of it and mounting up to Heaven, as we say that blood, guiltily shed, does.

Turning back towards his Lock (he had not gone out of view of it), the Rogue pondered as deeply as it was within the contracted power of such a fellow to do. "Why did he copy my clothes? He could have looked like what he wanted to look like, without that." This was the subject-matter in his thoughts; in which, too, there came lumbering up, by times, like any half-floating and half-sinking rubbish in the river, the question, Was it done by accident? The setting of a trap for finding out whether it was accidentally done, soon superseded, as a practical piece of cunning, the abstruser inquiry why otherwise it was done. And he devised a means.

Rogue Riderhood went into his Lock-house, and brought forth, into the now sober grey light, his chest of clothes. Sitting on the grass beside it, he turned out, one by one, the articles it contained, until he came to a conspicuous bright red neckerchief stained black here and there by wear. It arrested his attention, and he sat pausing over it, until he took off the rusty colourless wisp that he wore round his throat, and substituted the red neckerchief, leaving the long ends flowing. "Now," said the Rogue, "if arter he sees me in this neckhankecher, I see him in a sim'lar neckhankecher, it won't be accident!" Elated by his device, he carried his chest in again and went to supper.

"Lock ho! Lock!" It was a light night, and a barge coming down summoned him out of a long doze. In due course he had let the barge through and was alone again, looking to the closing of his gates, when Bradley Headstone appeared before him, standing on the brink of the Lock.

"Halloa!" said Riderhood. "Back a'ready, T'otherest?"

"He has put up for the night, at an Angler's Inn," was the fatigued and hoarse reply. "He goes on, up the river, at six in the morning. I have come back for a couple of hours' rest."

"You want 'em," said Riderhood, making towards the schoolmaster by his plank bridge.

"I don't want them," returned Bradley, irritably, "because I would rather not have them, but would much prefer to follow him all night. However, if he won't lead, I can't follow. I have been waiting about, until I could discover, for a certainty, at what time he starts; if I couldn't have made sure of it, I should have stayed there.—This would be a bad pit for a man to be flung into with his hands tied. These slippery smooth walls would give him no chance. And I suppose those gates would suck him down?"

"Suck him down, or swaller him up, he wouldn't get out," said Riderhood. "Not even if his hands warn't tied, he wouldn't. Shut him in at both ends, and I'd give him a pint o' old ale ever to come up to me standing here."

Bradley looked down with a ghastly relish. "You run about the brink, and run across it, in this uncertain light, on a few inches' width of rotten wood," said he. "I wonder you have no thought of being drowned."

269

"I can't be!" said Riderhood.

"You can't be drowned?"

"No!" said Riderhood, shaking his head with an air of thorough conviction, "it's well known. I have been brought out o' drowning, and I can't be drowned. I wouldn't have that there busted B'lowbridger aware on it, or her people might make it tell agin the damages I mean to get. But it's well known to water-side characters like myself, that him as has been brought out o' drowning, can never be drowned."

Bradley smiled sourly at the ignorance he would have corrected in one of his pupils, and continued to look down into the water, as if the place had a gloomy fascination for him.

"You seem to like it," said Riderhood.

He took no notice, but stood looking down, as if he had not heard the words. There was a very dark expression on his face; an expression that the Rogue found it hard to understand. It was fierce, and full of purpose; but the purpose might have been as much against himself as against another. If he had stepped back for a spring, taken a leap, and thrown himself in, it would have been no surprising sequel to the look. Perhaps his troubled soul, set upon some violence, did hover for the moment between that violence and another.

"Didn't you say," asked Riderhood, after watching him for a while with a sidelong glance, "as you had come back for a couple o' hours' rest?" But even then he had to jog him with his elbow before he answered.

"Eh? Yes."

"Hadn't you better come in and take your couple o' hours' rest?"

"Thank you. Yes."

With the look of one just awakened, he followed Riderhood into the Lock-house, where the latter produced from a cupboard some cold salt beef and half a loaf, some gin in a bottle, and some water in a jug. The last he brought in, cool and dripping, from the river.

270

THE TEST OF THE RED NECKERCHIEF

" There, T'otherest," said Riderhood, stooping over him to put it on the table. " You'd better take a bite and a sup, afore you takes your snooze." The draggling ends of the red neckerchief caught the schoolmaster's eyes. Riderhood saw him look at it.

" Oh ! " thought that worthy. " You're a-taking notice, are you ? Come ! You shall have a good squint at it then." With which reflection he sat down on the other side of the table, threw open his vest, and made a pretence of re-tying the neckerchief with much deliberation.

Bradley ate and drank. As he sat at his platter and mug, Riderhood saw him, again and again, steal a look at the neckerchief, as if he were correcting his slow observation and prompting his sluggish memory. " When you're ready for your snooze," said the honest creature, " chuck yourself on my bed in the corner, T'otherest. It'll be broad day afore three. I'll call you early."

" I shall require no calling," answered Bradley. And soon afterwards, divesting himself only of his shoes and coat, laid himself down.

Riderhood, leaning back in his wooden arm-chair with his arms folded on his breast, looked at him lying with his right hand clenched in his sleep and his teeth set, until a film came over his own sight, and he slept too. He awoke to find that it was daylight, and that his visitor was already astir, and going out to the river-side to cool his head :—" Though I'm blest," muttered Riderhood at the Lock-house door, looking after him, " if I think there's water enough in all the Thames to do *that* for you ! " Within five minutes he had taken his departure, and was passing on into the calm distance as he had passed yesterday. Riderhood knew when a fish leaped, by his starting and glancing round.

" Lock ho ! Lock ! " at intervals all day, and " Lock ho ! Lock ! " thrice in the ensuing night, but no return of Bradley. The second day was sultry and oppressive. In the afternoon, a thunderstorm came up, and had but newly broken into a furious sweep of rain when he rushed in at the door, like the storm itself.

"You've seen him with her!" exclaimed Riderhood, starting up.

"I have."

"Where?"

"At his journey's end. His boat's hauled up for three days. I heard him give the order. Then, I saw him wait for her and meet her. I saw them"—he stopped as though he were suffocating, and began again—"I saw them walking side by side, last night."

"What did you do?"

"Nothing."

"What are you going to do?"

He dropped into a chair, and laughed. Immediately afterwards, a great spirt of blood burst from his nose.

"How does that happen?" asked Riderhood.

"I don't know. I can't keep it back. It has happened twice—three times—four times—I don't know how many times—since last night. I taste it, smell it, see it, it chokes me, and then it breaks out like this."

He went into the pelting rain again with his head bare, and, bending low over the river, and scooping up the water with his two hands, washed the blood away. All beyond his figure, as Riderhood looked from the door, was a vast dark curtain in solemn movement towards one quarter of the heavens. He raised his head and came back, wet from head to foot, but with the lower part of his sleeves, where he had dipped into the river, streaming water.

"Your face is like a ghost's," said Riderhood.

"Did you ever see a ghost?" was the sullen retort.

"I mean to say, you're quite wore out."

"That may well be. I have had no rest since I left here. I don't remember that I have so much as sat down since I left here."

"Lie down now, then," said Riderhood.

In the Lock-keeper's House

" I will if you'll give me something to quench my thirst first."

The bottle and jug were again produced, and he mixed a weak draught, and another, and drank both in quick succession. "You asked me something," he said then.

" No, I didn't," replied Riderhood.

" I tell you," retorted Bradley, turning upon him in a wild and desperate manner, "you asked me something, before I went out to wash my face in the river."

" Oh ! Then ? " said Riderhood, backing a little. " I asked you wot you wos a-going to do."

" How can a man in this state know ? " he answered, protesting with both his tremulous hands, with an action so vigorously angry that he shook the water from his sleeves upon the floor, as if he had wrung them. " How can I plan anything, if I haven't sleep ? "

" Why, that's what I as good as said," returned the other. " Didn't I say lie down ? "

" Well, perhaps you did."

" Well ! Anyways I says it again. Sleep where you slept last ; the sounder and longer you can sleep, the better you'll know arterwards what you're up to."

His pointing to the truckle bed in the corner seemed gradually to bring that poor couch to Bradley's wandering remembrance. He slipped off his worn down-trodden shoes, and cast himself heavily, all wet as he was, upon the bed.

Riderhood sat down in his wooden arm-chair, and looked through the window at the lightning, and listened to the thunder. But his thoughts were far from being absorbed by the thunder and the lightning, for again, and again, and again he looked very curiously at the exhausted man upon the bed. The man had turned up the collar of the rough coat he wore, to shelter himself from the storm, and had buttoned it about his neck. Unconscious of that, and of most things, he had left the coat so, both when he had laved his face in the river, and when he had cast himself upon the bed ; though it would have been much easier to him if he had loosened it.

The thunder rolled heavily, and the forked lightning seemed to make jagged rents in every part of the vast curtain without, as Riderhood sat by the window, glancing at the bed. Sometimes he saw the man upon the bed, by a red light; sometimes by a blue ; sometimes he scarcely saw him in the darkness of the storm ; sometimes he saw nothing of him in the blinding glare of palpitating white fire. Anon, the rain would come again with a tremendous rush, and the river would seem to rise to meet it, and a blast of wind, bursting upon the door, would flutter the hair and dress of the man, as if invisible messengers were come around the bed to carry him away. From all these phases of the storm, Riderhood would turn, as if they were interruptions—rather striking interruptions possibly, but interruptions still—of his scrutiny of the sleeper.

" He sleeps sound," he said within himself; " yet he's that up to me and that noticing of me that my getting out of my chair may awake him, when a rattling peal won't; let alone my touching of him."

He very cautiously rose to his feet. " T'otherest," he said, in a low, calm voice, " are you a-lying easy ? There's a chill in the air, governor. Shall I put a coat over you ? "

No answer.

" That's about what it is a'ready, you see," muttered Riderhood in a lower and a different voice; " a coat over you, a coat over you ! "

The sleeper moving an arm, he sat down again in his chair, and feigned to watch the storm from the window. It was a grand spectacle, but not so grand as to keep his eyes, for half a minute together, from stealing a look at the man upon the bed.

It was at the concealed throat of the sleeper that Riderhood so often looked so curiously, until the sleep seemed to deepen into the stupor of the dead-tired in mind and body.

Then, Riderhood came from the window cautiously, and stood by the bed.

"Poor man!" he murmured in a low tone, with a crafty face, and a very watchful eye and ready foot, lest he should start up; "this here coat of his must make him uneasy in his sleep. Shall I loosen it for him, and make him more comfortable? Ah! I think I ought to do it, poor man. I think I will."

He touched the first button with a very cautious hand, and a step backward. But the sleeper remaining in profound unconsciousness, he touched the other buttons with a more assured hand, and perhaps the more lightly on that account. Softly and slowly, he opened the coat and drew it back.

The draggling ends of a bright-red neckerchief were then disclosed, and he had even been at the pains of dipping parts of it in some liquid, to give it the appearance of having become stained by wear. With a much-perplexed face, Riderhood looked from it to the sleeper, and from the sleeper to it, and finally crept back to his chair, and there, with his hand to his chin, sat long in a brown study, looking at both.

CHAPTER II

MR. and Mrs. Lammle had come to breakfast with Mr. and Mrs. Boffin. They were not absolutely uninvited, but had pressed themselves with so much urgency on the golden couple, that evasion of the honour and pleasure of their company would have been difficult, if desired. They were in a charming state of mind, were Mr. and Mrs. Lammle, and almost as fond of Mr. and Mrs. Boffin as of one another.

"My dear Mrs. Boffin," said Mrs. Lammle, "it imparts new life to me, to see my Alfred in confidential communication with Mr. Boffin. The two were formed to become intimate. So much simplicity combined with so much force of character, such natural sagacity united to such amiability and gentleness—those are the distinguishing characteristics of both."

This being said aloud, gave Mr. Lammle an opportunity, as he came with Mr. Boffin from the window to the breakfast table, of taking up his dear and honoured wife.

"My Sophronia," said that gentleman, "your too partial estimate of your poor husband's character—— "

"No! Not too partial, Alfred," urged the lady, tenderly moved; "never say that."

"My child, your favourable opinion, then, of your husband —you don't object to that phrase, darling?"

"How can I, Alfred?"

" Your favourable opinion, then, my Precious, does less than justice to Mr. Boffin, and more than justice to me."

" To the first charge, Alfred, I plead guilty. But to the second, oh no, no ! "

" Less than justice to Mr. Boffin, Sophronia," said Mr. Lammle, soaring into a tone of moral grandeur, " because it represents Mr. Boffin as on my lower level; more than justice to me, Sophronia, because it represents me as on Mr. Boffin's higher level. Mr. Boffin bears and forbears far more than I could."

" Far more than you could for yourself, Alfred ? "

" My love, that is not the question."

" Not the question, Lawyer ? " said Mrs. Lammle, archly.

" No, dear Sophronia. From my lower level, I regard Mr. Boffin as too generous, as possessed of too much clemency, as being too good to persons who are unworthy of him and ungrateful to him. To those noble qualities I can lay no claim. On the contrary, they rouse my indignation when I see them in action."

" Alfred ! "

" They rouse my indignation, my dear, against the unworthy persons, and give me a combative desire to stand between Mr. Boffin and all such persons. Why ? Because in my lower nature I am more worldly and less delicate. Not being so magnanimous as Mr. Boffin, I feel his injuries more than he does himself, and feel more capable of opposing his injurers."

It struck Mrs. Lammle that it appeared rather difficult this morning to bring Mr. and Mrs. Boffin into agreeable conversation. Here had been several lures thrown out, and neither of them had uttered a word. Here were she, Mrs. Lammle, and her husband discoursing at once affectingly and effectively, but discoursing alone. Assuming that the dear old creatures were impressed by what they heard, still one would like to be sure of it, the more so, as at least one of the dear old creatures was somewhat pointedly referred to.

If the dear old creatures were too bashful or too dull to assume their required places in the discussion, why then it would seem desirable that the dear old creatures should be taken by their heads and shoulders and brought into it.

"But is not my husband saying, in effect," asked Mrs. Lammle, therefore, with an innocent air, of Mr. and Mrs. Boffin, "that he becomes unmindful of his own temporary misfortunes in his admiration of another whom he is burning to serve? And is not that making an admission that his nature is a generous one? I am wretched in argument, but surely this is so, dear Mr. and Mrs. Boffin?"

Still, neither Mr. nor Mrs. Boffin said a word. He sat with his eyes on his plate, eating his muffins and ham, and she sat shyly looking at the teapot. Mrs. Lammle's innocent appeal was merely thrown into the air to mingle with the steam of the urn. Glancing towards Mr. and Mrs. Boffin, she very slightly raised her eyebrows, as though inquiring of her husband: "Do I notice anything wrong here?"

Mr. Lammle, who had found his chest effective on a variety of occasions, manœuvred his capacious shirt-front into the largest demonstration possible, and then smiling, retorted on his wife, thus:

"Sophronia, darling, Mr. and Mrs. Boffin will remind you of the old adage, that self-praise is no recommendation."

"Self-praise, Alfred? Do you mean because we are one and the same?"

"No, my dear child. I mean that you cannot fail to remember, if you reflect for a single moment, that what you are pleased to compliment me upon feeling in the case of Mr. Boffin, you have yourself confided to me as your own feeling in the case of Mrs. Boffin."

("I shall be beaten by this Lawyer," Mrs. Lammle gaily whispered to Mrs. Boffin. "I am afraid I must admit it, if he presses me, for it's damagingly true.")

Several white dints began to come and go about Mr. Lammle's nose, as he observed that Mrs. Boffin merely looked up from the teapot for a moment with an embarrassed smile, which was no smile, and then looked down again.

"Do you admit the charge, Sophronia?" inquired Alfred, in a rallying tone.

"Really, I think," said Mrs. Lammle, still gaily, "I must throw myself on the protection of the Court. Am I bound to answer that question, my Lord?" To Mr. Boffin.

"You needn't if you don't like, ma'am," was his answer. "It's not of the least consequence."

Both husband and wife glanced at him very doubtfully. His manner was grave, but not coarse, and derived some dignity from a certain repressed dislike of the tone of the conversation.

Again Mrs. Lammle raised her eyebrows for instruction from her husband. He replied in a slight nod, "Try 'em again."

"To protect myself against the suspicion of covert self-laudation, my dear Mrs. Boffin," said the airy Mrs. Lammle, "therefore, I must tell you how it was."

"No. Pray don't," Mr. Boffin interposed.

Mrs. Lammle turned to him laughingly. "The Court objects?"

"Ma'am," said Mr. Boffin, "the Court (if I am the Court) does object. The Court objects for two reasons. First, because the Court don't think it fair. Secondly, because the dear old lady, Mrs. Court (if I am Mr.) gets distressed by it."

A very remarkable wavering between two bearings—between her propitiatory bearing there, and her defiant bearing at Mr. Twemlow's—was observable on the part of Mrs. Lammle as she said: "What does the Court not consider fair?"

"Letting you go on," replied Mr. Boffin, nodding his head soothingly, as who should say, We won't be harder on you than we can help; we'll make the best of it. "It's not above-board and it's not fair. When the old lady is uncomfortable, there's sure to be good reason for it. I see she is uncomfortable, and I plainly see this is the good reason wherefore. *Have* you breakfasted, ma'am?"

Mrs. Lammle, settling into her defiant manner, pushed her plate away, looked at her husband, and laughed; but by no means gaily.

"Have *you* breakfasted, sir?" inquired Mr. Boffin.

"Thank you," replied Alfred, showing all his teeth. "If Mrs. Boffin will oblige me, I'll take another cup of tea."

He spilled a little of it over the chest which ought to have been so effective, and which had done so little; but on the whole drank it with something of an air, though the coming and going dints got almost as large, the while, as if they had been made by pressure of the teaspoon. "A thousand thanks," he then observed. "I have breakfasted."

"Now, which," said Mr. Boffin softly, taking out a pocket-book, "which of you two is Cashier?"

"Sophronia, my dear," remarked her husband, as he leaned back in his chair, waving his right hand towards her, while he hung his left hand by the thumb in the arm-hole of his waistcoat: "it shall be your department."

"I would rather," said Mr. Boffin, "that it was your husband's, ma'am, because—but never mind because. I would rather have to do with him. However, what I have to say, I will say with as little offence as possible: if I can say it without any, I shall be heartily glad. You two have done me a service, a very great service, in doing what you did (my old lady knows what it was), and I have put into this envelope a bank note for a hundred pound. I consider the service well worth a hundred pound, and I am well pleased to pay the money. Would you do me the favour to take it, and likewise to accept my thanks?"

With a haughty action, and without looking towards him, Mrs. Lammle held out her left hand, and into it Mr. Boffin put the little packet. When she had conveyed it to her bosom, Mr. Lammle had the appearance of feeling relieved, and breathing more freely, as not having been quite certain that the hundred pounds were his, until the note had been safely transferred out of Mr. Boffin's keeping into his own Sophronia's.

"It is not impossible," said Mr. Boffin, addressing Alfred, "that you have had some general idea, sir, of replacing Rokesmith, in course of time?"

"It is not," assented Alfred, with a glittering smile and a great deal of nose, "not impossible."

"And perhaps, ma'am," pursued Mr. Boffin, addressing Sophronia, "you have been so kind as to take up my old lady in your own mind, and to do her the honour of turning the question over whether you mightn't one of these days have her in charge, like? Whether you mightn't be a sort of Miss Bella Wilfer to her, and something more?"

"I should hope," returned Mrs. Lammle, with a scornful look and in a loud voice, "that if I were anything to your wife, sir, I could hardly fail to be something more than Miss Bella Wilfer, as you call her."

"What do *you* call her, ma'am?" asked Mr. Boffin.

Mrs. Lammle disdained to reply, and sat defiantly beating one foot on the ground.

"Again I think I may say, that's not impossible. Is it, sir?" asked Mr. Boffin, turning to Alfred.

"It is not," said Alfred, smiling assent as before, "not impossible."

"Now," said Mr. Boffin, gently, "it won't do. I don't wish to say a single word that might be afterwards remembered as unpleasant; but it won't do."

"Sophronia, my love," her husband repeated in a bantering manner, "you hear? It won't do."

"No," said Mr. Boffin, with his voice still dropped, "it really won't. You positively must excuse us. If you'll go your way, we'll go ours, and so I hope this affair ends to the satisfaction of all parties."

Mrs. Lammle gave him a look of a decidedly dissatisfied

281

party demanding exemption from the category; but said nothing.

"The best thing we can make of the affair," said Mr. Boffin, "is a matter of business, and as a matter of business it's brought to a conclusion. You have done me a great service, a very great service, and I have paid you for it. Is there any objection to the price?"

Mr. and Mrs. Lammle looked at one another across the table, but neither could say that there was. Mr. Lammle shrugged his shoulders, and Mrs. Lammle sat rigid.

"Very good," said Mr. Boffin. "We hope (my old lady and me) that you'll give us credit for taking the plainest and honestest short-cut that could be taken under the circumstances. We have talked it over with a deal of care (my old lady and me), and we have felt that at all to lead you on, or even at all to let you go on of your own selves, wouldn't be the right thing. So I have openly given you to understand that—" Mr. Boffin sought for a new turn of speech, but could find none so expressive as his former one, repeated in a confidential tone, "—that it won't do. If I could have put the case more pleasantly I would; but I hope I haven't put it very unpleasantly; at all events I haven't meant to. So," said Mr. Boffin, by way of peroration, "wishing you well in the way you go, we now conclude with the observation that perhaps you'll go it."

Mr. Lammle rose with an impudent laugh on his side of the table, and Mrs. Lammle rose with a disdainful frown on hers. At this moment a hasty foot was heard on the staircase, and Georgiana Podsnap broke into the room, unannounced and in tears.

"Oh, my dear Sophronia," cried Georgiana, wringing her hands as she ran up to embrace her, "to think that you and Alfred should be ruined! Oh, my poor dear Sophronia, to think that you should have had a Sale at your house after all your kindness to me! Oh, Mr. and Mrs. Boffin, pray forgive me for this intrusion, but you don't know how fond

I was of Sophronia when Pa wouldn't let me go there any more, or what I have felt for Sophronia since I heard from Ma of her having been brought low in the world. You don't, you can't, you never can, think how I have lain awake at night and cried for my good Sophronia, my first and only friend!"

Mrs. Lammle's manner changed under the poor silly girl's embraces, and she turned extremely pale: directing one appealing look, first to Mrs. Boffin, and then to Mr. Boffin. Both understood her instantly, with a more delicate subtlety than much better educated people, whose perception came less directly from the heart, could have brought to bear upon the case.

"I haven't a minute," said poor little Georgiana, "to stay. I am out shopping early with Ma, and I said I had a head-ache and got Ma to leave me outside in the phaeton, in Piccadilly, and ran round to Sackville Street, and heard that Sophronia was here, and then Ma came to see, oh, such a dreadful old stony woman from the country in a turban in Portland Place, and I said I wouldn't go up with Ma, but would drive round and leave cards for the Boffins, which is taking a liberty with the name ; but oh, my goodness ! I am distracted, and the phaeton's at the door, and what would Pa say if he knew it ! "

"Don't ye be timid, my dear," said Mrs. Boffin. "You came in to see us."

"Oh, no, I didn't," cried Georgiana. "It's very impolite, I know, but I came to see my poor Sophronia, my only friend. Oh! how I felt the separation, my dear Sophronia, before I knew you were brought low in the world, and how much more I feel it now ! "

There were actually tears in the bold woman's eyes, as the soft-headed and soft-hearted girl twined her arms about her neck.

"But I've come on business," said Georgiana, sobbing and drying her face, and then searching in a little reticule, "and

283

OUR MUTUAL FRIEND

if I don't despatch it I shall have come for nothing, and oh good gracious! what would Pa say if he knew of Sackville Street, and what would Ma say if she was kept waiting on the doorsteps of that dreadful turban, and there never were such pawing horses as ours unsettling my mind every moment more and more when I want more mind than I have got, by pawing up Mr. Boffin's street where they have no business to be. Oh! where is, where is it? Oh! I can't find it!" All this time sobbing, and searching in the little reticule.

"What do you miss, my dear?" asked Mr. Boffin, stepping forward.

"Oh! it's little enough," replied Georgiana, "because Ma always treats me as if I was in the nursery (I am sure I wish I was!), but I hardly ever spend it, and it has mounted up to fifteen pounds, Sophronia, and I hope three five-pound notes are better than nothing, though so little, so little! And now I have found that—oh, my goodness! there's the other gone next! Oh no, it isn't, here it is!"

With that, always sobbing and searching in the reticule, Georgiana produced a necklace.

"Ma says chits and jewels have no business together," pursued Georgiana, "and that's the reason why I have no trinkets except this; but I suppose my aunt Hawkinson was of a different opinion, because she left me this, though I used to think she might just as well have buried it, for it's always kept in jeweller's cotton. However, here it is, I am thankful to say, and of use at last, and you'll sell it, dear Sophronia, and buy things with it."

"Give it to me," said Mr. Boffin, gently taking it. "I'll see that it's properly disposed of."

"Oh! are you such a friend of Sophronia's, Mr. Boffin?" cried Georgiana. "Oh, how good of you! Oh, my gracious! there was something else, and it's gone out of my head! Oh no, it isn't, I remember what it was. My grandmamma's property, that'll come to me when I am of age, Mr. Boffin, will be all my own, and neither Pa nor Ma nor anybody else will have any control over it, and what I wish to do is to make some of it over somehow to Sophronia and Alfred, by signing something somewhere that'll prevail on somebody to advance them something. I want them to have something handsome to bring them up in the world again. Oh, my goodness me! Being such a friend of my dear Sophronia's, you won't refuse me, will you?"

"No, no," said Mr. Boffin, "it shall be seen to."

"Oh, thank you, thank you!" cried Georgiana. "If my maid had a little note and half a crown, I could run round to the pastrycook's to sign something, or I could sign something in the square if somebody would come and cough for me to let 'em in with the key, and would bring a pen and ink with 'em and a bit of blotting-paper. Oh, my gracious! I must tear myself away, or Pa and Ma will both find out! Dear, dear Sophronia good, good-bye!"

The credulous little creature again embraced Mrs. Lammle most affectionately, and then held out her hand to Mr. Lammle.

"Good-bye, dear Mr. Lammle—I mean Alfred. You won't think after to-day that I have deserted you and Sophronia because you have been brought low in the world, will you? Oh me! oh me! I have been crying my eyes out of my head, and Ma will be sure to ask me what's the matter. Oh, take me down, somebody, please, please, please!"

Mr. Boffin took her down, and saw her driven away, with her poor little red eyes and weak chin peering over the great apron of the custard-coloured phaeton, as if she had been ordered to expiate some childish misdemeanour by going to bed in the daylight, and were peeping over the counterpane in a miserable flutter of repentance and low spirits. Returning to the breakfast-room, he found Mrs. Lammle still standing on her side of the table, and Mr. Lammle on his side.

"I'll take care," said Mr. Boffin, showing the money and the necklace, "that these are soon given back."

Mrs. Lammle had taken up her parasol from a side table, and stood sketching with it on the pattern of the damask cloth, as she had sketched on the pattern of Mr. Twemlow's papered wall.

"You will not undeceive her, I hope, Mr. Boffin?" she said, turning her head towards him, but not her eyes.

"No," said Mr. Boffin.

"I mean, as to the worth and value of her friend," Mrs. Lammle explained, in a measured voice, and with an emphasis on her last word.

"No," he returned. "I may try to give a hint at her home that she is in want of kind and careful protection, but I shall say no more than that to her parents, and I shall say nothing to the young lady herself."

"Mr. and Mrs. Boffin," said Mrs. Lammle, still sketching, and seeming to bestow great pains upon it, "there are not many people, I think, who, under the circumstances, would have been so considerate and sparing as you have been to me just now. Do you care to be thanked?"

"Thanks are always worth having," said Mrs. Boffin, in her ready good nature.

"Then thank you both."

"Sophronia," asked her husband, mockingly, "are you sentimental?"

"Well, well, my good sir," Mr. Boffin interposed, "it's a very good thing to think well of another person, and it's a very good thing to be thought well of *by* another person. Mrs. Lammle will be none the worse for it, if she is."

"Much obliged. But I asked Mrs. Lammle if she was."

She stood sketching on the table-cloth, with her face clouded and set, and was silent.

"Because," said Alfred, "I am disposed to be sentimental myself, on your appropriation of the jewels and the money, Mr. Boffin. As our little Georgiana said, three five-pound notes are better than nothing, and if you sell a necklace you can buy things with the produce."

"*If* you sell it," was Mr. Boffin's comment, as he put it in his pocket.

Alfred followed it with his looks, and also greedily pursued the notes until they vanished into Mr. Boffin's waistcoat pocket. Then he directed a look, half exasperating and half jeering, at his wife. She still stood sketching; but, as she sketched, there was a struggle within her, which found expression in the depth of the few last lines of the parasol point indented into the table-cloth, and then some tears fell from her eyes.

" Why, confound the woman," exclaimed Lammle, " she *is* sentimental ! "

She walked to the window, flinching under his angry stare, looked out for a moment, and turned round quite coldly.

" You have had no former cause of complaint on the sentimental score, Alfred, and you will have none in future. It is not worth your noticing. We go abroad soon, with the money we have earned here ? "

" You know we do ; you know we must."

" There is no fear of my taking any sentiment with me. I should soon be eased of it, if I did. But it will be all left behind. It *is* all left behind. Are you ready, Alfred ? "

" What the deuce have I been waiting for but you, Sophronia ? "

" Let us go then. I am sorry I have delayed our dignified departure."

She passed out and he followed her. Mr. and Mrs. Boffin had the curiosity softly to raise a window and look after them as they went down the long street. They walked arm in arm, showily enough, but without appearing to interchange a syllable. It might have been fanciful to suppose that under their outer bearing there was something of the shamed air of two cheats who were linked together by concealed hand-cuffs ; but not so, to suppose that they were haggardly weary of one another, of themselves, and of all this world. In turning the street corner they might have turned out of this world, for anything Mr. and Mrs. Boffin ever saw of them to the contrary ; for they set eyes on the Lammles never more.

287

CHAPTER III

THE evening of that day being one of the reading evenings at the Bower, Mr. Boffin kissed Mrs. Boffin after a five-o'clock dinner, and trotted out, nursing his big stick in both arms, so that, as of old, it seemed to be whispering in his ear. He carried so very attentive an expression on his counte-nance, that it appeared as if the confidential discourse of the big stick required to be followed closely. Mr. Boffin's face was like the face of a thoughtful listener to an intricate com-munication, and, in trotting along, he occasionally glanced at that companion with the look of a man who was inter-posing the remark, "You don't mean it!"

Mr. Boffin and his stick went on alone together, until they arrived at certain cross-ways where they would be likely to fall in with any one coming, at about the same time, from Clerkenwell to the Bower. Here they stopped, and Mr. Boffin consulted his watch.

"It wants five minutes, good, to Venus's appointment," said he. "I'm rather early."

But Venus was a punctual man, and, even as Mr. Boffin replaced his watch in its pocket, was to be descried coming towards him. He quickened his pace on seeing Mr. Boffin already at the place of meeting, and was soon at his side.

"Thank'ee, Venus," said Mr. Boffin. "Thank'ee, thank'ee, thank'ee!"

It would not have been very evident why he thanked the anatomist, but for his furnishing the explanation in what he went on to say.

" All right, Venus, all right. Now, that you've been to see me, and have consented to keep up the appearance before Wegg of remaining in it for a time, I have got a sort of a backer. All right, Venus. Thank'ee, Venus. Thank'ee, thank'ee, thank'ee ! "

Mr. Venus shook the proffered hand with a modest air, and they pursued the direction of the Bower.

" Do you think Wegg is likely to drop down upon me to-night, Venus ? " inquired Mr. Boffin, wistfully, as they went along.

" I think he is, sir."

" Have you any particular reason for thinking so, Venus ? "

" Well, sir," returned the personage, " the fact is, he has given me another look-in, to make sure of what he calls our stock-in-trade being correct, and he has mentioned his intention that he was not to be put off beginning with you the very next time you should come. And this," hinted Mr. Venus, delicately, " being the very next time, you know, sir—— "

" —Why, therefore, you suppose he'll turn to at the grind-stone, eh, Venus ? " said Mr. Boffin.

" Just so, sir."

Mr. Boffin took his nose in his hand, as if it were already excoriated, and the sparks were beginning to fly out of that feature. " He's a terrible fellow, Venus ; he's an awful fellow. I don't know how ever I shall go through with it. You must stand by me, Venus, like a good man and true. You'll do all you can to stand by me, Venus ; won't you ? "

Mr. Venus replied with the assurance that he would ; and Mr. Boffin, looking anxious and dispirited, pursued the way in silence until they rang at the Bower gate. The stumping approach of Wegg was soon heard behind it, and as it turned upon its hinges he became visible with his hand on the lock.

"Mr. Boffin, sir?" he remarked. "You're quite a stranger!"

"Yes. I've been otherwise occupied, Wegg."

"Have you indeed, sir?" returned the literary gentleman, with a threatening sneer. "Hah! I've been looking for you, sir, rather what I may call specially."

"You don't say so, Wegg?"

"Yes, I do say so, sir. And if you hadn't come round to me to-night, dash my wig if I wouldn't have come round to you to-morrow. Now! I tell you!"

"Nothing wrong, I hope, Wegg?"

"Oh no, Mr. Boffin," was the ironical answer. "Nothing wrong! What should be wrong in Boffinses Bower! Step in, sir.

'If you'll come to the Bower I've shaded for you,
  Your bed shan't be roses all spangled with doo :
  Will you, will you, will you, will you, come to the Bower?
  Oh, won't you, won't you, won't you, won't you, come to the Bower?'"

An unholy glare of contradiction and offence shone in the eyes of Mr. Wegg, as he turned the key on his patron, after ushering him into the yard with this vocal quotation. Mr. Boffin's air was crestfallen and submissive. Whispered Wegg to Venus, as they crossed the yard behind him : "Look at the worm and minion; he's down in the mouth already." Whispered Venus to Wegg : "That's because I've told him. I've prepared the way for you."

Mr. Boffin, entering the usual chamber, laid his stick upon the settle usually reserved for him, thrust his hands into his pockets, and, with his shoulders raised and his hat drooping back upon them, looked disconsolately at Wegg. "My friend and partner, Mr. Venus, gives me to understand," remarked that man of might, addressing him, "that you are aware of our power over you. Now, when you have took your hat off, we'll go into that pint."

Mr. Boffin shook it off with one shake, so that it dropped on the floor behind him, and remained in his former attitude with his former rueful look upon him.

" First of all, I'm a-going to call you Boffin, for short," said Wegg. " If you don't like it, it's open to you to lump it."

" I don't mind it, Wegg," Mr. Boffin replied.

" That's lucky for you, Boffin. Now, do you want to be read to ? "

" I don't particularly care about it to-night, Wegg."

" Because if you did want," pursued Mr. Wegg, the brilliancy of whose point was dimmed by his having been unexpectedly answered : " you wouldn't be. I've been your slave long enough. I'm not to be trampled under-foot by a dustman any more. With the single exception of the salary, I renounce the whole and total sitiwation."

" Since you say it is to be so, Wegg," returned Mr. Boffin, with folded hands, " I suppose it must be."

" *I* suppose it must be," Wegg retorted. " Next (to clear the ground before coming to business), you've placed in this yard a skulking, a sneaking, and a sniffing menial."

" He hadn't a cold in his head when I sent him here," said Mr. Boffin.

" Boffin ! " retorted Wegg, " I warn you not to attempt a joke with me ! "

Here Mr. Venus interposed, and remarked that he conceived Mr. Boffin to have taken the description literally ; the rather, forasmuch as he, Mr. Venus, had himself supposed the menial to have contracted an affliction or a habit of the nose, involving a serious drawback on the pleasures of social intercourse, until he had discovered that Mr. Wegg's description of him was to be accepted as merely figurative.

" Any how, and every how," said Wegg, " he has been planted here, and he is here. Now, I won't have him here. So I call upon Boffin, before I say another word, to fetch him in and send him packing to the right-about."

The unsuspecting Sloppy was at that moment airing his

291

many buttons within view of the window. Mr. Boffin, after a short interval of impassive discomfiture, opened the window and beckoned him to come in.

"I call upon Boffin," said Wegg, with one arm a-kimbo and his head on one side, like a bullying counsel pausing for an answer from a witness, "to inform that menial that I am Master here."

In humble obedience, when the button-gleaming Sloppy entered, Mr. Boffin said to him : "Sloppy, my fine fellow, Mr. Wegg is Master here. He doesn't want you, and you are to go from here."

"For good ! " Mr. Wegg severely stipulated.

"For good," said Mr. Boffin.

Sloppy stared, with both his eyes and all his buttons, and his mouth wide open ; but was without loss of time escorted forth by Silas Wegg, pushed out at the yard gate by the shoulders, and locked out.

"The atmospere," said Wegg, stumping back into the room again, a little reddened by his late exertion, "is now freer for the purposes of respiration. Mr. Venus, sir, take a chair. Boffin, you may sit down."

Mr. Boffin, still with his hands ruefully stuck in his pockets, sat on the edge of the settle, shrunk into a small compass, and eyed the potent Silas with conciliatory looks.

"This gentleman," said Silas Wegg, pointing out Venus, "this gentleman, Boffin, is more milk and watery with you than I'll be. But he hasn't borne the Roman yoke as I have, nor yet he hasn't been required to pander to your depraved appetite for miserly characters."

"I never meant, my dear Wegg—" Mr. Boffin was beginning, when Silas stopped him.

"Hold your tongue, Boffin ! Answer when you're called upon to answer. You'll find you've got quite enough to do. Now, you're aware—are you—that you're in possession of property to which you've no right at all? Are you aware of that ? "

"Venus tells me so," said Mr. Boffin, glancing towards him for any support he could give.

"*I* tell you so," returned Silas. "Now, here's my hat, Boffin, and here's my walking-stick. Trifle with me, and instead of making a bargain with you, I'll put on my hat and take up my walking-stick, and go out and make a bargain with the rightful owner. Now, what do you say?"

"I say," returned Mr. Boffin, leaning forward in alarmed appeal, with his hands on his knees, "that I am sure I don't want to trifle, Wegg. I have said so to Venus."

"You certainly have, sir," said Venus.

"You're too milk and watery with our friend, you are indeed," remonstrated Silas, with a disapproving shake of his wooden head. "Then at once you confess yourself desirous to come to terms, do you, Boffin? Before you answer, keep this hat well in your mind, and also this walking-stick."

"I am willing, Wegg, to come to terms."

"Willing won't do, Boffin. I won't take willing. Are you desirous to come to terms? Do you ask to be allowed as a favour to come to terms?" Mr. Wegg again planted his arm, and put his head on one side.

"Yes."

"Yes what?" said the inexorable Wegg: "I won't take yes. I'll have it out of you in full, Boffin."

"Dear me!" cried that unfortunate gentleman. "I am so worried! I ask to be allowed to come to terms, supposing your document is all correct."

"Don't you be afraid of that," said Silas, poking his head at him. "You shall be satisfied by seeing it. Mr. Venus will show it you, and I'll hold you the while. Then you want to know what the terms are. Is that about the sum and substance of it? Will you or won't you answer, Boffin?" For he had paused a moment.

"Dear me!" cried that unfortunate gentleman again, "I am worrited to that degree that I'm almost off my head. You hurry me so. Be so good as name the terms, Wegg."

"Now, mark, Boffin," returned Silas: "Mark 'em well, because they're the lowest terms and the only terms. You'll throw your Mound (the little Mound as comes to you any way) into the general estate, and then you'll divide the whole property into three parts, and you'll keep one and hand over the others."

Mr. Venus's mouth screwed itself up, as Mr. Boffin's face lengthened itself; Mr. Venus not having been prepared for such a rapacious demand.

"Now, wait a bit, Boffin," Wegg proceeded, "there's something more. You've been a squandering this property—laying some of it out on yourself. *That* won't do. You've bought a house. You'll be charged for it."

"I shall be ruined, Wegg!" Mr. Boffin faintly protested.

"Now, wait a bit, Boffin; there's something more. You'll leave me in sole custody of these Mounds till they're all laid low. If any waluables should be found in 'em, I'll take care of such waluables. You'll produce your contract for the sale of the Mounds, that we may know to a penny what they're worth, and you'll make out likewise an exact list of all the other property. When the Mounds is cleared away to the last shovel-full, the final diwision will come off."

"Dreadful, dreadful, dreadful! I shall die in a work-house!" cried the Golden Dustman, with his hands to his head.

"Now, wait a bit, Boffin; there's something more. You've been unlawfully ferreting about this yard. You've been seen in the act of ferreting about this yard. Two pair of eyes at the present moment brought to bear upon you, have seen you dig up a Dutch bottle."

"It was mine, Wegg," protested Mr. Boffin. "I put it there myself."

"What was in it, Boffin?" inquired Silas.

"Not gold, not silver, not bank notes, not jewels, nothing that you could turn into money, Wegg; upon my soul!"

"Prepared, Mr. Venus," said Wegg, turning to his partner

with a knowing and superior air, " for an ewasive answer on the part of our dusty friend here, I have hit out a little idea which I think will meet your views. We charge that bottle against our dusty friend at a thousand pound."

Mr. Boffin drew a deep groan.

" Now, wait a bit, Boffin; there's something more. In your employment is an under-handed sneak, named Rokesmith. It won't answer to have *him* about, while this business of ours is about. He must be discharged."

" Rokesmith is already discharged," said Mr. Boffin, speaking in a muffled voice, with his hands before his face, as he rocked himself on the settle.

" Already discharged, is he?" returned Wegg, surprised. " Oh! Then, Boffin, I believe there's nothing more at present."

The unlucky gentleman continuing to rock himself to and fro, and to utter an occasional moan, Mr. Venus besought him to bear up against his reverses, and to take time to accustom himself to the thought of his new position. But, his taking time was exactly the thing of all others that Silas Wegg could not be induced to hear of. " Yes or no, and no half-measures!" was the motto which that obdurate person many times repeated; shaking his fist at Mr. Boffin, and pegging his motto into the floor with his wooden leg, in a threatening and alarming manner.

At length Mr. Boffin entreated to be allowed a quarter of an hour's grace, and a cooling walk of that duration in the yard. With some difficulty Mr. Wegg granted this great favour, but only on condition that he accompanied Mr. Boffin in his walk, as not knowing what he might fraudulently unearth if he were left to himself. A more absurd sight than Mr. Boffin in his mental irritation trotting very nimbly, and Mr. Wegg hopping after him with great exertion, eager to watch the slightest turn of an eyelash, lest it should indicate a spot rich with some secret, assuredly had never been seen in the shadow of the Mounds. Mr. Wegg was much distressed when the quarter of an hour expired, and came hopping in, a very bad second.

"I can't help myself?" cried Mr. Boffin, flouncing on the settle in a forlorn manner, with his hands deep in his pockets, as if his pockets had sunk. "What's the good of my pretending to stand out, when I can't help myself? I must give in to the terms. But I should like to see the document."

Wegg, who was all for clinching the nail he had so strongly driven home, announced that Boffin should see it without an hour's delay. Taking him into custody for that purpose, or overshadowing him as if he really were his Evil Genius in visible form, Mr. Wegg clapped Mr. Boffin's hat upon the back of his head, and walked him out by the arm, asserting a proprietorship over his soul and body that was at once more grim and more ridiculous than anything in Mr. Venus's rare collection. That light-haired gentleman followed close upon their heels, at least backing up Mr. Boffin in a literal sense, if he had not had recent opportunities of doing so spiritually; while Mr. Boffin, trotting on as hard as he could trot, involved Silas Wegg in frequent collisions with the public, much as a pre-occupied blind man's dog may be seen to involve his master.

Thus they reached Mr. Venus's establishment, somewhat heated by the nature of their progress thither. Mr. Wegg, especially, was in a flaming glow, and stood in the little shop, panting and mopping his head with his pocket-handkerchief, speechless for several minutes.

Meanwhile, Mr. Venus, who had left the duelling frogs to fight it out in his absence by candlelight for the public delectation, put the shutters up. When all was snug, and the shop-door fastened, he said to the perspiring Silas: "I suppose, Mr. Wegg, we may now produce the paper?"

"Hold on a minute, sir," replied that discreet character; "hold on a minute. Will you obligingly shove that box—which you mentioned on a former occasion as containing miscellanies—towards me in the midst of the shop here?"

Mr. Venus did as he was asked.

"Very good," said Silas, looking about: "ve—ry good. Will you hand me that chair, sir, to put a-top of it?"

Venus handed him the chair.

"Now, Boffin," said Wegg, "mount up here and take your seat, will you?"

Mr. Boffin, as if he were about to have his portrait painted, or to be electrified, or to be made a Freemason, or to be placed at any other solitary disadvantage, ascended the rostrum prepared for him.

"Now, Mr. Venus," said Silas, taking off his coat, "when I catches our friend here round the arms and body, and pins him tight to the back of the chair, you may show him what he wants to see. If you'll open it and hold it well up in one hand, sir, and a candle in the other, he can read it charming."

Mr. Boffin seemed rather inclined to object to these precautionary arrangements, but, being immediately embraced by Wegg, resigned himself. Venus then produced the document, and Mr. Boffin slowly spelt it out aloud : so very slowly, that Wegg, who was holding him in the chair with the grip of a wrestler, became again exceedingly the worse for his exertions. "Say when you've put it safe back, Mr. Venus," he uttered with difficulty, "for the strain of this is terrimenjious."

At length the document was restored to its place ; and Wegg, whose uncomfortable attitude had been that of a very persevering man unsuccessfully attempting to stand upon his head, took a seat to recover himself. Mr. Boffin, for his part, made no attempt to come down, but remained aloft disconsolate.

"Well, Boffin!" said Wegg, as soon as he was in a condition to speak. "Now you know!"

"Yes, Wegg," said Mr. Boffin, meekly. "Now I know."

"You have no doubts about it, Boffin?"

"No, Wegg. No, Wegg. None," was the slow and sad reply.

"Then, take care, you," said Wegg, "that you stick to your conditions. Mr. Venus, if on this auspicious occasion you should happen to have a drop of anything not quite so mild as tea in the 'ouse, I think I'd take the friendly liberty of asking you for a specimen of it."

Mr. Venus, reminded of the duties of hospitality, produced some rum. In answer to the inquiry, "Will you mix it, Mr. Wegg?" that gentleman pleasantly rejoined, "I think not, sir. On so auspicious an occasion, I prefer to take it in the form of a Gum-Tickler."

Mr. Boffin, declining rum, being still elevated on his pedestal, was in a convenient position to be addressed. Wegg having eyed him with an impudent air at leisure, addressed him, therefore, while refreshing himself with his dram.

"Bof—fin!"

"Yes, Wegg," he answered, coming out of a fit of abstraction, with a sigh.

"I haven't mentioned one thing, because it's a detail that comes of course. You must be followed up, you know. You must be kept under inspection."

"I don't quite understand," said Mr. Boffin.

"Don't you?" sneered Wegg. "Where's your wits, Boffin? Till the Mounds is down and this business completed, you're accountable for all the property, recollect. Consider yourself accountable to me. Mr. Venus here being too milk and watery with you, I am the boy for you."

"I've been a-thinking," said Mr. Boffin, in a tone of despondency, "that I must keep the knowledge from my old lady."

"The knowledge of the division, d'ye mean?" inquired Wegg, helping himself to a third Gum-Tickler—for he had already taken a second.

"Yes. If she was to die first of us two she might then think all her life, poor thing, that I had got the rest of the fortune still, and was saving it."

"I suspect, Boffin," returned Wegg, shaking his head

sagaciously, and bestowing a wooden wink upon him, "that you've found out some account of some old chap, supposed to be a Miser, who got himself the credit of having much more money than he had. However, *I* don't mind."

"Don't you see, Wegg?" Mr. Boffin feelingly represented to him: "don't you see? My old lady has got so used to the property. It would be such a hard surprise."

"I don't see it at all," blustered Wegg. "You'll have as much as I shall. And who are you?"

"But then, again," Mr. Boffin gently represented; "my old lady has very upright principles."

"Who's your old lady," returned Wegg, "to set herself up for having uprighter principles than mine?"

Mr. Boffin seemed a little less patient at this point than at any other of the negotiations. But he commanded himself, and said tamely enough: "I think it must be kept from my old lady, Wegg."

"Well," said Wegg, contemptuously, though, perhaps, perceiving some hint of danger otherwise, "keep it from your old lady. *I* ain't going to tell her. I can have you under close inspection without that. I'm as good a man as you, and better. Ask me to dinner. Give me the run of your 'ouse. I was good enough for you and your old lady once, when I helped you out with your weal and hammers. Was there no Miss Elizabeth, Master George, Aunt Jane, and Uncle Parker, before *you* two?"

"Gently, Mr. Wegg, gently," Venus urged.

"Milk and water-erily you mean, sir," he returned, with some little thickness of speech, in consequence of the Gum-Ticklers having tickled it. "I've got him under inspection, and I'll inspect him.

> 'Along the line the signal ran,
> England expects as this present man
> Will keep Boffin to his duty.'

—Boffin, I'll see you home."

Mr. Boffin descended with an air of resignation, and gave

himself up, after taking friendly leave of Mr. Venus. Once more, Inspector and Inspected went through the streets together, and so arrived at Mr. Boffin's door.

But even there, when Mr. Boffin had given his keeper good-night, and had let himself in with his key, and had softly closed the door, even there and then, the all-powerful Silas must needs claim another assertion of his newly-asserted power.

" Bof—fin ! " he called through the keyhole.

" Yes, Wegg," was the reply through the same channel.

" Come out. Show yourself again. Let's have another look at you ! "

Mr. Boffin—ah, how fallen from the high estate of his honest simplicity !—opened the door and obeyed.

" Go in. You may get to bed now," said Wegg, with a grin.

The door was hardly closed, when he again called through the keyhole :

" Bof—fin ! "

" Yes, Wegg."

This time Silas made no reply, but laboured with a will at turning an imaginary grindstone outside the keyhole, while Mr. Boffin stooped at it within ; he then laughed silently, and stumped home.

CHAPTER IV

CHERUBIC Pa arose with as little noise as possible from beside majestic Ma, one morning early, having a holiday before him. Pa and the lovely woman had a rather particular appointment to keep.

Yet Pa and the lovely woman were not going out together. Bella was up before four, but had no bonnet on. She was waiting at the foot of the stairs—was sitting on the bottom stair, in fact—to receive Pa when he came down, but her only object seemed to be to get Pa well out of the house.

" Your breakfast is ready, sir," whispered Bella, after greeting him with a hug, " and all you have to do, is, to eat it up and drink it up, and escape. How do you feel, Pa? "

" To the best of my judgment, like a housebreaker new to the business, my dear, who can't make himself quite comfortable till he is off the premises."

Bella tucked her arm in his with a merry noiseless laugh, and they went down to the kitchen on tiptoe; she stopping on every separate stair to put the tip of her forefinger on her rosy lips, and then lay it on his lips, according to her favourite petting way of kissing Pa.

" How do *you* feel, my love? " asked R. W., as she gave him his breakfast.

" I feel as if the Fortune-teller was coming true, dear Pa, and the fair little man was turning out as was predicted."

"Ho! Only the fair little man?" said her father.

Bella put another of those finger-seals upon his lips, and then said, kneeling down by him as he sat at table : "Now, look here, sir. If you keep well up to the mark this day, what do you think you deserve? What did I promise you should have, if you were good, upon a certain occasion?"

"Upon my word I don't remember, Precious. Yes, I do, though. Wasn't it one of those beau—tiful tresses?" with his caressing hand upon her hair.

"Wasn't it, too!" returned Bella, pretending to pout. "Upon my word! Do you know, sir, that the Fortune-teller would give five thousand guineas (if it was quite convenient to him, which it isn't) for the lovely piece I have cut off for you? You can form no idea, sir, of the number of times he kissed quite a scrubby little piece—in comparison —that I cut off for *him.* And he wears it, too, round his neck, I can tell you! Near his heart!" said Bella, nodding. "Ah! very near his heart. However, you have been a good, good boy, and you are the best of all the dearest boys that ever were, this morning, and here's the chain I have made of it, Pa, and you must let me put it round your neck with my own loving hands."

As Pa bent his head, she cried over him a little, and then said (after having stopped to dry her eyes on his white waistcoat, the discovery of which incongruous circumstance made her laugh): "Now, darling Pa, give me your hands that I may fold them together, and do you say after me:—My little Bella."

"My little Bella," repeated Pa.

"I am very fond of you."

"I am very fond of you, my darling," said Pa.

"You mustn't say anything not dictated to you, sir. You daren't do it in your responses at Church, and you mustn't do it in your responses out of Church."

"I withdraw the darling," said Pa.

"That's a pious boy! Now again :—You were always—"

" You were always," repeated Pa.

" A vexatious—— "

" No, you weren't," said Pa.

" A vexatious (do you hear, sir ?), a vexatious, capricious, thankless, troublesome, Animal ; but I hope you'll do better in the time to come, and I bless you and forgive you ! " Here, she quite forgot that it was Pa's turn to make the responses, and clung to his neck. " Dear Pa, if you knew how much I think this morning of what you told me once, about the first time of our seeing old Mr. Harmon, when I stamped and screamed and beat you with my detestable little bonnet ! I feel as if I had been stamping and screaming and beating you with my hateful little bonnet, ever since I was born, darling ! "

" Nonsense, my love. And as to your bonnets, they have always been nice bonnets, for they have always become you —or you have become them ; perhaps it was that—at every age."

" Did I hurt you much, poor little Pa ? " asked Bella, laughing (notwithstanding her repentance), with fantastic pleasure in the picture, " when I beat you with my bonnet ? "

" No, my child. Wouldn't have hurt a fly ! "

" Ay, but I am afraid I shouldn't have beat you at all, unless I had meant to hurt you, " said Bella. " Did I pinch your legs, Pa ? "

" Not much, my dear ; but I think it's almost time I—— "

" Oh, yes ! " cried Bella. " If I go on chattering, you'll be taken alive. Fly, Pa, fly ! "

So, they went softly up the kitchen stairs on tiptoe, and Bella with her light hand softly removed the fastenings of the house door, and Pa, having received a parting hug, made off. When he had gone a little way, he looked back. Upon which, Bella set another of those finger-seals upon the air, and thrust out her little foot expressive of the mark. Pa, in appropriate action, expressed fidelity to the mark, and made off as fast as he could go.

Bella walked thoughtfully in the garden for an hour and more, and then, returning to the bedroom where Lavvy the Irrepressible still slumbered, put on a little bonnet of quiet, but on the whole of sly appearance, which she had yesterday made. " I am going for a walk, Lavvy," she said, as she stooped down and kissed her. The Irrepressible, with a bounce in the bed, and a remark that it wasn't time to get up yet, relapsed into unconsciousness, if she had come out of it.

Behold Bella tripping along the streets, the dearest girl afoot under the summer sun ! Behold Pa waiting for Bella behind a pump, at least three miles from the parental roof-tree. Behold Bella and Pa aboard an early steamboat bound for Greenwich.

Were they expected at Greenwich ? Probably. At least, Mr. John Rokesmith was on the pier looking out, about a couple of hours before the coaly (but to him gold-dusty) little steamboat got her steam up in London. Probably. At least, Mr. John Rokesmith seemed perfectly satisfied when he descried them on board. Probably. At least, Bella no sooner stepped ashore than she took Mr. John Rokesmith's arm, without evincing surprise, and the two walked away together with an ethereal air of happiness which, as it were, wafted up from the earth and drew up after them a gruff and glum old pensioner to see it out. Two wooden legs had this gruff and glum old pensioner, and, a minute before Bella stepped out of the boat, and drew that confiding little arm of hers through Rokesmith's, he had had no object in life but tobacco, and not enough of that. Stranded was Gruff and Glum in a harbour of everlasting mud, when all in an instant Bella floated him, and away he went.

Say, cherubic parent taking the lead, in what direction do we steer first ? With some such inquiry in his thoughts, Gruff and Glum, stricken by so sudden an interest that he perked his neck and looked over the intervening people, as if he were trying to stand on tiptoe with his two wooden legs, took an observation of R. W. There was no "first" in the case, Gruff and Glum made out; the cherubic parent was bearing down and crowding on direct for Greenwich church, to see his relations.

For, Gruff and Glum, though most events acted on him simply as tobacco-stoppers, pressing down and condensing the quids within him, might be imagined to trace a family resemblance between the cherubs in the church architecture, and the cherub in the white waistcoat. Some resemblance of old Valentines, wherein a cherub, less appropriately attired for a proverbially uncertain climate, had been seen conducting lovers to the altar, might have been fancied to inflame the ardour of his timber toes. Be it as it might, he gave his moorings the slip, and followed in chase.

The cherub went before, all beaming smiles; Bella and John Rokesmith followed; Gruff and Glum stuck to them like wax. For years, the wings of his mind had gone to look after the legs of his body; but Bella had brought them back for him per steamer, and they were spread again.

He was a slow sailer on a wind of happiness, but he took a cross cut for the rendezvous, and pegged away as if he were scoring furiously at cribbage. When the shadow of the church-porch swallowed them up, victorious Gruff and Glum likewise presented himself to be swallowed up. And by this time the cherubic parent was so fearful of surprise, that, but for the two wooden legs on which Gruff and Glum was re-assuringly mounted, his conscience might have introduced, in the person of that pensioner, his own stately lady disguised, arrived at Greenwich in a car and griffins, like the spiteful Fairy at the christenings of the Princesses, to do something dreadful to the marriage service. And truly he had a momentary reason to be pale of face, and to whisper to Bella, "You don't think that can be your Ma; do you, my dear?" on account of a mysterious rustling and a stealthy movement somewhere in the remote neighbourhood of the organ, though it was gone directly and was heard no more. Albeit it was heard of afterwards, as will afterwards be read in this veracious register of marriage.

Who taketh? I, John, and so do I, Bella. Who giveth? I, R. W. Forasmuch, Gruff and Glum, as John and Bella, have consented together in holy wedlock, you may (in short) consider it done, and withdraw your two wooden legs from this temple. To the foregoing purport, the Minister speaking, as directed by the Rubric, to the People, selectly represented in the present instance by G. and G. above mentioned.

And now, the church-porch having swallowed up Bella Wilfer for ever and ever, had it not in its power to relinquish that young woman, but slid into the happy sunlight, Mrs. John Rokesmith instead. And long on the bright steps stood Gruff and Glum, looking after the pretty bride, with a narcotic consciousness of having dreamed a dream.

After which, Bella took out from her pocket a little letter, and read it aloud to Pa and John: this being a true copy of the same.

"DEAREST MA,

"I hope you won't be angry, but I am most happily married to Mr. John Rokesmith, who loves me better than I can ever deserve, except by loving him with all my heart. I thought it best not to mention it beforehand, in case it should cause any little difference at home. Please tell darling Pa. With love to Lavvy,

"Ever dearest Ma, your affectionate daughter,
"BELLA
"(P.S.—Rokesmith)."

Then, John Rokesmith put the queen's countenance on the letter—when had Her Gracious Majesty looked so benign as on that blessed morning!—and then Bella popped it into the post-office, and said merrily, "Now, dearest Pa, you are safe, and will never be taken alive!"

Pa was, at first, in the stirred depths of his conscience, so

306

far from sure of being safe yet, that he made out majestic matrons lurking in ambush among the harmless trees of Greenwich Park, and seemed to see a stately countenance tied up in a well-known pocket-handkerchief glooming down at him from a window of the Observatory, where the Familiars of the Astronomer Royal nightly outwatch the winking stars. But, the minutes passing on and no Mrs. Wilfer in the flesh appearing, he became more confident, and so repaired with good heart and appetite to Mr. and Mrs. John Rokesmith's cottage on Blackheath, where breakfast was ready.

A modest little cottage but a bright and a fresh, and on the snowy table-cloth the prettiest of little breakfasts. In waiting, too, like an attendant summer breeze, a fluttering young damsel, all pink and ribbons, blushing as if she had been married instead of Bella, and yet asserting the triumph of her sex over John and Pa, in an exulting and exalted flurry: as who should say, "This is what you must all come to, gentlemen, when we choose to bring you to book." This same young damsel was Bella's serving-maid, and unto her did deliver a bunch of keys, commanding treasures in the way of drysaltery, groceries, jams and pickles, the investigation of which made pastime after breakfast, when Bella declared that "Pa must taste everything, John dear, or it will never be lucky," and when Pa had all sorts of things poked into his mouth, and didn't quite know what to do with them when they were put there.

Then they, all three, out for a charming ride, and for a charming stroll among heath and bloom, and there behold the identical Gruff and Glum with his wooden legs horizontally disposed before him, apparently sitting meditating on the vicissitudes of life! To whom said Bella, in her light-hearted surprise: "Oh! How do you again? What a dear old pensioner you are!" To which Gruff and Glum responded that he see her married this morning, my Beauty, and that if it warn't a liberty he wished her ji and the fairest of fair wind and weather; further, in a general way requesting to know what cheer? and scrambling up on his two wooden legs to salute, hat in hand, ship-shape, with the gallantry of a man-of-wars-man and a heart of oak.

It was a pleasant sight, in the midst of the golden bloom, to see this salt old Gruff and Glum waving his shovel hat at Bella, while his thin white hair flowed free, as if she had once more launched him into blue water again. "You are a charming old pensioner," said Bella, "and I am so happy that I wish I could make you happy, too." Answered Gruff and Glum, "Give me leave to kiss your hand, my Lovely, and it's done!" So it was done to the general content-ment; and if Gruff and Glum didn't in the course of the afternoon splice the main brace, it was not for want of the means of inflicting that outrage on the feelings of the Infant Bands of Hope.

But, the marriage dinner was the crowning success, for what had bride and bridegroom plotted to do, but to have and to hold that dinner in the very room of the very hotel where Pa and the lovely woman had once dined together! Bella sat between Pa and John, and divided her attentions pretty equally, but felt it necessary (in the waiter's absence before dinner) to remind Pa that she was *his* lovely woman no longer.

"I am well aware of it, my dear," returned the cherub, "and I resign you willingly."

"Willingly, sir? You ought to be broken-hearted."

"So I should be, my dear, if I thought that I was going to lose you."

"But you know you are not; don't you, poor dear Pa? You know that you have only made a new relation who will be as fond of you and as thankful to you—for my sake and your own sake both—as I am; don't you, dear little Pa? Look here, Pa!" Bella put her finger on her own lip, and then on Pa's, then on her own lip again, and then on her husband's. "Now, we are a partnership of three, dear Pa."

The appearance of dinner here cut Bella short in one of

The Wedding Dinner at Greenwich

her disappearances : the more effectually, because it was put on under the auspices of a solemn gentleman in black clothes and a white cravat, who looked much more like a clergyman than *the* clergyman, and seemed to have mounted a great deal higher in the church : not to say, scaled the steeple. This dignitary, conferring in secrecy with John Rokesmith on the subject of punch and wines, bent his head as though stooping to the Papistical practice of receiving auricular confession. Likewise, on John's offering a suggestion which didn't meet his views, his face became overcast and reproachful, as enjoining penance.

What a dinner! Specimens of all the fishes that swim in the sea, surely had swum their way to it, and if samples of the fishes of divers colours that made a speech in the Arabian Nights (quite a ministerial explanation in respect of cloudiness), and then jumped out of the frying-pan, were not to be recognised, it was only because they had all become of one hue by being cooked in batter among the whitebait. And the dishes being seasoned with Bliss—an article which they are sometimes out of, at Greenwich—were of perfect flavour, and the golden drinks had been bottled in the golden age and hoarding up their sparkles ever since.

The best of it was, that Bella and John and the cherub had made a covenant that they would not reveal to mortal eyes any appearance whatever of being a wedding party. Now, the supervising dignitary, the Archbishop of Greenwich, knew this as well as if he had performed the nuptial ceremony. And the loftiness with which his Grace entered into their confidence without being invited, and insisted on a show of keeping the waiters out of it, was the crowning glory of the entertainment.

There was an innocent young waiter of a slender form and with weakish legs, as yet unversed in the wiles of waiterhood, and but too evidently of a romantic temperament, and deeply (it were not too much to add hopelessly) in love with some young female not aware of his merit. This guileless youth,

309

descrying the position of affairs, which even his innocence could not mistake, limited his waiting to languishing admiringly against the sideboard when Bella didn't want anything, and swooping at her when she did. Him, his Grace the Archbishop perpetually obstructed, cutting him out with his elbow in the moment of success, despatching him in degrading quest of melted butter, and, when by any chance he got hold of any dish worth having, bereaving him of it, and ordering him to stand back.

"Pray excuse him, madam," said the Archbishop in a low stately voice; "he is a very young man on liking, and we *don't* like him."

This induced John Rokesmith to observe—by way of making the thing more natural—"Bella, my love, this is so much more successful than any of our past anniversaries, that I think we must keep our future anniversaries here."

Whereunto Bella replied, with probably the least successful attempt at looking matronly that ever was seen: "Indeed, I think so, John, dear."

Here the Archbishop of Greenwich coughed a stately cough to attract the attention of three of his ministers present, and staring at them, seemed to say: "I call upon you by your fealty to believe this!"

With his own hands he afterwards put on the dessert, as remarking to the three guests, "The period has now arrived at which we can dispense with the assistance of those fellows who are not in our confidence," and would have retired with complete dignity but for a daring action issuing from the misguided brain of the young man on liking. He finding, by ill-fortune, a piece of orange-flower somewhere in the lobbies, now approached undetected with the same in a finger-glass, and placed it on Bella's right hand. The Archbishop instantly ejected and excommunicated him; but the thing was done.

"I trust, madam," said his Grace, returning alone, "that you will have the kindness to overlook it, in consideration of its being the act of a very young man who is merely here on liking, and who will never answer."

With that, he solemnly bowed and retired, and they all burst into laughter, long and merry. "Disguise is of no use," said Bella; "they all find me out; I think it must be, Pa and John dear, because I look so happy!"

Her husband feeling it necessary at this point to demand one of those mysterious disappearances on Bella's part, she dutifully obeyed; saying in a softened voice from her place of concealment:

"You remember how we talked about the ships that day, Pa?"

"Yes, my dear."

"Isn't it strange, now, to think that there was no John in all the ships, Pa?"

"Not at all, my dear."

"Oh, Pa! Not at all?"

"No, my dear. How can we tell what coming people are aboard the ships that may be sailing to us now from the unknown seas!"

Bella remaining invisible and silent, her father remained at his dessert and wine, until he remembered it was time for him to get home to Holloway. "Though I positively cannot tear myself away," he cherubically added, "—it would be a sin—without drinking to many, many happy returns of this most happy day."

"Hear! ten thousand times!" cried John. "I fill my glass and my precious wife's."

"Gentlemen," said the cherub, inaudibly addressing, in his Anglo-Saxon tendency to throw his feelings into the form of a speech, the boys down below, who were bidding against each other to put their heads in the mud for sixpence: "Gentlemen—and Bella and John—you will readily suppose that it is not my intention to trouble you with many observations on the present occasion. You will also at once infer the nature and even the terms of the toast I am about to propose on the present occasion. Gentlemen—and Bella and John—the present occasion is an occasion fraught with feelings that I cannot trust myself to express. But, gentlemen—and Bella and John—for the part I have had in it, for the confidence you have placed in me, and for the affectionate good-nature and kindness with which you have determined not to find me in the way, when I am well aware that I cannot be otherwise than in it more or less, I do most heartily thank you. Gentlemen—and Bella and John—my love to you, and may we meet, as on the present occasion, on many future occasions; that is to say, gentlemen —and Bella and John—on many happy returns of the present happy occasion."

Having thus concluded his address, the amiable cherub embraced his daughter, and took his flight to the steamboat which was to convey him to London, and was then lying at the floating pier, doing its best to bump the same to bits. But, the happy couple were not going to part with him in that way, and before he had been on board two minutes, there they were, looking down at him from the wharf above.

"Pa, dear!" cried Bella, beckoning him with her parasol to approach the side, and bending gracefully to whisper.

" Yes, my darling."

" Did I beat you much with that horrid little bonnet, Pa ? "

"Nothing to speak of, my dear."

"Did I pinch your legs, Pa ? "

"Only nicely, my pet."

"You are sure you quite forgive me, Pa? Please, Pa, please, forgive me quite!" Half laughing at him and half crying to him, Bella besought him in the prettiest manner; in a manner so engaging and so playful and so natural, that her cherubic parent made a coaxing face as if she had never grown up, and said, " What a silly little Mouse it is !"

"But you do forgive me that, and everything else; don't you, Pa ? "

" Yes, my dearest."

312

"And you don't feel solitary or neglected, going away by yourself; do you, Pa?"

"Lord bless you! No, my Life!"

"Good-bye, dearest Pa. Good-bye!"

"Good-bye, my darling! Take her away, my dear John. Take her home!"

So, she leaning on her husband's arm, they turned homeward by a rosy path which the gracious sun struck out for them in its setting. And oh! there are days in this life worth life and worth death. And oh! what a bright old song it is, that Oh, 'tis love, 'tis love, 'tis love, that makes the world go round!

CHAPTER V

CONCERNING THE MENDICANT'S BRIDE

THE impressive gloom with which Mrs. Wilfer received her husband on his return from the wedding, knocked so hard at the door of the cherubic conscience, and likewise so impaired the firmness of the cherubic legs, that the culprit's tottering condition of mind and body might have roused suspicion in less occupied persons than the grimly heroic lady, Miss Lavinia, and that esteemed friend of the family, Mr. George Sampson. But, the attention of all three being fully possessed by the main fact of the marriage, they had happily none to bestow on the guilty conspirator; to which fortunate circumstance he owed the escape for which he was in nowise indebted to himself.

"You do not, R. W.," said Mrs. Wilfer from her stately corner, "inquire for your daughter Bella."

"To be sure, my dear," he returned, with a most flagrant assumption of unconsciousness, "I did omit it. How—or perhaps I should rather say where—*is* Bella ? "

"Not here," Mrs. Wilfer proclaimed, with folded arms.

The cherub faintly muttered something to the abortive effect of " Oh, indeed, my dear ! "

"Not here," repeated Mrs. Wilfer, in a stern, sonorous voice. " In a word, R. W., you have no daughter Bella."

" No daughter Bella, my dear ? "

"No. Your daughter Bella," said Mrs. Wilfer, with a lofty air of never having had the least copartnership in that

314

young lady: of whom she now made reproachful mention as an article of luxury which her husband had set up entirely on his own account, and in direct opposition to her advice: " —your daughter Bella has bestowed herself upon a Mendicant."

" Good gracious, my dear ! "

"Show your father his daughter Bella's letter, Lavinia," said Mrs. Wilfer, in her monotonous Act of Parliament tone, and waving her hand. " I think your father will admit it to be documentary proof of what I tell him. I believe your father is acquainted with his daughter Bella's writing. But I do not know. He may tell you he is not. Nothing will surprise me."

" Posted at Greenwich, and dated this morning," said the Irrepressible, flouncing at her father in handing him the evidence. " Hopes Ma won't be angry, but is happily married to Mr. John Rokesmith, and didn't mention it beforehand to avoid words, and please tell darling you, and love to me, and I should like to know what you'd have said if any other unmarried member of the family had done it ! "

He read the letter, and faintly exclaimed " Dear me ! "

" You may well say Dear me ! " rejoined Mrs. Wilfer, in a deep tone. Upon which encouragement he said it again, though scarcely with the success he had expected ; for the scornful lady then remarked, with extreme bitterness: " You said that before."

" It's very surprising. But I suppose, my dear," hinted the cherub, as he folded the letter after a disconcerting silence, " that we must make the best of it ! Would you object to my pointing out, my dear, that Mr. John Rokesmith is not (so far as I am acquainted with him), strictly speaking, a Mendicant."

" Indeed ? " returned Mrs. Wilfer, with an awful air of politeness. " Truly so ? I was not aware that Mr. John Rokesmith was a gentleman of landed property. But I am much relieved to hear it."

"I doubt if you *have* heard it, my dear," the cherub submitted with hesitation.

"Thank you," said Mrs. Wilfer, "I make false statements, it appears? So be it. If my daughter flies in my face, surely my husband may. The one thing is not more unnatural than the other. There seems a fitness in the arrangement. By all means!" Assuming, with a shiver of resignation, a deadly cheerfulness.

But, here the Irrepressible skirmished into the conflict, dragging the reluctant form of Mr. Sampson after her.

"Ma," interposed the young lady, "I must say I think it would be much better if you would keep to the point, and not hold forth about people's flying into people's faces, which is nothing more nor less than impossible nonsense."

"How!" exclaimed Mrs. Wilfer, knitting her dark brows.

"Just im-possible nonsense, Ma," returned Lavvy, "and George Sampson knows it is, as well as I do."

Mrs. Wilfer suddenly becoming petrified, fixed her indignant eyes upon the wretched George: who, divided between the support due from him to his love, and the support due from him to his love's mamma, supported nobody, not even himself.

"The true point is," pursued Lavinia, "that Bella has behaved in a most unsisterly way to me, and might have severely compromised me with George and with George's family, by making off and getting married in this very low and disreputable manner—with some pew-opener or other, I suppose, for a bridesmaid—when she ought to have confided in me, and ought to have said, 'If, Lavvy, you consider it due to your engagement with George, that you should countenance the occasion by being present, then, Lavvy, I beg you to *be* present, keeping my secret from Ma and Pa.' As of course I should have done."

"As of course you would have done? Ingrate!" exclaimed Mrs. Wilfer. "Viper!"

"I say! You know, ma'am! Upon my honour you

316

mustn't!" Mr. Sampson remonstrated, shaking his head seriously. "With the highest respect for you, ma'am, upon my life you mustn't. No really, you know. When a man with the feelings of a gentleman finds himself engaged to a young lady, and it comes (even on the part of a member of the family) to vipers, you know!—I would merely put it to your own good feeling, you know," said Mr. Sampson, in rather lame conclusion.

Mrs. Wilfer's baleful stare at the young gentleman in acknowledgment of his obliging interference was of such a nature that Miss Lavinia burst into tears, and caught him round the neck for his protection.

"My own unnatural mother," screamed the young lady, "wants to annihilate George! But you shan't be annihilated, George. I'll die first!"

Mr. Sampson, in the arms of his mistress, still struggled to shake his head at Mrs. Wilfer, and to remark: "With every sentiment of respect for you, you know, ma'am—vipers really doesn't do you credit."

"You shall not be annihilated, George!" cried Miss Lavinia. "Ma shall destroy me first, and then she'll be contented. Oh, oh, oh! Have I lured George from his happy home to expose him to this! George dear, be free! Leave me, ever dearest George, to Ma and to my fate. Give my love to your aunt, George dear, and implore her not to curse the viper that has crossed your path and blighted your existence. Oh, oh, oh!" The young lady, who, hysterically speaking, was only just come of age, and had never gone off yet, here fell into a highly creditable crisis, which, regarded as a first performance, was very successful; Mr. Sampson, bending over the body meanwhile, in a state of distraction, which induced him to address Mrs. Wilfer in the inconsistent expressions: "Demon—with the highest respect for you— behold your work!"

The cherub stood helplessly rubbing his chin and looking on, but on the whole was inclined to welcome this diversion as one in which, by reason of the absorbent properties of hysterics, the previous question would become absorbed. And so, indeed, it proved, for the Irrepressible gradually coming to herself, and asking with wild emotion, "George dear, are you safe?" and further, "George love, what has happened? Where is Ma?" Mr. Sampson, with words of comfort, raised her prostrate form, and handed her to Mrs. Wilfer as if the young lady were something in the nature of refreshments. Mrs. Wilfer with dignity partaking of the refreshments, by kissing her once on the brow (as if accepting an oyster), Miss Lavvy, tottering, returned to the protection of Mr. Sampson: to whom she said, "George dear, I am afraid I have been foolish; but I am still a little weak and giddy; don't let go my hand, George!" And whom she afterwards greatly agitated at intervals, by giving utterance, when least expected, to a sound between a sob and a bottle of soda-water, that seemed to rend the bosom of her frock.

Among the most remarkable effects of this crisis may be mentioned its having, when peace was restored, an inexplicable moral influence, of an elevating kind, on Miss Lavinia, Mrs. Wilfer, and Mr. George Sampson, from which R. W. was altogether excluded, as an outsider and non-sympathiser. Miss Lavinia assumed a modest air of having distinguished herself; Mrs. Wilfer, a serene air of forgiveness and resignation; Mr. Sampson, an air of having been improved and chastened. The influence pervaded the spirit in which they returned to the previous question.

"George dear," said Lavvy, with a melancholy smile, "after what has passed, I am sure Ma will tell Pa that he may tell Bella we shall all be glad to see her and her husband."

Mr. Sampson said he was sure of it too; murmuring how eminently he respected Mrs. Wilfer, and ever must, and ever would. Never more eminently, he added, than after what had passed.

"Far be it from me," said Mrs. Wilfer, making deep

proclamation from her corner, "to run counter to the feelings of a child of mine, and of a Youth," Mr. Sampson hardly seemed to like that word, "who is the object of her maiden preference. I may feel—nay, know—that I have been deluded and deceived. I may feel—nay, know—that I have been set aside and passed over. I may feel—nay, know—that after having so far overcome my repugnance towards Mr. and Mrs. Boffin as to receive them under this roof, and to consent to your daughter Bella's," here turning to her husband, "residing under theirs, it were well if your daughter Bella," again turning to her husband, "had profited in a worldly point of view by a connection so distasteful, so disreputable. I may feel—nay, know—that in uniting herself to Mr. Rokesmith she has united herself to one who is, in spite of shallow sophistry, a Mendicant. And I may feel well assured that your daughter Bella," again turning to her husband, "does not exalt her family by becoming a Mendicant's bride. But I suppress what I feel, and say nothing of it."

Mr. Sampson murmured that this was the sort of thing you might expect from one who had ever in her own family been an example and never an outrage. And ever more so (Mr. Sampson added, with some degree of obscurity), and never more so, than in and through what had passed. He must take the liberty of adding, that what was true of the mother, was true of the youngest daughter, and that he could never forget the touching feelings that the conduct of both had awakened within him. In conclusion, he did hope that there wasn't a man with a beating heart who was capable of something that remained undescribed, in consequence of Miss Lavinia's stopping him as he reeled in his speech.

"Therefore, R. W.," said Mrs. Wilfer, resuming her discourse and turning to her lord again, "let your daughter Bella come when she will, and she will be received. So," after a short pause, and an air of having taken medicine in it, "so will her husband."

"And I beg, Pa," said Lavinia, "that you will not tell Bella what I have undergone. It can do no good, and it might cause her to reproach herself."

"My dearest girl," urged Mr. Sampson, "she ought to know it."

"No, George," said Lavinia, in a tone of resolute self-denial. "No, dearest George, let it be buried in oblivion."

Mr. Sampson considered that "too noble."

"Nothing is too noble, dearest George," returned Lavinia. "And, Pa, I hope you will be careful not to refer before Bella, if you can help it, to my engagement to George. It might seem like reminding her of her having cast herself away. And I hope, Pa, that you will think it equally right to avoid mentioning George's rising prospects when Bella is present. It might seem like taunting her with her own poor fortunes. Let me ever remember that I am her younger sister, and ever spare her painful contrasts, which could not but wound her sharply."

Mr. Sampson expressed his belief that such was the demeanour of Angels. Miss Lavvy replied with solemnity, "No, dearest George, I am but too well aware that I am merely human."

Mrs. Wilfer, for her part, still further improved the occasion by sitting with her eyes fastened on her husband, like two great black notes of interrogation, severely inquiring, Are you looking into your breast? Do you deserve your blessings? Can you lay your hand upon your heart and say that you are worthy of so hysterical a daughter? I do not ask you if you are worthy of such a wife—put Me out of the question—but are you sufficiently conscious of, and thankful for, the pervading moral grandeur of the family spectacle on which you are gazing? These inquiries proved very harassing to R. W., who, besides being a little disturbed by wine, was in perpetual terror of committing himself by the utterance of stray words that would betray his guilty foreknowledge. However, the scene being over, and—all things considered—well over, he sought refuge in a doze; which gave his lady immense offence.

"Can you think of your daughter Bella, and sleep?" she disdainfully inquired.

To which he mildly answered, "Yes, I think I can, my dear."

"Then," said Mrs. Wilfer, with solemn indignation, "I would recommend you, if you have a human feeling, to retire to bed."

"Thank you, my dear," he replied; "I think it *is* the best place for me." And with these unsympathetic words very gladly withdrew.

Within a few weeks afterwards, the Mendicant's bride (arm-in-arm with the Mendicant) came to tea, in fulfilment of an engagement made through the father. And the way in which the Mendicant's bride dashed at the unassailable position so considerately to be held by Miss Lavvy, and scattered the whole of the works in all directions in a moment, was triumphant.

"Dearest Ma," cried Bella, running into the room with a radiant face, "how do you do, dearest Ma?" And then embraced her joyously. "And Lavvy darling, how do *you* do, and how's George Sampson, and how is he getting on, and when are you going to be married, and how rich are you going to grow? You must tell me all about it, Lavvy dear, immediately. John love, kiss Ma and Lavvy, and then we shall all be at home and comfortable."

Mrs. Wilfer stared, but was helpless. Miss Lavinia stared, but was helpless. Apparently with no compunction, and assuredly with no ceremony, Bella tossed her bonnet away, and sat down to make the tea.

"Dearest Ma and Lavvy, you both take sugar, I know. And, Pa (you good little Pa), you don't take milk. John does. I didn't before I was married; but I do now, because John does. John dear, did you kiss Ma and Lavvy? Oh, you did! Quite correct, John dear; but I didn't see you do

321

it, so I asked. Cut some bread and butter, John, that's a love. Ma likes it doubled. And now you must tell me, dearest Ma and Lavvy, upon your words and honours! didn't you for a moment—just a moment—think I was a dreadful little wretch when I wrote to say I had run away?"

Before Mrs. Wilfer could wave her gloves, the Mendicant's bride in her merriest affectionate manner went on again.

"I think it must have made you rather cross, dear Ma and Lavvy, and I know I deserved that you should be very cross. But you see I had been such a heedless, heartless creature, and had led you so to expect that I should marry for money, and so to make sure that I was incapable of marrying for love, that I thought you couldn't believe me. Because, you see, you didn't know how much of Good, Good, Good, I had learnt from Jonn. Well! So I was sly about it, and ashamed of what you supposed me to be, and fearful that we couldn't understand one another and might come to words, which we should all be sorry for afterwards, and so I said to John that if he liked to take me without any fuss, he might. And as he did like, I let him. And we were married at Greenwich church in the presence of nobody— except an unknown individual who dropped in," here her eyes sparkled more brightly, "and half a pensioner. And now, isn't it nice, dearest Ma and Lavvy, to know that no words have been said which any of us can be sorry for, and that we are all the best of friends at the pleasantest of teas!"

Having got up and kissed them again, she slipped back to her chair (after a loop on the road to squeeze her husband round the neck) and again went on.

"And now you will naturally want to know, dearest Ma and Lavvy, how we live, and what we have got to live upon. Well! And so we live on Blackheath, in the charm—ingest of dolls' houses, de—lightfully furnished, and we have a clever little servant, who is de—cidedly pretty, and we are

322

economical and orderly, and do everything by clockwork, and we have a hundred and fifty pounds a year, and we have all we want, and more. And lastly, if you would like to know in confidence, as perhaps you may, what is my opinion of my husband, my opinion is—that I almost love him!"

"And if you would like to know in confidence, as perhaps you may," said her husband, smiling, as he stood by her side, without her having detected his approach, "my opinion of my wife, my opinion is——" But Bella started up, and put her hand upon his lips.

"Stop, sir! No, John dear! Seriously! Please not yet awhile! I want to be something so much worthier than the doll in the doll's house."

"My darling, are you not?"

"Not half, not a quarter, so much worthier as I hope you may some day find me! Try me through some reverse, John—try me through some trial—and tell them after *that*, what you think of me."

"I will, my Life," said John. "I promise it."

"That's my dear John. And you won't speak a word now; will you?"

"And I won't," said John, with a very expressive look of admiration around him, "speak a word now!"

She laid her laughing cheek upon his breast to thank him, and said, looking at the rest of them sideways out of her bright eyes: "I'll go further, Pa and Ma and Lavvy. John don't suspect it—he had no idea of it—but I quite love him!"

Even Mrs. Wilfer relaxed under the influence of her married daughter, and seemed in a majestic manner to imply remotely that if R. W. had been a more deserving object, she too might have condescended to come down from her pedestal for his beguilement. Miss Lavinia, on the other hand, had strong doubts of the policy of the course of treatment, and whether it might not spoil Mr. Sampson, if experimented on in the case of that young gentleman. R. W.

himself was for his part convinced that he was father of one of the most charming of girls, and that Rokesmith was the most favoured of men; which opinion, if propounded to him, Rokesmith would probably not have contested.

The newly-married pair left early, so that they might walk at leisure to their starting-place from London, for Greenwich. At first they were very cheerful and talked much; but after a while, Bella fancied that her husband was turning somewhat thoughtful. So she asked him:

"John dear, what's the matter?"

"Matter, my love?"

"Won't you tell me," said Bella, looking up into his face, "what you are thinking of?"

"There's not much in the thought, my soul. I was thinking whether you wouldn't like me to be rich?"

"You rich, John?" repeated Bella, shrinking a little.

"I mean, really rich. Say, as rich as Mr. Boffin. You would like that?"

"I should be almost afraid to try, John dear. Was he much the better for his wealth? Was I much the better for the little part I once had in it?"

"But all people are not the worse for riches, my own."

"Most people?" Bella musingly suggested with raised eyebrows.

"Nor even most people, it may be hoped. If you were rich, for instance, you would have a great power of doing good to others."

"Yes, sir, for instance," Bella playfully rejoined; "but should I exercise the power, for instance? And again, sir, for instance; should I, at the same time, have a great power of doing harm to myself?"

Laughing and pressing her arm, he retorted: "But still, again for instance; would you exercise that power?"

"I don't know," said Bella, thoughtfully shaking her head. "I hope not. I think not. But it's so easy to hope not, and think not, without the riches."

" Why don't you say, my darling—instead of that phrase—being poor ? " he asked, looking earnestly at her.

" Why don't I say, being poor ? Because I am not poor. Dear John, it's not possible that you suppose I think we are poor ? "

" I do, my love."

" Oh, John ! "

" Understand me, sweetheart. I know that I am rich beyond all wealth in having you; but I think *of* you, and think *for* you. In such a dress as you are wearing now, you first charmed me, and in no dress could you ever look, to my thinking, more graceful or more beautiful. But you have admired many finer dresses this very day ; and is it not natural that I wish I could give them to you ? "

" It's very nice that you should wish it, John. It brings these tears of grateful pleasure into my eyes, to hear you say so with such tenderness. But I don't want them."

" Again," he pursued, " we are now walking through the muddy streets. I love those pretty feet so dearly that I feel as if I could not bear the dirt to soil the sole of your shoe. Is it not natural that I wish you could ride in a carriage ? "

" It's very nice," said Bella, glancing downward at the feet in question, " to know that you admire them so much, John dear, and since you do, I am sorry that these shoes are a full size too large. But I don't want a carriage, believe me."

" You would like one, if you could have one, Bella ? "

" I shouldn't like it for its own sake, half so well as such a wish for it. Dear John, your wishes are as real to me as the wishes in the Fairy story, that were all fulfilled as soon as spoken. Wish me everything that you can wish for the woman you dearly love, and I have as good as got it, John. I have better than got it, John ! "

They were not the less happy for such talk, and home was not the less home for coming after it. Bella was fast developing a perfect genius for home. All the loves and graces seemed (her husband thought) to have taken domestic service with her, and to help her to make home engaging.

Her married life glided happily on. She was all alone all day, for, after an early breakfast her husband repaired every morning to the City, and did not return until their late dinner hour. He was "in a China house," he explained to Bella: which she found quite satisfactory, without pursuing the China house into minuter details than a wholesale vision of tea, rice, odd-smelling silks, carved boxes, and tight-eyed people in more than double-soled shoes, with their pigtails pulling their heads of hair off, painted on transparent porcelain. She always walked with her husband to the railroad, and was always there again to meet him; her old coquettish ways a little sobered down (but not much), and her dress as daintily managed as if she managed nothing else. But, John gone to business and Bella returned home, the dress would be lain aside, trim little wrappers and aprons would be substituted, and Bella, putting back her hair with both hands, as if she were making the most business-like arrangements for going dramatically distracted, would enter on the household affairs of the day. Such weighing and mixing and chopping and grating, such dusting and washing and polishing, such snipping and weeding and trowelling and other small gardening, such making and mending and folding and airing, such diverse arrangements, and above all such severe study! For Mrs. J. R., who had never been wont to do too much at home as Miss B. W., was under the constant necessity of referring for advice and support to a sage volume entitled The Complete British Family Housewife, which she would sit consulting, with her elbows on the table and her temples on her hands, like some perplexed enchantress poring over the Black Art. This, principally because the Complete British Housewife, however sound a Briton at heart, was by no means an expert Briton at expressing herself with clearness in the British tongue, and sometimes might have issued her directions to equal purpose in the Kamskatchan language

326

BELLA'S MARRIED LIFE

In any crisis of this nature, Bella would suddenly exclaim aloud, " Oh, you ridiculous old thing, what do you mean by that? You must have been drinking!" And having made this marginal note, would try the Housewife again, with all her dimples screwed into an expression of profound research.

There was likewise a coolness on the part of the British Housewife, which Mrs. John Rokesmith found highly exasperating. She would say, " Take a salamander," as if a general should command a private to catch a Tartar. Or, she would casually issue the order, " Throw in a handful— " of something entirely unattainable. In these, the Housewife's most glaring moments of unreason, Bella would shut her up and knock her on the table, apostrophising her with the compliment, " Oh, you ARE a stupid old donkey! Where am I to get it, do you think ?"

Another branch of study claimed the attention of Mrs. John Rokesmith for a regular period every day. This was the mastering of the newspaper, so that she might be close up with John on general topics when John came home. In her desire to be in all things his companion, she would have set herself with equal zeal to master Algebra, or Euclid, if he had divided his soul between her and either. Wonderful was the way in which she would store up the City Intelligence, and beamingly shed it upon John in the course of the evening, incidentally mentioning the commodities that were looking up in the markets, and how much gold had been taken to the Bank, and trying to look wise and serious over it until she would laugh at herself most charmingly, and would say, kissing him : " It all comes of my love, John dear."

For a City man, John certainly did appear to care as little as might be for the looking up or looking down of things, as well as for the gold that got taken to the Bank. But he cared, beyond all expression, for his wife, as a most precious and sweet commodity that was always looking up, and that never was worth less than all the gold in the world. And she, being inspired by her affection, and having a quick wit and a fine ready instinct, made amazing progress in her domestic efficiency, though, as an endearing creature, she made no progress at all. This was her husband's verdict, and he justified it by telling her that she had begun her married life as the most endearing creature that could possibly be.

"And you have such a cheerful spirit!" he said, fondly. "You are like a bright light in the house."

"Am I truly, John?"

"Are you truly? Yes, indeed. Only much more, and much better."

"Do you know, John dear," said Bella, taking him by a button of his coat, "that I sometimes, at odd moments—don't laugh, John, please."

Nothing should induce John to do it, when she asked him not to do it.

"—That I sometimes think, John, I feel a little serious."

"Are you too much alone, my darling?"

"Oh dear, no, John! The time is so short that I have not a moment too much in the week."

"Why serious, my life, then? When serious?"

"When I laugh, I think," said Bella, laughing as she laid her head upon his shoulder. "You wouldn't believe, sir, that I feel serious now? But I do." And she laughed again, and something glistened in her eyes.

"Would you like to be rich, pet?" he asked her coaxingly.

"Rich, John! How *can* you ask such goose's questions?"

"Do you regret anything, my love?"

"Regret anything? No!" Bella confidently answered. But then, suddenly changing, she said, between laughing and glistening: "Oh yes, I do, though. I regret Mrs. Boffin."

"I, too, regret that separation very much. But perhaps it is only temporary. Perhaps things may so fall out, as that you may sometimes see her again—as that we may sometimes see her again." Bella might be very anxious on the subject, but she scarcely seemed so at the moment. With an absent

328

air, she was investigating that button on her husband's coat, when Pa came in to spend the evening.

Pa had his special chair and his special corner reserved for him on all occasions, and—without disparagement of his domestic joys—was far happier there than anywhere. It was always pleasantly droll to see Pa and Bella together; but on this present evening her husband thought her more than usually fantastic with him.

"You are a very good little boy," said Bella, "to come unexpectedly as soon as you could get out of school. And how have they used you at school to-day, you dear?"

"Well, my pet," replied the cherub, smiling and rubbing his hands, as she sat him down in his chair, "I attend two schools. There's the Mincing Lane establishment, and there's your mother's Academy. Which might you mean, my dear?"

"Both," said Bella.

"Both, eh? Why, to say the truth, both have taken a little out of me to-day, my dear, but that was to be expected. There's no royal road to learning; and what is life but learning?"

"And what do you do with yourself when you have got your learning by heart, you silly child?"

"Why then, my dear," said the cherub, after a little consideration, "I suppose I die."

"You are a very bad boy," retorted Bella, "to talk about dismal things and be out of spirits."

"My Bella," rejoined her father, "I am not out of spirits. I am as gay as a lark." Which his face confirmed.

"Then if you are sure and certain it's not you, I suppose it must be I," said Bella; "so I won't do so any more. John dear, we must give this little fellow his supper, you know."

"Of course we must, my darling."

"He has been grubbing and grubbing at school," said Bella, looking at her father's hand and lightly slapping it, "till he's not fit to be seen. Oh, what a grubby child!"

329

"Indeed, my dear," said her father, "I was going to ask to be allowed to wash my hands, only you find me out so soon."

"Come here, sir!" cried Bella, taking him by the front of his coat, "come here and be washed directly. You are not to be trusted to do it for yourself. Come here, sir!"

The cherub, to his genial amusement, was accordingly conducted to a little washing-room, where Bella soaped his face and rubbed his face, and soaped his hands and rubbed his hands, and splashed him and rinsed him and towelled him, until he was as red as beetroot, even to his very ears: "Now you must be brushed and combed, sir," said Bella, busily. "Hold the light, John. Shut your eyes, sir, and let me take hold of your chin. Be good directly, and do as you are told!"

Her father being more than willing to obey, she dressed his hair in her most elaborate manner, brushing it out straight, parting it, winding it over her fingers, sticking it up on end, and constantly falling back on John to get a good look at the effect of it. Who always received her on his disengaged arm, and detained her, while the patient cherub stood waiting to be finished.

"There!" said Bella, when she had at last completed the final touches. "Now, you are something like a genteel boy! Put your jacket on, and come and have your supper."

The cherub investing himself with his coat was led back to his corner—where, but for having no egotism in his pleasant nature, he would have answered well enough for that radiant though self-sufficient boy, Jack Horner—Bella with her own hands laid a cloth for him, and brought him his supper on a tray. "Stop a moment," said she, "we must keep his little clothes clean;" and tied a napkin under his chin, in a very methodical manner.

While he took his supper, Bella sat by him, sometimes admonishing him to hold his fork by the handle, like a polite child, and at other times carving for him, or pouring out his drink. Fantastic as it all was, and accustomed as she ever had been to make a plaything of her good father, ever delighted that she should put him to that account, still there was an occasional something on Bella's part that was new. It could not be said that she was less playful, whimsical, or natural, than she always had been; but it seemed, her husband thought, as if there were some rather graver reason than he had supposed for what she had so lately said, and as if, throughout all this, there were glimpses of an underlying seriousness.

It was a circumstance in support of this view of the case, that when she had lighted her father's pipe, and mixed him his glass of grog, she sat down on a stool between her father and her husband, leaning her arm upon the latter, and was very quiet. So quiet, that when her father rose to take his leave, she looked round with a start, as if she had forgotten his being there.

" You go a little way with Pa, John ? "

" Yes, my dear. Do you ? "

" I have not written to Lizzie Hexam since I wrote and told her that I really had a lover—a whole one. I have often thought I would like to tell her how right she was when she pretended to read in the live coals that I would go through fire and water for him. I am in the humour to tell her so to-night, John, and I'll stay at home and do it."

" You are tired."

" Not at all tired, John dear, but in the humour to write to Lizzie. Good night, dear Pa. Good night, you dear, good, gentle Pa ! "

Left to herself, she sat down to write, and wrote Lizzie a long letter. She had but completed it and read it over, when her husband came back. " You are just in time, sir," said Bella ; " I am going to give you your first curtain lecture. It shall be a parlour-curtain lecture. You shall take this chair of mine when I have folded my letter, and I will take the stool (though you ought to take it, I can tell you, sir, if it's the stool of repentance), and you'll soon find yourself taken to task soundly."

Her letter folded, sealed, and directed, and her pen wiped, and her middle finger wiped, and her desk locked up and put away, and these transactions performed with an air of severe business sedateness, which the Complete British Housewife might have assumed, and certainly would not have rounded off and broken down in with a musical laugh, as Bella did : she placed her husband in his chair, and placed herself upon her stool.

" Now, sir ! To begin at the beginning. What is your name ? "

A question more decidedly rushing at the secret he was keeping from her, could not have astounded him. But he kept his countenance and his secret, and answered, " John Rokesmith, my dear."

" Good boy ! Who gave you that name ? "

With a returning suspicion that something might have betrayed him to her, he answered, interrogatively, " My godfathers and my godmothers, dear love ? "

" Pretty good ! " said Bella. " Not goodest good, because you hesitate about it. However, as you know your Catechism fairly, so far, I'll let you off the rest. Now, I am going to examine you out of my own head. John dear, why did you go back, this evening, to the question you once asked me before—would I like to be rich ? "

Again, his secret ! He looked down at her as she looked up at him, with her hands folded on his knee, and it was as nearly told as ever secret was.

Having no reply ready, he could do no better than embrace her.

" In short, dear John," said Bella, " this is the topic of my lecture : I want nothing on earth, and I want you to believe it."

" If that's all, the lecture may be considered over, for I do."

" It's not all, John dear," Bella hesitated. " It's only

Firstly. There's a dreadful Secondly, and a dreadful Thirdly to come—as I used to say to myself in sermon-time when I was a very small-sized sinner at church."

" Let them come, my dearest."

" Are you sure, John dear; are you absolutely certain in your innermost heart of hearts—— ? "

" Which is not in my keeping," he rejoined.

" No, John, but the key is.—Are you absolutely certain that down at the bottom of that heart of hearts, which you have given to me as I have given mine to you, there is no remembrance that I was once very mercenary ? "

" Why, if there were no remembrance in me of the time you speak of," he softly asked her with his lips to hers, " could I love you quite as well as I do; could I have in the Calendar of my life the brightest of its days ; could I whenever I look at your dear face, or hear your dear voice, see and hear my noble champion ? It can never have been that which made you serious, darling ? "

" No, John, it wasn't that, and still less was it Mrs. Boffin, though I love her. Wait a moment, and I'll go on with the lecture. Give me a moment, because I like to cry for joy. It's so delicious, John dear, to cry for joy."

She did so on his neck, and, still clinging there, laughed a little when she said, " I think I am ready now for Thirdly, John."

" *I* am ready for Thirdly," said John, " whatever it is."

" I believe, John," pursued Bella, " that you believe that I believe—— "

" My dear child," cried her husband gaily, " what a quantity of believing ! "

" Isn't there ? " said Bella, with another laugh. " I never knew such a quantity ! It's like verbs in an exercise. But I can't get on with less believing. I'll try again. I believe, dear John, that you believe that I believe that we have as much money as we require, and that we want for nothing."

" It is strictly true, Bella."

"But if our money should by any means be rendered not so much—if we had to stint ourselves a little in purchases that we can afford to make now—would you still have the same confidence in my being quite contented, John?"

"Precisely the same confidence, my soul."

"Thank you, John dear, thousands upon thousands of times. And I may take it for granted, no doubt," with a little faltering, "that you would be quite as contented yourself, John. But, yes, I know I may. For, knowing that I should be so, how surely I may know that you would be so; you who are so much stronger, and firmer, and more reasonable and more generous, than I am."

"Hush!" said her husband, "I must not hear that. You are all wrong there, though otherwise as right as can be. And now I am brought to a little piece of news, my dearest, that I might have told you earlier in the evening. I have strong reason for confidently believing that we shall never be in the receipt of a smaller income than our present income."

She might have shown herself more interested in the intelligence; but she had returned to the investigation of the coat-button that had engaged her attention a few hours before, and scarcely seemed to heed what he said.

"And now we have got to the bottom of it at last," cried her husband, rallying her, "and this is the thing that made you serious?"

"No, dear," said Bella, twisting the button and shaking her head, "it wasn't this."

"Why then, Lord bless this little wife of mine, there's a Fourthly!" exclaimed John.

"This worried me a little, and so did Secondly," said Bella, occupied with the button, "but it was quite another sort of seriousness—a much deeper and quieter sort of seriousness—that I spoke of, John dear."

As he bent his face to hers, she raised hers to meet it, and laid her little right hand on his eyes, and kept it there.

"Do you remember, John, on the day we were married,

Pa's speaking of the ships that might be sailing towards us from the unknown seas?"

"Perfectly, my darling!"

"I think . . . . . among them . . . . . there is a ship upon the ocean . . . . . bringing . . . . . to you and me . . . . . a little baby, John."

CHAPTER VI

THE Paper Mill had stopped work for the night, and the paths and roads in its neighbourhood were sprinkled with clusters of people going home from their day's labour in it. There were men, women, and children in the groups, and there was no want of lively colour to flutter in the gentle evening wind. The mingling of various voices and the sound of laughter made a cheerful impression upon the ear, analogous to that of the fluttering colours upon the eye. Into the sheet of water reflecting the flushed sky in the foreground of the living picture, a knot of urchins were casting stones, and watching the expansion of the rippling circles. So, in the rosy evening, one might watch the ever-widening beauty of the landscape—beyond the newly-released workers wending home—beyond the silver river—beyond the deep green fields of corn, so prospering, that the loiterers in their narrow threads of pathway seemed to float immersed breast-high—beyond the hedgerows and the clumps of trees—beyond the windmills on the ridge—away to where the sky appeared to meet the earth, as if there were no immensity of space between mankind and Heaven.

It was a Saturday evening, and at such a time the village dogs, always much more interested in the doings of humanity than in the affairs of their own species, were particularly active. At the general shop, at the butcher's, and at the

336

public-house, they evinced an inquiring spirit never to be satiated. Their especial interest in the public-house would seem to imply some latent rakishness in the canine character; for little was eaten there, and they, having no taste for beer or tobacco (Mrs. Hubbard's dog is said to have smoked, but proof is wanting), could only have been attracted by sympathy with loose convivial habits. Moreover, a most wretched fiddle played within; a fiddle so unutterably vile, that one lean long-bodied cur, with a better ear than the rest, found himself under compulsion at intervals to go round the corner and howl. Yet even he returned to the public-house on each occasion with the tenacity of a confirmed drunkard.

Fearful to relate, there was even a sort of little Fair in the village. Some despairing gingerbread that had been vainly trying to dispose of itself all over the country, and had cast a quantity of dust upon its head in its mortification, again appealed to the public from an infirm booth. So did a heap of nuts, long, long exiled from Barcelona, and yet speaking English so indifferently as to call fourteen of themselves a pint. A Peep-show which had originally started with the Battle of Waterloo, and had since made it every other battle of later date by altering the Duke of Wellington's nose, tempted the student of illustrated history. A Fat Lady, perhaps in part sustained upon postponed pork, her professional associate being a Learned Pig, displayed her life-size picture in a low dress as she appeared when presented at Court, several yards round. All this was a vicious spectacle, as any poor idea of amusement on the part of the rougher hewers of wood and drawers of water in this land of England ever is and shall be. They *must not* vary the rheumatism with amusement. They may vary it with fever and ague, or with as many rheumatic variations as they have joints; but positively not with entertainment after their own manner.

The various sounds arising from this scene of depravity,

and floating away into the still evening air, made the evening, at any point which they just reached fitfully, mellowed by the distance, more still by contrast. Such was the stillness of the evening to Eugene Wrayburn, as he walked by the river with his hands behind him.

He walked slowly, and with the measured step and pre-occupied air of one who was waiting. He walked between the two points, an osier-bed at this end and some floating lilies at that, and at each point stopped and looked ex-pectantly in one direction.

"It is very quiet," said he.

It was very quiet. Some sheep were grazing on the grass by the river-side, and it seemed to him that he had never before heard the crisp, tearing sound with which they cropped it. He stopped idly, and looked at them.

"You are stupid enough, I suppose. But if you are clever enough to get through life tolerably to your satisfaction, you have got the better of me, Man as I am, and Mutton as you are!"

A rustle in a field beyond the hedge attracted his attention. "What's here to do?" he asked himself, leisurely going towards the gate and looking over. "No jealous paper-miller? No pleasures of the chase in this part of the country? Mostly fishing hereabouts!"

The field had been newly mown, and there were yet the marks of the scythe on the yellow-green ground, and the track of wheels where the hay had been carried. Following the tracks with his eyes, the view closed with the new hayrick in a corner.

Now, if he had gone on to the hayrick, and gone round it? But, say that the event was to be, as the event fell out, and how idle are such suppositions! Besides, if he had gone; what is there of warning in a bargeman lying on his face?

"A bird flying to the hedge," was all he thought about it; and came back, and resumed his walk.

"If I had not a reliance on her being truthful," said Eugene, after taking some half-dozen turns, "I should begin to think she had given me the slip for the second time. But she promised, and she is a girl of her word."

Turning again at the water-lilies, he saw her coming, and advanced to meet her.

"I was saying to myself, Lizzie, that you were sure to come, though you were late."

"I had to linger through the village as if I had no object before me, and I had to speak to several people in passing along, Mr. Wrayburn."

"Are the lads of the village—and the ladies—such scandal-mongers?" he asked, as he took her hand and drew it through his arm.

She submitted to walk slowly on, with downcast eyes. He put her hand to his lips, and she quietly drew it away.

"Will you walk beside me, Mr. Wrayburn, and not touch me?" For, his arm was already stealing round her waist.

She stopped again, and gave him an earnest supplicating look. "Well, Lizzie, well!" said he, in an easy way, though ill at ease with himself, "don't be unhappy, don't be reproachful."

"I cannot help being unhappy, but I do not mean to be reproachful. Mr. Wrayburn, I implore you to go away from this neighbourhood to-morrow morning."

"Lizzie, Lizzie, Lizzie!" he remonstrated. "As well be reproachful as wholly unreasonable. I can't go away."

"Why not?"

"Faith!" said Eugene in his airily candid manner. "Because you won't let me. Mind! I don't mean to be reproachful either. I don't complain that you design to keep me here. But you do it, you do it."

"Will you walk beside me, and not touch me," for his arm was coming about her again; "while I speak to you very seriously, Mr. Wrayburn?"

"I will do anything within the limits of possibility, for

339

you, Lizzie," he answered with pleasant gaiety as he folded his arms. "See here! Napoleon Buonaparte at St. Helena."

"When you spoke to me as I came from the Mill the night before last," said Lizzie, fixing her eyes upon him with a look of supplication which troubled his better nature, "you told me that you were much surprised to see me, and that you were on a solitary fishing excursion. Was it true?"

"It was not," replied Eugene composedly, "in the least true. I came here because I had information that I should find you here."

"Can you imagine why I left London, Mr. Wrayburn?"

"I am afraid, Lizzie," he openly answered, "that you left London to get rid of me. It is not flattering to my self-love, but I am afraid you did."

"I did."

"How could you be so cruel?"

"Oh, Mr. Wrayburn," she answered, suddenly breaking into tears, "is the cruelty on my side? Oh, Mr. Wrayburn, Mr. Wrayburn, is there no cruelty in your being here to-night?"

"In the name of all that's good—and that is not conjuring you in my own name—for Heaven knows I am not good"—said Eugene, "don't be distressed!"

"What else can I be, when I know the distance and the difference between us? What else can I be, when to tell me why you came here, is to put me to shame!" said Lizzie, covering her face.

He looked at her with a real sentiment of remorseful tenderness and pity. It was not strong enough to impel him to sacrifice himself and spare her, but it was a strong emotion.

"Lizzie! I never thought before, that there was a woman in the world who could affect me so much by saying so little. But don't be hard in your construction of me. You don't know what my state of mind towards you is. You don't know how you haunt me and bewilder me. You don't know how the cursed carelessness that is over-officious in helping me at every other turning of my life, won't help me here. You have struck it dead, I think, and I sometimes almost wish you had struck me dead along with it."

She had not been prepared for such passionate expressions, and they awakened some natural sparks of feminine pride and joy in her breast. To consider, wrong as he was, that he could care so much for her, and that she had the power to move him so!

"It grieves you to see me distressed, Mr. Wrayburn; it grieves me to see you distressed. I don't reproach you. Indeed I don't reproach you. You have not felt this as I feel it, being so different from me, and beginning from another point of view. You have not thought. But I entreat you to think now, think now!"

"What am I to think of?" asked Eugene bitterly.

"Think of me."

"Tell me how *not* to think of you, Lizzie, and you'll change me altogether."

"I don't mean in that way. Think of me, as belonging to another station, and quite cut off from you in honour. Remember that I have no protector near me, unless I have one in your noble heart. Respect my good name. If you feel towards me, in one particular, as you might if I was a lady, give me the full claims of a lady upon your generous behaviour. I am removed from you and your family by being a working girl. How true a gentleman to be as considerate of me as if I was removed by being a Queen!"

He would have been base indeed to have stood untouched by her appeal. His face expressed contrition and indecision as he asked:

"Have I injured you so much, Lizzie?"

"No, no. You may set me quite right. I don't speak of the past, Mr. Wrayburn, but of the present and the future. Are we not here now, because through two days you have followed me so closely where there are so many eyes to see you, that I consented to this appointment as an escape?"

"Again, not very flattering to my self-love," said Eugene moodily; "but yes. Yes. Yes."

"Then I beseech you, Mr. Wrayburn, I beg and pray you, leave this neighbourhood. If you do not, consider to what you will drive me."

He did consider within himself for a moment or two, and then retorted, "Drive you? To what shall I drive you, Lizzie?"

"You will drive me away. I live here peacefully and respected, and I am well employed here. You will force me to quit this place as I quitted London, and—by following me again—will force me to quit the next place in which I may find refuge, as I quitted this."

"Are you so determined, Lizzie—forgive the word I am going to use, for it's literal truth—to fly from a lover?"

"I am so determined," she answered resolutely, though trembling, "to fly from such a lover. There was a poor woman died here but a little while ago, scores of years older than I am, whom I found by chance, lying on the wet earth. You may have heard some account of her?"

"I think I have," he answered, "if her name was Higden."

"Her name was Higden. Though she was so weak and old, she kept true to one purpose to the very last. Even at the very last, she made me promise that her purpose should be kept to, after she was dead, so settled was her determination. What she did, I can do. Mr. Wrayburn, if I believed—but I do not believe—that you could be so cruel to me as to drive me from place to place to wear me out, you should drive me to death and not do it."

He looked full at her handsome face, and in his own handsome face there was a light of blended admiration, anger, and reproach, which she—who loved him so in secret—whose heart had long been so full, and he the cause of its overflowing—drooped before. She tried hard to retain her firmness, but he saw it melting away under his eyes. In the

342

moment of its dissolution, and of his first full knowledge of his influence upon her, she dropped, and he caught her on his arm.

"Lizzie! Rest so a moment. Answer what I ask you. If I had not been what you call removed from you and cut off from you, would you have made this appeal to me to leave you?"

"I don't know, I don't know. Don't ask me, Mr. Wrayburn. Let me go back."

"I swear to you, Lizzie, you shall go directly. I swear to you, you shall go alone. I'll not accompany you, I'll not follow you, if you will reply."

"How can I, Mr. Wrayburn? How can I tell you what I should have done, if you had not been what you are?"

"If I had not been what you make me out to be," he struck in, skilfully changing the form of words, "would you still have hated me?"

"O Mr. Wrayburn," she replied appealingly, and weeping, "you know me better than to think I do!"

"If I had not been what you make me out to be, Lizzie, would you still have been indifferent to me?"

"O Mr. Wrayburn," she answered as before, "you know me better than that too!"

There was something in the attitude of her whole figure as he supported it, and she hung her head, which besought him to be merciful and not force her to disclose her heart. He was not merciful with her, and he made her do it.

"If I know you better than quite to believe (unfortunate dog though I am!) that you hate me, or even that you are wholly indifferent to me, Lizzie, let me know so much more from yourself before we separate. Let me know how you would have dealt with me if you had regarded me as being what you would have considered on equal terms with you."

"It is impossible, Mr. Wrayburn. How can I think of you as being on equal terms with me? If my mind could put you on equal terms with me, you could not be yourself.

343

How could I remember, then, the night when I first saw you, and when I went out of the room because you looked at me so attentively? Or, the night that passed into the morning when you broke to me that my father was dead? Or, the nights when you used to come to see me at my next home? Or, your having known how uninstructed I was, and having caused me to be taught better? Or, my having so looked up to you and wondered at you, and at first thought you so good to be at all mindful of me?"

"Only 'at first' thought me so good, Lizzie? What did you think me after 'at first'? So bad?"

"I don't say that. I don't mean that. But after the first wonder and pleasure of being noticed by one so different from any one who had ever spoken to me, I began to feel that it might have been better if I had never seen you."

"Why?"

"Because you *were* so different," she answered in a lower voice. "Because it was so endless, so hopeless. Spare me."

"Did you think for me at all, Lizzie?" he asked, as if he were a little stung.

"Not much, Mr. Wrayburn. Not much until to-night."

"Will you tell me why?"

"I never supposed until to-night that you needed to be thought for. But if you do need to be; if you do truly feel at heart that you have indeed been towards me what you have called yourself to-night, and that there is nothing for us in this life but separation; then Heaven help you, and Heaven bless you!"

The purity with which in these words she expressed something of her own love and her own suffering, made a deep impression on him for the passing time. He held her, almost as if she were sanctified to him by death, and kissed her, once, almost as he might have kissed the dead.

"I promised that I would not accompany you, nor follow you. Shall I keep you in view? You have been agitated, and it's growing dark."

The Parting by the River

"I am used to be out alone at this hour, and I entreat you not to do so."

"I promise. I can bring myself to promise nothing more to-night, Lizzie, except that I will try what I can do."

"There is but one means, Mr. Wrayburn, of sparing yourself and of sparing me, every way. Leave this neighbourhood to-morrow morning."

"I will try."

As he spoke the words in a grave voice, she put her hand in his, removed it, and went away by the river-side.

"Now, could Mortimer believe this?" murmured Eugene, still remaining, after a while, where she had left him. "Can I even believe it myself?"

He referred to the circumstance that there were tears upon his hand, as he stood covering his eyes. "A most ridiculous position this, to be found out in!" was his next thought. And his next struck its root in a little rising resentment against the cause of the tears.

"Yet I have gained a wonderful power over her, too, let her be as much in earnest as she will!"

The reflection brought back the yielding of her face and form as she had drooped under his gaze. Contemplating the reproduction, he seemed to see, for the second time, in the appeal and in the confession of weakness, a little fear.

"And she loves me. And so earnest a character must be very earnest in that passion. She cannot choose for herself to be strong in this fancy, wavering in that, and weak in the other. She must go through with her nature, as I must go through with mine. If mine exacts its pains and penalties all round, so must hers, I suppose."

Pursuing the inquiry into his own nature, he thought, "Now, if I married her. If, outfacing the absurdity of the situation in correspondence with M. R. F., I astonished M. R. F. to the utmost extent of his respected powers, by informing him that I had married her, how would M. R. F. reason with the legal mind? 'You wouldn't marry for

some money and some station, because you were frightfully
likely to become bored. Are you less frightfully likely to
become bored, marrying for no money and no station? Are
you sure of yourself?' Legal mind, in spite of forensic protestations, must secretly admit, 'Good reasoning on the part
of M. R. F. *Not* sure of myself.'"

In the very act of calling this tone of levity to his aid,
he felt it to be profligate and worthless, and asserted her
against it.

"And yet," said Eugene, "I should like to see the fellow
(Mortimer excepted) who would undertake to tell me that
this was not a real sentiment on my part, won out of me by
her beauty and her worth, in spite of myself, and that I
would not be true to her. I should particularly like to see
the fellow to-night who would tell me so, or who would tell
me anything that could be construed to her disadvantage;
for I am wearily out of sorts with one Wrayburn who cuts a
sorry figure, and I would far rather be out of sorts with somebody else. 'Eugene, Eugene, Eugene, this is a bad business.'
Ah! So go the Mortimer Lightwood bells, and they sound
melancholy to-night."

Strolling on, he thought of something else to take himself
to task for. "Where is the analogy, Brute Beast," he said
impatiently, "between a woman whom your father coolly
finds out for you and a woman whom you have found out for
yourself, and have ever drifted after with more and more of
constancy since you first set eyes upon her? Ass! Can you
reason no better than that?"

But, again he subsided into a reminiscence of his first full
knowledge of his power just now, and of her disclosure of her
heart. To try no more to go away, and to try her again,
was the reckless conclusion it turned uppermost. And yet
again, "Eugene, Eugene, Eugene, this is a bad business!"
And, "I wish I could stop the Lightwood peal, for it
sounds like a knell."

Looking above, he found that the young moon was up, and

346

that the stars were beginning to shine in the sky from which the tones of red and yellow were flickering out, in favour of the calm blue of a summer night. He was still by the riverside. Turning suddenly, he met a man, so close upon him that Eugene, surprised, stepped back, to avoid a collision. The man carried something over his shoulder which might have been a broken oar, or spar, or bar, and took no notice of him, but passed on.

"Halloa, friend!" said Eugene, calling after him, "are you blind?"

The man made no reply, but went his way.

Eugene Wrayburn went the opposite way, with his hands behind him and his purpose in his thoughts. He passed the sheep, and passed the gate, and came within hearing of the village sounds, and came to the bridge. The inn where he stayed, like the village and the mill, was not across the river, but on that side of the stream on which he walked. However, knowing the rushy bank and the backwater on the other side to be a retired place, and feeling out of humour for noise or company, he crossed the bridge, and sauntered on: looking up at the stars as they seemed one by one to be kindled in the sky, and looking down at the river as the same stars seemed to be kindled deep in the water. A landing-place overshadowed by a willow, and a pleasure-boat lying moored there among some stakes, caught his eye as he passed along. The spot was in such dark shadow, that he paused to make out what was there, and then passed on again.

The rippling of the river seemed to cause a correspondent stir in his uneasy reflections. He would have laid them asleep if he could, but they were in movement, like the stream, and all tending one way with a strong current. As the ripple under the moon broke unexpectedly now and then, and palely flashed in a new shape and with a new sound, so parts of his thoughts started, unbidden, from the rest, and revealed their wickedness. "Out of the question to marry

347

her," said Eugene, "and out of the question to leave her. The crisis!"

He had sauntered far enough. Before turning to retrace his steps, he stopped upon the margin, to look down at the reflected night. In an instant, with a dreadful crash, the reflected night turned crooked, flames shot jaggedly across the air, and the moon and stars came bursting from the sky.

Was he struck by lightning? With some incoherent half-formed thought to that effect, he turned under the blows that were blinding him and mashing his life, and closed with a murderer, whom he caught by a red neckerchief—unless the raining down of his own blood gave it that hue.

Eugene was light, active, and expert; but his arms were broken, or he was paralysed, and could do no more than hang on to the man, with his head swung back, so that he could see nothing but the heaving sky. After dragging at the assailant, he fell on the bank with him, and then there was another great crash, and then a splash, and all was done.

Lizzie Hexam, too, had avoided the noise, and the Saturday movement of people in the straggling street, and chose to walk alone by the water until her tears should be dry, and she could so compose herself as to escape remark upon her looking ill or unhappy on going home. The peaceful serenity of the hour and place, having no reproaches or evil intentions within her breast to contend against, sank healingly into its depths. She had meditated and taken comfort. She, too, was turning homeward, when she heard a strange sound.

It startled her, for it was like a sound of blows. She stood still and listened. It sickened her, for blows fell heavily and cruelly on the quiet of the night. As she listened, undecided, all was silent. As she yet listened, she heard a faint groan, and a fall into the river.

Her old bold life and habit instantly inspired her. Without vain waste of breath in crying for help where there were none to hear, she ran towards the spot from which the sounds had come. It lay between her and the bridge, but it was

348

more removed from her than she had thought; the night being so very quiet, and sound travelling far with the help of the water.

At length, she reached a part of the green bank, much and newly trodden, where there lay some broken splintered pieces of wood and some torn fragments of clothes. Stooping, she saw that the grass was bloody. Following the drops and smears, she saw that the watery margin of the bank was bloody. Following the current with her eyes, she saw a bloody face turned up towards the moon, and drifting away.

Now, merciful Heaven be thanked for that old time, and grant, O Blessed Lord, that through thy wonderful workings it may turn to good at last! To whomsoever the drifting face belongs, be it man's or woman's, help my humble hands, Lord God, to raise it from death and restore it to some one to whom it must be dear!

It was thought, fervently thought, but not for a moment did the prayer check her. She was away before it welled up in her mind, away, swift and true, yet steady above all—for without steadiness it could never be done—to the landing-place under the willow-tree, where she also had seen the boat lying moored among the stakes.

A sure touch of her old practised hand, a sure step of her old practised foot, a sure light balance of her body, and she was in the boat. A quick glance of her practised eye showed her, even through the deep dark shadow, the sculls in a rack against the red-brick garden-wall. Another moment, and she had cast off (taking the line with her), and the boat had shot out into the moonlight, and she was rowing down the stream as never other woman rowed on English water.

Intently over her shoulder, without slackening speed, she looked ahead for the driving face. She passed the scene of the struggle—yonder it was, on her left, well over the boat's stern—she passed on her right, the end of the village street, a hilly street that almost dipped into the river; its sounds were growing faint again, and she slackened; looking as the boat drove everywhere, everywhere, for the floating face.

She merely kept the boat before the stream now, and rested on her oars, knowing well that if the face were not soon visible, it had gone down, and she would overshoot it. An untrained sight would never have seen by the moonlight what she saw at the length of a few strokes astern. She saw the drowning figure rise to the surface, slightly struggle, and as if by instinct turn over on its back to float. Just so had she first dimly seen the face which she now dimly saw again.

Firm of look and firm of purpose, she intently watched its coming on, until it was very near; then, with a touch unshipped her sculls, and crept aft in the boat, between kneeling and crouching. Once, she let the body evade her, not being sure of her grasp. Twice, and she had seized it by its bloody hair.

It was insensible, if not virtually dead; it was mutilated, and streaked the water all about it with dark red streaks. As it could not help itself, it was impossible for her to get it on board. She bent over the stern to secure it with the line, and then the river and its shores rang to the terrible cry she uttered.

But, as if possessed by supernatural spirit and strength, she lashed it safe, resumed her seat, and rowed in, desperately, for the nearest shallow water where she might run the boat aground. Desperately, but not wildly, for she knew that if she lost distinctness of intention, all was lost and gone.

She ran the boat ashore, went into the water, released him from the line, and by main strength lifted him in her arms and laid him in the bottom of the boat. He had fearful wounds upon him, and she bound them up with her dress torn into strips. Else, supposing him to be still alive, she foresaw that he must bleed to death before he could be landed at his inn, which was the nearest place for succour. This done very rapidly, she kissed his disfigured forehead, looked up in anguish to the stars, and blessed him and forgave him, "if she had anything to forgive." It was only in that instant that she thought of herself, and then she thought of herself only for him.

Now, merciful Heaven be thanked for that old time, enabling me, without a wasted moment, to have got the boat afloat again, and to row back against the stream! And grant, O Blessed Lord God, that through poor me he may be raised from death, and preserved to some one else to whom he may be dear one day, though never dearer than to me!

She rowed hard—rowed desperately, but never wildly—and seldom removed her eyes from him in the bottom of the boat. She had so laid him there, as that she might see his disfigured face; it was so much disfigured that his mother might have covered it, but it was above and beyond disfigurement in her eyes.

The boat touched the edge of the patch of inn lawn, sloping gently to the water. There were lights in the windows, but there chanced to be no one out of doors. She made the boat fast, and again by main strength took him up, and never laid him down until she laid him down in the house.

Surgeons were sent for, and she sat supporting his head. She had oftentimes heard in days that were gone, how doctors would lift the hand of an insensible wounded person, and would drop it if the person were dead. She waited for the awful moment when the doctors might lift this hand, all broken and bruised, and let it fall.

The first of the surgeons came, and asked, before proceeding to his examination, "Who brought him in?"

"I brought him in, sir," answered Lizzie, at whom all present looked.

"You, my dear? You could not lift, far less carry, this weight."

"I think I could not, at another time, sir; but I am sure I did."

The surgeon looked at her with great attention, and with

some compassion. Having with a grave face touched the wounds upon the head, and the broken arms, he took the hand.

Oh! would he let it drop?

He appeared irresolute. He did not retain it, but laid it gently down, took a candle, looked more closely at the injuries on the head, and at the pupils of the eyes. That done, he replaced the candle and took the hand again. Another surgeon then coming in, the two exchanged a whisper, and the second took the hand. Neither did he let it fall at once, but kept it for a while and laid it gently down.

"Attend to the poor girl," said the first surgeon then. "She is quite unconscious. She sees nothing and hears nothing. All the better for her! Don't rouse her, if you can help it; only move her. Poor girl, poor girl! She must be amazingly strong of heart, but it is much to be feared that she has set her heart upon the dead. Be gentle with her."

CHAPTER VII

DAY was breaking at Plashwater Weir-Mill Lock. Stars were yet visible, but there was dull light in the east that was not the light of night. The moon had gone down, and a mist crept along the banks of the river, seen through which the trees were the ghosts of trees, and the water was the ghost of water. This earth looked spectral, and so did the pale stars: while the cold eastern glare, expressionless as to heat or colour, with the eye of the firmament quenched, might have been likened to the stare of the dead.

Perhaps it was so likened by the lonely Bargeman, standing on the brink of the lock. For certain, Bradley Headstone looked that way, when a chill air came up, and when it passed on murmuring, as if it whispered something that made the phantom trees and water tremble—or threaten—for fancy might have made it either.

He turned away, and tried the Lock-house door. It was fastened on the inside.

" Is he afraid of me ? " he muttered, knocking.

Rogue Riderhood was soon roused, and soon undrew the bolt and let him in.

" Why, T'otherest, I thought you had been and got lost ! Two nights away ! I a'most believed as you'd giv' me the slip, and I had as good as half a mind for to advertise you in the newspapers to come for'ard."

353

Bradley's face turned so dark on this hint, that Riderhood deemed it expedient to soften it into a compliment.

"But not you, governor, not you," he went on, stolidly shaking his head. "For what did I say to myself arter having amused myself with that there stretch of a comic idea, as a sort of a playful game? Why, I says to myself, 'He's a man o' honour.' That's what *I* says to myself. 'He's a man o' double honour.'"

Very remarkably, Riderhood put no question to him. He had looked at him on opening the door, and he now looked at him again (stealthily this time), and the result of his looking was, that he asked him no question.

"You'll be for another forty on 'em, governor, as I judges, afore you turns your mind to breakfast," said Riderhood, when his visitor sat down, resting his chin on his hand, with his eyes on the ground. And very remarkably again: Riderhood feigned to set the scanty furniture in order, while he spoke, to have a show of reason for not looking at him.

"Yes, I had better sleep, I think," said Bradley, without changing his position.

"I myself should recommend it, governor," assented Riderhood. "Might you be anyways dry?"

"Yes. I should like a drink," said Bradley; but without appearing to attend much.

Mr. Riderhood got out his bottle, and fetched his jug-full of water, and administered a potation. Then, he shook the coverlet of his bed and spread it smooth, and Bradley stretched himself upon it in the clothes he wore. Mr. Riderhood poetically remarking that he would pick the bones of his night's rest in his wooden chair, sat in the window as before; but, as before, watched the sleeper narrowly until he was very sound asleep. Then, he rose and looked at him close, in the bright daylight, on every side, with great minuteness. He went out to his Lock to sum up what he had seen.

"One of his sleeves is tore right away below the elber, and the t'other's had a good rip at the shoulder. He's been

354

hung on to, pretty tight, for his shirt's all tore out of the neck-gathers. He's been in the grass and he's been in the water. And he's spotted, and I know with what, and with whose. Hooroar ! "

Bradley slept long. Early in the afternoon a barge came down. Other barges had passed through, both ways, before it ; but the Lock-keeper hailed only this particular barge, for news, as if he had made a time calculation with some nicety. The men on board told him a piece of news, and there was a lingering on their part to enlarge upon it.

Twelve hours had intervened since Bradley's lying down, when he got up. " Not that I swaller it," said Riderhood, squinting at his Lock, when he saw Bradley coming out of the house, " as you've been a-sleeping all the time, old boy ! "

Bradley came to him, sitting on his wooden lever, and asked what o'clock it was ? Riderhood told him it was between two and three.

" When are you relieved ? " asked Bradley.

" Day arter to-morrow, governor."

" Not sooner ? "

" Not a inch sooner, governor."

On both sides importance seemed attached to this question of relief. Riderhood quite petted his reply ; saying a second time, and prolonging a negative roll of his head, " n—n—not a inch sooner, governor."

" Did I tell you I was going on to-night ? " asked Bradley.

" No, governor," returned Riderhood, in a cheerful, affable, and conversational manner, " you did not tell me so. But most like you meant to it and forgot to it. How, otherways, could a doubt have come into your head about it, governor ? "

" As the sun goes down, I intend to go on," said Bradley.

" So much the more necessairy is a Peck," returned Riderhood. " Come in and have it, T'otherest ? "

The formality of spreading a table-cloth not being observed in Mr. Riderhood's establishment, the serving of the " peck " was the affair of a moment ; it merely consisted in the handing down of a capacious baking-dish with three-fourths of an immense meat pie in it, and the production of two pocket-knives, an earthenware mug, and a large brown bottle of beer.

Both ate and drank, but Riderhood much the more abundantly. In lieu of plates, that honest man cut two triangular pieces from the thick crust of the pie, and laid them, inside uppermost, upon the table: the one before himself, and the other before his guest. Upon these platters he placed two goodly portions of the contents of the pie, thus imparting the unusual interest to the entertainment that each partaker scooped out the inside of his plate, and consumed it with his other fare, besides having the sport of pursuing the clots of congealed gravy over the plain of the table, and successfully taking them into his mouth at last from the blade of his knife, in case of their not first sliding off it.

Bradley Headstone was so remarkably awkward at these exercises, that the Rogue observed it.

" Look out, T'otherest!" he cried, " you'll cut your hand!"

But the caution came too late, for Bradley gashed it at the instant. And, what was more unlucky, in asking Riderhood to tie it up, and in standing close to him for the purpose, he shook his hand under the smart of the wound, and shook blood over Riderhood's dress.

When dinner was done, and when what remained of the platters and what remained of the congealed gravy had been put back into what remained of the pie, which served as an economical investment for all miscellaneous savings, Riderhood filled the mug with beer and took a long drink. And now he did look at Bradley, and with an evil eye.

" T'otherest!" he said, hoarsely, as he bent across the table to touch his arm. " The news has gone down the river afore you."

" What news?"

" Who do you think," said Riderhood, with a hitch of his

head, as if he disdainfully jerked the feint away, "picked up the body? Guess."

"I am not good at guessing anything."

"She did. Hooroar! You had him there agin. She did."

The convulsive twitching of Bradley Headstone's face, and the sudden hot humour that broke out upon it, showed how grimly the intelligence touched him. But he said not a single word, good or bad. He only smiled in a lowering manner, and got up and stood leaning at the window, looking through it. Riderhood followed him with his eyes. Riderhood cast down his eyes on his own besprinked clothes. Riderhood began to have an air of being better at a guess than Bradley owned to being.

"I have been so long in want of rest," said the schoolmaster, "that with your leave I'll lie down again."

"And welcome, T'otherest!" was the hospitable answer of his host. He had laid himself down without waiting for it, and he remained upon the bed until the sun was low. When he arose and came out to resume his journey, he found his host waiting for him on the grass by the towing-path outside the door.

"Whenever it may be necessary that you and I should have any further communication together," said Bradley, "I will come back. Good-night!"

"Well, since no better can be," said Riderhood, turning on his heel, "Good-night!" But he turned again as the other set forth, and added under his breath, looking after him with a leer: "You wouldn't be let to go like that, if my Relief warn't as good as come. I'll catch you up in a mile."

In a word, his real time of relief being that evening at sunset, his mate came lounging in, within a quarter of an hour. Not staying to fill up the utmost margin of his time, but borrowing an hour or so, to be repaid again when he should relieve his reliever, Riderhood straightway followed on the track of Bradley Headstone.

He was a better follower than Bradley. It had been the calling of his life to slink, and skulk, and dog, and waylay, and he knew his calling well. He effected such a forced march on leaving the Lock-house that he was close up with him—that is to say, as close up with him as he deemed it convenient to be—before another Lock was passed. His man looked back pretty often as he went, but got no hint of him. *He* knew how to take advantage of the ground, and where to put the hedge between them, and where the wall, and when to duck, and when to drop, and had a thousand arts beyond the doomed Bradley's slow conception.

But, all his arts were brought to a standstill, like himself, when Bradley, turning into a green lane or riding by the river-side, a solitary spot run wild in nettles, briars, and brambles, and encumbered with the scathed trunks of a whole hedgerow of felled trees, on the outskirts of a little wood—began stepping on these trunks and dropping down among them and stepping on them again, apparently as a schoolboy might have done, but assuredly with no schoolboy purpose, or want of purpose.

" What are you up to ? " muttered Riderhood, down in the ditch, and holding the hedge a little open with both hands. And soon his actions made a most extraordinary reply. " By George and the Draggin ! " cried Riderhood, " if he ain't a-going to bathe ! "

He had passed back, on and among the trunks of trees again, and had passed on to the water-side and had begun undressing on the grass. For a moment it had a suspicious look of suicide, arranged to counterfeit accident. " But you wouldn't have fetched a bundle under your arm, from among that timber, if such was your game ! " said Riderhood. Nevertheless it was a relief to him when the bather, after a plunge and a few strokes, came out. " For I shouldn't," he said, in a feeling manner, " have liked to lose you till I had made more money out of you neither."

Prone in another ditch (he had changed his ditch as his

man had changed his position), and holding apart so small a patch of the hedge that the sharpest eyes could not have detected him, Rogue Riderhood watched the bather dressing. And now gradually came the wonder that he stood up, completely clothed, another man, and not the Bargeman.

"Aha!" said Riderhood. "Much as you was dressed that night. I see. You're a-taking me with you, now. You're deep. But I knows a deeper."

When the bather had finished dressing, he kneeled on the grass, doing something with his hands, and again stood up with his bundle under his arm. Looking all around him with great attention, he then went to the river's edge, and flung it in as far, and yet as lightly as he could. It was not until he was so decidedly upon his way again as to be beyond a bend of the river, and for the time out of view, that Riderhood scrambled from the ditch.

"Now," was his debate with himself, "shall I foller you on, or shall I let you loose for this once, and go a-fishing?" The debate continuing, he followed, as a precautionary measure in any case and got him again in sight. "If I was to let you loose this once," said Riderhood then, still following, "I could make you come to me agin, or I could find you out in one way or another. If I wasn't to go a-fishing, others might.—I'll let you loose this once, and go a-fishing?" With that, he suddenly dropped the pursuit and turned.

The miserable man whom he had released for the time, but not for long, went on towards London. Bradley was suspicious of every sound he heard, and of every face he saw, but was under a spell which very commonly falls upon the shedder of blood, and had no suspicion of the real danger that lurked in his life, and would have it yet. Riderhood was much in his thoughts—had never been out of his thoughts since the night-adventure of their first meeting; but Riderhood occupied a very different place there, from the place of pursuer; and Bradley had been at the pains of devising so many means of fitting that place to him, and of

359

wedging him into it, that his mind could not compass the possibility of his occupying any other. And this is another spell against which the shedder of blood for ever strives in vain. There are fifty doors by which discovery may enter. With infinite pains and cunning, he double locks and bars forty-nine of them, and cannot see the fiftieth standing wide open.

Now, too, was he cursed with a state of mind more wearing and more wearisome than remorse. He had no remorse ; but the evil-doer who can hold that avenger at bay, cannot escape the slower torture of incessantly doing the evil deed again and doing it more efficiently. In the defensive declarations and pretended confessions of murderers, the pursuing shadow of this torture may be traced through every lie they tell. If I had done it as alleged, is it conceivable that I would have made this and this mistake? If I had done it as alleged, should I have left that unguarded place which that false and wicked witness against me so infamously deposed to? The state of that wretch who continually finds the weak spots in his own crime, and strives to strengthen them when it is unchangeable, is a state that aggravates the offence by doing the deed a thousand times instead of once ; but it is a state, too, that tauntingly visits the offence upon a sullen unrepentant nature with its heaviest punishment every time.

Bradley toiled on, chained heavily to the idea of his hatred and his vengeance, and thinking how he might have satiated both in many better ways than the way he had taken. The instrument might have been better, the spot and the hour might have been better chosen. To batter a man down from behind in the dark, on the brink of a river, was well enough, but he ought to have been instantly disabled, whereas he had turned and seized his assailant ; and so, to end it before chance help came, and to be rid of him, he had been hurriedly thrown backward into the river before the life was fully beaten out of him. Now if it could be done again, it must not be so done. Supposing his head had been held down under water for a while. Supposing the first blow had been truer. Supposing he had been shot. Supposing he had been strangled. Suppose this way, that way, the other way. Suppose anything but getting unchained from the one idea, for that was inexorably impossible.

The school re-opened next day. The scholars saw little or no change in their master's face, for it always wore its slowly labouring expression. But, as he heard his classes, he was always doing the deed and doing it better. As he paused with his piece of chalk at the black board before writing on it, he was thinking of the spot, and whether the water was not deeper and the fall straighter, a little higher up, or a little lower down. He had half a mind to draw a line or two upon the board, and show himself what he meant. He was doing it again and improving on the manner, at prayers, in his mental arithmetic, all through his questioning, all through the day.

Charley Hexam was a master now, in another school, under another head. It was evening, and Bradley was walking in his garden observed from behind a blind by gentle little Miss Peecher, who contemplated offering him a loan of her smelling salts for headache, when Mary Anne, in faithful attendance, held up her arm.

" Yes, Mary Anne ? "

" Young Mr. Hexam, if you please, ma'am, coming to see Mr. Headstone."

" Very good, Mary Anne."

Again Mary Anne held up her arm.

" You may speak, Mary Anne ? "

" Mr. Headstone has beckoned young Mr. Hexam into his house, ma'am, and he has gone in himself without waiting for young Mr. Hexam to come up, and now *he* has gone in too, ma'am, and has shut the door."

" With all my heart, Mary Anne."

Again Mary Anne's telegraphic arm worked.

"What more, Mary Anne?"

"They must find it rather dull and dark, Miss Peecher, for the parlour blind's down, and neither of them pulls it up."

"There is no accounting," said good Miss Peecher with a little sad sigh which she repressed by laying her hand on her neat methodical bodice, "there is no accounting for tastes, Mary Anne."

Charley, entering the dark room, stopped short when he saw his old friend in its yellow shade.

"Come in, Hexam, come in."

Charley advanced to take the hand that was held out to him; but stopped again, short of it. The heavy, blood-shot eyes of the schoolmaster, rising to his face with an effort, met his look of scrutiny.

"Mr. Headstone, what's the matter?"

"Matter? Where?"

"Mr. Headstone, have you heard the news? This news about the fellow, Mr. Eugene Wrayburn? That he is killed?"

"He is dead, then!" exclaimed Bradley.

Young Hexam standing looking at him, he moistened his lips with his tongue, looked about the room, glanced at his former pupil, and looked down. "I heard of the outrage," said Bradley, trying to constrain his working mouth, "but I had not heard the end of it."

"Where were you," said the boy, advancing a step as he lowered his voice, "when it was done? Stop! I don't ask that. Don't tell me. If you force your confidence upon me, Mr. Headstone, I'll give up every word of it. Mind! Take notice. I'll give it up, and I'll give up you. I will."

The wretched creature seemed to suffer acutely under this renunciation. A desolate air of utter and complete loneliness fell upon him, like a visible shade.

"It's for me to speak, not you," said the boy. "If you do, you'll do it at your peril. I am going to put your selfishness before you, Mr. Headstone—your passionate, violent, and

362

ungovernable selfishness—to show you why I can, and why I will, have nothing more to do with you."

He looked at young Hexam as if he were waiting for a scholar to go on with a lesson that he knew by heart and was deadly tired of. But he had said his last word to him.

"If you had any part—I don't say what—in this attack," pursued the boy; "or if you know anything about it—I don't say how much—or if you know who did it—I go no closer— you did an injury to me that's never to be forgiven. You know that I took you with me to his chambers in the Temple when I told him my opinion of him, and made myself responsible for my opinion of you. You know that I took you with me when I was watching him, with a view to recovering my sister and bringing her to her senses; you know that I have allowed myself to be mixed up with you all through this business, in favouring your desire to marry my sister. And how do you know that, pursuing the ends of your own violent temper, you have not laid me open to suspicion? Is that your gratitude to me, Mr. Headstone?"

Bradley sat looking steadily before him at the vacant air. As often as young Hexam stopped, he turned his eyes towards him, as if he were waiting for him to go on with the lesson, and get it done. As often as the boy resumed, Bradley resumed his fixed face.

"I am going to be plain with you, Mr. Headstone," said young Hexam, shaking his head in a half-threatening manner, "because this is no time for affecting not to know things that I do know—except certain things at which it might not be very safe for you to hint again. What I mean is this: if you were a good master, I was a good pupil. I have done you plenty of credit, and in improving my own reputation I have improved yours quite as much. Very well then. Starting on equal terms, I want to put before you how you have shown your gratitude to me, for doing all I could to further your wishes with reference to my sister. You have compromised me by being seen about with me, endeavouring to counteract this Mr. Eugene Wrayburn. That's the first thing you have done. If my character, and my now dropping you, help me out of that, Mr. Headstone, the deliverance is to be attributed to me, and not to you. No thanks to you for it !"

The boy stopping again, he moved his eyes again.

"I am going on, Mr. Headstone, don't you be afraid. I am going on to the end, and I have told you beforehand what the end is. Now, you know my story. You are as well aware as I am, that I have had many disadvantages to leave behind me in life. You have heard me mention my father, and you are sufficiently acquainted with the fact that the home from which I, as I may say, escaped, might have been a more creditable one than it was. My father died, and then it might have been supposed that my way to respectability was pretty clear. No. For then my sister begins."

He spoke as confidently, and with as entire an absence of any tell-tale colour in his cheek, as if there were no softening old time behind him. Not wonderful, for there *was* none in his hollow, empty heart. What is there but self, for selfishness to see behind it ?

"When I speak of my sister, I devoutly wish that you had never seen her, Mr. Headstone. However, you did see her, and that's useless now. I confided in you about her. I explained her character to you, and how she interposed some ridiculous, fanciful notions in the way of our being as respectable as I tried for. You fell in love with her, and I favoured you with all my might. She could not be induced to favour you, and so we came into collision with this Mr. Eugene Wrayburn. Now, what have you done ? Why, you have justified my sister in being firmly set against you from first to last, and you have put me in the wrong again ! And why have you done it ? Because, Mr. Headstone, you are in all your passions so selfish, and so concentrated upon yourself, that you have not bestowed one proper thought on me."

Better to be Abel than Cain

The cool conviction with which the boy took up and held his position, could have been derived from no other vice in human nature.

"It is," he went on, actually with tears, " an extraordinary circumstance attendant on my life, that every effort I make towards perfect respectability, is impeded by somebody else through no fault of mine! Not content with doing what I have put before you, you will drag my name into notoriety through dragging my sister's—which you are pretty sure to do, if my suspicions have any foundation at all—and the worse you prove to be, the harder it will be for me to detach myself from being associated with you in people's minds."

When he had dried his eyes and heaved a sob over his injuries, he began moving towards the door.

" However, I have made up my mind that I will become respectable in the scale of society, and that I will not be dragged down by others. I have done with my sister as well as with you. Since she cares so little for me as to care nothing for undermining my respectability, she shall go her way and I will go mine. My prospects are very good, and I mean to follow them alone. Mr. Headstone, I don't say what you have got upon your conscience, for I don't know. Whatever lies upon it, I hope you will see the justice of keeping wide and clear of me, and will find a consolation in completely exonerating all but yourself. I hope before many years are out, to succeed the master in my present school, and the mistress being a single woman, though some years older than I am, I might even marry her. If it is any comfort to you to know what plans I may work out by keeping myself strictly respectable in the scale of society, these are the plans at present occurring to me. In conclusion, if you feel a sense of having injured me, and a desire to make some small reparation, I hope you will think how respectable you might have been yourself, and will contemplate your blighted existence."

Was it strange that the wretched man should take this

heavily to heart? Perhaps he had taken the boy to heart, first, through some long laborious years ; perhaps through the same years he had found his drudgery lightened by communication with a brighter and more apprehensive spirit than his own ; perhaps a family resemblance of face and voice between the boy and his sister, smote him hard in the gloom of his fallen state. For whichsoever reason, or for all, he drooped his devoted head when the boy was gone, and shrank together on the floor, and grovelled there, with the palms of his hands tight-clasping his hot temples, in unutterable misery, and unrelieved by a single tear.

Rogue Riderhood had been busy with the river that day. He had fished with assiduity on the previous evening, but the light was short, and he had fished unsuccessfully. He had fished again that day with better luck, and had carried his fish home to Plashwater Weir-Mill Lock-house, in a bundle.

CHAPTER VIII.

THE dolls' dressmaker went no more to the business-premises of Pubsey and Co. in Saint Mary Axe, after chance had disclosed to her (as she supposed) the flinty and hypocritical character of Mr. Riah. She often moralised over her work on the tricks and the manners of that venerable cheat, but made her little purchases elsewhere, and lived a secluded life. After much consultation with herself, she decided not to put Lizzie Hexam on her guard against the old man, arguing that the disappointment of finding him out would come upon her quite soon enough. Therefore, in her communication with her friend by letter, she was silent on this theme, and principally dilated on the backslidings of her bad child, who every day grew worse and worse.

"You wicked old boy," Miss Wren would say to him, with a menacing forefinger; "you'll force me to run away from you, after all, you will; and then you'll shake to bits, and there'll be nobody to pick up the pieces!"

At this foreshadowing of a desolate decease, the wicked old boy would whine and whimper, and would sit shaking himself into the lowest of low spirits, until such time as he could shake himself out of the house and shake another threepennyworth into himself. But dead drunk or dead sober (he had come to such a pass that he was least alive in the latter state), it was always on the conscience of the

367

paralytic scarecrow that he had betrayed his sharp parent for sixty threepennyworths of rum, which were all gone, and that her sharpness would infallibly detect his having done it sooner or later. All things considered, therefore, and addition made of the state of his body to the state of his mind, the bed on which Mr. Dolls reposed was a bed of roses from which the flowers and leaves had entirely faded, leaving him to lie upon the thorns and stalks.

On a certain day, Miss Wren was alone at her work, with the house-door set open for coolness, and was trolling in a small sweet voice a mournful little song, which might have been the song of the doll she was dressing, bemoaning the brittleness and meltability of wax, when whom should she descry standing on the pavement, looking in at her, but Mr. Fledgeby.

"I thought it was you!" said Fledgeby, coming up the two steps.

"Did you?" Miss Wren retorted. "And I thought it was you, young man. Quite a coincidence. You're not mistaken, and I'm not mistaken. How clever we are!"

"Well, and how are you?" said Fledgeby.

"I am pretty much as usual, sir," replied Miss Wren. "A very unfortunate parent, worried out of my life and senses by a very bad child."

Fledgeby's small eyes opened so wide that they might have passed for ordinary-sized eyes, as he stared about him for the very young person whom he supposed to be in question.

"But you're not a parent," said Miss Wren, "and consequently it's of no use talking to you upon a family subject. To what am I to attribute the honour and favour?"

"To a wish to improve your acquaintance," Mr. Fledgeby replied.

Miss Wren, stopping to bite her thread, looked at him very knowingly.

"We never meet now," said Fledgeby; "do we?"

"No," said Miss Wren, chopping off the word.

368

"So I had a mind," pursued Fledgeby, "to come and have a talk with you about our dodging friend, the child of Israel."

"So *he* gave you my address; did he?" asked Miss Wren.

"I got it out of him," said Fledgeby, with a stammer.

"You seem to see a good deal of him," remarked Miss Wren, with shrewd distrust. "A good deal of him you seem to see, considering."

"Yes, I do," said Fledgeby. "Considering."

"Haven't you," inquired the dressmaker, bending over the doll on which her art was being exercised, "done interceding with him yet?"

"No," said Fledgeby, shaking his head.

"La! Been interceding with him all this time, and sticking to him still?" said Miss Wren, busy with her work.

"Sticking to him is the word," said Fledgeby.

Miss Wren pursued her occupation with a concentrated air, and asked, after an interval of silent industry:

"Are you in the army?"

"Not exactly," said Fledgeby, rather flattered by the question.

"Navy?" asked Miss Wren.

"N—no," said Fledgeby. He qualified these two negatives, as if he were not absolutely in either service, but was almost in both.

"What are you then?" demanded Miss Wren.

"I am a gentleman, I am," said Fledgeby.

"Oh!" assented Jenny, screwing up her mouth with an appearance of conviction. "Yes, to be sure! That accounts for your having so much time to give to interceding. But only to think how kind and friendly a gentleman you must be!"

Mr. Fledgeby found that he was skating round a board marked Dangerous, and had better cut out a fresh track. "Let's get back to the dodgerest of the dodgers," said he. "What's he up to in the case of your friend the handsome gal? He must have some object. What's his object?"

369

"Cannot undertake to say, sir, I am sure!" returned Miss Wren, composedly.

"He won't acknowledge where she's gone," said Fledgeby; "and I have a fancy that I should like to have another look at her. Now I know he knows where she is gone."

"Cannot undertake to say, sir, I am sure!" Miss Wren again rejoined.

"And you know where she is gone?" hazarded Fledgeby.

"Cannot undertake to say, sir, really," replied Miss Wren.

The quaint little chin met Mr. Fledgeby's gaze with such a baffling hitch, that that agreeable gentleman was for some time at a loss how to resume his fascinating part in the dialogue. At length he said:

"Miss Jenny!—That's your name, if I don't mistake?"

"Probably you don't mistake, sir," was Miss Wren's cool answer; "because you had it on the best authority. Mine, you know."

"Miss Jenny! Instead of coming up and being dead, let's come out and look alive. It'll pay better, I assure you," said Fledgeby, bestowing an inveigling twinkle or two upon the dressmaker. "You'll find it pay better."

"Perhaps," said Miss Jenny, holding out her doll at arm's length, and critically contemplating the effect of her art with her scissors on her lips and her head thrown back, as if her interest lay there, and not in the conversation; "perhaps you'll explain your meaning, young man, which is Greek to me.—You must have another touch of blue in your trimming, my dear." Having addressed the last remark to her fair client, Miss Wren proceeded to snip at some blue fragments that lay before her, among fragments of all colours, and to thread a needle from a skein of blue silk.

"Look here," said Fledgeby.—"Are you attending?"

"I am attending, sir," replied Miss Wren, without the slightest appearance of so doing. "Another touch of blue in your trimming, my dear."

"Well, look here," said Fledgeby, rather discouraged by

370

the circumstances under which he found himself pursuing the conversation. " If you're attending—— "

("Light blue, my sweet young lady," remarked Miss Wren, in a sprightly tone, " being best suited to your fair complexion and your flaxen curls.")

" I say, if you're attending," proceeded Fledgeby, " it'll pay better in this way. It'll lead in a roundabout manner to your buying damage and waste of Pubsey and Co. at a nominal price, or even getting it for nothing."

" Aha ! " thought the dressmaker. " But you are not so roundabout, Little Eyes, that I don't notice your answering for Pubsey and Co. after all ! Little Eyes, Little Eyes, you're too cunning by half."

" And I take it for granted," pursued Fledgeby, " that to get the most of your materials for nothing would be well worth your while, Miss Jenny ? "

" You may take it for granted," returned the dressmaker with many knowing nods, " that it's always well worth my while to make money."

" Now," said Fledgeby approvingly, " you're answering to a sensible purpose. Now, you're coming out and looking alive ! So I make so free, Miss Jenny, as to offer the remark, that you and Judah were too thick together to last. You can't come to be intimate with such a deep file as Judah without beginning to see a little way into him, you know," said Fledgeby with a wink.

" I must own," returned the dressmaker, with her eyes upon her work, " that we are not good friends at present."

" I know you're not good friends at present," said Fledgeby. " I know all about it. I should like to pay off Judah, by not letting him have his own deep way in everything. In most things he'll get it by hook or by crook, but—hang it all!—don't let him have his own deep way in everything. That's too much." Mr. Fledgeby said this with some display of indignant warmth, as if he was counsel in the cause for Virtue.

371

"How can I prevent his having his own way?" began the dressmaker.

"Deep way, I called it," said Fledgeby.

" —His own deep way, in anything?"

"I'll tell you," said Fledgeby. "I like to hear you ask it, because it's looking alive. It's what I should expect to find in one of your sagacious understanding. Now, candidly."

"Eh?" cried Miss Jenny.

"I said, now candidly," Mr. Fledgeby explained, a little put out.

"Oh-h!"

"I should be glad to countermine him, respecting the handsome gal, your friend. He means something there. You may depend upon it, Judah means something there. He has a motive, and of course his motive is a dark motive. Now, whatever his motive is, it's necessary to his motive"— Mr. Fledgeby's constructive powers were not equal to the avoidance of some tautology here—"that it should be kept from me, what he has done with her. So I put it to you, who know: What *has* he done with her? I ask no more. And is that asking much, when you understand that it will pay?"

Miss Jenny Wren, who had cast her eyes upon the bench again after her last interruption, sat looking at it, needle in hand but not working, for some moments. She then briskly resumed her work, and said, with a side-long glance of her eyes and chin at Mr. Fledgeby:

"Where d'ye live?"

"Albany, Piccadilly," replied Fledgeby.

"When are you at home?"

"When you like."

"Breakfast-time?" said Jenny, in her abruptest and shortest manner.

"No better time in the day," said Fledgeby.

"I'll look in upon you to-morrow, young man. Those two ladies," pointing to dolls, "have an appointment in Bond

372

Street at ten precisely. When I've dropped 'em there, I'll drive round to you." With a weird little laugh, Miss Jenny pointed to her crutch-stick as her equipage.

"This is looking alive indeed!" cried Fledgeby, rising.

"Mark you! I promise you nothing," said the dolls' dressmaker, dabbing two dabs at him with her needle, as if she put out both his eyes.

"No, no. *I* understand," returned Fledgeby. "The damage and waste question shall be settled first. It shall be made to pay; don't you be afraid. Good-day, Miss Jenny."

"Good-day, young man."

Mr. Fledgeby's prepossessing form withdrew itself: and the little dressmaker, clipping and snipping and stitching, and stitching and snipping and clipping, fell to work at a great rate; musing and muttering all the time.

"Misty, misty, misty. Can't make it out. Little Eyes and the wolf in a conspiracy? Or Little Eyes and the wolf against one another? Can't make it out. My poor Lizzie, have they both designs against you, either way? Can't make it out. Is Little Eyes Pubsey, and the wolf Co? Can't make it out. Pubsey true to Co, and Co to Pubsey? Pubsey false to Co, and Co to Pubsey? Can't make it out. What said Little Eyes? 'Now, candidly?' Ah! However the cat jumps, *he's* a liar. That's all I can make out at present; but you may go to bed in the Albany, Piccadilly, with *that* for your pillow, young man!" Thereupon, the little dressmaker again dabbed out his eyes separately, and making a loop in the air of her thread and deftly catching it into a knot with her needle, seemed to bowstring him into the bargain.

For the terrors undergone by Mr. Dolls that evening when his little parent sat profoundly meditating over her work, and when he imagined himself found out, as often as she changed her attitude, or turned her eyes towards him, there is no adequate name. Moreover it was her habit to shake her head at that wretched old boy whenever she caught his eye as he shivered and shook. What are popularly called "the trembles" being in full force upon him that evening, and likewise what are popularly called "the horrors," he had a very bad time of it; which was not made better by his being so remorseful as frequently to moan "Sixty three-penn'orths." This imperfect sentence not being at all intelligible as a confession, but sounding like a Gargantuan order for a dram, brought him into new difficulties by occasioning his parent to pounce at him in a more than usually snappish manner, and to overwhelm him with bitter reproaches.

What was a bad time for Mr. Dolls, could not fail to be a bad time for the dolls' dressmaker. However, she was on the alert next morning, and drove to Bond Street, and set down the two ladies punctually, and then directed her equipage to conduct her to the Albany. Arrived at the doorway of the house in which Mr. Fledgeby's chambers were, she found a lady standing there in a travelling dress, holding in her hand—of all things in the world—a gentleman's hat.

"You want some one?" said the lady in a stern manner.

"I am going up-stairs to Mr. Fledgeby's."

"You cannot do that at this moment. There is a gentleman with him. I am waiting for the gentleman. His business with Mr. Fledgeby will very soon be transacted, and then you can go up. Until the gentleman comes down, you must wait here."

While speaking, and afterwards, the lady kept watchfully between her and the staircase, as if prepared to oppose her going up, by force. The lady being of a stature to stop her with a hand, and looking mightily determined, the dressmaker stood still.

"Well? Why do you listen?" asked the lady.

"I am not listening," said the dressmaker.

"What do you hear?" asked the lady, altering her phrase.

"Is it a kind of a spluttering somewhere?" said the dressmaker, with an inquiring look.

" Mr. Fledgeby in his shower-bath, perhaps," remarked the lady, smiling.

" And somebody's beating a carpet, I think ? "

" Mr. Fledgeby's carpet, I dare say," replied the smiling lady.

Miss Wren had a reasonably good eye for smiles, being well accustomed to them on the part of her young friends, though their smiles mostly ran smaller than in nature. But she had never seen so singular a smile as that upon this lady's face. It twitched her nostrils open in a remarkable manner, and contracted her lips and eyebrows. It was a smile of enjoyment too, though of such a fierce kind that Miss Wren thought she would rather not enjoy herself than do it in that way.

" Well ! " said the lady, watching her. " What now ? "

" I hope there's nothing the matter ! " said the dressmaker.

" Where ? " inquired the lady.

" I don't know where," said Miss Wren, staring about her. " But I never heard such odd noises. Don't you think I had better call somebody ? "

" I think you had better not," returned the lady with a significant frown, and drawing closer.

On this hint, the dressmaker relinquished the idea, and stood looking at the lady as hard as the lady looked at her. Meanwhile the dressmaker listened with amazement to the odd noises which still continued, and the lady listened too, but with a coolness in which there was no trace of amazement.

Soon afterwards, came a slamming and banging of doors ; and then came running down-stairs, a gentleman with whiskers, and out of breath, who seemed to be red-hot.

" Is your business done, Alfred ? " inquired the lady.

" Very thoroughly done," replied the gentleman, as he took his hat from her.

" You can go up to Mr. Fledgeby as soon as you like," said the lady, moving haughtily away.

" Oh ! And you can take these three pieces of stick with

375

you," added the gentleman, politely, "and say, if you please, that they come from Mr. Alfred Lammle, with his compliments, on leaving England. Mr. Alfred Lammle. Be so good as not to forget the name."

The three pieces of stick were three broken and frayed fragments of a stout lithe cane. Miss Jenny taking them wonderingly, and the gentleman repeating with a grin, "Mr. Alfred Lammle, if you'll be so good. Compliments, on leaving England," the lady and gentleman walked away quite deliberately, and Miss Jenny and her crutch-stick went up-stairs. "Lammle, Lammle, Lammle?" Miss Jenny repeated as she panted from stair to stair, "where have I heard that name? Lammle, Lammle? I know! Saint Mary Axe!"

With a gleam of new intelligence in her sharp face, the dolls' dressmaker pulled at Fledgeby's bell. No one answered; but, from within the chambers, there proceeded a continuous spluttering sound of a highly singular and unintelligible nature.

"Good gracious! Is Little Eyes choking?" cried Miss Jenny.

Pulling at the bell again and getting no reply, she pushed the outer door, and found it standing ajar. No one being visible on her opening it wider, and the spluttering continuing, she took the liberty of opening an inner door, and then beheld the extraordinary spectacle of Mr. Fledgeby in his shirt, a pair of Turkish trousers, and a Turkish cap, rolling over and over on his own carpet, and spluttering wonderfully.

"Oh Lord!" gasped Mr. Fledgeby. "Oh, my eye! Stop thief! I am strangling. Fire! Oh, my eye! A glass of water. Give me a glass of water. Shut the door. Murder! Oh Lord!" and then rolled and spluttered more than ever.

Hurrying into another room, Miss Jenny got a glass of water, and brought it for Fledgeby's relief: who, gasping, spluttering, and rattling in his throat between whiles, drank some water, and laid his head faintly on her arm.

376

"Oh, my eye!" cried Fledgeby, struggling anew. "It's salt and snuff. It's up my nose, and down my throat, and in my windpipe. Ugh! Ow! Ow! Ow! Ah—h—h—h!" And here, crowing fearfully, with his eyes starting out of his head, appeared to be contending with every mortal disease incidental to poultry.

"And, Oh, my Eye, I'm so sore!" cried Fledgeby, starting over on his back, in a spasmodic way that caused the dressmaker to retreat to the wall. "Oh, I smart so! Do put something to my back and arms, and legs and shoulders. Ugh! It's down my throat again and can't come up. Ow! Ow! Ow! Ah—h—h—h! Oh, I smart so!" Here Mr. Fledgeby bounded up, and bounded down, and went rolling over and over again.

The dolls' dressmaker looked on until he rolled himself into a corner with his Turkish slippers uppermost, and then, resolving in the first place to address her ministration to the salt and snuff, gave him more water and slapped his back. But, the latter application was by no means a success, causing Mr. Fledgeby to scream, and to cry out, "Oh, my eye! don't slap me! I'm covered with weales and I smart so!"

However, he gradually ceased to choke and crow, saving at intervals, and Miss Jenny got him into an easy-chair: where, with his eyes red and watery, with his features swollen, and with some half-dozen livid bars across his face, he presented a most rueful sight.

"What ever possessed you to take salt and snuff, young man?" inquired Miss Jenny.

"I didn't take it," the dismal youth replied. "It was crammed into my mouth."

"Who crammed it?" asked Miss Jenny.

"He did," answered Fledgeby. "The assassin. Lammle. He rubbed it into my mouth and up my nose and down my throat—Ow! Ow! Ow! Ah—h—h—h! Ugh!—to prevent my crying out, and then cruelly assaulted me."

"With this?" asked Miss Jenny, showing the pieces of cane.

377

"That's the weapon," said Fledgeby, eyeing it with the air of an acquaintance. "He broke it over me. Oh, I smart so! How did you come by it?"

"When he ran down-stairs and joined the lady he had left in the hall with his hat"—Miss Jenny began.

"Oh!" groaned Mr. Fledgeby, writhing. "She was holding his hat, was she? I might have known she was in it."

"When he came down-stairs and joined the lady who wouldn't let me come up, he gave me the pieces for you, and I was to say, 'With Mr. Alfred Lammle's compliments on his leaving England.'" Miss Jenny said it with such spiteful satisfaction, and such a hitch of her chin and eyes as might have added to Mr. Fledgeby's miseries, if he could have noticed either, in his bodily pain with his hand to his head.

"Shall I go for the police?" inquired Miss Jenny, with a nimble start towards the door.

"Stop! No, don't!" cried Fledgeby. "Don't, please. We had better keep it quiet. Will you be so good as shut the door? Oh, I do smart so!"

In testimony of the extent to which he smarted, Mr. Fledgeby came wallowing out of the easy-chair, and took another roll on the carpet.

"Now the door's shut," said Mr. Fledgeby, sitting up in anguish, with his Turkish cap half on and half off, and the bars on his face getting bluer, "do me the kindness to look at my back and shoulders. They must be in an awful state, for I hadn't got my dressing-gown on, when the brute came rushing in. Cut my shirt away from the collar; there's a pair of scissors on that table. Oh!" groaned Mr. Fledgeby, with his hand to his head again. "How I do smart, to be sure!"

"There?" inquired Miss Jenny, alluding to the back and shoulders.

"Oh Lord, yes!" moaned Fledgeby, rocking himself. "And all over! Everywhere!"

The busy little dressmaker quickly snipped the shirt away,

and laid bare the results of as furious and sound a thrashing as even Mr. Fledgeby merited. "You may well smart, young man!" exclaimed Miss Jenny. And stealthily rubbed her little hands behind him, and poked a few exultant pokes with her two forefingers over the crown of his head.

"What do you think of vinegar and brown paper?" inquired the suffering Fledgeby, still rocking and moaning. "Does it look as if vinegar and brown paper was the sort of application?"

"Yes," said Miss Jenny, with a silent chuckle. "It looks as if it ought to be Pickled."

Mr. Fledgeby collapsed under the word "Pickled," and groaned again. "My kitchen is on this floor," he said; "you'll find brown paper in a dresser-drawer there, and a bottle of vinegar on a shelf. Would you have the kindness to make a few plasters and put 'em on? It can't be kept too quiet."

"One, two—hum—five, six. You'll want six," said the dressmaker.

"There's smart enough," whimpered Mr. Fledgeby, groaning and writhing again, "for sixty."

Miss Jenny repaired to the kitchen, scissors in hand, found the brown paper and found the vinegar, and skilfully cut out and steeped six large plasters. When they were all lying ready on the dresser, an idea occurred to her as she was about to gather them up.

"I think," said Miss Jenny, with a silent laugh, "he ought to have a little pepper? Just a few grains? I think the young man's tricks and manners make a claim upon his friends for a little pepper?"

Mr. Fledgeby's evil star showing her the pepper-box on the chimney-piece, she climbed upon a chair, and got it down, and sprinkled all the plasters with a judicious hand. She then went back to Mr. Fledgeby, and stuck them all on him: Mr. Fledgeby uttering a sharp howl as each was put in its place.

"There, young man!" said the dolls' dressmaker. "Now I hope you feel pretty comfortable?"

Apparently Mr. Fledgeby did not, for he cried by way of answer, "Oh—h, how I do smart!"

Miss Jenny got his Persian gown upon him, extinguished his eyes crookedly with his Persian cap, and helped him to his bed: upon which he climbed groaning. "Business between you and me being out of the question to-day, young man, and my time being precious," said Miss Jenny then, "I'll make myself scarce. Are you comfortable now?"

"Oh, my eye!" cried Mr. Fledgeby. "No, I ain't. Oh—h—h! how I do smart!"

The last thing Miss Jenny saw, as she looked back before closing the room door, was Mr. Fledgeby in the act of plunging and gambolling all over his bed, like a porpoise or dolphin in its native element. She then shut the bedroom door, and all the other doors, and going down-stairs and emerging from the Albany into the busy streets, took omnibus for Saint Mary Axe: pressing on the road all the gaily-dressed ladies whom she could see from the window, and making them unconscious lay-figures for dolls, while she mentally cut them out and basted them.

CHAPTER IX

SET down by the omnibus at the corner of Saint Mary Axe, and trusting to her feet and her crutch-stick within its precincts, the dolls' dressmaker proceeded to the place of business of Pubsey and Co. All there was sunny and quiet externally, and shady and quiet internally. Hiding herself in the entry outside the glass door, she could see from that post of observation the old man in his spectacles sitting writing at his desk.

"Boh!" cried the dressmaker, popping in her head at the glass door. "Mr. Wolf at home?"

The old man took his glasses off, and mildly laid them down beside him. "Ah Jenny, is it you? I thought you had given me up."

"And so I had given up the treacherous wolf of the forest," she replied; "but, godmother, it strikes me you have come back. I am not quite sure, because the wolf and you change forms. I want to ask you a question or two, to find out whether you are really godmother or really wolf. May I?"

"Yes, Jenny, yes." But Riah glanced towards the door, as if he thought his principal might appear there, unseasonably.

"If you're afraid of the fox," said Miss Jenny, "you may dismiss all present expectations of seeing that animal. *He* won't show himself abroad for many a day."

"What do you mean, my child?"

381

"I mean, godmother," replied Miss Wren, sitting down beside the Jew, "that the fox has caught a famous flogging, and that if his skin and bones are not tingling, aching, and smarting at this present instant, no fox did ever tingle, ache, and smart." Therewith Miss Jenny related what had come to pass in the Albany, omitting the few grains of pepper.

"Now, godmother," she went on, "I particularly wish to ask you what has taken place here, since I left the wolf here? Because I have an idea about the size of a marble, rolling about in my little noddle. First and foremost, are you Pubsey and Co., or are you either? Upon your solemn word and honour."

The old man shook his head.

"Secondly, isn't Fledgeby both Pubsey and Co.?"

The old man answered with a reluctant nod.

"My idea," exclaimed Miss Wren, "is now about the size of an orange. But before it gets any bigger, welcome back, dear godmother!"

The little creature folded her arms about the old man's neck with great earnestness, and kissed him. "I humbly beg your forgiveness, godmother. I am truly sorry. I ought to have had more faith in you. But what could I suppose when you said nothing for yourself, you know? I don't mean to offer that as a justification, but what could I suppose, when you were a silent party to all he said? It did look bad; now didn't it?"

"It looked so bad, Jenny," responded the old man, with gravity, "that I will straightway tell you what an impression it wrought upon me. I was hateful in mine own eyes. I was hateful to myself, in being so hateful to the debtor and to you. But more than that, and worse than that, and to pass out far and broad beyond myself—I reflected that evening, sitting alone in my garden on the housetop, that I was doing dishonour to my ancient faith and race. I reflected—clearly reflected for the first time, that in bending my neck to the yoke I was willing to wear, I bent the unwilling necks of the whole Jewish people. For it is not, in Christian countries, with the Jews as with other peoples. Men say, ' This is a bad Greek, but there are good Greeks. This is a bad Turk, but there are good Turks.' Not so with the Jews. Men find the bad among us easily enough—among what peoples are the bad not easily found?—but they take the worst of us as samples of the best; they take the lowest of us as presentations of the highest; and they say ' All Jews are alike.' If, doing what I was content to do here, because I was grateful for the past and have small need of money now, I had been a Christian, I could have done it, compromising no one but my individual self. But doing it as a Jew, I could not choose but compromise the Jews of all conditions and all countries. It is a little hard upon us, but it is the truth. 1 would that all our people remembered it! Though I have little right to say so, seeing that it came home so late to me."

The dolls' dressmaker sat holding the old man by the hand, and looking thoughtfully in his face.

" Thus I reflected, I say, sitting that evening in my garden on the housetop. And passing the painful scene of that day in review before me many times, I always saw that the poor gentleman believed the story readily, because I was one of the Jews—that you believed the story readily, my child, because I was one of the Jews—that the story itself first came into the invention of the originator thereof, because I was one of the Jews. This was the result of my having had you three before me, face to face, and seeing the thing visibly presented as upon a theatre. Wherefore I perceived that the obligation was upon me to leave this service. But, Jenny, my dear," said Riah, breaking off, " I promised that you should pursue your questions, and I obstruct them."

" On the contrary, godmother; my idea is as large now as a pumpkin—and *you* know what a pumpkin is, don't you? So you gave notice that you were going? Does that come next?" asked Miss Jenny, with a look of close attention.

" I indited a letter to my master. Yes. To that effect."

"And what said Tingling - Tossing - Aching - Screaming-Scratching-Smarter?" asked Miss Wren, with an unspeakable enjoyment in the utterance of those honourable titles and in the recollection of the pepper.

"He held me to certain months of servitude, which were his lawful term of notice. They expire to-morrow. Upon their expiration—not before—I had meant to set myself right with my Cinderella."

"My idea is getting so immense now," cried Miss Wren, clasping her temples, "that my head won't hold it! Listen, godmother; I am going to expound. Little Eyes (that's Screaming-Scratching-Smarter) owes you a heavy grudge for going. Little Eyes casts about how best to pay you off. Little Eyes thinks of Lizzie. Little Eyes says to himself, 'I'll find out where he has placed that girl, and I'll betray his secret because it's dear to him.' Perhaps Little Eyes thinks, 'I'll make love to her myself too;' but that I can't swear—all the rest I can. So, Little Eyes comes to me, and I go to Little Eyes. That's the way of it. And now the murder's all out, I'm sorry," added the dolls' dressmaker, rigid from head to foot with energy as she shook her little fist before her eyes, "that I didn't give him Cayenne pepper and chopped pickled Capsicum!"

This expression of regret being but partially intelligible to Mr. Riah, the old man reverted to the injuries Fledgeby had received, and hinted at the necessity of his at once going to tend that beaten cur.

"Godmother, godmother, godmother!" cried Miss Wren, irritably, "I really lose all patience with you. One would think you believed in the Good Samaritan. How can you be so inconsistent?"

"Jenny dear," began the old man, gently, "it is the custom of our people to help——"

"Oh! Bother your people!" interposed Miss Wren, with a toss of her head. "If your people don't know better than to go and help Little Eyes, it's a pity they ever got out of

Egypt. Over and above that," she added, " he wouldn't take your help if you offered it. Too much ashamed. Wants to keep it close and quiet, and to keep you out of the way."

They were still debating this point when a shadow darkened the entry, and the glass door was opened by a messenger who brought a letter unceremoniously addressed, " Riah." To which he said there was an answer wanted.

The letter, which was scrawled in pencil uphill and down-hill and round crooked corners, ran thus :

" OLD RIAH,

" Your accounts being all squared, go. Shut up the place, turn out directly, and send me the key by bearer. Go. You are an unthankful dog of a Jew. Get out.

" F."

The dolls' dressmaker found it delicious to trace the screaming and smarting of Little Eyes in the distorted writing of this epistle. She laughed over it and jeered at it in a convenient corner (to the great astonishment of the messenger) while the old man got his few goods together in a black bag. That done, the shutters of the upper windows closed, and the office blind pulled down, they issued forth upon the steps with the attendant messenger. There, while Miss Jenny held the bag, the old man locked the house door, and handed over the key to him ; who at once retired with the same.

" Well, godmother," said Miss Wren, as they remained upon the steps together, looking at one another. " And so you're thrown upon the world ! "

" It would appear so, Jenny, and somewhat suddenly."

" Where are you going to seek your fortune ? " asked Miss Wren.

The old man smiled, but looked about him with a look of having lost his way in life, which did not escape the dolls' dressmaker.

385

"Verily, Jenny," said he, "the question is to the purpose, and more easily asked than answered. But as I have experience of the ready goodwill and good help of those who have given occupation to Lizzie, I think I will seek them out for myself."

"On foot?" asked Miss Wren, with a chop.

"Ay!" said the old man. "Have I not my staff?"

It was exactly because he had his staff, and presented so quaint an aspect, that she mistrusted his making the journey.

"The best thing you can do," said Jenny, "for the time being, at all events, is to come home with me, godmother. Nobody's there but my bad child, and Lizzie's lodging stands empty." The old man, when satisfied that no inconvenience could be entailed on any one by his compliance, readily complied: and the singularly-assorted couple once more went through the streets together.

Now the bad child having been strictly charged by his parent to remain at home in her absence, of course went out; and, being in the very last stage of mental decrepitude, went out with two objects; firstly, to establish a claim he conceived himself to have upon any licensed victualler living, to be supplied with threepennyworth of rum for nothing; and secondly, to bestow some maudlin remorse on Mr. Eugene Wrayburn, and see what profit came of it. Stumblingly pursuing these two designs—they both meant rum, the only meaning of which he was capable—the degraded creature staggered into Covent Garden Market and there bivouacked, to have an attack of the trembles succeeded by an attack of the horrors, in a doorway.

This market of Covent Garden was quite out of the creature's line of road, but it had the attraction for him which it has for the worst of the solitary members of the drunken tribe. It may be the companionship of the nightly stir, or it may be the companionship of the gin and beer that slop about among carters and hucksters, or it may be the companionship of the trodden vegetable refuse, which is so like their own dress that perhaps they take the Market for a great wardrobe; but be it what it may, you shall see no such individual drunkards on doorsteps anywhere, as there. Of dozing women-drunkards especially, you shall come upon such specimens there, in the morning sunlight, as you might seek out of doors in vain through London. Such stale vapid rejected cabbage-leaf and cabbage-stalk dress, such damaged-orange countenance, such squashed pulp of humanity, are open to the day nowhere else. So the attraction of the Market drew Mr. Dolls to it, and he had out his two fits of trembles and horrors in a doorway on which a woman had had out her sodden nap a few hours before.

There is a swarm of young savages always flitting about this same place, creeping off with fragments of orange-chests, and mouldy litter—Heaven knows into what holes they can convey them, having no home!—whose bare feet fall with a blunt dull softness on the pavement as the policeman hunts them, and who are (perhaps for that reason) little heard by the Powers that be, whereas in top-boots they would make a deafening clatter. These, delighting in the trembles and the horrors of Mr. Dolls, as in a gratuitous drama, flocked about him in his doorway, butted at him, leaped at him, and pelted him. Hence, when he came out of his invalid retirement and shook off that ragged train, he was much bespattered, and in worse case than ever. But, not yet at his worst; for, going into a public-house, and being supplied in stress of business with his rum, and seeking to vanish without payment, he was collared, searched, found penniless, and admonished not to try that again, by having a pail of dirty water cast over him. This application superinduced another fit of the trembles; after which Mr. Dolls, as finding himself in good cue for making a call on a professional friend, addressed himself to the Temple.

There was nobody at the chambers but Young Blight. That discreet youth, sensible of a certain incongruity in the association of such a client with the business that might be

387

coming some day, with the best intentions temporised with Dolls, and offered a shilling for coach hire home. Mr. Dolls, accepting the shilling, promptly laid it out in two threepenny-worths of conspiracy against his life, and two threepenny-worths of raging repentance. Returning to the Chambers with which burden, he was descried coming round into the court, by the wary young Blight watching from the window: who instantly closed the outer door, and left the miserable object to expend his fury on the panels.

The more the door resisted him, the more dangerous and imminent became that bloody conspiracy against his life. Force of police arriving, he recognised in them the conspirators, and laid about him hoarsely, fiercely, staringly, convulsively, foamingly. A humble machine, familiar to the conspirators and called by the expressive name of Stretcher, being unavoidably sent for, he was rendered a harmless bundle of torn rags by being strapped down upon it, with voice and consciousness gone out of him, and life fast going. As this machine was borne out at the Temple gate by four men, the poor little dolls' dressmaker and her Jewish friend were coming up the street.

"Let us see what it is," cried the dressmaker. "Let us make haste and look, godmother."

The brisk little crutch-stick was but too brisk. "Oh, gentlemen, gentlemen, he belongs to me!"

"Belongs to you?" said the head of the party, stopping it.

"Oh yes, dear gentlemen, he's my child, out without leave. My poor bad, bad boy! and he don't know me, he don't know me! Oh, what shall I do," cried the little creature, wildly beating her hands together, "when my own child don't know me!"

The head of the party looked (as well he might) to the old man for explanation. He whispered, as the dolls' dressmaker bent over the exhausted form and vainly tried to extract some sign of recognition from it: "It's her drunken father."

388

As the load was put down in the street, Riah drew the head of the party aside, and whispered that he thought the man was dying. "No, surely not?" returned the other. But he became less confident, on looking, and directed the bearers to "bring him to the nearest doctor's shop."

Thither he was brought; the window becoming from within a wall of faces, deformed into all kinds of shapes through the agency of globular red bottles, green bottles, blue bottles, and other coloured bottles. A ghastly light shining upon him that he didn't need, the beast so furious but a few minutes gone was quiet enough now, with a strange mysterious writing on his face, reflected from one of the great bottles, as if Death had marked him: "Mine."

The medical testimony was more precise and more to the purpose than it sometimes is in a Court of Justice. "You had better send for something to cover it. All's over."

Therefore, the police sent for something to cover it, and it was covered and borne through the streets, the people falling away. After it, went the dolls' dressmaker, hiding her face in the Jewish skirts, and clinging to them with one hand, while with the other she plied her stick. It was carried home, and, by reason that the staircase was very narrow, it was put down in the parlour—the little working-bench being set aside to make room for it—and there, in the midst of the dolls with no speculation in their eyes, lay Mr. Dolls with no speculation in his.

Many flaunting dolls had to be gaily dressed, before the money was in the dressmaker's pocket to get mourning for Mr. Dolls. As the old man, Riah, sat by, helping her in such small ways as he could, he found it difficult to make out whether she really did realise that the deceased had been her father.

"If my poor boy," she would say, "had been brought up better, he might have done better. Not that I reproach myself. I hope I have no cause for that."

"None indeed, Jenny, I am very certain."

389

"Thank you, godmother. It cheers me to hear you say so. But you see it is so hard to bring up a child well, when you work, work, work, all day. When he was out of employment, I couldn't always keep him near me. He got fractious and nervous, and I was obliged to let him go into the streets. And he never did well in the streets, he never did well out of sight. How often it happens with children!"

"Too often, even in this sad sense!" thought the old man.

"How can I say what I might have turned out myself, but for my back having been so bad and my legs so queer when I was young!" the dressmaker would go on. "I had nothing to do but work, and so I worked. I couldn't play. But my poor unfortunate child could play, and it turned out the worse for him."

"And not for him alone, Jenny."

"Well! I don't know, godmother. He suffered heavily, did my unfortunate boy. He was very, very ill sometimes. And I called him a quantity of names;" shaking her head over her work, and dropping tears. "I don't know that his going wrong was much the worse for me. If it ever was, let us forget it."

"You are a good girl, you are a patient girl."

"As for patience," she would reply with a shrug, "not much of that, godmother. If I had been patient, I should never have called him names. But I hope I did it for his good. And besides, I felt my responsibility as a mother so much. I tried reasoning, and reasoning failed. I tried coaxing, and coaxing failed. I tried scolding, and scolding failed. But I was bound to try everything, you know, with such a charge upon my hands. Where would have been my duty to my poor lost boy, if I had not tried everything'

With such talk, mostly in a cheerful tone on the part of the industrious little creature, the day-work and the night-work were beguiled until enough of smart dolls had gone forth to bring into the kitchen, where the working-bench now stood, the sombre stuff that the occasion required, and to bring into the house the other sombre preparations. "And now," said Miss Jenny, "having knocked off my rosy-cheeked young friends, I'll knock off my white-cheeked self." This referred to her making her own dress, which at last was done. "The disadvantage of making for yourself," said Miss Jenny, as she stood upon a chair to look at the result in the glass, "is, that you can't charge anybody else for the job, and the advantage is, that you haven't to go out to try on. Humph! Very fair indeed! If He could see me now (whoever he is) I hope he wouldn't repent of his bargain!"

The simple arrangements were of her own making, and were stated to Riah thus:

"I mean to go alone, godmother, in my usual carriage, and you'll be so kind as keep house while I am gone. It's not far off. And when I return, we'll have a cup of tea and a chat over future arrangements. It's a very plain last house that I have been able to give my poor unfortunate boy; but he'll accept the will for the deed, if he knows anything about it, and if he doesn't know anything about it," with a sob, and wiping her eyes, "why, it won't matter to him. I see the service in the Prayer-book says, that we brought nothing into this world, and it is certain we can take nothing out. It comforts me for not being able to hire a lot of stupid undertaker's things for my poor child, and seeming as if I was trying to smuggle 'em out of this world with him, when of course I must break down in the attempt, and bring 'em all back again. As it is, there'll be nothing to bring back but me, and that's quite consistent, for I shan't be brought back some day!"

After that previous carrying of him in the streets, the wretched old fellow seemed to be twice buried. He was taken on the shoulders of half-a-dozen blossom-faced men, who shuffled with him to the churchyard, and who were preceded by another blossom-faced man, affecting a stately stalk, as if he were a Policeman of the D(eath) Division, and ceremoniously pretending not to know his intimate acquaintances as he led the pageant. Yet, the spectacle of only one little mourner hobbling after caused many people to turn their heads with a look of interest.

At last the troublesome deceased was got into the ground, to be buried no more, and the stately stalker stalked back before the solitary dressmaker, as if she were bound in honour to have no notion of the way home. Those Furies, the conventionalities, being thus appeased, he left her.

"I must have a very short cry, godmother, before I cheer up for good," said the little creature, coming in. "Because after all a child is a child, you know."

It was a longer cry than might have been expected. Howbeit, it wore itself out in a shadowy corner, and then the dressmaker came forth, and washed her face, and made the tea. "You wouldn't mind my cutting out something while we are at tea, would you?" she asked her Jewish friend, with a coaxing air.

"Cinderella, dear child," the old man expostulated, "will you never rest?"

"Oh! It's not work, cutting out a pattern isn't," said Miss Jenny, with her busy little scissors already snipping at some paper. "The truth is, godmother, I want to fix it while I have it correct in my mind."

"Have you seen it to-day, then?" asked Riah.

"Yes, godmother. Saw it just now. It's a surplice, that's what it is. Thing our clergymen wear, you know," explained Miss Jenny, in consideration of his professing another faith.

"And what have you to do with that, Jenny?"

"Why, godmother," replied the dressmaker, "you must know that we Professors who live upon our taste and invention, are obliged to keep our eyes always open. And you know already that I have many extra expenses to meet just now. So, it came into my head while I was weeping at my poor boy's grave, that something in my way might be done with a clergyman."

"What can be done?" asked the old man.

"Not a funeral, never fear!" returned Miss Jenny, anticipating his objection with a nod. "The public don't like to be made melancholy, I know very well. I am seldom called upon to put my young friends into mourning; not into real mourning, that is; Court mourning they are rather proud of. But a doll clergyman, my dear,—glossy black curls and whiskers,—uniting two of my young friends in matrimony," said Miss Jenny, shaking her forefinger, "is quite another affair. If you don't see those three at the altar in Bond Street, in a jiffy, my name's Jack Robinson!"

With her expert little ways in sharp action, she had got a doll into whitey-brown paper orders, before the meal was over, and was displaying it for the edification of the Jewish mind, when a knock was heard at the street-door. Riah went to open it, and presently came back, ushering in, with a grave and courteous air that sat so well upon him, a gentleman.

The gentleman was a stranger to the dressmaker; but even in the moment of his casting his eyes upon her, there was something in his manner which brought to her remembrance Mr. Eugene Wrayburn.

"Pardon me," said the gentleman. "You are the dolls' dressmaker?"

"I am the dolls' dressmaker, sir."

"Lizzie Hexam's friend?"

"Yes, sir," replied Miss Jenny, instantly on the defensive. "And Lizzie Hexam's friend."

"Here is a note from her, entreating you to accede to the request of Mr. Mortimer Lightwood, the bearer. Mr. Riah chances to know that I am Mr. Mortimer Lightwood, and will tell you so."

Riah bent his head in corroboration.

"Will you read the note?"

"It's very short," said Jenny with a look of wonder, when she had read it.

"There was no time to make it longer. Time was so

very precious. My dear friend, Mr. Eugene Wrayburn, is dying."

The dressmaker clasped her hands, and uttered a little piteous cry.

"Is dying," repeated Lightwood, with emotion, "at some distance from here. He is sinking under injuries received at the hands of a villain who attacked him in the dark. I come straight from his bedside. He is almost always insensible. In a short restless interval of sensibility, or partial sensibility, I made out that he asked for you to be brought to sit by him. Hardly relying on my own interpretation of the indistinct sounds he made, I caused Lizzie to hear them. We were both sure that he asked for you."

The dressmaker, with her hands still clasped, looked affrightedly from the one to the other of her two companions.

"If you delay, he may die with his request ungratified, with his last wish—intrusted to me—we have long been much more than brothers—unfulfilled. I shall break down, if I try to say more."

In a few moments the black bonnet and the crutch-stick were on duty, the good Jew was left in possession of the house, and the dolls' dressmaker, side by side in a chaise with Mortimer Lightwood, was posting out of town.

CHAPTER X

A DARKENED and hushed room; the river outside the windows flowing on to the vast ocean; a figure on the bed, swathed and bandaged and bound, lying helpless on its back, with its two useless arms in splints at its sides. Only two days of usage so familiarised the little dressmaker with this scene, that it held the place occupied two days ago by the recollections of years.

He had scarcely moved since her arrival. Sometimes his eyes were open, sometimes closed. When they were open, there was no meaning in their unwinking stare at one spot straight before them, unless for a moment the brow knitted into a faint expression of anger, or surprise. Then, Mortimer Lightwood would speak to him, and on occasions he would be so far roused as to make an attempt to pronounce his friend's name. But, in an instant consciousness was gone again, and no spirit of Eugene was in Eugene's crushed outer form.

They provided Jenny with materials for plying her work, and she had a little table placed at the foot of his bed. Sitting there, with her rich shower of hair falling over the chair-back, they hoped she might attract his notice. With the same object, she would sing, just above her breath, when he opened his eyes, or she saw his brow knit into that faint expression, so evanescent that it was like a shape made in

395

water. But as yet he had not heeded. The "they" here mentioned were the medical attendant; Lizzie, who was there in all her intervals of rest; and Lightwood, who never left him.

The two days became three, and the three days became four. At length, quite unexpectedly, he said something in a whisper.

"What was it, my dear Eugene?"

"Will you, Mortimer——"

"Will I——?"

"Send for her?"

"My dear fellow, she is here."

Quite unconscious of the long blank, he supposed that they were still speaking together.

The little dressmaker stood up at the foot of the bed, humming her song, and nodded to him brightly. "I can't shake hands, Jenny," said Eugene, with something of his old look; "but I am very glad to see you."

Mortimer repeated this to her, for it could only be made out by bending over him and closely watching his attempts to say it. In a little while, he added:

"Ask her if she has seen the children?"

Mortimer could not understand this, neither could Jenny herself, until he added:

"Ask her if she has smelt the flowers?"

"Oh! I know!" cried Jenny. "I understand him now!" Then, Lightwood yielded his place to her quick approach, and she said, bending over the bed, with that better look: "You mean my long bright slanting rows of children, who used to bring me ease and rest? You mean the children, who used to take me up, and make me light?"

Eugene smiled, "Yes."

"I have not seen them since I saw you. I never see them now, but I am hardly ever in pain now."

"It was a pretty fancy," said Eugene.

"But I have heard my birds sing," cried the little creature,

396

Eugene's Bedside

"and I have smelt my flowers. Yes, indeed I have! And both were most beautiful and most Divine!"

"Stay and help to nurse me," said Eugene, quietly. "I should like you to have the fancy here, before I die."

She touched his lips with her hand, and shaded her eyes with that same hand as she went back to her work and her little low song. He heard the song with evident pleasure, until she allowed it gradually to sink away into silence.

"Mortimer."

"My dear Eugene."

"If you can give me anything to keep me here for only a few minutes——"

"To keep you here, Eugene?"

"To prevent my wandering away I don't know where—for I begin to be sensible that I have just come back, and that I shall lose myself again—do so, dear boy!"

Mortimer gave him such stimulants as could be given him with safety (they were always at hand, ready), and bending over him once more, was about to caution him, when he said:

"Don't tell me not to speak, for I must speak. If you knew the harassing anxiety that gnaws and wears me when I am wandering in those places—where are those endless places, Mortimer? They must be at an immense distance!"

He saw in his friend's face that he was losing himself; for he added after a moment: "Don't be afraid—I am not gone yet. What was it?"

"You wanted to tell me something, Eugene. My poor dear fellow, you wanted to say something to your old friend —to the friend who has always loved you, admired you, imitated you, founded himself upon you, been nothing without you, and who, God knows, would be here in your place if he could."

"Tut, tut!" said Eugene with a tender glance as the other put his hand before his face. "I am not worth it. I acknowledge that I like it, dear boy, but I am not worth it. This attack, my dear Mortimer; this murder ——"

His friend leaned over him with renewed attention, saying:
" You and I suspect some one."

" More than suspect. But, Mortimer, while I lie here, and
when I lie here no longer, I trust to you that the perpetrator
is never brought to justice."

" Eugene ? "

" Her innocent reputation would be ruined, my friend.
She would be punished, not he. I have wronged her enough
in fact : I have wronged her still more in intention. You
recollect what pavement is said to be made of good intentions.
It is made of bad intentions too. Mortimer, I am lying on
it, and I know ! "

" Be comforted, my dear Eugene."

" I will, when you have promised me. Dear Mortimer,
the man must never be pursued. If he should be accused,
you must keep him silent and save him. Don't think of
avenging me ; think only of hushing the story and protecting
her. You can confuse the case, and turn aside the circumstances. Listen to what I say to you. It was not the schoolmaster, Bradley Headstone. Do you hear me? Twice ; it
was not the schoolmaster, Bradley Headstone. Do you hear
me? Three times ; it was not the schoolmaster, Bradley
Headstone."

He stopped, exhausted. His speech had been whispered,
broken, and indistinct ; but by a great effort he had made it
plain enough to be unmistakable.

" Dear fellow, I am wandering away. Stay me for another
moment, if you can."

Lightwood lifted his head at the neck, and put a wine-glass
to his lips. He rallied.

" I don't know how long ago it was done, whether weeks,
days, or hours. No matter. There is inquiry on foot, and
pursuit. Say ! Is there not ? "

" Yes."

" Check it ; divert it ! Don't let her be brought in question.
Shield her. The guilty man, brought to justice, would poison

her name. Let the guilty man go unpunished. Lizzie and my reparation before all ! Promise me ! "

" Eugene, I do. I promise you."

In the act of turning his eyes gratefully towards his friend, he wandered away. His eyes stood still, and settled into that former intent unmeaning stare.

Hours and hours, days and nights, he remained in this same condition. There were times when he would calmly speak to his friend after a long period of unconsciousness, and would say he was better, and would ask for something. Before it could be given him, he would be gone again.

The dolls' dressmaker, all softened compassion now, watched him with an earnestness that never relaxed. She would regularly change the ice, or the cooling spirit, on his head, and would keep her ear at the pillow between whiles, listening for any faint words that fell from him in his wanderings. It was amazing through how many hours at a time she would remain beside him, in a crouching attitude, attentive to his slightest moan. As he could not move a hand, he could make no sign of distress; but, through this close watching (if through no secret sympathy or power) the little creature attained an understanding of him that Lightwood did not possess. Mortimer would often turn to her, as if she were an interpreter between this sentient world and the insensible man ; and she would change the dressing of a wound, or ease a ligature, or turn his face, or alter the pressure of the bedclothes on him, with an absolute certainty of doing right. The natural lightness and delicacy of touch which had become very refined by practice in her miniature work, no doubt was involved in this ; but her perception was at least as fine.

The one word, Lizzie, he muttered millions of times. In a certain phase of his distressful state, which was the worst to those who tended him, he would roll his head upon the pillow, incessantly repeating the name in a hurried and impatient manner, with the misery of a disturbed mind, and

399

the monotony of a machine. Equally, when he lay still and staring, he would repeat it for hours without cessation, but then, always in a tone of subdued warning and horror. Her presence and her touch upon his breast or face would often stop this, and then they learned to expect that he would for some time remain still, with his eyes closed, and that he would be conscious on opening them. But, the heavy disappointment of their hope—revived by the welcome silence of the room—was, that his spirit would glide away again and be lost, in the moment of their joy that it was there.

This frequent rising of a drowning man from the deep, to sink again, was dreadful to the beholders. But, gradually the change stole upon him that it became dreadful to himself. His desire to impart something that was on his mind, his unspeakable yearning to have speech with his friend and make a communication to him, so troubled him when he recovered consciousness, that its term was thereby shortened. As the man rising from the deep would disappear the sooner for fighting with the water, so he in his desperate struggle went down again.

One afternoon, when he had been lying still, and Lizzie, unrecognised, had just stolen out of the room to pursue her occupation, he uttered Lightwood's name.

"My dear Eugene, I am here."

"How long is this to last, Mortimer?"

Lightwood shook his head. "Still, Eugene, you are no worse than you were."

"But I know there's no hope. Yet I pray it may last long enough for you to do me one last service, and for me to do one last action. Keep me here a few moments, Mortimer. Try, try!"

His friend gave him what aid he could, and encouraged him to believe that he was more composed, though even then his eyes were losing the expression they so rarely recovered.

"Hold me here, dear fellow, if you can. Stop my wandering away. I am going!"

"Not yet, not yet. Tell me, dear Eugene, what is it I shall do?"

"Keep me here for only a single minute. I am going away again. Don't let me go. Hear me speak first. Stop me—stop me!"

"My poor Eugene, try to be calm."

"I do try. I try so hard. If you only knew how hard! Don't let me wander till I have spoken. Give me a little more wine."

Lightwood complied. Eugene, with a most pathetic struggle against the unconsciousness that was coming over him, and with a look of appeal that affected his friend profoundly, said:

"You can leave me with Jenny, while you speak to her and tell her what I beseech of her. You can leave me with Jenny, while you are gone. There's not much for you to do. You won't be long away."

"No, no, no. But tell me what it is that I shall do, Eugene!"

"I am going! You can't hold me."

"Tell me in a word, Eugene!"

His eyes were fixed again, and the only word that came from his lips was the word millions of times repeated. Lizzie, Lizzie, Lizzie.

But the watchful little dressmaker had been vigilant as ever in her watch, and she now came up and touched Lightwood's arm as he looked down at his friend, despairingly.

"Hush!" she said, with her finger on her lips. "His eyes are closing. He'll be conscious when he next opens them. Shall I give you a leading word to say to him?"

"Oh, Jenny, if you could only give me the right word!"

"I can. Stoop down."

He stooped, and she whispered in his ear. She whispered in his ear one short word of a single syllable. Lightwood started, and looked at her.

"Try it," said the little creature, with an excited and

401

exultant face. She then bent over the unconscious man, and, for the first time, kissed him on the cheek, and kissed the poor maimed hand that was nearest her. Then, she withdrew to the foot of the bed.

Some two hours afterwards, Mortimer Lightwood saw his friend's consciousness come back, and instantly, but very tranquilly, bent over him.

"Don't speak, Eugene. Do no more than look at me, and listen to me. You follow what I say?"

He moved his head in assent.

"I am going on from the point where we broke off. Is the word we should soon have come to—is it—Wife?"

"Oh, God bless you, Mortimer!"

"Hush! don't be agitated. Don't speak. Hear me, dear Eugene. Your mind will be more at peace, lying here, if you make Lizzie your wife. You wish me to speak to her, and tell her so, and entreat her to be your wife. You ask her to kneel at this bedside and be married to you, that your reparation may be complete. Is that so?"

"Yes. God bless you! Yes."

"It shall be done, Eugene. Trust it to me. I shall have to go away for some few hours, to give effect to your wishes. You see this is unavoidable?"

"Dear friend, I said so."

"True. But I had not the clue then. How do you think I got it?"

Glancing wistfully around, Eugene saw Miss Jenny at the foot of the bed, looking at him with her elbows on the bed, and her head upon her hands. There was a trace of his whimsical air upon him, as he tried to smile at her.

"Yes, indeed," said Lightwood, "the discovery was hers. Observe, my dear Eugene; while I am away you will know that I have discharged my trust with Lizzie, by finding her here, in my present place at your bedside, to leave you no more. A final word before I go. This is the right course of a true man, Eugene. And I solemnly believe, with all my soul, that if Providence should mercifully restore you to us, you will be blessed with a noble wife in the preserver of your life, whom you will dearly love."

"Amen. I am sure of that. But I shall not come through it, Mortimer."

"You will not be the less hopeful or less strong for this, Eugene."

"No. Touch my face with yours, in case I should not hold out till you come back. I love you, Mortimer. Don't be uneasy for me while you are gone. If my dear brave girl will take me, I feel persuaded that I shall live long enough to be married, dear fellow."

Miss Jenny gave up altogether on this parting taking place between the friends, and sitting with her back towards the bed in the bower made by her bright hair, wept heartily, though noiselessly. Mortimer Lightwood was soon gone. As the evening light lengthened the heavy reflections of the trees in the river, another figure came with a soft step into the sick room.

"Is he conscious?" asked the little dressmaker, as the figure took its station by the pillow. For, Jenny had given place to it immediately, and could not see the sufferer's face, in the dark room, from her new and removed position.

"He is conscious, Jenny," murmured Eugene for himself. "He knows his wife."

CHAPTER XI

MRS. JOHN ROKESMITH sat at needlework in her neat little room, beside a basket of neat little articles of clothing, which presented so much of the appearance of being in the dolls' dressmaker's way of business, that one might have supposed she was going to set up in opposition to Miss Wren. Whether the Complete British Family Housewife had imparted sage counsel anent them, did not appear, but probably not, as that cloudy oracle was nowhere visible. For certain, however, Mrs. John Rokesmith stitched at them with so dexterous a hand, that she must have taken lessons of somebody. Love is in all things a most wonderful teacher, and perhaps love (from a pictorial point of view, with nothing on but a thimble) had been teaching this branch of needlework to Mrs. John Rokesmith.

It was near John's time for coming home, but as Mrs. John was desirous to finish a special triumph of her skill before dinner, she did not go out to meet him. Placidly, though rather consequentially smiling, she sat stitching away with a regular sound, like a sort of dimpled little charming Dresden-china clock by the very best maker.

A knock at the door, and a ring at the bell. Not John; or Bella would have flown out to meet him. Then who, if not John? Bella was asking herself the question, when that fluttering little fool of a servant fluttered in, saying, " Mr. Lightwood ! "

404

Oh good gracious!

Bella had but time to throw a handkerchief over the basket, when Mr. Lightwood made his bow. There was something amiss with Mr. Lightwood, for he was strangely grave and looked ill.

With a brief reference to the happy time when it had been his privilege to know Mrs. Rokesmith as Miss Wilfer, Mr. Lightwood explained what was amiss with him and why he came. He came bearing Lizzie Hexam's earnest hope that Mrs. John Rokesmith would see her married.

Bella was so fluttered by the request, and by the short narrative he had feelingly given her, that there never was a more timely smelling-bottle than John's knock. " My husband," said Bella; " I'll bring him in."

But, that turned out to be more easily said than done; for, the instant she mentioned Mr. Lightwood's name, John stopped, with his hand upon the lock of the room door.

" Come up-stairs, my darling."

Bella was amazed by the flush in his face, and by his sudden turning away. " What can it mean?" she thought, as she accompanied him up-stairs.

" Now, my life," said John, taking her on his knee, " tell me all about it."

All very well to say, " Tell me all about it;" but John was very much confused. His attention evidently trailed off, now and then, even while Bella told him all about it. Yet she knew that he took a great interest in Lizzie and her fortunes. What could it mean?

" You will come to this marriage with me, John dear? "

" N—no, my love: I can't do that."

" You can't do that, John? "

" No, my dear, it's quite out of the question. Not to be thought of."

" Am I to go alone, John? "

" No, my dear, you will go with Mr. Lightwood."

"Don't you think it is time we went down to Mr. Lightwood, John dear?" Bella insinuated.

"My darling, it's almost time you went, but I must ask you to excuse me to him altogether."

"You never mean, John dear, that you are not going to see him? Why he knows you have come home. I told him so."

"That's a little unfortunate, but it can't be helped. Unfortunate or fortunate, I positively cannot see him, my love."

Bella cast about in her mind what could be his reason for this unaccountable behaviour, as she sat on his knee looking at him in astonishment and pouting a little. A weak reason presented itself.

"John dear, you never can be jealous of Mr. Lightwood?"

"Why, my precious child," returned her husband, laughing outright: "how could I be jealous of him? Why should I be jealous of him?"

"Because, you know, John," pursued Bella, pouting a little more, "though he did rather admire me once, it was not my fault."

"It was your fault that I admired you," returned her husband, with a look of pride in her, "and why not your fault that he admired you? But, I jealous on that account? Why, I must go distracted for life, if I turned jealous of every one who used to find my wife beautiful and winning!"

"I am half angry with you, John dear," said Bella, laughing a little, "and half pleased with you; because you are such a stupid old fellow, and yet you say nice things, as if you meant them. Don't be mysterious, sir. What harm do you know of Mr. Lightwood?"

"None, my love."

"What has he ever done to you, John?"

"He has never done anything to me, my dear. I know no more against him than I know against Mr. Wrayburn; he has never done anything to me; neither has Mr. Wrayburn. And yet I have exactly the same objection to both of them."

"Oh, John!" retorted Bella, as if she were giving him up for a bad job, as she used to give up herself. "You are nothing better than a sphinx! And a married sphinx isn't a—isn't a nice confidential husband," said Bella, in a tone of injury.

"Bella, my life," said John Rokesmith, touching her cheek, with a grave smile, as she cast down her eyes and pouted again; "look at me. I want to speak to you."

"In earnest, Blue Beard of the secret chamber?" asked Bella, clearing her pretty face.

"In earnest. And I confess to the secret chamber. Don't you remember that you asked me not to declare what I thought of your higher qualities until you had been tried?"

"Yes, John dear. And I fully meant it, and I fully mean it."

"The time will come, my darling—I am no prophet, but I say so,—when you *will* be tried. The time will come, I think, when you will undergo a trial through which you will never pass quite triumphantly for me, unless you can put perfect faith in me."

"Then you may be sure of me, John dear, for I can put perfect faith in you, and I do, and I always, always will. Don't judge me by a little thing like this, John. In little things, I am a little thing myself—I always was. But in great things, I hope not; I don't mean to boast, John dear, but I hope not!"

He was even better convinced of the truth of what she said than she was, as he felt her loving arms about him. If the Golden Dustman's riches had been his to stake, he would have staked them to the last farthing on the fidelity through good and evil of her affectionate and trusting heart.

"Now, I'll go down to, and go away with, Mr. Lightwood," said Bella, springing up. "You are the most creasing and tumbling Clumsy-Boots of a packer, John, that ever was; but if you're quite good, and will promise never to do so any more (though I don't know what you have done!)

you may pack me a little bag for a night, while I get my bonnet on."

He gaily complied, and she tied her dimpled chin up, and shook her head into her bonnet, and pulled out the bows of her bonnet-strings, and got her gloves on, finger by finger, and finally got them on her little plump hands, and bade him good-bye and went down. Mr. Lightwood's impatience was much relieved when he found her dressed for departure.

"Mr. Rokesmith goes with us?" he said, hesitating, with a look towards the door.

"Oh, I forgot!" replied Bella. "His best compliments. His face is swollen to the size of two faces, and he is to go to bed directly, poor fellow, to wait for the doctor, who is coming to lance him."

"It is curious," observed Lightwood, "that I have never yet seen Mr. Rokesmith, though we have been engaged in the same affairs."

"Really?" said the unblushing Bella.

"I begin to think," observed Lightwood, "that I never shall see him."

"These things happen so oddly sometimes," said Bella with a steady countenance, "that there seems a kind of fatality in them. But I am quite ready, Mr. Lightwood."

They started directly, in a little carriage that Lightwood had brought with him from never-to-be-forgotten Greenwich; and from Greenwich they started directly for London; and in London they waited at a railway station until such time as the Reverend Frank Milvey, and Margaretta his wife, with whom Mortimer Lightwood had been already in conference, should come and join them.

That worthy couple were delayed by a portentous old parishioner of the female gender, who was one of the plagues of their lives, and with whom they bore with most exemplary sweetness and good-humour, notwithstanding her having an infection of absurdity about her, that communicated itself to everything with which, and everybody with whom, she came in contact. She was a member of the Reverend Frank's congregation, and made a point of distinguishing herself in that body, by conspicuously weeping at everything, however cheering, said by the Reverend Frank in his public ministration ; also by applying to herself the various lamentations of David, and complaining in a personally injured manner (much in arrear of the clerk and the rest of the respondents) that her enemies were digging pitfalls about her, and breaking her with rods of iron. Indeed, this old widow discharged herself of that portion of the Morning and Evening Service as if she were lodging a complaint on oath and applying for a warrant before a magistrate. But this was not her most inconvenient characteristic, for that took the form of an impression, usually recurring in inclement weather and at about daybreak, that she had something on her mind and stood in immediate need of the Reverend Frank to come and take it off. Many a time had that kind creature got up, and gone out to Mrs. Sprodgkin (such was the disciple's name), suppressing a strong sense of her comicality by his strong sense of duty, and perfectly knowing that nothing but a cold would come of it. However, beyond themselves, the Reverend Frank Milvey and Mrs. Milvey seldom hinted that Mrs. Sprodgkin was hardly worth the trouble she gave ; but both made the best of her, as they did of all their troubles.

This very exacting member of the fold appeared to be endowed with a sixth sense, in regard of knowing when the Reverend Frank Milvey least desired her company, and with promptitude appearing in his little hall. Consequently, when the Reverend Frank had willingly engaged that he and his wife would accompany Lightwood back, he said, as a matter of course : " We must make haste to get out, Margaretta, my dear, or we shall be descended on by Mrs. Sprodgkin." To which Mrs. Milvey replied, in her pleasantly emphatic way, " Oh *yes*, for she *is* such a marplot, Frank, and *does* worry so ! " Words that were scarcely uttered when their theme was announced as in faithful attendance below, desiring

counsel on a spiritual matter. The points on which Mrs.
Sprodgkin sought elucidation being seldom of a pressing
nature (as Who begat Whom, or some information concerning
the Amorites), Mrs. Milvey on this special occasion resorted
to the device of buying her off with a present of tea and
sugar, and a loaf and butter. These gifts Mrs. Sprodgkin
accepted, but still insisted on dutifully remaining in the hall,
to curtsey to the Reverend Frank as he came forth. Who,
incautiously saying in his genial manner, " Well, Sally, there
you are ! " involved himself in a discursive address from Mrs.
Sprodgkin, revolving around the result that she regarded
tea and sugar in the light of myrrh and frankincense, and
considered bread and butter identical with locusts and wild
honey. Having communicated this edifying piece of information, Mrs. Sprodgkin was left still unadjourned in the hall,
and Mr. and Mrs. Milvey hurried in a heated condition to
the railway station. All of which is here recorded to the
honour of that good Christian pair, representatives of hundreds
of other good Christian pairs as conscientious and as useful,
who merge the smallness of their work in its greatness, and
feel in no danger of losing dignity when they adapt themselves to incomprehensible humbugs.

"Detained at the last moment by one who had a claim
upon me," was the Reverend Frank's apology to Lightwood,
taking no thought to himself. To which Mrs. Milvey added,
taking thought for him, like the championing little wife she
was : " Oh yes, detained at the last moment. But *as* to the
claim, Frank, I *must* say that I *do* think you are *over*-con-
siderate sometimes, and allow *that* to be a *little* abused."

Bella felt conscious, in spite of her late pledge for herself,
that her husband's absence would give disagreeable occasion
for surprise to the Milveys. Nor could she appear quite at
her ease when Mrs. Milvey asked :

" *How* is Mr. Rokesmith, and *is* he gone before us, or *does*
he follow us ? "

It becoming necessary, upon this, to send him to bed again

and hold him in waiting to be lanced again, Bella did it. But not half as well on the second occasion as on the first; for, a twice-told white one, seems almost to become a black one when you are not used to it.

"Oh *dear!*" said Mrs. Milvey, "I am *so* sorry! Mr. Rokesmith took *such* an interest in Lizzie Hexam, when we were there before. And if we had *only* known of his face, we *could* have given him something that would have kept it down long enough for so *short* a purpose."

By way of making the white one whiter, Bella hastened to stipulate that he was not in pain. Mrs. Milvey was *so* glad of it.

"I don't know *how* it is," said Mrs. Milvey, "and I am *sure* you don't, Frank, but the clergy and their wives seem to *cause* swelled faces. Whenever I take notice of a child in the school, it seems to me as if its face swelled *instantly*. Frank *never* makes acquaintance with a new old woman, but she gets the face-ache. And another thing is, we *do* make the poor children sniff so. I don't know *how* we do it, and I should be so glad not to; but the *more* we take notice of them, the *more* they sniff. Just as they do when the text is given out.—Frank, that's a schoolmaster. I have seen him somewhere."

The reference was to a young man of reserved appearance, in a coat and waistcoat of black and pantaloons of pepper and salt. He had come into the office of the station, from its interior, in an unsettled way, immediately after Lightwood had gone out to the train; and he had been hurriedly reading the printed bills and notices on the wall. He had had a wandering interest in what was said among the people waiting there and passing to and fro. He had drawn nearer, at about the time when Mrs. Milvey mentioned Lizzie Hexam, and had remained near since, though always glancing towards the door by which Lightwood had gone out. He stood with his back towards them, and his gloved hands clasped behind him. There was now so evident a faltering upon him, expressive of

411

indecision whether or no he should express his having heard himself referred to, that Mr. Milvey spoke to him.

"I cannot recall your name," he said, "but I remember to have seen you in your school."

"My name is Bradley Headstone, sir," he replied, backing into a more retired place.

"I ought to have remembered it," said Mr. Milvey, giving him his hand. "I hope you are well? A little overworked, I am afraid?"

"Yes, I am overworked just at present, sir."

"Had no play in your last holiday time?"

"No, sir."

"All work and no play, Mr. Headstone, will not make dulness, in your case, I dare say; but it will make dyspepsia, if you don't take care."

"I will endeavour to take care, sir. Might I beg leave to speak to you, outside, a moment?"

"By all means."

It was evening, and the office was well lighted. The schoolmaster, who had never remitted his watch on Lightwood's door, now moved by another door to a corner without, where there was more shadow than light; and said, plucking at his gloves:

"One of your ladies, sir, mentioned within my hearing a name that I am acquainted with; I may say, well acquainted with. The name of the sister of an old pupil of mine. He was my pupil for a long time, and has got on and gone upward rapidly. The name of Hexam. The name of Lizzie Hexam." He seemed to be a shy man, struggling against nervousness, and spoke in a very constrained way. The break he set between his last two sentences was quite embarrassing to his hearer.

"Yes," replied Mr. Milvey. "We are going down to see her."

"I gathered as much, sir. I hope there is nothing amiss with the sister of my old pupil? I hope no bereavement has befallen her. I hope she is in no affliction? Has lost no—relation?"

Mr. Milvey thought this a man with a very odd manner, and a dark downward look: but he answered in his usual open way.

"I am glad to tell you, Mr. Headstone, that the sister of your old pupil has not sustained any such loss. You thought I might be going down to bury some one?"

"That may have been the connection of ideas, sir, with your clerical character, but I was not conscious of it.—Then you are not, sir?"

A man with a very odd manner indeed, and with a lurking look that was quite oppressive.

"No. In fact," said Mr. Milvey, "since you are so interested in the sister of your old pupil, I may as well tell you that I am going down to marry her."

The schoolmaster started back. "Not to marry her myself," said Mr. Milvey, with a smile, "because I have a wife already. To perform the marriage service at her wedding."

Bradley Headstone caught hold of a pillar behind him. If Mr. Milvey knew an ashy face when he saw it, he saw it then.

"You are quite ill, Mr. Headstone!"

"It is not much, sir. It will pass over very soon. I am accustomed to be seized with giddiness. Don't let me detain you, sir; I stand in need of no assistance, I thank you. Much obliged by your sparing me these minutes of your time."

As Mr. Milvey, who had no more minutes to spare, made a suitable reply and turned back into the office, he observed the schoolmaster to lean against the pillar with his hat in his hand, and to pull at his neckcloth as if he were trying to tear it off. The Reverend Frank accordingly directed the notice of one of the attendants to him, by saying: "There is a person outside who seems to be really ill, and to require some help, though he says he does not."

Lightwood had by this time secured their places, and the

413

departure-bell was about to be rung. They took their seats, and were beginning to move out of the station, when the same attendant came running along the platform looking into all the carriages.

"Oh! You are here, sir!" he said, springing on the step, and holding the window-frame by his elbow, as the carriage moved. "That person you pointed out to me is in a fit."

"I infer from what he told me that he is subject to such attacks. He will come to, in the air, in a little while."

He was took very bad to be sure, and was biting and knocking about him (the man said) furiously. Would the gentleman give him his card, as he had seen him first? The gentleman did so, with the explanation that he knew no more of the man attacked than that he was a man of very respectable occupation, who had said he was out of health, as his appearance would of itself have indicated. The attendant received the card, watched his opportunity for sliding down, slid down, and so it ended.

Then, the train rattled among the house-tops, and among the ragged sides of houses torn down to make way for it, and over the swarming streets, and under the fruitful earth, until it shot across the river: bursting over the quiet surface like a bomb-shell, and gone again as if it had exploded in the rush of smoke and steam and glare. A little more, and again it roared across the river, a great rocket: spurning the watery turnings and doublings with ineffable contempt, and going straight to its end, as Father Time goes to his. To whom it is no matter what living waters run high or low, reflect the heavenly lights and darknesses, produce their little growth of weeds and flowers, turn here, turn there, are noisy or still, are troubled or at rest, for their course has one sure termination, though their sources and devices are many.

Then, a carriage ride succeeded, near the solemn river, stealing away by night, as all things steal away, by night and by day, so quietly yielding to the attraction of the loadstone rock of Eternity; and the nearer they drew to the chamber where Eugene lay, the more they feared that they might find his wanderings done. At last they saw its dim light shining out, and it gave them hope: though Lightwood faltered as he thought: "If he were gone, she would still be sitting by him."

But he lay quiet, half in stupor, half in sleep. Bella, entering with a raised admonitory finger, kissed Lizzie softly, but said not a word. Neither did any of them speak, but all sat down at the foot of the bed, silently waiting. And now, in this night-watch, mingling with the flow of the river and with the rush of the train, came the questions into Bella's mind again: What could be in the depths of that mystery of John's? Why was it that he had never been seen by Mr. Lightwood, whom he still avoided? When would that trial come, through which her faith in, and her duty to, her dear husband, was to carry her, rendering him triumphant? For that had been his term. Her passing through the trial was to make the man she loved with all her heart, triumphant. Term not to sink out of sight in Bella's breast.

Far on in the night, Eugene opened his eyes. He was sensible, and said at once: "How does the time go? Has our Mortimer come back?"

Lightwood was there immediately, to answer for himself. "Yes, Eugene, and all is ready."

"Dear boy!" returned Eugene, with a smile, "we both thank you heartily. Lizzie, tell them how welcome they are, and that I would be eloquent if I could."

"There is no need," said Mr. Milvey. "We know it. Are you better, Mr. Wrayburn?"

"I am much happier," said Eugene.

"Much better too, I hope?"

Eugene turned his eyes towards Lizzie, as if to spare her, and answered nothing.

Then they all stood around the bed, and Mr. Milvey, opening his book, began the service; so rarely associated with the shadow of death; so inseparable in the mind from a flush of life and gaiety and hope and health and joy. Bella thought how different from her own sunny little wedding, and wept. Mrs. Milvey overflowed with pity, and wept too. The dolls' dressmaker, with her hands before her face, wept in her golden bower. Reading in a low clear voice, and bending over Eugene, who kept his eyes upon him, Mr. Milvey did his office with suitable simplicity. As the bridegroom could not move his hand, they touched his fingers with the ring, and so put it on the bride. When the two plighted their troth, she laid her hand on his, and kept it there. When the ceremony was done, and all the rest departed from the room, she drew her arm under his head, and laid her own head down upon the pillow by his side.

"Undraw the curtains, my dear girl," said Eugene, after a while, "and let us see our wedding-day."

The sun was rising, and his first rays struck into the room as she came back and put her lips to his. "I bless the day!" said Eugene. "I bless the day!" said Lizzie.

"You have made a poor marriage of it, my sweet wife," said Eugene. "A shattered, graceless fellow, stretched at his length here, and next to nothing for you when you are a young widow."

"I have made the marriage that I would have given all the world to dare to hope for," she replied.

"You have thrown yourself away," said Eugene, shaking his head. "But you have followed the treasure of your heart. My justification is, that you had thrown that away first, dear girl!"

"No. I had given it to you."

"The same thing, my poor Lizzie!"

"Hush, hush! A very different thing."

There were tears in his eyes, and she besought him to close them. "No," said Eugene, again shaking his head; "let me look at you, Lizzie, while I can. You brave, devoted girl! You heroine!"

Her own eyes filled under his praises. And when he

mustered strength to move his wounded head a very little way, and lay it on her bosom, the tears of both fell.

"Lizzie," said Eugene, after a silence : "when you see me wandering away from this refuge that I have so ill deserved, speak to me by my name, and I think I shall come back."

"Yes, dear Eugene."

"There!" he exclaimed, smiling. "I should have gone then but for that!"

A little while afterwards, when he appeared to be sinking into insensibility, she said, in a calm loving voice : "Eugene, my dear husband!" He immediately answered : "There again! You see how you can recall me!" and afterwards, when he could not speak, he still answered by a slight movement of his head upon her bosom.

The sun was high in the sky when she gently disengaged herself to give him the stimulants and nourishment he required. The utter helplessness of the wreck of him that lay cast ashore there now alarmed her, but he himself appeared a little more hopeful.

"Ah, my beloved Lizzie!" he said, faintly. "How shall I ever pay all I owe you, if I recover!"

"Don't be ashamed of me," she replied, "and you will have more than paid all."

"It would require a life, Lizzie, to pay all; more than a life."

"Live for that, then; live for me, Eugene; live to see how hard I will try to improve myself, and never to discredit you."

"My darling girl," he replied, rallying more of his old manner than he had ever yet got together. "On the contrary, I have been thinking whether it is not the best thing I can do, to die."

"The best thing you can do, to leave me with a broken heart?"

"I don't mean that, my dear girl. I was not thinking of that. What I was thinking of was this. Out of your compassion for me, in this maimed and broken state, you make

417

so much of me—you think so well of me—you love me so dearly!"

"Heaven knows I love you dearly!"

"And Heaven knows I prize it! Well. If I live, you'll find me out."

"I shall find out that my husband has a mine of purpose and energy, and will turn it to the best account?"

"I hope so, dearest Lizzie," said Eugene, wistfully, and yet somewhat whimsically. "I hope so. But I can't summon the vanity to think so. How can I think so, looking back on such a trifling, wasted youth as mine! I humbly hope it; but I daren't believe it. There is a sharp misgiving in my conscience that if I were to live, I should disappoint your good opinion and my own—and that I ought to die, my dear!"

CHAPTER XII

THE winds and tides rose and fell a certain number of times, the earth moved round the sun a certain number of times, the ship upon the ocean made her voyage safely, and brought a baby-Bella home. Then who so blest and happy as Mrs. John Rokesmith, saving and excepting Mr. John Rokesmith!

" Would you not like to be rich *now*, my darling ? "

" How can you ask me such a question, John dear ? Am I not rich ? "

These were among the first words spoken near the baby-Bella as she lay asleep. She soon proved to be a baby of wonderful intelligence, evincing the strongest objection to her grandmother's society, and being invariably seized with a painful acidity of the stomach when that dignified lady honoured her with any attention.

It was charming to see Bella contemplating this baby, and finding out her own dimples in that tiny reflection, as if she were looking in the glass without personal vanity. Her cherubic father justly remarked to her husband that the baby seemed to make her younger than before, reminding him of the days when she had a pet doll and used to talk to it as she carried it about. The world might have been challenged to produce another baby who had such a store of pleasant nonsense said and sung to it, as Bella said and sung to this baby; or who was dressed and undressed as often in four-and-twenty

419

hours as Bella dressed and undressed this baby; or who was held behind doors and poked out to stop its father's way when he came home, as this baby was; or, in a word, who did half the number of baby things, through the lively invention of a gay and proud young mother, that this inexhaustible baby did.

The inexhaustible baby was two or three months old, when Bella began to notice a cloud upon her husband's brow. Watching it, she saw a gathering and deepening anxiety there, which caused her great disquiet. More than once, she awoke him muttering in his sleep; and, though he muttered nothing worse than her own name, it was plain to her that his restlessness originated in some load of care. Therefore, Bella at length put in her claim to divide this load, and bear her half of it.

"You know, John dear," she said, cheerily reverting to their former conversation, "that I hope I may safely be trusted in great things. And it surely cannot be a little thing that causes you so much uneasiness. It's very considerate of you to try to hide from me that you are uncomfortable about something, but it's quite impossible to be done, John love."

"I admit that I am rather uneasy, my own."

"Then please to tell me what about, sir."

But no, he evaded that. "Never mind!" thought Bella, resolutely. "John requires me to put perfect faith in him, and he shall not be disappointed."

She went up to London one day, to meet him, in order that they might make some purchases. She found him waiting for her at her journey's end, and they walked away together through the streets. He was in gay spirits, though still harping on that notion of their being rich; and he said, now let them make believe that yonder fine carriage was theirs, and that it was waiting to take them home to a fine house they had; what would Bella, in that case, best like to find in the house? Well! Bella didn't know: already having everything she wanted, she couldn't say. But, by degrees she was led on to confess that she would like to have for the inexhaustible baby such a nursery as never was seen. It was to be " a very rainbow for colours," as she was quite sure baby noticed colours ; and the staircase was to be adorned with the most exquisite flowers, as she was absolutely certain baby noticed flowers ; and there was to be an aviary somewhere, of the loveliest little birds, as there was not the smallest doubt in the world that baby noticed birds. Was there nothing else ? No, John dear. The predilections of the inexhaustible baby being provided for, Bella could think of nothing else.

They were chatting on in this way, and John had suggested, " No jewels for your own wear, for instance ? " and Bella had replied laughing, Oh ! if he came to that, yes, there might be a beautiful ivory case of jewels on the dressing-table ; when these pictures were in a moment darkened and blotted out.

They turned a corner and met Mr. Lightwood.

He stopped as if he were petrified by the sight of Bella's husband, who in the same moment had changed colour.

" Mr. Lightwood and I have met before," he said.

" Met before, John ? " Bella repeated in a tone of wonder. " Mr. Lightwood told me he had never seen you."

" I did not then know that I had," said Lightwood, discomposed on her account. " I believed that I had only heard of——Mr. Rokesmith." With an emphasis on the name.

" When Mr. Lightwood saw me, my love," observed her husband, not avoiding his eye, but looking at him, " my name was Julius Handford."

Julius Handford ! The name that Bella had so often seen in old newspapers, when she was an inmate of Mr. Boffin's house ! Julius Handford, who had been publicly entreated to appear, and for intelligence of whom a reward had been publicly offered !

" I would have avoided mentioning it in your presence," said Lightwood to Bella, delicately ; " but since your husband mentions it himself, I must confirm his strange admission. I saw him as Mr. Julius Handford, and I afterwards (unquestionably to his knowledge) took great pains to trace him out."

"Quite true. But it was not my object or my interest," said Rokesmith, quietly, "to be traced out."

Bella looked from the one to the other, in amazement.

"Mr. Lightwood," pursued her husband, "as chance has brought us face to face at last—which is not to be wondered at, for the wonder is, that, in spite of all my pains to the contrary, chance has not confronted us together sooner—I have only to remind you that you have been at my house, and to add that I have not changed my residence."

"Sir," returned Lightwood, with a meaning glance towards Bella, "my position is a truly painful one. I hope that no complicity in a very dark transaction may attach to you, but you cannot fail to know that your own extraordinary conduct has laid you under suspicion."

"I know it has," was all the reply.

"My professional duty," said Lightwood, hesitating, with another glance towards Bella, "is greatly at variance with my personal inclination : but I doubt, Mr. Handford, or Mr. Rokesmith, whether I am justified in taking leave of you here, with your whole course unexplained."

Bella caught her husband by the hand.

"Don't be alarmed, my darling. Mr. Lightwood will find that he is quite justified in taking leave of me here. At all events," added Rokesmith, "he will find that I mean to take leave of him here."

"I think, sir," said Lightwood, "you can scarcely deny that when I came to your house on the occasion to which you have referred, you avoided me of a set purpose."

"Mr. Lightwood, I assure you, I have no disposition to deny it, or intention to deny it. I should have continued to avoid you, in pursuance of the same set purpose, for a short time longer, if we had not met now. I am going straight home, and shall remain at home to-morrow until noon. Hereafter, I hope we may be better acquainted. Good-day."

Lightwood at last

Lightwood stood irresolute, but Bella's husband passed him in the steadiest manner, with Bella on his arm; and they went home without encountering any further remonstrance or molestation from any one.

When they had dined and were alone, John Rokesmith said to his wife, who had preserved her cheerfulness : " And you don't ask me, my dear, why I bore that name ? "

" No, John love. I should dearly like to know, of course ; " (which her anxious face confirmed ;) " but I wait until you can tell me of your own free will. You asked me if I could have perfect faith in you, and I said yes, and I meant it."

It did not escape Bella's notice that he began to look triumphant. She wanted no strengthening in her firmness ; but if she had had need of any, she would have derived it from his kindling face.

" You cannot have been prepared, my dearest, for such a discovery as that this mysterious Mr. Handford was identical with your husband ? "

" No, John dear, of course not. But you told me to prepare to be tried, and I prepared myself."

He drew her to nestle closer to him, and told her it would soon be over, and the truth would soon appear. " And now," he went on, " lay stress, my dear, on these words that I am going to add. I stand in no kind of peril, and I can by possibility be hurt at no one's hand."

" You are quite, quite sure of that, John dear ? "

" Not a hair of my head ! Moreover, I have done no wrong, and have injured no man. Shall I swear it ?

" No, John ! " cried Bella, laying her hand upon his lips, with a proud look. " Never to me ! "

" But circumstances," he went on—" I can, and I will, disperse them in a moment—have surrounded me with one of the strangest suspicions ever known. You heard Mr. Lightwood speak of a dark transaction ? "

" Yes, John."

" You are prepared to hear explicitly what he meant ? "

423

"Yes, John."

"My life, he meant the murder of John Harmon, your allotted husband."

With a fast palpitating heart, Bella grasped him by the arm. "You cannot be suspected, John?"

"Dear love, I can be—for I am!"

There was silence between them, as she sat looking in his face, with the colour quite gone from her own face and lips. "How dare they!" she cried at length, in a burst of generous indignation. "My beloved husband, how dare they!"

He caught her in his arms as she opened hers, and held her to his heart. "Even knowing this, you can trust me, Bella?"

"I can trust you, John dear, with all my soul. If I could not trust you, I should fall dead at your feet."

The kindling triumph in his face was bright indeed, as he looked up and rapturously exclaimed, what had he done to deserve the blessing of this dear, confiding creature's heart! Again she put her hand upon his lips, saying, "Hush!" and then told him, in her own little natural pathetic way, that if all the world were against him, she would be for him; that if all the world repudiated him, she would believe him; that if he were infamous in other eyes, he would be honoured in hers; and that, under the worst unmerited suspicion, she could devote her life to consoling him, and imparting her own faith in him to their little child.

A twilight calm of happiness then succeeding to their radiant noon, they remained at peace, until a strange voice in the room startled them both. The room being by that time dark, the voice said, "Don't let the lady be alarmed by my striking a light," and immediately a match rattled, and glimmered in a hand. The hand and the match and the voice were then seen by John Rokesmith to belong to Mr. Inspector, once meditatively active in this chronicle.

"I take the liberty," said Mr. Inspector, in a business-like manner, "to bring myself to the recollection of Mr. Julius

A VISIT FROM MR. INSPECTOR

Handford, who gave me his name and address down at our place a considerable time ago. Would the lady object to my lighting the pair of candles on the chimney-piece, to throw a further light upon the subject? No? Thank you, ma'am. Now, we look cheerful."

Mr. Inspector, in a dark-blue buttoned-up frock coat and pantaloons, presented a serviceable, half-pay, Royal Arms kind of appearance, as he applied his pocket-handkerchief to his nose and bowed to the lady.

"You favoured me, Mr. Handford," said Mr. Inspector, "by writing down your name and address, and I produce the piece of paper on which you wrote it. Comparing the same with the writing on the fly-leaf of this book on the table—and a sweet pretty volume it is—I find the writing of the entry, 'Mrs. John Rokesmith. From her husband on her birth-day'—and very gratifying to the feelings such memorials are—to correspond exactly. Can I have a word with you?"

"Certainly. Here, if you please," was the reply.

"Why," retorted Mr. Inspector, again using his pocket-handkerchief, "though there's nothing for the lady to be at all alarmed at, still, ladies are apt to take alarm at matters of business—being of that fragile sex that they're not accustomed to them when not of a strictly domestic character—and I do generally make it a rule to propose retirement from the presence of ladies, before entering upon business topics. Or, perhaps," Mr. Inspector hinted, "if the lady was to step up-stairs, and take a look at baby now!"

"Mrs. Rokesmith,"—her husband was beginning; when Mr. Inspector, regarding the words as an introduction, said, "Happy, I am sure, to have the honour." And bowed, with gallantry.

"Mrs. Rokesmith," resumed her husband, "is satisfied that she can have no reason for being alarmed, whatever the business is."

"Really? Is that so?" said Mr. Inspector. "But it's a sex to live and learn from, and there's nothing a lady can't accomplish when she once fully gives her mind to it. It's the case with my own wife. Well, ma'am, this good gentleman of yours has given rise to a rather large amount of trouble which might have been avoided if he had come forward and explained himself. Well, you see! he *didn't* come forward and explain himself. Consequently, now that we meet, him and me, you'll say—and say right—that there's nothing to be alarmed at in my proposing to him to come forward—or, putting the same meaning in another form, to come along with me—*and* explain himself."

When Mr. Inspector put it in that other form, "to come along with me," there was a relishing roll in his voice, and his eye beamed with an official lustre.

"Do you propose to take me into custody?" inquired John Rokesmith, very coolly.

"Why argue?" returned Mr. Inspector, in a comfortable sort of remonstrance; "ain't it enough that I propose that you shall come along with me?"

"For what reason?"

"Lord bless my soul and body!" returned Mr. Inspector, "I wonder at it in a man of your education. Why argue?"

"What do you charge against me?"

"I wonder at you before a lady," said Mr. Inspector, shaking his head reproachfully: "I wonder, brought up as you have been, you haven't a more delicate mind! I charge you, then, with being some way concerned in the Harmon Murder. I don't say whether before, or in, or after, the fact. I don't say whether with having some knowledge of it that hasn't come out."

"You don't surprise me. I foresaw your visit this afternoon."

"Don't!" said Mr. Inspector. "Why, why argue? It's my duty to inform you that whatever you say, will be used against you."

"I don't think it will."

"But I tell you it will," said Mr. Inspector. "Now, having

426

received the caution, do you still say that you foresaw my visit this afternoon?"

"Yes. And I will say something more if you will step with me into the next room."

With a reassuring kiss on the lips of the frightened Bella, her husband (to whom Mr. Inspector obligingly offered his arm) took up a candle, and withdrew with that gentleman. They were a full half-hour in conference. When they returned, Mr. Inspector looked considerably astonished.

"I have invited this worthy officer, my dear," said John, "to make a short excursion with me in which you shall be a sharer. He will take something to eat and drink, I dare say, on your invitation, while you are getting your bonnet on."

Mr. Inspector declined eating, but assented to the proposal of a glass of brandy and water. Mixing this cold, and pensively consuming it, he broke at intervals into such soliloquies as that he never did know such a move, that he never had been so gravelled, and that what a game was this to try the sort of stuff a man's opinion of himself was made of! Concurrently with these comments, he more than once burst out a laughing, with the half-enjoying, and half-piqued air of a man who had given up a good conundrum, after much guessing, and been told the answer. Bella was so timid of him, that she noted these things in a half-shrinking, half-perceptive way, and similarly noted that there was a great change in his manner towards John. That coming-along-with-him deportment was now lost in long musing looks at John and at herself, and sometimes in slow heavy rubs of his hand across his forehead, as if he were ironing out the creases which his deep pondering made there. He had had some coughing and whistling satellites, secretly gravitating towards him about the premises, but they were now dismissed, and he eyed John as if he had meant to do him a public service, but had unfortunately been anticipated. Whether Bella might have noted anything more, if she had been less afraid of him, she could not determine; but it was all inexplicable to her, and not the faintest flash of the real state of the case broke in upon her mind. Mr. Inspector's increased notice of herself, and knowing way of raising his eyebrows when their eyes by any chance met, as if he put the question "Don't you see?" augmented her timidity, and, consequently, her perplexity. For all these reasons, when he and she and John, at towards nine o'clock of a winter evening, went to London, and began driving from London Bridge, among low-lying water-side wharves and docks and strange places, Bella was in the state of a dreamer; perfectly unable to account for her being there, perfectly unable to forecast what would happen next, or whither she was going, or why; certain of nothing in the immediate presence, but that she confided in John, and that John seemed somehow to be getting more triumphant. But what a certainty was that!

They alighted at last at the corner of a court, where there was a building with a bright lamp and a wicket gate. Its orderly appearance was very unlike that of the surrounding neighbourhood, and was explained by the inscription POLICE STATION.

"We are not going in here, John?" said Bella, clinging to him.

"Yes, my dear; but of our own accord. We shall come out again as easily, never fear."

The whitewashed room was pure white as of old, the methodical book-keeping was in peaceful progress as of old, and some distant howler was banging against a cell-door as of old. The sanctuary was not a permanent abiding-place, but a kind of criminal Pickford's. The lower passions and vices were regularly ticked off in the books, warehoused in the cells, carted away as per accompanying invoice, and left little mark upon it.

Mr. Inspector placed two chairs for his visitors, before the fire, and communed in a low voice with a brother of his order (also of a half-pay and Royal Arms aspect), who, judged only by his occupation at the moment, might have been a writing-master, setting copies. Their conference done, Mr. Inspector returned to the fireplace, and, having observed that he would step round to the Fellowships and see how matters stood, went out. He soon came back again, saying, "Nothing could be better, for they're at supper with Miss Abbey in the bar;" and then they all three went out together.

Still, as in a dream, Bella found herself entering a snug, old-fashioned public-house, and found herself smuggled into a little three-cornered room nearly opposite the bar of that establishment. Mr. Inspector achieved the smuggling of herself and John into this queer room, called Cosy in an inscription on the door, by entering in the narrow passage first in order, and suddenly turning round upon them with extended arms, as if they had been two sheep. The room was lighted for their reception.

"Now," said Mr. Inspector to John, turning the gas lower; "I'll mix with 'em in a casual way, and when I say Identification, perhaps you'll show yourself."

John nodded, and Mr. Inspector went alone to the half-door of the bar. From the dim doorway of Cosy, within which Bella and her husband stood, they could see a comfortable little party of three persons sitting at supper in the bar, and could hear everything that was said.

The three persons were Miss Abbey and two male guests. To whom collectively, Mr. Inspector remarked that the weather was getting sharp for the time of year.

"It need be sharp to suit your wits, sir," said Miss Abbey. "What have you got in hand now?"

"Thanking you for your compliment: not much, Miss Abbey," was Mr. Inspector's rejoinder.

"Who have you got in Cosy?" asked Miss Abbey.

"Only a gentleman and his wife, Miss."

"And who are they? If one may ask it without detriment to your deep plans in the interests of the honest public?" said Miss Abbey, proud of Mr. Inspector as an administrative genius.

"They are strangers in this part of the town, Miss Abbey. They are waiting till I shall want the gentleman to show himself somewhere, for half a moment."

"While they're waiting," said Miss Abbey, "couldn't you join us?"

Mr. Inspector immediately slipped into the bar, and sat down at the side of the half-door, with his back towards the passage, and directly facing the two guests. "I don't take my supper till later in the night," said he, "and therefore I won't disturb the compactness of the table. But I'll take a glass of flip, if that's flip in the jug in the fender."

"That's flip," replied Miss Abbey, "and it's my making, and if even you can find out better, I shall be glad to know where." Filling him, with hospitable hands, a steaming tumbler, Miss Abbey replaced the jug by the fire; the company not having yet arrived at the flip-stage of their supper, but being as yet skirmishing with strong ale.

"Ah—h!" cried Mr. Inspector. "That's the smack! There's not a Detective in the Force, Miss Abbey, that could find out better stuff than that."

"Glad to hear you say so," rejoined Miss Abbey. "You ought to know, if anybody does."

"Mr. Job Potterson," Mr. Inspector continued, "I drink your health. Mr. Jacob Kibble, I drink yours. Hope you have made a prosperous voyage home, gentlemen both."

Mr. Kibble, an unctuous broad man of few words and many mouthfuls, said, more briefly than pointedly, raising his ale to his lips: "Same to you." Mr. Job Potterson, a semi-seafaring man of obliging demeanour, said, "Thank you, sir."

"Lord bless my soul and body!" cried Mr. Inspector. "Talk of trades, Miss Abbey, and the way they set their marks on men" (a subject which nobody had approached); "who wouldn't know your brother to be a Steward! There's a bright and ready twinkle in his eye, there's a neatness in his action, there's a smartness in his figure, there's an air of

430

reliability about him in case you wanted a basin, which points out the steward! And Mr. Kibble; ain't he Passenger, all over? While there's that mercantile cut upon him which would make you happy to give him credit for five hundred pound, don't you see the salt sea shining on him too?"

"*You* do, I dare say," returned Miss Abbey, "but *I* don't. And as for stewarding, I think it's time my brother gave that up, and took this House in hand on his sister's retiring. The House will go to pieces if he don't. I wouldn't sell it for any money that could be told out, to a person that I couldn't depend upon to be a Law to the Porters, as I have been."

"There you're right, Miss," said Mr. Inspector. "A better-kept house is not known to our men. What do I say? Half so well a kept house is not known to our men. Show the Force the Six Jolly Fellowship Porters, and the Force— to a constable—will show you a piece of perfection, Mr. Kibble."

That gentleman, with a very serious shake of his head, subscribed the article.

"And talk of Time slipping by you, as if it was an animal at rustic sports with his tail soaped," said Mr. Inspector (again, a subject which nobody had approached); "why, well you may. Well you may. How has it slipped by us, since the time when Mr. Job Potterson here present, Mr. Jacob Kibble here present, and an Officer of the Force here present, first came together on a matter of Identification!"

Bella's husband stepped softly to the half-door of the bar, and stood there.

"How has Time slipped by us," Mr. Inspector went on slowly, with his eyes narrowly observant of the two guests, "since we three very men, at an Inquest in this very house— Mr. Kibble? Taken ill, sir?"

Mr. Kibble had staggered up, with his lower jaw dropped, catching Potterson by the shoulder, and pointing to the half-door. He now cried out: "Potterson! Look! Look

431

there!" Potterson started up, started back, and exclaimed: "Heaven defend us, what's that?" Bella's husband stepped back to Bella, took her in his arms (for she was terrified by the unintelligible terror of the two men), and shut the door of the little room. A hurry of voices succeeded, in which Mr. Inspector's voice was busiest; it gradually slackened and sank; and Mr. Inspector reappeared. "Sharp's the word, sir!" he said, looking in with a knowing wink. "We'll get your lady out at once." Immediately, Bella and her husband were under the stars, making their way back, alone, to the vehicle they had kept in waiting.

All this was most extraordinary, and Bella could make nothing of it but that John was in the right. How in the right, and how suspected of being in the wrong, she could not divine. Some vague idea that he had never really assumed the name of Handford, and that there was a remarkable likeness between him and that mysterious person, was her nearest approach to any definite explanation. But John was triumphant; that much was made apparent; and she could wait for the rest.

When John came home to dinner next day, he said, sitting down on the sofa by Bella and baby-Bella: "My dear, I have a piece of news to tell you. I have left the China House."

As he seemed to like having left it, Bella took it for granted that there was no misfortune in the case.

"In a word, my love," said John, "the China House is broken up and abolished. There is no such thing any more."

"Then, are you already in another House, John?"

"Yes, my darling. I am in another way of business. And I am rather better off."

The inexhaustible baby was instantly made to congratulate him, and to say, with appropriate action on the part of a very limp arm and a speckled fist: "Three cheers, ladies and gemplemorums. Hoo—ray!"

JOHN AND BELLA MUST MOVE

"I am afraid, my life," said John, "that you have become very much attached to this cottage."

"Afraid I have, John? Of course I have."

"The reason why I said afraid," returned John, "is, because we must move."

"Oh, John!"

"Yes, my dear, we must move. We must have our head-quarters in London now. In short, there's a dwelling-house, rent-free, attached to my new position, and we must occupy it."

"That's a gain, John."

"Yes, my dear, it is undoubtedly a gain."

He gave her a very blithe look, and a very sly look. Which occasioned the inexhaustible baby to square at him with the speckled fists, and demand in a threatening manner what he meant?

"My love, you said it was a gain, and *I* said it was a gain. A very innocent remark, surely."

"I won't," said the inexhaustible baby, "—allow—you—to make—game—of—my—venerable—Ma." At each division administering a soft facer with one of the speckled fists.

John having stooped down to receive these punishing visitations, Bella asked him, would it be necessary to move soon? Why, yes, indeed (said John) he did propose that they should move very soon. Taking the furniture with them, of course? (said Bella). Why, no (said John), the fact was, that the house was—in a sort of a kind of a way—furnished already.

The inexhaustible baby, hearing this, resumed the offensive: and said, "But there's no nursery for me, sir. What do you mean, marble-hearted parent?" To which the marble-hearted parent rejoined that there was a—sort of a kind of a nursery—and it might be "made to do." "Made to do?" returned the Inexhaustible, administering more punishment, "what do you take me for?" And was then turned over on its back in Bella's lap, and smothered with kisses.

433

"But really, John dear," said Bella, flushed in quite a lovely manner by these exercises, "will the new house, just as it stands, do for baby? That's the question?"

"I felt that to be the question," he returned, "and therefore I arranged that you should come with me and look at it, to-morrow morning." Appointment made, accordingly, for Bella to go up with him to-morrow morning; John kissed; and Bella delighted.

When they reached London in pursuance of their little plan, they took coach and drove westward. Not only drove westward, but drove into that particular westward division which Bella had seen last when she turned her face from Mr. Boffin's door. Not only drove into that particular division, but drove at last into that very street. Not only drove into that very street, but stopped at last at that very house.

"John dear!" cried Bella, looking out of the window in a flutter. "Do you see where we are?"

"Yes, my love. The coachman's quite right."

The house-door was opened without any knocking or ringing, and John promptly helped her out. The servant who stood holding the door asked no question of John, neither did he go before them or follow them as they went straight up-stairs. It was only her husband's encircling arm, urging her on, that prevented Bella from stopping at the foot of the staircase. As they ascended, it was seen to be tastefully ornamented with most beautiful flowers.

"Oh, John!" said Bella, faintly. "What does this mean?"

"Nothing, my darling, nothing. Let us go on."

Going on a little higher, they came to a charming aviary, in which a number of tropical birds, more gorgeous in colour than the flowers, were flying about; and among those birds were gold and silver fish, and mosses, and water-lilies, and a fountain, and all manner of wonders.

"Oh, my dear John!" said Bella. "What does this mean?"

"Nothing, my darling, nothing. Let us go on."

They went on, until they came to a door. As John put out his hand to open it, Bella caught his hand.

"I don't know what it means, but it's too much for me. Hold me, John love!"

John caught her up in his arm, and lightly dashed into the room with her.

Behold Mr. and Mrs. Boffin beaming! Behold Mrs. Boffin clapping her hands in an ecstasy, running to Bella, with tears of joy pouring down her comely face, and folding her to her breast, with the words: "My deary, deary, deary girl, that Noddy and me saw married and couldn't wish joy to, or so much as speak to! My deary, deary, deary, wife of John, and mother of his little child! My loving, loving, bright bright, Pretty Pretty. Welcome to your house and home, my deary!"

CHAPTER XIII

SHOWING HOW THE GOLDEN DUSTMAN HELPED TO SCATTER DUST

In all the first bewilderment of her wonder, the most bewilderingly wonderful thing to Bella was the shining countenance of Mr. Boffin. That his wife should be joyous, open-hearted, and genial, or that her face should express every quality that was large and trusting, and no quality that was little or mean, was accordant with Bella's experience. But, that he, with a perfectly beneficent air and a plump rosy face, should be standing there, looking at her and John, like some jovial good spirit, was marvellous. For, how had he looked when she last saw him in that very room (it was the room in which she had given him that piece of her mind at parting), and what had become of all those crooked lines of suspicion, avarice, and distrust, that twisted his visage then?

Mrs. Boffin seated Bella on the large ottoman, and seated herself beside her, and John, her husband, seated himself on the other side of her, and Mr. Boffin stood beaming at every one and everything he could see, with surpassing jollity and enjoyment. Mrs. Boffin was then taken with a laughing fit of clapping her hands and clapping her knees, and rocking herself to and fro, and then with another laughing fit of embracing Bella, and rocking her to and fro—both fits of considerable duration.

"Old lady, old lady," said Mr. Boffin, at length; "if you don't begin somebody else must."

"I'm a-going to begin, Noddy, my dear," returned Mrs. Boffin. "Only it isn't easy for a person to know where to begin, when a person is in this state of delight and happiness. Bella, my dear. Tell me, who's this?"

"Who is this?" repeated Bella. "My husband."

"Ah! But tell me his name, deary!" cried Mrs. Boffin. "Rokesmith."

"No, it ain't!" cried Mrs. Boffin, clapping her hands and shaking her head. "Not a bit of it."

"Handford then," suggested Bella.

"No, it ain't!" cried Mrs. Boffin, again clapping her hands and shaking her head. "Not a bit of it."

"At least, his name is John, I suppose?" said Bella.

"Ah! I should think so, deary!" cried Mrs. Boffin. "I should hope so! Many and many is the time I have called him by his name of John. But what's his other name, his true other name? Give a guess, my pretty."

"I can't guess," said Bella, turning her pale face from one to another.

"*I* could," cried Mrs. Boffin, "and what's more, I did! I found him out all in a flash, as I may say, one night. Didn't I, Noddy?"

"Ay! That the old lady did!" said Mr. Boffin, with stout pride in the circumstance.

"Harkee to me, deary," pursued Mrs. Boffin, taking Bella's hands betweeen her own, and gently beating on them from time to time. "It was after a particular night when John had been disappointed—as he thought—in his affections. It was after a night when John had made an offer to a certain young lady, and the certain young lady had refused it. It was after a particular night, when he felt himself cast-away-like, and had made up his mind to go seek his fortune. It was the very next night. My Noddy wanted a paper out of his Secretary's room, and I says to Noddy, 'I am going by the door, and I'll ask him for it.' I tapped at his door, and he didn't hear me. I looked in, and saw him a-sitting lonely

437

by his fire, brooding over it. He chanced to look up with a pleased kind of smile in my company when he saw me, and then in a single moment, every grain of the gunpowder that had been lying sprinkled thick about him ever since I first set eyes upon him as a man at the Bower, took fire! Too many a time had I seen him sitting lonely, when he was a poor child, to be pitied, heart and hand! Too many a time had I seen him in need of being brightened up with a comforting word! Too many and too many a time to be mistaken, when that glimpse of him come at last! No! no! I just makes out to cry, 'I know you now! You're John!' And he catches me as I drops.—So what," said Mrs. Boffin, breaking off in the rush of her speech to smile most radiantly, "might you think by this time that your husband's name was, dear?"

"Not," returned Bella, with quivering lips; "not Harmon? That's not possible?"

"Don't tremble. Why not possible, deary, when so many things are possible?" demanded Mrs. Boffin, in a soothing tone.

"He was killed," gasped Bella.

"Thought to be," said Mrs. Boffin. "But if ever John Harmon drew the breath of life on earth, that is certainly John Harmon's arm round your waist now, my pretty. If ever John Harmon had a wife on earth, that wife is certainly you. If ever John Harmon and his wife had a child on earth, that child is certainly this."

By a master-stroke of secret arrangement, the inexhaustible baby here appeared at the door, suspended in mid-air by invisible agency. Mrs. Boffin plunging at it, brought it to Bella's lap, where both Mrs. and Mr. Boffin (as the saying is) "took it out of" the Inexhaustible in a shower of caresses. It was only this timely appearance that kept Bella from swooning. This, and her husband's earnestness in explaining further to her how it had come to pass that he had been supposed to be slain, and had even been suspected of his own murder; also, how he had put a pious fraud upon her which had preyed upon his mind, as the time for its disclosure approached, lest she might not make full allowance for the object with which it had originated, and in which it had fully developed.

"But bless ye, my beauty!" cried Mrs. Boffin, taking him up short at this point, with another hearty clap of her hands. "It wasn't John only that was in it. We was all of us in it."

"I don't," said Bella, looking vacantly from one to another, "yet understand——"

"Of course you don't, my deary," exclaimed Mrs. Boffin. "How can you till you're told? So now I am a-going to tell you. So you put your two hands between my two hands again," cried the comfortable creature, embracing her, "with that blessed little picter lying on your lap, and you shall be told all the story. Now, I'm a-going to tell the story. Once, twice, three times, and the horses is off. Here they go! When I cries out that night, 'I know you now, you're John!'—which was my exact words; wasn't they, John?"

"Your exact words," said John, laying his hand on hers.

"That's a very good arrangement," cried Mrs. Boffin. "Keep it there, John. And as we was all of us in it, Noddy, you come and lay yours a-top of his, and we won't break the pile till the story's done."

Mr. Boffin hitched up a chair, and added his broad brown right hand to the heap.

"That's capital!" said Mrs. Boffin, giving it a kiss. "Seems quite a family building; don't it? But the horses is off. Well! When I cries out that night, 'I know you now! you're John!' John catches of me, it is true; but I ain't a light weight, bless ye, and he's forced to let me down. Noddy, he hears a noise, and in he trots, and as soon as I anyways comes to myself I calls to him, 'Noddy, well I might say as I did say, that night at the Bower, for, the Lord be thankful this is John!' On which he gives a heave, and down he goes likewise, with his head under the writing-table. This brings me round comfortable, and that brings him round comfortable, and then John and him and me we all fall a-crying for joy."

" Yes! They cry for joy, my darling," her husband struck in. " You understand? These two, whom I come to life to disappoint and dispossess, cry for joy!"

Bella looked at him confusedly, and looked again at Mrs. Boffin's radiant face.

"That's right, my dear, don't you mind him," said Mrs. Boffin; "stick to me. Well! Then we sits down, gradually gets cool, and holds a confabulation. John, he tells us how he is despairing in his mind on accounts of a certain fair young person, and how, if I hadn't found him out, he was going away to seek his fortune far and wide, and had fully meant never to come to life, but to leave the property as our wrongful inheritance for ever and a day. At which you never see a man so frightened as my Noddy was. For to think that he should have come in to the property wrongful, however innocent, and—more than that—might have gone on keeping it to his dying day, turned him whiter than chalk."

" And you too," said Mr. Boffin.

" Don't you mind him, neither, my deary," resumed Mrs. Boffin; "stick to me. This brings up a certain confabulation regarding a certain fair young person; when Noddy he gives it as his opinion that she is a deary creetur. 'She may be a leetle spoilt, and nat'rally spoilt,' he says, 'by circumstances, but that's only on the surface, and I lay my life,' he says, 'that she's the true golden gold at heart.'"

" So did you," said Mr. Boffin.

" Don't you mind him a single morsel, my dear," proceeded Mrs. Boffin, " but stick to me. Then says John, Oh, if he could but prove so! Then we both of us ups and says, that minute, ' Prove so!'"

With a start, Bella directed a hurried glance towards Mr. Boffin. But, he was sitting thoughtfully smiling at that broad brown hand of his, and either didn't see it or would take no notice of it.

"'Prove it, John!' we says," repeated Mrs. Boffin. "'Prove it and overcome your doubts with triumph, and be happy for the first time in your life, and for the rest of your life.' This puts John in a state, to be sure. Then we says, 'What will content you? If she was to stand up for you when you was slighted, if she was to show herself of a generous mind when you was oppressed, if she was to be truest to you when you was poorest and friendliest, and all this against her own seeming interest, how would that do?' 'Do?' says John, 'it would raise me to the skies.' 'Then,' says my Noddy, 'make your preparations for the ascent, John, it being my firm belief that up you go!'"

Bella caught Mr. Boffin's twinkling eye for half an instant; but he got it away from her, and restored it to his broad brown hand.

"From the first, you was always a special favourite of Noddy's," said Mrs. Boffin, shaking her head. "O you were! And if I had been inclined to be jealous, I don't know what I mightn't have done to you. But as I wasn't—why, my beauty," with a hearty laugh and an embrace, "I made you a special favourite of my own too. But the horses is coming round the corner. Well! Then says my Noddy, shaking his sides till he was fit to make 'em ache again: 'Look out for being slighted and oppressed, John, for if ever a man had a hard master, you shall find me from this present time to be such to you.' And then he began!" cried Mrs. Boffin, in an ecstasy of admiration. "Lord bless you, then he began! And how he *did* begin; didn't he!"

Bella looked half frightened, and yet half laughed.

"But, bless you," pursued Mrs. Boffin, "if you could have seen him of a night, at that time of it! The way he'd sit and chuckle over himself! The way he'd say, 'I've been a regular brown bear to-day,' and take himself in his arms and hug himself at the thoughts of the brute he had pretended. But every night he says to me: 'Better and better, old lady. What did we say of her? She'll come through it,

441

the true golden gold. This'll be the happiest piece of work we ever done.' And then he'd say, 'I'll be a grislier old growler to-morrow!' and laugh, he would, till John and me was often forced to slap his back, and bring it out of his windpipes with a little water."

Mr. Boffin, with his face bent over his heavy hand, made no sound, but rolled his shoulders when thus referred to, as if he were vastly enjoying himself.

"And so, my good and pretty," pursued Mrs. Boffin, "you was married, and there was we hid up in the church-organ by this husband of yours; for he wouldn't let us out with it then, as was first meant. 'No,' he says, 'she's so unselfish and contented, that I can't afford to be rich yet. I must wait a little longer.' Then, when baby was expected, he says, 'She is such a cheerful, glorious housewife, that I can't afford to be rich yet. I must wait a little longer.' Then, when baby was born, he says, 'She is so much better than she ever was, that I can't afford to be rich yet. I must wait a little longer.' And so he goes on and on, till I says outright, 'Now, John, if you don't fix a time for setting her up in her own house and home, and letting us walk out of it, I'll turn Informer.' Then he says, he'll only wait to triumph beyond what we ever thought possible, and to show her to us better than even we ever supposed; and he says, 'She shall see me under suspicion of having murdered myself, and *you* shall see how trusting and how true she'll be.' Well! Noddy and me agreed to that, and he was right, and here you are, and the horses is in, and the story is done, and God bless you, my Beauty, and God bless us all!"

The pile of hands dispersed, and Bella and Mrs. Boffin took a good long hug of one another: to the apparent peril of the inexhaustible baby, lying staring in Bella's lap.

"But *is* the story done?" said Bella, pondering. "Is there no more of it?"

"What more of it should there be, deary?" returned Mrs. Boffin, full of glee.

"Are you sure you have left nothing out of it?" asked Bella.

"I don't think I have," said Mrs. Boffin, archly.

"John dear," said Bella, "you're a good nurse; will you please hold baby?" Having deposited the Inexhaustible in his arms with those words, Bella looked hard at Mr. Boffin, who had moved to a table where he was leaning his head upon his hand with his face turned away, and, quietly settling herself on her knees at his side, and drawing one arm over his shoulder, said : "Please I beg your pardon, and I made a small mistake of a word when I took leave of you last. Please I think you are better (not worse) than Hopkins, better (not worse) than Dancer, better (not worse) than Blackberry Jones, better (not worse) than any of them! Please something more!" cried Bella, with an exultant ringing laugh as she struggled with him and forced him to turn his delighted face to hers. "Please I have found out something not yet mentioned. Please I don't believe you are a hard-hearted miser at all, and please I don't believe you ever for one single minute were!"

At this Mrs. Boffin fairly screamed with rapture, and sat beating her feet upon the floor, clapping her hands, and bobbing herself backwards and forwards, like a demented member of some Mandarin's family.

"O, I understand you now, sir!" cried Bella. "I want neither you nor any one else to tell me the rest of the story. I can tell it to *you*, now, if you would like to hear it."

"Can you, my dear?" said Mr. Boffin. "Tell it then."

"What?" cried Bella, holding him prisoner by the coat with both hands. "When you saw what a greedy little wretch you were the patron of, you determined to show her how much misused and misprized riches could do, and often had done, to spoil people; did you? Not caring what she thought of you (and Goodness knows *that* was of no consequence!) you showed her, in yourself, the most detestable sides of wealth, saying in your own mind, 'This shallow creature would never work the truth out of her own weak soul, if she had a hundred years to do it in ; but a glaring instance kept before her may open even her eyes and set her thinking.' That was what you said to yourself; was it, sir ? "

" I never said anything of the sort," Mr. Boffin declared in a state of the highest enjoyment.

" Then you ought to have said it, sir," returned Bella, giving him two pulls and one kiss, " for you must have thought and meant it. You saw that good fortune was turning my stupid head and hardening my silly heart—was making me grasping, calculating, insolent, insufferable—and you took the pains to be the dearest and kindest finger-post that ever was set up anywhere, pointing out the road that I was taking and the end it led to. Confess instantly ! "

" John," said Mr. Boffin, one broad piece of sunshine from head to foot, " I wish you'd help me out of this."

" You can't be heard by counsel, sir," returned Bella. " You must speak for yourself. Confess instantly ! "

" Well, my dear," said Mr. Boffin, " the truth is, that when we did go in for the little scheme that my old lady has pinted out, I did put it to John, what did he think of going in for some such general scheme as *you* have pinted out ? But I didn't in any way so word it, because I didn't in any way so mean it. I only said to John, wouldn't it be more consistent, me going in for being a reg'lar brown bear respecting him, to go in as a reg'lar brown bear all round ? "

" Confess this minute, sir," said Bella, " that you did it to correct and amend me ! "

" Certainly, my dear child," said Mr. Boffin, " I didn't do it to harm you; you may be sure of that. And I did hope it might just hint a caution. Still, it ought to be mentioned that no sooner had my old lady found out John, than John made known to her and me that he had had his eye upon a thankless person by the name of Silas Wegg. Partly for the punishment of which Wegg, by leading him on in a very un-handsome and underhanded game that he was playing, them

444

books that you and me bought so many of together (and, by-the-bye, my dear, he wasn't Blackberry Jones, but Blewberry) was read aloud to me by that person of the name of Silas Wegg aforesaid."

Bella, who was still on her knees at Mr. Boffin's feet, gradually sank down in a sitting posture on the ground, as she meditated more and more thoughtfully, with her eyes upon his beaming face.

"Still," said Bella, after this meditative pause, "there remain two things that I cannot understand. Mrs. Boffin never supposed any part of the change in Mr. Boffin to be real; did she? You never did; did you?" asked Bella, turning to her.

"No!" returned Mrs. Boffin with a most rotund and glowing negative.

"And yet you took it very much to heart," said Bella. "I remember its making you very uneasy, indeed."

"Ecod, you see Mrs. John has a sharp eye, John!" cried Mr. Boffin, shaking his head with an admiring air. "You're right, my dear. The old lady nearly blowed us into shivers and smithers, many times."

"Why?" asked Bella. "How did that happen when she was in your secret?"

"Why, it was a weakness in the old lady," said Mr. Boffin: "and yet, to tell you the whole truth and nothing but the truth, I'm rather proud of it. My dear, the old lady thinks so high of me that she couldn't abear to see and hear me coming out as a regular brown one. Couldn't abear to make-believe as I meant it! In consequence of which, we was everlastingly in danger with her."

Mrs. Boffin laughed heartily at herself; but a certain glistening in her honest eyes revealed that she was by no means cured of that dangerous propensity.

"I assure you, my dear," said Mr. Boffin, "that on the celebrated day when I made what has since been agreed upon to be my grandest demonstration—I allude to Mew says

445

the cat, Quack-quack says the duck, and Bow-wow-wow says the dog—I assure you, my dear, that on that celebrated day, them flinty and unbelieving words hit my old lady so hard on my account, that I had to hold her, to prevent her running out after you, and defending me by saying I was playing a part."

Mrs. Boffin laughed heartily again, and her eyes glistened again, and it then appeared, not only that in that burst of sarcastic eloquence Mr. Boffin was considered by his two fellow-conspirators to have outdone himself, but that in his own opinion it was a remarkable achievement. "Never thought of it afore the moment, my dear!" he observed to Bella. "When John said, if he had been so happy as to win your affections and possess your heart, it come into my head to turn round upon him with 'Win her affections and possess her heart! Mew says the cat, Quack-quack says the duck, and Bow-wow-wow says the dog.' I couldn't tell you how it come into my head or where from, but it had so much the sound of a rasper that I own to you it astonished myself. I was awful nigh bursting out a laughing though, when it made John stare!"

"You said, my pretty," Mrs. Boffin reminded Bella, "that there was one other thing you couldn't understand."

"O yes!" cried Bella, covering her face with her hands; "but that I never shall be able to understand as long as I live. It is, how John could love me so when I so little deserved it, and how you, Mr. and Mrs. Boffin, could be so forgetful of yourselves, and take such pains and trouble, to make me a little better, and after all to help him to so unworthy a wife. But I am very, very grateful."

It was John Harmon's turn then—John Harmon now for good, and John Rokesmith for nevermore—to plead with her (quite unnecessarily) in behalf of his deception, and to tell her, over and over again, that it had been prolonged by her own winning graces in her supposed station of life. This led on to many interchanges of endearment and enjoyment on all

446

Mr. Boffin does the Honours of the Nursery Door

sides, in the midst of which the Inexhaustible being observed staring in a most imbecile manner, on Mrs. Boffin's breast, was pronounced to be supernaturally intelligent as to the whole transaction, and was made to declare to the ladies and gemplemorums, with a wave of the speckled fist (with difficulty detached from an exceedingly short waist), "I have already informed my venerable Ma that I know all about it."

Then, said John Harmon, would Mrs. John Harmon come and see her house? And a dainty house it was, and a tastefully beautiful; and they went through it in procession; the Inexhaustible on Mrs. Boffin's bosom (still staring) occupying the middle station, and Mr. Boffin bringing up the rear. And on Bella's exquisite toilette table was an ivory casket, and in the casket were jewels the like of which she had never dreamed of, and aloft on an upper floor was a nursery garnished as with rainbows; "though we were hard put to it," said John Harmon, "to get it done in so short a time."

The house inspected, emissaries removed the Inexhaustible, who was shortly afterwards heard screaming among the rainbows; whereupon Bella withdrew herself from the presence and knowledge of gemplemorums, and the screaming ceased, and smiling Peace associated herself with that young olive branch.

"Come and look in, Noddy!" said Mrs. Boffin to Mr. Boffin.

Mr. Boffin, submitting to be led on tiptoe to the nursery door, looked in with immense satisfaction, although there was nothing to see but Bella in a musing state of happiness, seated in a little low chair upon the hearth, with her child in her fair young arms, and her soft eyelashes shading her eyes from the fire.

"It looks as if the old man's spirit had found rest at last; don't it?" said Mrs. Boffin.

"Yes, old lady."

"And as if his money had turned bright again, after a

long, long rust in the dark, and was at last beginning to sparkle in the sunlight?"

"Yes, old lady."

"And it makes a pretty and a promising picter; don't it?"

"Yes, old lady."

But, aware at the instant of a fine opening for a point, Mr. Boffin quenched that observation in this—delivered in the grisliest growling of the regular brown bear. "A pretty and a hopeful picter? Mew, Quack-quack, Bow-wow!" And then trotted silently down-stairs, with his shoulders in a state of the liveliest commotion.

CHAPTER XIV

Mr. and Mrs. John Harmon had so timed their taking possession of their rightful name and their London house, that the event befell on the very day when the last waggon-load of the last Mound was driven out at the gates of Boffin's Bower. As it jolted away, Mr. Wegg felt that the last load was correspondingly removed from his mind, and hailed the auspicious season when that black sheep, Boffin, was to be closely sheared.

Over the whole slow process of levelling the Mounds, Silas had kept watch with rapacious eyes. But, eyes no less rapacious had watched the growth of the Mounds in years bygone, and had vigilantly sifted the dust of which they were composed. No valuables turned up. How should there be any, seeing that the old hard jailer of Harmony Jail had coined every waif and stray into money, long before?

Though disappointed by this bare result, Mr. Wegg felt too sensibly relieved by the close of the labour, to grumble to any great extent. A foreman-representative of the dust contractors, purchasers of the Mounds, had worn Mr. Wegg down to skin and bone. This supervisor of the proceedings asserting his employers' rights to cart off by daylight, night-light, torchlight, when they would, must have been the death of Silas if the work had lasted much longer. Seeming never to need sleep himself, he would reappear, with a tied-up broken head, in fantail hat and velveteen smalls, like an accursed goblin, at the most unholy and untimely hours. Tired out by keeping close ward over a long day's work in fog and rain, Silas would have just crawled to bed and be dozing, when a horrid shake and rumble under his pillow would announce an approaching train of carts, escorted by this Demon of Unrest, to fall to work again. At another time, he would be rumbled up out of his soundest sleep, in the dead of the night; at another, would be kept at his post eight-and-forty hours on end. The more his persecutor besought him not to trouble himself to turn out, the more suspicious was the crafty Wegg that indications had been observed of something hidden some-where, and that attempts were on foot to circumvent him. So continually broken was his rest through these means, that he led the life of having wagered to keep ten thousand dog-watches in ten thousand hours, and looked piteously upon himself as always getting up and yet never going to bed. So gaunt and haggard had he grown at last, that his wooden leg showed disproportionate, and presented a thriving appear-ance in contrast with the rest of his plagued body, which might almost have been termed chubby.

However, Wegg's comfort was, that all his disagreeables were now over, and that he was immediately coming into his property. Of late the Grindstone did undoubtedly appear to have been whirling at his own nose rather than Boffin's, but Boffin's nose was now to be sharpened fine. Thus far, Mr. Wegg had let his dusty friend off lightly, having been baulked in that amiable design of frequently dining with him, by the machinations of the sleepless dustman. He had been constrained to depute Mr. Venus to keep their dusty friend, Boffin, under inspection, while he himself turned lank and lean at the Bower.

To Mr. Venus's museum Mr. Wegg repaired when at length the Mounds were down and gone. It being evening, he found that gentleman, as he expected, seated over his fire; but did not find him, as he expected, floating his powerful mind in tea.

"Why, you smell rather comfortable here!" said Wegg seeming to take it ill, and stopping and sniffing as he entered.

"I *am* rather comfortable, sir," said Venus.

"You don't use lemon in your business, do you?" asked Wegg, sniffing again.

"No, Mr. Wegg," said Venus. "When I use it at all, I mostly use it in cobblers' punch."

"What do you call cobblers' punch?" demanded Wegg, in a worse humour than before.

"It's difficult to impart the receipt for it, sir," returned Venus, "because, however particular you may be in allotting your materials, so much will still depend upon the individual gifts, and there being a feeling thrown into it. But the groundwork is gin."

"In a Dutch bottle?" said Wegg gloomily, as he sat himself down.

"Very good, sir, very good!" cried Venus. "Will you partake, sir?"

"Will I partake?" returned Wegg very surlily. "Why, of course I will! *Will* a man partake, as has been tormented out of his five senses by an everlasting dustman with his head tied up! *Will* he, too! As if he wouldn't!"

"Don't let it put you out, Mr. Wegg. You don't seem in your usual spirits."

"If you come to that, you don't seem in your usual spirits," growled Wegg. "You seem to be setting up for lively."

This circumstance appeared, in his then state of mind, to give Mr. Wegg uncommon offence.

"And you've been having your hair cut!" said Wegg, missing the usual dusty shock.

"Yes, Mr. Wegg. But don't let that put you out, either."

"And I am blest if you ain't getting fat!" said Wegg, with culminating discontent. "What are you going to do next?"

"Well, Mr. Wegg," said Venus, smiling in a sprightly manner, "I suspect you could hardly guess what I am going to do next."

"I don't want to guess," retorted Wegg. "All I've got to say is, that it's well for you that the diwision of labour has been what it has been. It's well for you to have had so light a part in this business, when mine has been so heavy. You haven't had *your* rest broke, I'll be bound."

"Not at all, sir," said Venus. "Never rested so well in all my life, I thank you."

"Ah!" grumbled Wegg, "you should have been me. If you had been me, and had been fretted out of your bed, and your sleep, and your meals, and your mind, for a stretch of months together, *you*'d have been out of condition and out of sorts."

"Certainly it has trained you down, Mr. Wegg," said Venus, contemplating his figure with an artist's eye. "Trained you down very low, it has! So weazen and yellow is the kivering upon your bones, that one might almost fancy you had come to give a look-in upon the French gentleman in the corner, instead of me."

Mr. Wegg, glancing in great dudgeon towards the French gentleman's corner, seemed to notice something new there, which induced him to glance at the opposite corner, and then to put on his glasses and stare at all the nooks and corners of the dim shop in succession.

"Why, you've been having the place cleaned up!" he exclaimed.

"Yes, Mr. Wegg. By the hand of adorable woman."

"Then what you're going to do next, I suppose, is to get married?"

"That's it, sir."

Silas took off his glasses again—finding himself too intensely disgusted by the sprightly appearance of his friend and partner to bear a magnified view of him, and made the inquiry:

"To the old party."

"Mr. Wegg!" said Venus, with a sudden flush of wrath. "The lady in question is not a old party."

"I meant," explained Wegg, testily, "to the party as formerly objected?"

"Mr. Wegg," said Venus, "in a case of so much delicacy, I must trouble you to say what you mean. There are strings that must not be played upon. No, sir! Not sounded, unless in the most respectful and tuneful manner. Of such melodious strings is Miss Pleasant Riderhood formed."

"Then it *is* the lady as formerly objected?" said Wegg.

"Sir," returned Venus with dignity, "I accept the altered phrase. It is the lady as formerly objected."

"When is it to come off?" asked Silas.

"Mr. Wegg," said Venus, with another flush, "I cannot permit it to be put in the form of a Fight. I must temperately but firmly call upon you, sir, to amend that question."

"When is the lady," Wegg reluctantly demanded, constraining his ill-temper in remembrance of the partnership and its stock in trade, "a-going to give her 'and where she has already given her 'art."

"Sir," returned Venus, "I again accept the altered phrase, and with pleasure. The lady is a-going to give her 'and where she has already given her 'art, next Monday."

"Then the lady's objection has been met?" said Silas.

"Mr. Wegg," said Venus, "as I did name to you, I think, on a former occasion, if not on former occasions——"

"On former occasions," interrupted Wegg.

"——What," pursued Venus, "what the nature of the lady's objection was, I may impart, without violating any of the tender confidences since sprung up between the lady and myself, how it has been met, through the kind interference of two good friends of mine : one previously acquainted with the lady : and one, not. The pint was thrown out, sir, by those two friends when they did me the great service of waiting on the lady to try if a union betwixt the lady and

453

me could not be brought to bear—the pint, I say, was thrown out by them, sir, whether if, after marriage, I confined myself to the articulation of men, children, and the lower animals, it might not relieve the lady's mind of her feeling respecting being—as a lady—regarded in a bony light. It was a happy thought, sir, and it took root."

"It would seem, Mr. Venus," observed Wegg, with a touch of distrust, "that you are flush of friends?"

"Pretty well, sir," that gentleman answered, in a tone of placid mystery. "So-so, sir. Pretty well."

"However," said Wegg, after eyeing him with another touch of distrust, "I wish you joy. One man spends his fortune in one way, and another in another. You are going to try matrimony. I mean to try travelling."

"Indeed, Mr. Wegg?"

"Change of air, sea-scenery, and my natural rest, I hope may bring me round after the persecutions I have undergone from the dustman with his head tied up, which I just now mentioned. The tough job being ended and the Mounds laid low, the hour is come for Boffin to stump up. Would ten to-morrow morning suit you, partner, for finally bringing Boffin's nose to the grindstone?"

Ten to-morrow morning would quite suit Mr. Venus for that excellent purpose.

"You have had him well under inspection, I hope?" said Silas.

Mr. Venus had had him under inspection pretty well every day.

"Suppose you was just to step round to-night then, and give him orders from me—I say from me, because he knows *I* won't be played with—to be ready with his papers, his accounts, and his cash, at that time in the morning?" said Wegg. "As a matter of form, which will be agreeable to your own feelings, before we go out (for I'll walk with you part of the way, though my leg gives under me with weariness), let's have a look at the stock in trade."

Mr. Venus produced it, and it was perfectly correct; Mr. Venus undertook to produce it again in the morning, and to keep tryst with Mr. Wegg on Boffin's doorstep as the clock struck ten. At a certain point of the road between Clerkenwell and Boffin's house (Mr. Wegg expressly insisted that there should be no prefix to the Golden Dustman's name) the partners separated for the night.

It was a very bad night; to which succeeded a very bad morning. The streets were so unusually slushy, muddy, and miserable in the morning, that Wegg rode to the scene of action; arguing that a man who was, as it were, going to the Bank to draw out a handsome property, could well afford that trifling expense.

Venus was punctual, and Wegg undertook to knock at the door, and conduct the conference. Door knocked at. Door opened.

"Boffin at home?"

The servant replied that *Mr.* Boffin was at home.

"He'll do," said Wegg; "though it ain't what I call him."

The servant inquired if they had any appointment?

"Now, I tell you what, young fellow," said Wegg, "I won't have it. This won't do for me. I don't want menials. I want Boffin."

They were shown into a waiting-room, where the all-powerful Wegg wore his hat, and whistled, and with his fore-finger stirred up a clock that stood upon the chimney-piece, until he made it strike. In a few minutes they were shown up-stairs into what used to be Boffin's room; which, besides the door of entrance, had folding-doors in it, to make it one of a suite of rooms when occasion required. Here, Boffin was seated at a library-table, and here Mr. Wegg, having imperiously motioned the servant to withdraw, drew up a chair and seated himself, in his hat, close beside him. Here, also, Mr. Wegg instantly underwent the remarkable experience of having his hat twitched off his head and thrown out of a window, which was opened and shut for the purpose.

"Be careful what insolent liberties you take in that gentleman's presence," said the owner of the hand which had done this, "or I will throw you after it."

Wegg involuntarily clapped his hand to his bare head, and stared at the Secretary. For, it was he addressed him with a severe countenance, and who had come in quietly by the folding-doors.

"Oh!" said Wegg, as soon as he recovered his suspended power of speech. "Very good! I gave directions for *you* to be dismissed. And you ain't gone, ain't you? Oh! We'll look into this presently. Very good!"

"No, nor *I* ain't gone," said another voice.

Somebody else had come in quietly by the folding-doors. Turning his head, Wegg beheld his persecutor, the ever-wakeful dustman, accoutred with fantail hat and velveteen smalls complete. Who, untying his tied-up broken head, revealed a head that was whole, and a face that was Sloppy's.

"Ha, ha, ha, gentlemen!" roared Sloppy, in a peal of laughter, and with immeasurable relish. "He never thought as I could sleep standing, and often done it when I turned for Mrs. Higden! He never thought as I used to give Mrs. Higden the Police-news in different voices! But I did lead him a life all through it, gentlemen, I hope I really and truly DID!" Here, Mr. Sloppy opening his mouth to a quite alarming extent, and throwing back his head to peal again, revealed incalculable buttons.

"Oh!" said Wegg, slightly discomfited, but not much as yet: "one and one is two not dismissed, is it? Bof—fin! Just let me ask a question. Who set this chap on, in this dress, when the carting began? Who employed this fellow?"

"I say!" remonstrated Sloppy, jerking his head forward. "No fellows, or *I'll* throw you out of winder!"

Mr. Boffin appeased him with a wave of his hand, and said: "I employed him, Wegg."

"Oh! You employed him, Boffin? Very good. Mr. Venus, we raise our terms, and we can't do better than

456

proceed to business. Bof—fin! I want the room cleared of these two scum."

"That's not going to be done, Wegg," replied Mr. Boffin, sitting composedly on the library-table, at one end, while the Secretary sat composedly on it at the other.

"Bof—fin! Not going to be done?" repeated Wegg. "Not at your peril?"

"No, Wegg," said Mr. Boffin, shaking his head good-humouredly. "Not at my peril, and not on any other terms."

Wegg reflected a moment, and then said: "Mr. Venus, will you be so good as hand me over that same dockyment?"

"Certainly, sir," replied Venus, handing it to him with much politeness. "There it is. Having now, sir, parted with it, I wish to make a small observation: not so much because it is anyways necessary, or expresses any new doctrine or discovery, as because it is a comfort to my mind. Silas Wegg, you are a precious old rascal."

Mr. Wegg, who, as if anticipating a compliment, had been beating time with the paper to the other's politeness until this unexpected conclusion came upon him, stopped rather abruptly.

"Silas Wegg," said Venus, "know that I took the liberty of taking Mr. Boffin into our concern as a sleeping partner, at a very early period of our firm's existence."

"Quite true," added Mr. Boffin; "and I tested Venus by making him a pretended proposal or two; and I found him on the whole, a very honest man, Wegg."

"So Mr. Boffin, in his indulgence, is pleased to say," Venus remarked: "though in the beginning of this dirt, my hands were not, for a few hours, quite as clean as I could wish. But I hope I made early and full amends."

"Venus, you did," said Mr. Boffin. "Certainly, certainly, certainly."

Venus inclined his head with respect and gratitude. "Thank you, sir. I am much obliged to you, sir, for all. For your good opinion now, for your way of receiving and encouraging me when I first put myself in communication with you, and for the influence since so kindly brought to bear upon a certain lady, both by yourself and by Mr. John Harmon." To whom, when thus making mention of him, he also bowed.

Wegg followed the name with sharp ears, and the action with sharp eyes, and a certain cringing air was infusing itself into his bullying air, when his attention was re-claimed by Venus.

"Everything else between you and me, Mr. Wegg," said Venus, "now explains itself, and you can now make out, sir, without further words from me. But totally to prevent any unpleasantness or mistake that might arise on what I consider an important point, to be made quite clear at the close of our acquaintance, I beg the leave of Mr. Boffin and Mr. John Harmon to repeat an observation which I have already had the pleasure of bringing under your notice. You are a precious old rascal!"

"You are a fool," said Wegg, with a snap of his fingers, "and I'd have got rid of you before now, if I could have struck out any way of doing it. I have thought it over, I can tell you. You may go and welcome. You leave the more for me. Because, you know," said Wegg, dividing his next observation between Mr. Boffin and Mr. Harmon, "I am worth my price, and I mean to have it. This getting off is all very well in its way, and it tells with such an anatomical Pump as this one," pointing out Mr. Venus, "but it won't do with a Man. I am here to be bought off, and I have named my figure. Now, buy me, or leave me."

"I'll leave you, Wegg," said Mr. Boffin, laughing, "as far as I am concerned."

"Bof—fin!" replied Wegg, turning upon him with a severe air. "I understand *your* new-born boldness. I see the brass underneath *your* silver plating. *You* have got *your* nose put out of joint. Knowing that you've nothing at stake, you can afford to come the independent game. Why, you're just so much smeary glass to see through, you know!

458

But Mr. Harmon is in another sitiwation. What Mr. Harmon risks, is quite another pair of shoes. Now, I've heerd something lately about this being Mr. Harmon—I make out now, some hints that I've met on that subject in the newspaper—and I drop you, Bof—fin, as beneath my notice. I ask Mr. Harmon whether he has any idea of the contents of this present paper?"

"It is a will of my late father's, of more recent date than the will proved by Mr. Boffin (address whom again, as you have addressed him already, and I'll knock you down), leaving the whole of his property to the Crown," said John Harmon, with as much indifference as was compatible with extreme sternness.

"Right you are!" cried Wegg. "Then," screwing the weight of his body upon his wooden leg, and screwing his wooden head very much on one side, and screwing up one eye: "then, I put the question to you, what's this paper worth?"

"Nothing," said John Harmon.

Wegg had repeated the word with a sneer, and was entering on some sarcastic retort, when, to his boundless amazement, he found himself gripped by the cravat; shaken until his teeth chattered; shoved back, staggering, into a corner of the room; and pinned there.

"You scoundrel!" said John Harmon, whose seafaring hold was like that of a vice.

"You're knocking my head against the wall," urged Silas faintly.

"I mean to knock your head against the wall," returned John Harmon, suiting his action to his words, with the heartiest good-will; "and I'd give a thousand pounds for leave to knock your brains out. Listen, you scoundrel, and look at that Dutch bottle."

Sloppy held it up, for his edification.

"That Dutch bottle, scoundrel, contained the latest will of the many wills made by my unhappy self-tormenting father.

That will gives everything absolutely to my noble benefactor and yours, Mr. Boffin, excluding and reviling me, and
my sister (then already dead of a broken heart), by name.
That Dutch bottle was found by my noble benefactor and
yours, after he entered on possession of the estate. That
Dutch bottle distressed him beyond measure, because, though
I and my sister were both no more, it cast a slur upon our
memory which he knew we had done nothing in our miserable
youth, to deserve. That Dutch bottle, therefore, he buried
in the Mound belonging to him, and there it lay while you,
you thankless wretch, were prodding and poking—often very
near it, I dare say. His intention was, that it should never
see the light; but he was afraid to destroy it, lest to destroy
such a document, even with his great generous motive, might
be an offence at law. After the discovery was made here who
I was, Mr. Boffin, still restless on the subject, told me, upon
certain conditions impossible for such a hound as you to
appreciate, the secret of that Dutch bottle. I urged upon him
the necessity of its being dug up and the paper being legally
produced and established. The first thing you saw him do,
and the second thing has been done without your knowledge.
Consequently, the paper now rattling in your hand as I shake
you—and I should like to shake the life out of you—is worth
less than the rotten cork of the Dutch bottle, do you understand?"

Judging from the fallen countenance of Silas as his head
wagged backwards and forwards in a most uncomfortable
manner, he did understand.

"Now, scoundrel," said John Harmon, taking another
sailor-like turn on his cravat and holding him in his corner
at arm's length, "I shall make two more short speeches to
you, because I hope they will torment you. Your discovery
was a genuine discovery (such as it was), for nobody had
thought of looking into that place. Neither did we know you
had made it, until Venus spoke to Mr. Boffin, though I kept
you under good observation from my first appearance here,

and though Sloppy has long made it the chief occupation and delight of his life, to attend you like your shadow. I tell you this, that you may know we knew enough of you to persuade Mr. Boffin to let us lead you on, deluded to the last possible moment, in order that your disappointment might be the heaviest possible disappointment. That's the first short speech, do you understand?"

Here John Harmon assisted his comprehension with another shake.

"Now, scoundrel," he pursued, "I am going to finish. You supposed me just now to be the possessor of my father's property.—So I am. But through any act of my father's or by any right I have? No. Through the munificence of Mr. Boffin. The conditions that he made with me, before parting with the secret of the Dutch bottle, were, that I should take the fortune, and that he should take his Mound and no more. I owe everything I possess, solely to the disinterestedness, uprightness, tenderness, goodness (there are no words to satisfy me) of Mr. and Mrs. Boffin. And when, knowing what I knew, I saw such a mud-worm as you presume to rise in this house against this noble soul, the wonder is," added John Harmon through his clenched teeth, and with a very ugly turn indeed on Wegg's cravat, "that I didn't try to twist your head off, and fling *that* out of window! So. That's the last short speech, do you understand?"

Silas, released, put his hand to his throat, cleared it, and looked as if he had rather a large fishbone in that region. Simultaneously with this action on his part in his corner, a singular, and on the surface an incomprehensible, movement was made by Mr. Sloppy: who began backing towards Mr. Wegg along the wall, in the manner of a porter or heaver who is about to lift a sack of flour or coals.

"I am sorry, Wegg," said Mr. Boffin, in his clemency, "that my old lady and I can't have a better opinion of you than the bad one we are forced to entertain. But I shouldn't like to leave you, after all said and done, worse off

461

in life than I found you. Therefore say in a word, before we part, what it'll cost to set you up in another stall."

"And in another place," John Harmon struck in. "You don't come outside these windows."

"Mr. Boffin," returned Wegg in avaricious humiliation: "when I first had the honour of making your acquaintance, I had got together a collection of ballads which was, I may say, above price."

"Then they can't be paid for," said John Harmon, "and you had better not try, my dear sir."

"Pardon me, Mr. Boffin," resumed Wegg, with a malignant glance in the last speaker's direction, "I was putting the case to you, who, if my senses did not deceive me, put the case to me. I had a very choice collection of ballads, and there was a new stock of gingerbread in the tin box. I say no more, but would rather leave it to you."

"But it's difficult to name what's right," said Mr. Boffin uneasily, with his hand in his pocket, "and I don't want to go beyond what's right, because you really have turned out such a very bad fellow. So artful, and so ungrateful you have been, Wegg; for when did I ever injure you?"

"There was also," Mr. Wegg went on, in a meditative manner, "a errand connection, in which I was much respected. But I would not wish to be deemed covetous, and I would rather leave it to you, Mr. Boffin."

"Upon my word, I don't know what to put it at," the Golden Dustman muttered.

"There was likewise," resumed Wegg, "a pair of trestles, for which alone a Irish person, who was deemed a judge of trestles, offered five and six—a sum I would not hear of, for I should have lost by it—and there was a stool, a umbrella, a clothes-horse, and a tray. But I leave it to you, Mr. Boffin."

The Golden Dustman seeming to be engaged in some abstruse calculation, Mr. Wegg assisted him with the following additional items.

462

"There was, further, Miss Elizabeth, Master George, Aunt Jane, and Uncle Parker. Ah! When a man thinks of the loss of such patronage as that; when a man finds so fair a garden rooted up by pigs; he finds it hard indeed, without going high, to work it into money. But I leave it wholly to you, sir."

Mr. Sloppy still continued his singular, and on the surface his incomprehensible, movement.

"Leading on has been mentioned," said Wegg with a melancholy air, "and it's not easy to say how far the tone of my mind may have been lowered by unwholesome reading on the subject of Misers, when you was leading me and others on to think you one yourself, sir. All I can say is, that I felt my tone of mind a-lowering at the time. And how can a man put a price upon his mind! There was likewise a hat just now. But I leave the ole to you, Mr. Boffin."

"Come!" said Mr. Boffin. "Here's a couple of pound."

"In justice to myself, I couldn't take it, sir."

The words were but out of his mouth when John Harmon lifted his finger, and Sloppy, who was now close to Wegg, backed to Wegg's back, stooped, grasped his coat collar behind with both hands, and deftly swung him up like the sack of flour or coals before mentioned. A countenance of special discontent and amazement Mr. Wegg exhibited in this position, with his buttons almost as prominently on view as Sloppy's own, and with his wooden leg in a highly unaccommodating state. But, not for many seconds was his countenance visible in the room; for, Sloppy lightly trotted out with him and trotted down the staircase, Mr. Venus attending to open the street door. Mr. Sloppy's instructions had been to deposit his burden in the road; but a scavenger's cart happening to stand unattended at the corner, with its little ladder planted against the wheel, Mr. S. found it impossible to resist the temptation of shooting Mr. Silas Wegg into the cart's contents. A somewhat difficult feat, achieved with great dexterity, and with a prodigious splash.

463

CHAPTER XV

WHAT WAS CAUGHT IN THE TRAPS THAT WERE SET

How Bradley Headstone had been racked and riven in his mind since the quiet evening when by the river-side he had risen, as it were, out of the ashes of the Bargeman, none but he could have told. Not even he could have told, for such misery can only be felt.

First, he had to bear the combined weight of the knowledge of what he had done, of that haunting reproach that he might have done it so much better, and of the dread of discovery. This was load enough to crush him, and he laboured under it day and night. It was as heavy on him in his scanty sleep, as in his red-eyed waking hours. It bore him down with a dread, unchanging monotony, in which there was not a moment's variety. The overweighted beast of burden, or the overweighted slave, can for certain instants shift the physical load, and find some slight respite even in enforcing additional pain upon such a set of muscles or such a limb. Not even that poor mockery of relief could the wretched man obtain, under the steady pressure of the infernal atmosphere into which he had entered.

Time went by, and no visible suspicion dogged him; time went by, and in such public accounts of the attack as were renewed at intervals, he began to see Mr. Lightwood (who acted as lawyer for the injured man) straying further from the fact, going wider of the issue, and evidently slackening in his zeal. By degrees, a glimmering of the cause of this

464

began to break on Bradley's sight. Then came the chance encounter with Mr. Milvey at the railway station (where he often lingered in his leisure hours, as a place where any fresh news of his deed would be circulated, or any placard referring to it would be posted), and then he saw in the light what he had brought about.

For, then he saw that through his desperate attempt to separate those two for ever, he had been made the means of uniting them. That he had dipped his hands in blood, to mark himself a miserable fool and tool. That Eugene Wrayburn, for his wife's sake, set him aside and left him to crawl along his blasted course. He thought of Fate, or Providence, or be the directing Power what it might, as having put a fraud upon him—overreached him—and in his impotent mad rage bit, and tore, and had his fit.

New assurance of the truth came upon him in the next few following days, when it was put forth how the wounded man had been married on his bed, and to whom ; and how, though always in a dangerous condition, he was a shade better. Bradley would far rather have been seized for his murder, than he would have read that passage, knowing himself spared, and knowing why.

But, not to be still further defrauded and overreached—which he would be, if implicated by Riderhood, and punished by the law for his abject failure, as though it had been a success—he kept close in his school during the day, ventured out warily at night, and went no more to the railway station. He examined the advertisements in the newspapers for any sign that Riderhood acted on his hinted threat of so summoning him to renew their acquaintance, but found none. Having paid him handsomely for the support and accommodation he had had at the Lock-house, and knowing him to be a very ignorant man who could not write, he began to doubt whether he was to be feared at all, or whether they need ever meet again.

All this time, his mind was never off the rack, and his

465

raging sense of having been made to fling himself across the chasm which divided those two, and bridge it over for their coming together, never cooled down. This horrible condition brought on other fits. He could not have said how many, or when; but he saw in the faces of his pupils that they had seen him in that state, and that they were possessed by a dread of his relapsing.

One winter day when a slight fall of snow was feathering the sills and frames of the school-room windows, he stood at his black board, crayon in hand, about to commence with a class; when, reading in the countenances of those boys that there was something wrong, and that they seemed in alarm for him, he turned his eyes to the door towards which they faced. He then saw a slouching man of forbidding appearance standing in the midst of the school, with a bundle under his arm; and saw that it was Riderhood.

He sat down on a stool which one of the boys put for him, and he had a passing knowledge that he was in danger of falling, and that his face was becoming distorted. But, the fit went off for that time, and he wiped his mouth, and stood up again.

"Beg your pardon, governor! By your leave!" said Riderhood, knuckling his forehead, with a chuckle and a leer. "What place may this be?"

"This is a school."

"Where young folks learns wot's right?" said Riderhood, gravely nodding. "Beg your pardon, governor! By your leave! But who teaches this school?"

"I do."

"You're the master, are you, learned governor?"

"Yes. I am the master."

"And a lovely thing it must be," said Riderhood, "fur to learn young folks wot's right, and fur to know wot *they* know wot you do it. Beg your pardon, learned governor! By your leave!—That there black board; wot's it for?"

"It is for drawing on, or writing on."

RIDERHOOD VISITS THE SCHOOL

"Is it though!" said Riderhood. "Who'd have thought it, from the looks on it! *Would* you be so kind as write your name upon it, learned governor?" (In a wheedling tone.)

Bradley hesitated for a moment; but placed his usual signature, enlarged, upon the board.

"I ain't a learned character myself," said Riderhood, surveying the class, "but I do admire learning in others. I should dearly like to hear these here young folks read that there name off, from the writing."

The arms of the class went up. At the miserable master's nod, the shrill chorus arose: "Bradley Headstone!"

"No?" cried Riderhood. "You don't mean it? Head-stone! Why, that's in a churchyard. Hooroar for another turn!"

Another tossing of arms, another nod, and another shrill chorus: "Bradley Headstone!"

"I've got it now!" said Riderhood, after attentively listening, and internally repeating: "Bradley. I see. Chris'en name, Bradley, sim'lar to Roger which is my own. Eh? Family name, Headstone, sim'lar to Riderhood which is my own. Eh?"

Shrill chorus: "Yes!"

"Might you be acquainted, learned governor," said Riderhood, "with a person of about your own heighth and breadth, and wot 'ud pull down in a scale about your own weight, answering to a name sounding summat like T'otherest?"

With a desperation in him that made him perfectly quiet, though his jaw was heavily squared; with his eyes upon Riderhood; and with traces of quickened breathing in his nostrils, the schoolmaster replied, in a suppressed voice, after a pause: "I think I know the man you mean."

"I thought you knowed the man I mean, learned governor. I want the man."

With a half glance around him at his pupils, Bradley returned: "Do you suppose he is here?"

"Begging your pardon, learned governor, and by your

467

leave," said Riderhood, with a laugh, "how could I suppose he's here, when there's nobody here but you, and me, and these young lambs wot you're a-learning on? But he is most excellent company, that man, and I want him to come and see me at my Lock, up the river."

"I'll tell him so."

"D'ye think he'll come?" asked Riderhood.

"I am sure he will."

"Having got your word for him," said Riderhood, "I shall count upon him. P'raps you'd so far obleege me, learned governor, as tell him that if he don't come precious soon, I'll look him up."

"He shall know it."

"Thankee. As I says a while ago," pursued Riderhood, changing his hoarse tone and leering round upon the class again, "though not a learned character my own self, I do admire learning in others, to be sure! Being here and having met with your kind attention, Master, might I, afore I go, ask a question of these here young lambs of yourn?"

"If it is in the way of school," said Bradley, always sustaining his dark look at the other, and speaking in his suppressed voice, "you may."

"Oh! It's in the way of school!" cried Riderhood. "I'll pound it, Master, to be in the way of school. Wot's the diwisions of water, my lambs? Wot sorts of water is there on the land?"

Shrill chorus: "Seas, rivers, lakes, and ponds."

"Seas, rivers, lakes, and ponds," said Riderhood. "They've got all the lot, Master! Blowed if I shouldn't have left out lakes, never having clapped eyes upon one, to my knowledge. Seas, rivers, lakes, and ponds. Wot is it, lambs, as they ketches in seas, rivers, lakes, and ponds?"

Shrill chorus (with some contempt for the ease of the question): "Fish!"

"Good agin!" said Riderhood. "But what else is it, my lambs, as they sometimes ketches in rivers?"

468

Chorus at a loss. One shrill voice: " Weed ! "

" Good agin ! " cried Riderhood. " But it ain't weed neither. You'll never guess, my dears. Wot is it, besides fish, as they sometimes ketches in rivers? Well! I'll tell you. It's suits o' clothes."

Bradley's face changed.

" Leastways, lambs," said Riderhood, observing him out of the corners of his eyes, "that's wot I my own self sometimes ketches in rivers. For strike me blind, my lambs, if I didn't ketch in a river the wery bundle under my arm ! "

The class looked at the master, as if appealing from the irregular entrapment of this mode of examination. The master looked at the examiner, as if he would have torn him to pieces.

" I ask your pardon, learned governor," said Riderhood, smearing his sleeve across his mouth as he laughed with a relish, " tain't fair to the lambs, I know. It wos a bit of fun of mine. But upon my soul I drawed this here bundle out of a river ! It's a Bargeman's suit of clothes. You see, it had been sunk there by the man as wore it, and I got it up."

" How do you know it was sunk there by the man who wore it ? " asked Bradley.

" 'Cause I see him do it," said Riderhood.

They looked at each other. Bradley, slowly withdrawing his eyes, turned his face to the black board and slowly wiped his name out.

" A heap of thanks, Master," said Riderhood, " for bestowing so much of your time, and of the lambses' time, upon a man as hasn't got no other recommendation to you than being a honest man. Wishing to see at my Lock up the river, the person as we've spoke of, and as you've answered for, I takes my leave of the lambs and of their learned governor both."

With those words, he slouched out of the school, leaving the master to get through his weary work as he might, and

469

leaving the whispering pupils to observe the master's face until he fell into the fit which had been long impending.

The next day but one was Saturday, and a holiday. Bradley rose early, and set out on foot for Plashwater Weir-Mill Lock. He rose so early that it was not yet light when he began his journey. Before extinguishing the candle by which he had dressed himself, he made a little parcel of his decent silver watch and its decent guard, and wrote inside the paper : "Kindly take care of these for me." He then addressed the parcel to Miss Peecher, and left it on the most protected corner of the little seat in her little porch.

It was a cold, hard, easterly morning when he latched the garden gate and turned away. The light snowfall which had feathered his school-room windows on the Thursday, still lingered in the air, and was falling white, while the wind blew black. The tardy day did not appear until he had been on foot two hours, and had traversed a great part of London from east to west. Such breakfast as he had, he took at the comfortless public-house where he had parted from Riderhood on the occasion of their night-walk. He took it, standing at the littered bar, and looked loweringly at a man who stood where Riderhood had stood that early morning.

He outwalked the short day, and was on the towing-path by the river, somewhat footsore, when the night closed in. Still two or three miles short of the Lock, he slackened his pace then, but went steadily on. The ground was now covered with snow, though thinly, and there were floating lumps of ice in the more exposed parts of the river, and broken sheets of ice under the shelter of the banks. He took heed of nothing but the ice, the snow, and the distance, until he saw a light ahead, which he knew gleamed from the Lock-house window. It arrested his steps, and he looked all around. The ice, and the snow, and he, and the one light, had absolute possession of the dreary scene. In the distance before him lay the place where he had struck the worse than useless blows that mocked him with Lizzie's presence there as

470

Eugene's wife. In the distance behind him, lay the place where the children with pointing arms had seemed to devote him to the demons in crying out his name. Within there, where the light was, was the man who as to both distances could give him up to ruin. To these limits had his world shrunk.

He mended his pace, keeping his eyes upon the light with a strange intensity, as if he were taking aim at it. When he approached it so nearly as that it parted into rays, they seemed to fasten themselves to him and draw him on. When he struck the door with his hand, his foot followed so quickly on his hand, that he was in the room before he was bidden to enter.

The light was the joint product of a fire and a candle. Between the two, with his feet on the iron fender, sat Riderhood, pipe in mouth.

He looked up with a surly nod when his visitor came in. His visitor looked down with a surly nod. His outer clothing removed, the visitor then took a seat on the opposite side of the fire.

" Not a smoker, I think ? " said Riderhood, pushing a bottle to him across the table.

" No."

They both lapsed into silence, with their eyes upon the fire.

" You don't need to be told I am here," said Bradley at length. " Who is to begin ? "

" I'll begin," said Riderhood, " when I've smoked this here pipe out."

He finished it with great deliberation, knocked out the ashes on the hob, and put it by.

" I'll begin," he then repeated, " Bradley Headstone, Master, if you wish it."

" Wish it ? I wish to know what you want with me."

" And so you shall." Riderhood had looked hard at his hands and his pockets, apparently as a precautionary measure lest he should have any weapon about him. But, he now

471

leaned forward, turning the collar of his waistcoat with an inquisitive finger, and asked, " Why, where's your watch ? "

" I have left it behind."

" I want it. But it can be fetched. I've took a fancy to it."

Bradley answered with a contemptuous laugh.

" I want it," repeated Riderhood, in a louder voice, " and I mean to have it."

" That is what you want of me, is it ? "

" No," said Riderhood, still louder ; " it's on'y part of what I want of you. I want money of you."

" Anything else ? "

" Everythink else ! " roared Riderhood, in a very loud and furious way. " Answer me like that, and I won't talk to you at all."

Bradley looked at him.

" Don't so much as look at me like that, or I won't talk to you at all," vociferated Riderhood. " But, instead of talking, I'll bring my hand down upon you with all its weight," heavily smiting the table with great force, " and smash you ! "

" Go on," said Bradley, after moistening his lips.

" Oh ! I'm a-going on. Don't you fear but I'll go on full-fast enough for you, and fur enough for you, without your telling. Look here, Bradley Headstone, Master. You might have split the T'other governor to chips and wedges without my caring, except that I might have come upon you for a glass or so now and then. Else why have to do with you at all ? But when you copied my clothes, and when you copied my neckhankercher, and when you shook blood upon me after you had done the trick, you did wot I'll be paid for, and paid heavy for. If it come to be throw'd upon you, you was to be ready to throw it upon me, was you ? Where else but in Plashwater Weir-Mill Lock was there a man dressed according as described ? Where else but in Plashwater Weir-Mill Lock was there a man as had had words

472

with him coming through in his boat? Look at the Lock-keeper in Plashwater Weir-Mill Lock, in them same answering clothes and with that same answering red neckhankercher, and see whether his clothes happens to be bloody or not. Yes, they do happen to be bloody. Ah, you sly devil!"

Bradley, very white, sat looking at him in silence.

"But two could play at your game," said Riderhood, snapping his fingers at him half a dozen times, "and I played it long ago; long afore you tried your clumsy hand at it; in days when you hadn't begun croaking your lecters or what not in your school. I know to a figure how you done it. Where you stole away, I could steal away arter you, and do it knowinger than you. I know how you come away from London in your own clothes, and where you changed your clothes, and hid your clothes. I see you with my own eyes take your own clothes from their hiding-place among them felled trees, and take a dip in the river to account for your dressing yourself, to any one as might come by. I see you rise up Bradley Headstone, Master, where you sat down Bargeman. I see you pitch your Bargeman's bundle into the river. I hooked your Bargeman's bundle out of the river. I've got your Bargeman's clothes, tore this way and that way with the scuffle, stained green with the grass, and spattered all over with what bust from the blows. I've got them, and I've got you. I don't care a curse for the T'other governor, alive or dead, but I care a many curses for my own self. And as you laid your plots agin me and was a sly devil agin me, I'll be paid for it—I'll be paid for it—I'll be paid for it—till I've drained you dry!"

Bradley looked at the fire, with a working face, and was silent for a while. At last he said, with what seemed an inconsistent composure of voice and feature:

"You can't get blood out of a stone, Riderhood."

"I can get money out of a schoolmaster though."

"You can't get out of me what is not in me. You can't wrest from me what I have not got. Mine is but a poor

473

calling. You have had more than two guineas from me, already. Do you know how long it has taken me (allowing for a long and arduous training) to earn such a sum?"

"I don't know, nor I don't care. Yours is a 'spectable calling. To save your 'spectability, it's worth your while to pawn every article of clothes you've got, sell every stick in your house, and beg and borrow every penny you can get trusted with. When you've done that and handed over, I'll leave you. Not afore."

"How do you mean, you'll leave me?"

"I mean as I'll keep you company, wherever you go, when you go away from here. Let the Lock take care of itself. I'll take care of you, once I've got you."

Bradley again looked at the fire. Eyeing him aside, Riderhood took up his pipe, refilled it, lighted it, and sat smoking. Bradley leaned his elbows on his knees, and his head upon his hands, and looked at the fire with a most intent abstraction.

"Riderhood," he said, raising himself in his chair, after a long silence, and drawing out his purse and putting it on the table. "Say I part with this, which is all the money I have; say I let you have my watch; say that every quarter, when I draw my salary, I pay you a certain portion of it."

"Say nothink of the sort," retorted Riderhood, shaking his head as he smoked. "You've got away once, and I won't run the chance agin. I've had trouble enough to find you, and shouldn't have found you if I hadn't seen you slipping along the street over-night, and watched you till you was safe housed. I'll have one settlement with you for good and all."

"Riderhood, I am a man who has lived a retired life. I have no resources beyond myself. I have absolutely no friends."

"That's a lie," said Riderhood. "You've got one friend as I knows of; one as is good for a Savings-Bank book, or I'm a blue monkey!"

474

Bradley's face darkened, and his hand slowly closed on the purse and drew it back, as he sat listening for what the other should go on to say.

"I went into the wrong shop, fust, last Thursday," said Riderhood. "Found myself among the young ladies, by George! Over the young ladies, I see a Missis. That Missis is sweet enough upon you, Master, to sell herself up, slap, to get you out of trouble. Make her do it then."

Bradley stared at him so very suddenly that Riderhood, not quite knowing how to take it, affected to be occupied with the encircling smoke from his pipe; fanning it away with his hand, and blowing it off.

"You spoke to the mistress, did you?" inquired Bradley, with that former composure of voice and feature that seemed inconsistent, and with averted eyes.

"Poof! Yes," said Riderhood, withdrawing his attention from the smoke. "I spoke to her. I didn't say much to her. She was put in a fluster by my dropping in among the young ladies (I never did set up for a lady's man), and she took me into her parlour to hope as there were nothink wrong. I tells her, 'O no, nothink wrong. The master's my wery good friend.' But I see how the land laid, and that she was comfortable off."

Bradley put the purse in his pocket, grasped his left wrist with his right hand, and sat rigidly contemplating the fire.

"She couldn't live more handy to you than she does," said Riderhood, "and when I goes home with you (as of course I am a-going), I recommend you to clean her out without loss of time. You can marry her, arter you and me have come to a settlement. She's nice-looking, and I know you can't be keeping company with no one else, having been so lately disapinted in another quarter."

Not one other word did Bradley utter all that night. Not once did he change his attitude, or loosen his hold upon his wrist. Rigid before the fire, as if it were a charmed flame that was turning him old, he sat, with the dark lines deepening

475

ın his face, its stare becoming more and more haggard, its surface turning whiter and whiter as if it were being overspread with ashes, and the very texture and colour of his hair degenerating.

Not until the late daylight made the window transparent, did this decaying statue move. Then it slowly arose, and sat in the window looking out.

Riderhood had kept his chair all night. In the earlier part of the night he had muttered twice or thrice that it was bitter cold; or that the fire burnt fast, when he got up to mend it; but, as he could elicit from his companion neither sound nor movement, he had afterwards held his peace. He was making some disorderly preparations for coffee, when Bradley came from the window and put on his outer coat and hat.

"Hadn't us better have a bit o' breakfast afore we start?" said Riderhood. "It ain't good to freeze a empty stomach, Master."

Without a sign to show that he heard, Bradley walked out of the Lock-house. Catching up from the table a piece of bread, and taking his Bargeman's bundle under his arm, Riderhood immediately followed him. Bradley turned towards London. Riderhood caught him up, and walked at his side.

The two men trudged on, side by side, in silence, full three miles. Suddenly, Bradley turned to retrace his course. Instantly, Riderhood turned likewise, and they went back side by side.

Bradley re-entered the Lock-house. So did Riderhood. Bradley sat down in the window. Riderhood warmed himself at the fire. After an hour or more, Bradley abruptly got up again, and again went out, but this time turned the other way. Riderhood was close after him, caught him up in a few paces, and walked at his side.

This time, as before, when he found his attendant not to be shaken off, Bradley suddenly turned back. This time, as before, Riderhood turned back along with him. But, not this time, as before, did they go into the Lock-house, for Bradley came to a stand on the snow-covered turf by the Lock, looking up the river and down the river. Navigation was impeded by the frost, and the scene was a mere white and yellow desert.

"Come, come, Master," urged Riderhood, at his side. "'This is a dry game. And where's the good of it? You can't get rid of me, except by coming to a settlement. I am a-going along with you wherever you go."

Without a word of reply, Bradley passed quickly from him over the wooden bridge on the Lock gates. "Why, there's even less sense in this move than t'other," said Riderhood, following. "The Weir's there, and you'll have to come back, you know."

Without taking the least notice, Bradley leaned his body against a post, in a resting attitude, and there rested with his eyes cast down. "Being brought here," said Riderhood, gruffly, "I'll turn it to some use by changing my gates." With a rattle and a rush of water, he then swung-to the Lock gates that were standing open, before opening the others. So, both sets of gates were, for the moment, closed.

"You'd better by far be reasonable, Bradley Headstone, Master," said Riderhood, passing him, "or I'll drain you all the drier for it, when we do settle.—Ah! Would you!"

Bradley had caught him round the body. He seemed to be girdled with an iron ring. They were on the brink of the Lock, about midway between the two sets of gates.

"Let go!" said Riderhood, "or I'll get my knife out and slash you wherever I can cut you. Let go!"

Bradley was drawing to the Lock-edge. Riderhood was drawing away from it. It was a strong grapple, and a fierce struggle, arm and leg. Bradley got him round, with his back to the Lock, and still worked him backward.

"Let go!" said Riderhood. "Stop! What are you trying at? You can't drown Me. Ain't I told you that

477

the man as has come through drowning can never be drowned? I can't be drowned."

"I can be!" returned Bradley, in a desperate, clenched voice. "I am resolved to be. I'll hold you living, and I'll hold you dead. Come down!"

Riderhood went over into the smooth pit, backward, and Bradley Headstone upon him. When the two were found, lying under the ooze and scum behind one of the rotting gates, Riderhood's hold had relaxed, probably in falling, and his eyes were staring upward. But he was girdled still with Bradley's iron ring, and the rivets of the iron ring held tight.

CHAPTER XVI

PERSONS AND THINGS IN GENERAL

Mr. and Mrs. John Harmon's first delightful occupation was, to set all matters right that had strayed in any way wrong, or that might, could, would, or should, have strayed in any way wrong, while their name was in abeyance. In tracing out affairs for which John's fictitious death was to be considered in any way responsible, they used a very broad and free construction; regarding, for instance, the dolls' dressmaker as having a claim on their protection, because of her association with Mrs. Eugene Wrayburn, and because of Mrs. Eugene's old association, in her turn, with the dark side of the story. It followed that the old man, Riah, as a good and serviceable friend to both, was not to be disclaimed. Nor even Mr. Inspector, as having been trepanned into an industrious hunt on a false scent. It may be remarked, in connection with that worthy officer, that a rumour shortly afterwards pervaded the Force, to the effect that he had confided to Miss Abbey Potterson, over a jug of mellow flip in the bar of the Six Jolly Fellowship Porters, that he "didn't stand to lose a farthing" through Mr. Harmon's coming to life, but was quite as well satisfied as if that gentleman had been barbarously murdered, and he (Mr. Inspector) had pocketed the government reward.

In all their arrangements of such nature, Mr. and Mrs. John Harmon derived much assistance from their eminent solicitor,

Mr. Mortimer Lightwood; who laid about him professionally with such unwonted despatch and intention, that a piece of work was vigorously pursued as soon as cut out; whereby Young Blight was acted on as by that transatlantic dram which is poetically named An Eye-Opener, and found himself staring at real clients instead of out of window. The accessibility of Riah proving very useful as to a few hints towards the disentanglement of Eugene's affairs, Lightwood applied himself with infinite zest to attacking and harassing Mr. Fledgeby; who, discovering himself in danger of being blown into the air by certain explosive transactions in which he had been engaged, and having been sufficiently flayed under his beating, came to a parley and asked for quarter. The harmless Twemlow profited by the conditions entered into, though he little thought it. Mr. Riah unaccountably melted; waited in person on him over the stable-yard in Duke Street, Saint James's, no longer ravening but mild, to inform him that payment of interest as heretofore, but henceforth at Mr. Lightwood's offices, would appease his Jewish rancour; and departed with the secret that Mr. John Harmon had advanced the money and become the creditor. Thus was the sublime Snigsworth's wrath averted, and thus did he snort no larger amount of moral grandeur at the Corinthian column in the print over the fireplace, than was normally in his (and the British) constitution.

Mrs. Wilfer's first visit to the Mendicant's bride at the new abode of Mendicancy, was a grand event. Pa had been sent for into the City, on the very day of taking possession, and had been stunned with astonishment, and brought-to, and led about the house by one ear, to behold its various treasures, and had been enraptured and enchanted. Pa had also been appointed Secretary, and had been enjoined to give instant notice of resignation to Chicksey, Veneering, and Stobbles, for ever and ever. But Ma came later, and came, as was her due, in state.

A VISIT IN STATE

The carriage was sent for Ma, who entered it with a bearing worthy of the occasion, accompanied, rather than supported, by Miss Lavinia, who altogether declined to recognise the maternal majesty. Mr. George Sampson meekly followed. He was received in the vehicle, by Mrs. Wilfer, as if admitted to the honour of assisting at a funeral in the family, and she then issued the order, "Onward!" to the Mendicant's menial.

"I wish to goodness, Ma," said Lavvy, throwing herself back among the cushions, with her arms crossed, "that you'd loll a little."

"How!" repeated Mrs. Wilfer. "Loll!"

"Yes, Ma."

"I hope," said the impressive lady, "I am incapable of it."

"I am sure you look so, Ma. But why one should go out to dine with one's own daughter or sister, as if one's under-petticoat was a backboard, I do *not* understand."

"Neither do I understand," retorted Mrs. Wilfer, with deep scorn, "how a young lady can mention the garment in the name in which you have indulged. I blush for you."

"Thank you, Ma," said Lavvy, yawning, "but I can do it for myself, I am obliged to you, when there's any occasion."

Here, Mr. Sampson, with the view of establishing harmony, which he never under any circumstances succeeded in doing, said with an agreeable smile: "After all, you know, ma'am, we know it's there." And immediately felt that he had committed himself.

"We know it's there!" said Mrs. Wilfer, glaring.

"Really, George," remonstrated Miss Lavinia, "I must say that I don't understand your allusions, and that I think you might be more delicate and less personal."

"Go it!" cried Mr. Sampson, becoming, on the shortest notice, a prey to despair. "Oh yes! Go it, Miss Lavinia Wilfer!"

"What you may mean, George Sampson, by your omnibus-

driving expressions, I cannot pretend to imagine. Neither,"
said Miss Lavinia, "Mr. George Sampson, do I wish to
imagine. It is enough for me to know in my own heart that
I am not going to— " having imprudently got into a sentence
without providing a way out of it, Miss Lavinia was constrained to close with "going to go it." A weak conclusion
which, however, derived some appearance of strength from
disdain.

"Oh yes!" cried Mr. Sampson, with bitterness. "Thus it
ever is. I never—— "

"If you mean to say," Miss Lavvy cut him short, "that
you never brought up a young gazelle, you may save yourself
the trouble, because nobody in this carriage supposes that
you ever did. We know you better." (As if this were a
home-thrust.)

"Lavinia," returned Mr. Sampson, in a dismal vein, "I
did not mean to say so. What I did mean to say, was,
that I never expected to retain my favoured place in this
family, after Fortune shed her beams upon it. Why do you
take me," said Mr. Sampson, "to the glittering halls with
which I can never compete, and then taunt me with my
moderate salary? Is it generous? Is it kind?"

The stately lady, Mrs. Wilfer, perceiving her opportunity
of delivering a few remarks from the throne, here took up
the altercation.

"Mr. Sampson," she began, "I cannot permit you to
misrepresent the intentions of a child of mine."

"Let him alone, Ma," Miss Lavvy interposed with haughti-
ness. "It is indifferent to me what he says or does."

"Nay, Lavinia," quoth Mrs. Wilfer, "this touches the
blood of the family. If Mr. George Sampson attributes,
even to my youngest daughter—— "

("I don't see why you should use the word 'even,' Ma,"
Miss Lavvy interposed, "because I am quite as important as
any of the others.")

"Peace!" said Mrs. Wilfer, solemnly. "I repeat, if Mr.

482

George Sampson attributes, to my youngest daughter, grovelling motives, he attributes them equally to the mother of my youngest daughter. That mother repudiates them, and demands of Mr. George Sampson, as a youth of honour, what he *would* have? I may be mistaken—nothing is more likely —but Mr. George Sampson," proceeded Mrs. Wilfer, majestically waving her gloves, "appears to me to be seated in a first-class equipage. Mr. George Sampson appears to me to be on his way, by his own admission, to a residence that may be termed Palatial. Mr. George Sampson appears to me to be invited to participate in the—shall I say the—Elevation which has descended on the family with which he is ambitious, shall I say to Mingle? Whence, then, this tone on Mr. Sampson's part?"

"It is only, ma'am," Mr. Sampson explained, in exceedingly low spirits, "because, in a pecuniary sense, I am painfully conscious of my unworthiness. Lavinia is now highly connected. Can I hope that she will still remain the same Lavinia as of old? And is it not pardonable if I feel sensitive, when I see a disposition on her part to take me up short?"

"If you are not satisfied with your position, sir," observed Miss Lavinia, with much politeness, "we can set you down at any turning you may please to indicate to my sister's coachman."

"Dearest Lavinia," urged Mr. Sampson, pathetically, "I adore you."

"Then if you can't do it in a more agreeable manner," returned the young lady, "I wish you wouldn't."

"I also," pursued Mr. Sampson, "respect you, ma'am, to an extent which must ever be below your merits, I am well aware, but still up to an uncommon mark. Bear with a wretch, Lavinia, bear with a wretch, ma'am, who feels the noble sacrifices you make for him, but is goaded almost to madness"—Mr. Sampson slapped his forehead—"when he thinks of competing with the rich and influential."

483

"When you have to compete with the rich and influential, it will probably be mentioned to you," said Miss Lavvy, "in good time. At least, it will if the case is *my* case."

Mr. Sampson immediately expressed his fervent opinion that this was "more than human," and was brought upon his knees at Miss Lavinia's feet.

It was the crowning addition indispensable to the full enjoyment of both mother and daughter, to bear Mr. Sampson, a grateful captive, into the glittering halls he had mentioned, and to parade him through the same, at once a living witness of their glory, and a bright instance of their condescension. Ascending the staircase, Miss Lavinia permitted him to walk at her side, with the air of saying : "Notwithstanding all these surroundings, I am yours as yet, George. How long it may last is another question, but I am yours as yet." She also benignantly intimated to him, aloud, the nature of the objects upon which he looked, and to which he was unaccustomed : as, "Exotics, George," "An aviary, George," "An ormolu clock, George," and the like. While through the whole of the decorations, Mrs. Wilfer led the way with the bearing of a Savage Chief, who would feel himself compromised by manifesting the slightest token of surprise or admiration.

Indeed, the bearing of this impressive woman, throughout the day, was a pattern to all impressive women under similar circumstances. She renewed the acquaintance of Mr. and Mrs. Boffin, as if Mr. and Mrs. Boffin had said of her what she had said of them, and as if Time alone could quite wear her injury out. She regarded every servant who approached her, as her sworn enemy, expressly intending to offer her affronts with the dishes, and to pour forth outrages on her moral feelings from the decanters. She sat erect at table, on the right hand of her son-in-law, as half suspecting poison in the viands, and as bearing up with native force of character against other deadly ambushes. Her carriage towards Bella was as a carriage towards a young lady of good position whom she had met in society a few years ago. Even when, slightly thawing under the influence of sparkling champagne, she related to her son-in-law some passages of domestic interest concerning her papa, she infused into the narrative such Arctic suggestions of her having been an unappreciated blessing to mankind, since her papa's days, and also of that gentleman's having been a frosty impersonation of a frosty race, as struck cold to the very soles of the feet of the hearers. The Inexhaustible being produced, staring, and evidently intending a weak and washy smile shortly, no sooner beheld her, than it was stricken spasmodic and inconsolable. When she took her leave at last, it would have been hard to say whether it was with the air of going to the scaffold herself, or of leaving the inmates of the house for immediate execution. Yet, John Harmon enjoyed it all merrily, and told his wife, when he and she were alone, that her natural ways had never seemed so dearly natural as beside this foil, and that although he did not dispute her being her father's daughter, he should ever remain steadfast in the faith that she could not be her mother's.

This visit was, as has been said, a great event. Another event, not grand, but deemed in the house a special one, occurred at about the same period; and this was, the first interview between Mr. Sloppy and Miss Wren.

The dolls' dressmaker, being at work for the Inexhaustible upon a full-dressed doll some two sizes larger than that young person, Mr. Sloppy undertook to call for it, and did so.

" Come in, sir," said Miss Wren, who was working at her bench. " And who may you be ? "

Mr. Sloppy introduced himself by name and buttons.

" Oh indeed ! " cried Jenny. " Ah ! I have been looking forward to knowing you. I heard of your distinguishing yourself."

" Did you, Miss ? " grinned Sloppy. " I am sure I am glad to hear it, but I don't know how."

485

"Pitching somebody into a mud-cart," said Miss Wren.

"Oh! That way!" cried Sloppy. "Yes, Miss." And threw back his head and laughed.

"Bless us!" exclaimed Miss Wren, with a start. "Don't open your mouth as wide as that, young man, or it'll catch so, and not shut again some day."

Mr. Sloppy opened it, if possible, wider, and kept it open until his laugh was out.

"Why, you're like the giant," said Miss Wren, "when he came home in the land of Beanstalk, and wanted Jack for supper."

"Was he good-looking, Miss?" asked Sloppy.

"No," said Miss Wren. "Ugly."

Her visitor glanced round the room—which had many comforts in it now, that had not been in it before—and said: "This is a pretty place, Miss."

"Glad you think so, sir," returned Miss Wren. "And what do you think of Me?"

The honesty of Mr. Sloppy being severely taxed by the question, he twisted a button, grinned, and faltered.

"Out with it!" said Miss Wren, with an arch look. "Don't you think me a queer little comicality?" In shaking her head at him after asking the question, she shook her hair down.

"Oh!" cried Sloppy, in a burst of admiration. "What a lot, and what a colour!"

Miss Wren, with her usual expressive hitch, went on with her work. But, left her hair as it was; not displeased by the effect it had made.

"You don't live here alone; do you, Miss?" asked Sloppy.

"No," said Miss Wren, with a chop. "Live here with my fairy godmother."

"With;" Mr. Sloppy couldn't make it out; "with who did you say, Miss?"

"Well!" replied Miss Wren, more seriously. "With my second father. Or with my first, for that matter." And she shook her head, and drew a sigh. "If you had known a poor child I used to have here," she added, "you'd have understood me. But you didn't, and you can't. All the better!"

"You must have been taught a long time," said Sloppy, glancing at the array of dolls in hand, "before you came to work so neatly, Miss, and with such a pretty taste."

"Never was taught a stitch, young man!" returned the dressmaker, tossing her head. "Just gobbled and gobbled, till I found out how to do it. Badly enough at first, but better now."

"And here have I," said Sloppy, in something of a self-reproachful tone, "been a-learning and a-learning, and here has Mr. Boffin been a-paying and a-paying, ever so long!"

"I have heard what your trade is," observed Miss Wren; "it's cabinet-making."

Mr. Sloppy nodded. "Now that the Mounds is done with, it is. I'll tell you what, Miss. I should like to make you something."

"Much obliged. But what?"

"I could make you," said Sloppy, surveying the room, "I could make you a handy set of nests to lay the dolls in. Or I could make you a handy little set of drawers, to keep your silks and threads and scraps in. Or I could turn you a rare handle for that crutch-stick, if it belongs to him you call your father."

"It belongs to me," returned the little creature, with a quick flush of her face and neck. "I am lame."

Poor Sloppy flushed too, for there was an instinctive delicacy behind his buttons, and his own hand had struck it. He said, perhaps, the best thing in the way of amends that could be said. "I am very glad it's yours, because I'd rather ornament it for you than for any one else. Please may I look at it?"

Miss Wren was in the act of handing it to him over her bench, when she paused. "But you had better see me use it," she said, sharply. "This is the way. Hoppetty, Kicketty, Peg-peg-peg. Not pretty; is it?"

"It seems to me that you hardly want it at all," said Sloppy.

The little dressmaker sat down again, and gave it into his hand, saying, with that better look upon her, and with a smile: "Thank you!"

"And as concerning the nests and drawers," said Sloppy, after measuring the handle on his sleeve, and softly standing the stick aside against the wall, "why, it would be a real pleasure to me. I've heerd tell that you can sing most beautiful; and I should be better paid with a song than with any money, for I always loved the likes of that, and often giv' Mrs. Higden and Johnny a comic song myself, with 'Spoken' in it. Though that's not your sort, I'll wager."

"You are a very kind young man," returned the dressmaker, "a really kind young man. I accept your offer.—I suppose He won't mind," she added as an afterthought, shrugging her shoulders; "and if he does, he may!"

"Meaning him that you call your father, Miss?" asked Sloppy.

"No, no," replied Miss Wren. "Him, Him, Him!"

"Him, him, him?" repeated Sloppy; staring about, as if for Him.

"Him who is coming to court and marry me," returned Miss Wren. "Dear me, how slow you are!"

"Oh! *Him!*" said Sloppy. And seemed to turn thoughtful and a little troubled. "I never thought of him. When is he coming, Miss?"

"What a question!" cried Miss Wren. "How should *I* know!"

"Where is he coming from, Miss?"

"Why, good gracious, how can *I* tell! He is coming from somewhere or other, I suppose, and he is coming some day or other, I suppose. *I* don't know any more about him, at present."

This tickled Mr. Sloppy as an extraordinarily good joke, and he threw back his head and laughed with measureless enjoyment. At the sight of him laughing in that absurd way, the dolls' dressmaker laughed very heartily indeed. So they both laughed, till they were tired.

"There, there, there!" said Miss Wren. "For goodness' sake stop, Giant, or I shall be swallowed up alive, before I know it. And to this minute you haven't said what you've come for."

"I have come for little Miss Harmonses doll," said Sloppy.

"I thought as much," remarked Miss Wren, "and here is little Miss Harmonses doll waiting for you. She's folded up in silver paper, you see, as if she was wrapped from head to foot in new Bank notes. Take care of her, and there's my hand, and thank you again."

"I'll take more care of her than if she was a gold image," said Sloppy, "and there's both *my* hands, Miss, and I'll soon come back again."

But, the greatest event of all, in the new life of Mr. and Mrs. John Harmon, was a visit from Mr. and Mrs. Eugene Wrayburn. Sadly wan and worn was the once gallant Eugene, and walked resting on his wife's arm, and leaning heavily upon a stick. But, he was daily growing stronger and better, and it was declared by the medical attendants that he might not be much disfigured by-and-by. It was a grand event, indeed, when Mr. and Mrs. Eugene Wrayburn came to stay at Mr. and Mrs. John Harmon's house : where, by the way, Mr. and Mrs. Boffin (exquisitely happy, and daily cruising about, to look at shops) were likewise staying indefinitely.

To Mr. Eugene Wrayburn, in confidence, did Mrs. John Harmon impart what she had known of the state of his wife's affections, in his reckless time. And to Mrs. John Harmon, in confidence, did Mr. Eugene Wrayburn impart that, please God, she should see how his wife had changed him !

"I make no protestations," said Eugene; "—who does, who means them?—I have made a resolution."

"But would you believe, Bella," interposed his wife, coming to resume her nurse's place at his side, for he never got on well without her : "that on our wedding day he told me he almost thought the best thing he could do, was to die?"

"As I didn't do it, Lizzie," said Eugene, "I'll do that better thing you suggested—for your sake."

That same afternoon, Eugene lying on his couch in his own room up-stairs, Lightwood came to chat with him, while Bella took his wife out for a ride. "Nothing short of force will make her go," Eugene had said; so, Bella had playfully forced her.

"Dear old fellow," Eugene began with Lightwood, reaching up his hand, "you couldn't have come at a better time, for my mind is full, and I want to empty it. First, of my present, before I touch upon my future. M. R. F., who is a much younger cavalier than I, and a professed admirer of beauty, was so affable as to remark the other day (he paid us a visit of two days up the river there, and much objected to the accommodation of the hotel), that Lizzie ought to have her portrait painted. Which, coming from M. R. F., may be considered equivalent to a melodramatic blessing."

"You are getting well," said Mortimer, with a smile.

"Really," said Eugene, "I mean it. When M. R. F. said that, and followed it up by rolling the claret (for which he called, and I paid) in his mouth, and saying, 'My dear son, why do you drink this trash?' it was tantamount—in him— to a paternal benediction on our union, accompanied with a gush of tears. The coolness of M. R. F. is not to be measured by ordinary standards."

"True enough," said Lightwood.

"That's all," pursued Eugene, "that I shall ever hear from M. R. F. on the subject, and he will continue to saunter through the world with his hat on one side. My marriage being thus solemnly recognised at the family altar, I have no further trouble on that score. Next, you really have done wonders for me, Mortimer, in easing my money-perplexities, and with such a guardian and steward beside me, as the preserver of my life (I am hardly strong yet, you see, for I am not man enough to refer to her without a trembling voice —she is so inexpressibly dear to me, Mortimer!), the little that I can call my own will be more than it ever has been. It need be more, for you know what it always has been in my hands. Nothing."

" Worse than nothing, I fancy, Eugene. My own small income (I devoutly wish that my grandfather had left it to the Ocean rather than to me!) has been an effective Something, in the way of preventing me from turning to at Anything. And I think yours has been much the same."

" There spake the voice of wisdom," said Eugene. " We are shepherds both. In turning to at last, we turn to in earnest. Let us say no more of that, for a few years to come. Now, I have had an idea, Mortimer, of taking myself and my wife to one of the colonies, and working at my vocation there."

" I should be lost without you, Eugene ; but you may be right."

" No," said Eugene, emphatically. " Not right. Wrong! "

He said it with such a lively—almost angry—flash, that Mortimer showed himself greatly surprised.

" You think this thumped head of mine is excited ? " Eugene went on, with a high look ; " not so, believe me. I can say to you of the healthful music of my pulse what Hamlet said of his. My blood is up, but wholesomely up, when I think of it ! Tell me ! Shall I turn coward to Lizzie, and sneak away with her, as if I were ashamed of her ! Where would your friend's part in this world be, Mortimer, if she had turned coward to him, and on immeasurably better occasion ? "

" Honourable and staunch," said Lightwood. " And yet, Eugene—— "

491

"And yet what, Mortimer?"

"And yet, are you sure that you might not feel (for her sake, I say for her sake) any slight coldness towards her on the part of—Society?"

"Oh! You and I may well stumble at the word," returned Eugene, laughing. "Do we mean our Tippins?"

"Perhaps we do," said Mortimer, laughing also.

"Faith, we DO!" returned Eugene, with great animation. "We may hide behind the bush and beat about it, but we DO. Now, my wife is something nearer to my heart, Mortimer, than Tippins is, and I owe her a little more than I owe to Tippins, and I am rather prouder of her than I ever was of Tippins. Therefore, I will fight it out to the last gasp, with her and for her, here, in the open field. When I hide her, or strike for her, faint-heartedly, in a hole or a corner, do you, whom I love next best upon earth, tell me what I shall most righteously deserve to be told:—that she would have done well to have turned me over with her foot that night when I lay bleeding to death, and to have spat in my dastard face."

The glow that shone upon him as he spoke the words, so irradiated his features, that he looked, for the time, as though he had never been mutilated. His friend responded as Eugene would have had him respond, and they discoursed of the future, until Lizzie came back. After resuming her place at his side, and tenderly touching his hands and his head, she said:

"Eugene, dear, you made me go out, but I ought to have stayed with you. You are more flushed than you have been for many days. What have you been doing?"

"Nothing," replied Eugene, "but looking forward to your coming back."

"And talking to Mr. Lightwood," said Lizzie, turning to him with a smile. "But it cannot have been Society that disturbed you."

"Faith, my dear love!" retorted Eugene, in his old airy

manner, as he laughed and kissed her, " I rather think it *was* Society though ! "

The word ran so much in Mortimer Lightwood's thoughts as he went home to the Temple that night, that he resolved to take a look at Society, which he had not seen for a considerable period.

CHAPTER THE LAST

THE VOICE OF SOCIETY

BEHOVES Mortimer Lightwood, therefore, to answer a dinner card from Mr. and Mrs. Veneering, requesting the honour, and to signify that Mr. Mortimer Lightwood will be happy to have the other honour. The Veneerings have been, as usual, indefatigably dealing dinner cards to Society, and whoever desires to take a hand had best be quick about it, for it is written in the Books of the Insolvent Fates that Veneering shall make a resounding smash next week. Yes. Having found out the clue to that great mystery how people can contrive to live beyond their means, and having over-jobbed his jobberies as legislator deputed to the Universe by the pure electors of Pocket-Breaches, it shall come to pass next week that Veneering will accept the Chiltern Hundreds, that the legal gentleman in Britannia's confidence will again accept the Pocket-Breaches Thousands, and that the Veneerings will retire to Calais, there to live on Mrs. Veneering's diamonds (in which Mr. Veneering, as a good husband, has from time to time invested considerable sums), and to relate to Neptune and others, how that, before Veneering retired from Parliament, the House of Commons was composed of himself and the six hundred and fifty-seven dearest and oldest friends he had in the world. It shall likewise come to pass, at as nearly as possible the same period, that Society will discover that it always did despise Veneering, and distrust Veneering, and that when it went to Veneering's to dinner it always had misgivings—though very secretly at the time, it would seem, and in a perfectly private and confidential manner.

The next week's books of the Insolvent Fates, however, being not yet opened, there is the usual rush to the Veneerings, of the people who go to their house to dine with one another and not with them. There is Lady Tippins. There are Podsnap the Great, and Mrs. Podsnap. There is Twemlow. There are Buffer, Boots, and Brewer. There is the Contractor, who is Providence to five hundred thousand men. There is the Chairman, travelling three thousand miles per week. There is the brilliant genius who turned the shares into that remarkably exact sum of three hundred and seventy-five thousand pounds, no shillings, and nopence.

To whom, add Mortimer Lightwood, coming in among them with a resumption of his old languid air, founded on Eugene, and belonging to the days when he told the story of the man from Somewhere.

That fresh fairy, Tippins, all but screams at sight of her false swain. She summons the deserter to her with her fan; but the deserter, predetermined not to come, talks Britain with Podsnap. Podsnap always talks Britain, and talks as if he were a sort of Private Watchman employed, in the British interests, against the rest of the world. "We know what Russia means, sir," says Podsnap; "we know what France wants; we see what America is up to; but we know what England is. That's enough for us."

However, when dinner is served, and Lightwood drops into his old place over against Lady Tippins, she can be fended off no longer. "Long banished Robinson Crusoe," says the charmer, exchanging salutations, "how did you leave the Island?"

"Thank you," says Lightwood. "It made no complaint of being in pain anywhere."

"Say, how did you leave the savages?" asks Lady Tippins.

"They were becoming civilized when I left Juan Fernandez,"

says Lightwood. "At least they were eating one another, which looked like it."

"Tormentor!" returns the dear young creature. "You know what I mean, and you trifle with my impatience. Tell me something, immediately, about the married pair. You were at the wedding."

"Was I, by-the-bye?" Mortimer pretends, at great leisure, to consider. "So I was!"

"How was the bride dressed? In rowing costume?" Mortimer looks gloomy, and declines to answer.

"I hope she steered herself, skiffed herself, paddled herself, larboarded and starboarded herself, or whatever the technical term may be, to the ceremony?" proceeds the playful Tippins.

"However she got to it, she graced it," says Mortimer.

Lady Tippins with a skittish little scream, attracts the general attention. "Graced it! Take care of me if I faint, Veneering. He means to tell us, that a horrid female water-man is graceful!"

"Pardon me. I mean to tell you nothing, Lady Tippins," replies Lightwood. And keeps his word by eating his dinner with a show of the utmost indifference.

"You shall not escape me in this way, you morose back-woods-man," retorts Lady Tippins. "You shall not evade the question, to screen your friend Eugene, who has made this exhibition of himself. The knowledge shall be brought home to you that such a ridiculous affair is condemned by the voice of Society. My dear Mrs. Veneering, do let us resolve our-selves into a Committee of the whole House on the subject."

Mrs. Veneering, always charmed by this rattling sylph, cries: "Oh yes! Do let us resolve ourselves into a Com-mittee of the whole House! So delicious!" Veneering says, "As many as are of that opinion, say Aye,—contrary, No—the Ayes have it." But nobody takes the slightest notice of his joke.

"Now, I am Chairwoman of Committees!" cries Lady Tippins.

496

("What spirits she has!" exclaims Mrs. Veneering; to whom likewise nobody attends.)

"And this," pursues the sprightly one, "is a Committee of the whole House to what-you-may-call-it—elicit, I suppose —the voice of Society. The question before the Committee is, whether a young man of very fair family, good appearance, and some talent, makes a fool or a wise man of himself in marrying a female waterman, turned factory girl."

"Hardly so, I think," the stubborn Mortimer strikes in. "I take the question to be, whether such a man as you describe, Lady Tippins, does right or wrong in marrying a brave woman (I say nothing of her beauty), who has saved his life, with a wonderful energy and address; whom he knows to be virtuous, and possessed of remarkable qualities; whom he has long admired, and who is deeply attached to him."

"But, excuse me," says Podsnap, with his temper and his shirt-collar about equally rumpled; "was this young woman ever a female waterman?"

"Never. But she sometimes rowed in a boat with her father, I believe."

General sensation against the young woman. Brewer shakes his head. Boots shakes his head. Buffer shakes his head.

"And now, Mr. Lightwood, was she ever," pursues Podsnap, with his indignation rising high into those hair-brushes of his, "a factory girl?"

"Never. But she had some employment in a paper mill, I believe." General sensation repeated. Brewer says, "Oh dear!" Boots says, "Oh dear!" Buffer says, "Oh dear!" All, in a rumbling tone of protest.

"Then all *I* have to say is," returns Podsnap, putting the thing away with his right arm, "that my gorge rises against such a marriage—that it offends and disgusts me—that it makes me sick—and that I desire to know no more about it."

("Now I wonder," thinks Mortimer, amused, "whether *you* are the Voice of Society!")

"Hear, hear, hear!" cries Lady Tippins. "Your opinion

497

of this *mésalliance,* honourable colleague of the honourable member who has just sat down ? "

Mrs. Podsnap is of opinion that in these matters " there should be an equality of station and fortune, and that a man accustomed to Society should look out for a woman accustomed to Society and capable of bearing her part in it with —an ease and elegance of carriage—that." Mrs. Podsnap stops there, delicately intimating that every such man should look out for a fine woman as nearly resembling herself as he may hope to discover.

("Now I wonder," thinks Mortimer, "whether *you* are the Voice ! ")

Lady Tippins next canvasses the Contractor, of five hundred thousand power. It appears to this potentate, that what the man in question should have done, would have been, to buy the young woman a boat and a small annuity, and set her up for herself. These things are a question of beefsteaks and porter. You buy the young woman a boat. Very good. You buy her, at the same time, a small annuity. You speak of that annuity in pounds sterling, but it is in reality so many pounds of beefsteaks and so many pints of porter. On the one hand, the young woman has the boat. On the other hand, she consumes so many pounds of beefsteaks and so many pints of porter. Those beefsteaks and that porter are the fuel to that young woman's engine. She derives therefrom a certain amount of power to row the boat ; that power will produce so much money ; you add that to the small annuity ; and thus you get at the young woman's income. That (it seems to the Contractor) is the way of looking at it.

The fair enslaver having fallen into one of her gentle sleeps during this last exposition, nobody likes to wake her. Fortunately, she comes awake of herself, and puts the question to the Wandering Chairman. The Wanderer can only speak of the case as if it were his own. If such a young woman as the young woman described, had saved his own life, he

would have been very much obliged to her, wouldn't have
married her, and would have got her a berth in an Electric
Telegraph Office, where young women answer very well.

What does the Genius of the three hundred and seventy-
five thousand pounds, no shillings, and nopence, think? He
can't say what he thinks, without asking: Had the young
woman any money?

"No," says Lightwood, in an uncompromising voice: "no
money."

"Madness and moonshine," is then the compressed verdict
of the Genius. "A man may do anything lawful, for money.
But for no money!—Bosh!"

What does Boots say?

Boots says he wouldn't have done it under twenty thousand
pounds.

What does Brewer say?

Brewer says what Boots says.

What does Buffer say?

Buffer says he knows a man who married a bathing-woman,
and bolted.

Lady Tippins fancies she has collected the suffrages of the
whole Committee (nobody dreaming of asking the Veneerings
for their opinion), when, looking round the table through her
eye-glass, she perceives Mr. Twemlow with his hand to his
forehead.

Good gracious! My Twemlow forgotten! My dearest! My
own! What is his vote?

Twemlow has the air of being ill at ease, as he takes his
hand from his forehead and replies. "I am disposed to think,"
says he, "that this is a question of the feelings of a gentleman."

"A gentleman can have no feelings who contracts such a
marriage," flushes Podsnap.

"Pardon me, sir," says Twemlow, rather less mildly than
usual, "I don't agree with you. If this gentleman's feelings
of gratitude, of respect, of admiration, and affection, induced
him (as I presume they did) to marry this lady——"

"This lady!" echoes Podsnap.

"Sir," returns Twemlow, with his wristbands bristling a little, "*you* repeat the word; *I* repeat the word. This lady. What else would you call her, if the gentleman were present?"

This being something in the nature of a poser for Podsnap, he merely waves it away with a speechless wave.

"I say," resumes Twemlow, "if such feelings on the part of this gentleman, induced this gentleman to marry this lady, I think he is the greater gentleman for the action, and makes her the greater lady. I beg to say, that when I use the word, gentleman, I use it in the sense in which the degree may be attained by any man. The feelings of a gentleman I hold sacred, and I confess I am not comfortable when they are made the subject of sport or general discussion."

"I should like to know," sneers Podsnap, "whether your noble relation would be of your opinion."

"Mr. Podsnap," retorts Twemlow, "permit me. He might be, or he might not be. I cannot say. But, I could not allow even him to dictate to me on a point of great delicacy, on which I feel very strongly."

Somehow, a canopy of wet blanket seems to descend upon the company, and Lady Tippins was never known to turn so very greedy, or so very cross. Mortimer Lightwood alone brightens. He has been asking himself, as to every other member of the Committee in turn, "I wonder whether you are the Voice!" But he does not ask himself the question after Twemlow has spoken, and he glances in Twemlow's direction as if he were grateful. When the company disperse —by which time Mr. and Mrs. Veneering have had quite as much as they want of the honour, and the guests have had quite as much as *they* want of the other honour—Mortimer sees Twemlow home, shakes hands with him cordially at parting, and fares to the Temple, gaily.

POSTSCRIPT

WHEN I devised this story, I foresaw the likelihood that a class of readers and commentators would suppose that I was at great pains to conceal exactly what I was at great pains to suggest: namely, that Mr. John Harmon was not slain, and that Mr. John Rokesmith was he. Pleasing myself with the idea that the supposition might in part arise out of some ingenuity in the story, and thinking it worth while, in the interests of art, to hint to an audience that an artist (of whatever denomination) may perhaps be trusted to know what he is about in his vocation, if they will concede him a little patience, I was not alarmed by the anticipation.

To keep for a long time unsuspected, yet always working itself out, another purpose originating in that leading incident, and turning it to a pleasant and useful account at last, was at once the most interesting and the most difficult part of my design. Its difficulty was much enhanced by the mode of publication; for, it would be very unreasonable to expect that many readers, pursuing a story in portions from month to month through nineteen months, will, until they have it before them complete, perceive the relations of its finer

501

threads to the whole pattern which is always before the eyes of the story weaver at his loom. Yet, that I hold the advantages of the mode of publication to outweigh its disadvantages, may be easily believed of one who revived it in the Pickwick Papers after long disuse, and has pursued it ever since.

There is sometimes an odd disposition in this country to dispute as improbable in fiction, what are the commonest experiences in fact. Therefore, I note here, though it may not be at all necessary, that there are hundreds of Will Cases (as they are called), far more remarkable than that fancied in this book; and that the stores of the Prerogative Office teem with instances of testators who have made, changed, contradicted, hidden, forgotten, left cancelled, and left uncancelled, each many more wills than were ever made by the elder Mr. Harmon of Harmony Jail.

In my social experiences since Mrs. Betty Higden came upon the scene and left it, I have found Circumlocutional champions disposed to be warm with me on the subject of my view of the Poor Law. My friend Mr. Bounderby could never see any difference between leaving the Coketown "hands" exactly as they were, and requiring them to be fed with turtle soup and venison out of gold spoons. Idiotic propositions of a parallel nature have been freely offered for my acceptance, and I have been called upon to admit that I would give Poor Law relief to anybody, anywhere, anyhow. Putting this nonsense aside, I have observed a suspicious tendency in the champions to divide into two parties; the one, contending that there are no deserving Poor who prefer death by slow starvation and bitter weather, to the mercies of some Relieving Officers and some Union Houses; the other, admitting that there are such Poor, but denying that they have any cause or reason for what they do. The records in our newspapers, the late exposure by THE LANCET, and the common sense and senses of common people, furnish too abundant evidence against both defences. But, that my view of the Poor Law may not be mistaken or misrepresented, I will state it. I believe there has been in England, since the days of the STUARTS, no law so often infamously administered, no law so often openly violated, no law habitually so ill-supervised. In the majority of the shameful cases of disease and death from destitution, that shock the Public and disgrace the country, the illegality is quite equal to the inhumanity—and known language could say no more of their lawlessness.

On Friday the Ninth of June in the present year, Mr. and Mrs. Boffin (in their manuscript dress of receiving Mr. and Mrs. Lammle at breakfast) were on the South-Eastern Railway with me, in a terribly destructive accident. When I had done what I could to help others, I climbed back into my carriage—nearly turned over a viaduct, and caught aslant upon the turn—to extricate the worthy couple. They were much soiled, but otherwise unhurt. The same happy result attended Miss Bella Wilfer on her wedding day, and Mr. Riderhood inspecting Bradley Headstone's red neckerchief as he lay asleep. I remember with devout thankfulness that I can never be much nearer parting company with my readers for ever than I was then, until there shall be written against my life, the two words with which I have this day closed this book :—THE END.

September 2nd, 1865.

*This book
designed by William B. Taylor
is a production of
Heron Books, London*

*Printed in England by
Hazell Watson and Viney Limited
Aylesbury, Bucks*